THE QUIT LIST

A ROMANTIC COMEDY

KATIE BAILEY

Character cover art by
CINDY RAS

ELEVENTH AVENUE
PUBLISHING

HOLLY

Ever heard the saying, "Quit while you're ahead?"

It's very, very helpful. Like, when you're in Vegas for your sister's bachelorette party, and you're up fifty bucks on the slot machines, but then that last gin and tonic you just *knew* was a bad idea starts to make your head a little fuzzy, and you can't help but funnel that cash back into the machine, convinced that the little pieces of fruit are going to align and you're going to be the Strip's next instant millionaire.

For one glorious moment, you're invincible. Powerful. You can do anything.

As your fifty bucks whittles away and you fall behind, you begin to feed the beast with more and more cash, determined to regain your position in the lead...

Then, the next morning, you wake up *The Hangover*-style, with last night's mascara panda-ing your eye sockets, a slice of lime tangled in your hair, grease from the fried chicken sandwich you devoured at 3AM splattered all over your dress, and an email from your bank regarding unusual activity on your account.

Winner, winner, chicken dinner, you are not.

"I'm not following, honey. What does your drunken trip to Vegas have to do with us ordering dessert?" My date, Keith—because of course he's named *Keith*—frowns at me as he wipes the remnants of his lobster ravioli from his lips with a napkin.

Everything! I want to scream. *It has everything to do with it!*

But instead of screaming (because if I've learned anything from dating, it's that no one likes a madwoman), I calmly splay my hands on the linen tablecloth and force myself to look Keith straight in the eye. "We should've quit while we were ahead. Instead, we stuck out this date for the past two hours while we both wished we were somewhere else. Right?"

Keith stares at me blankly.

"So now," I continue reasonably, "we should cut our losses, settle the bill 50/50, and get on with our lives. Ordering dessert is only going to drag out the inevitable. We both know that you're not going to call in one day, or three, or seven, or whatever the recommended wait time is these days, and that we're never going to see each other again."

My dinner companion continues to stare at me like I have two heads and one mouth. Even in his stupor, he's actually quite nice looking with that thick blond hair and chiseled jawline. You know, objectively speaking. Like if you see him from a far, far distance that puts you nowhere near his personality.

Truth is, I can't say I blame him for seeming so flummoxed. This isn't how I usually end dates.

When a date goes badly, I tend to do what every other normal person does: I pretend that I had a lovely time, say that I look forward to him calling (when we both know he won't), and the night ends *after* dessert with a perfectly amicable—if a little disingenuous—parting of ways. Thereby avoiding all unnecessary conflict in the process.

But Keith, here, has officially frayed my last romantic nerve.

And in the interest of being the opposite of disingenuous —*ingenuous?*—I'd rather stab myself in the eye with my fork than prolong this evening.

Which is saying a lot because the Full Moon Bar & Bistro has insanely good peanut butter chocolate cheesecake.

I would know, because I've been here for the past ten (yes, I said *ten*) Saturday nights in a row on dates. None of which went particularly well. But also, none of them went so badly that I didn't want to round out the night with the universal bad-dates-silver-lining that is cheesecake.

Until now.

Keith blinks at me for a moment with watery blue eyes before his lips twist. "Still not following, love. Are you saying you don't put out or what?"

I don't know why I'm shocked by this. I really don't.

"What I'm *saying* is that we're completely incompatible." My voice is still calm and reasonable enough to mask my inner turmoil.

Keith showed up fifteen minutes late and went on to be incredibly rude to the waiter when he heard that there was, indeed, gluten in the pasta. He then proceeded to order said gluten-laden pasta before talking about himself for an hour. And if that wasn't bad enough, it was mostly in the third person.

Conversation topics ranged from humble-brags about his Very Important Job (something to do with bossing people around), to feminism (Keith does not appear to be a fan), to the minimum wage crisis (this mainly consisted of his thoughts on how if people "showed more initiative," they could be fancy-suit-wearing bossholes too, one day!).

And yes, he chose to rant about the latter while our waiter

uncorked our wine and poured our drinks, giving him the occasional smirk as he spoke.

Awkward and *mortifying* don't even begin to cover what I felt as the poor waiter walked away.

And after that particular moment of grossness, I had confirmation that I, for sure, could not stand this man.

What I should've done, right at that second, was to get up and leave.

Quit while I was ahead.

But, no. I continued to sit here, like an overdressed lemon, for the next hour, tuning out Keith's monologues while internally wondering why I'm cursed in the dating department.

Apparently by staying, all I've done is made him think that there's a snowball's chance in hell that I'm going home with him tonight.

Keith seems totally unphased by my proclamation as he reaches for yet another piece of bread. "Look, Hallie, I've got an early flight tomorrow. You and I gonna knock boots after this or not?"

And just like that, something deep within me snaps. Maybe it's the weeks of awkward bad dates in a row, filled with even more awkward silences. Or the fact that tonight is yet another evening spent with someone who has zero interest in me—and I in them. Or the fact that, despite my efforts over the past couple months, I seem to be making no progress towards finding what I want, and instead, I almost appear to be moving backwards.

But either way, I'm officially done trying to be *calm* and *reasonable* with this insufferable man.

"It's *Holly*. And to your incredibly inappropriate and rather offensive question, I'm gonna say... Not." I smile sweetly. And then, in case he's *still not following*, I add, "Absolutely no way

4

in hell. Not if you were the last living, breathing, sentient being on earth."

Keith stops licking butter off his fingers as he fixes me with that blue-eyed stare. *Finally*, something I've said has apparently gotten through that thick skull. And his jaw immediately sets in annoyance.

"What a waste of time," he mutters.

It's all I can do not to throw my hands in the air. *"At last*, we agree on something." I motion to our waiter for the bill. "Why don't you head out, Keith. I'll take care of the check."

I don't mean anything by this except that I want this man to leave my table once and for all, but Keith must take it as an attempt to emasculate him, because he quickly turns a violent shade of red. He fumbles for his wallet and proceeds to scatter a few twenties on the table before shooting me an incredulous glare. "I was about to leave, anyway."

"Goodbye, Keith," I reply, barely keeping from full-on rolling my eyes at him—apparently the two glasses of wine I've consumed are making me much braver than usual. That, or the thought of yet more of my time being wasted. "I'd say have a nice life, but I wouldn't mean it."

"No wonder you're single," Keith spits, before finally— thankfully—taking his leave, stepping right into our waiter's path and rudely demanding that *he* move out of the way.

I close my eyes for a moment and take a deep, calming breath. When I open them again, our waiter is hovering close by the table, his eyes darting nervously between me and Keith's swiftly retreating figure.

I smile blandly and nod at the leather check presenter in his hand. "I'll get that."

Inside, I find two mint chocolates and a hefty receipt.

It's not like I make the big bucks at my Guest Services job at the Pinnacle Hotel, and tonight's meal will certainly cut into the already modest "date budget" I've set for myself. I cram both chocolates into my mouth, hoping the sugar will take the edge off the sting. "I'll pay now. By card, if you've got the reader with you."

"Sure." The waiter looks like he's still debating running for his life.

I tap my card on the reader for the full amount of the dinner, then bundle up Keith's sloppy collection of twenties and slide them into the leather book as a tip.

The waiter's eyes widen. "Wow. That's, um..."

"Deserved," I finish for him. "Thanks for being a great server."

His expression shifts from twitchily nervous to positively delighted. "Thank you so much."

As he trots off, I pour myself another glass of the overpriced bottle of wine that still sits on the table, trying to appear composed. I'm happy to have made someone's night, but I'm not sure my tipping the waiter so generously was born from actual generosity or out of spite, given Keith's disgusting "minimum wage workers are lazy" spiel.

It's likely a bit of both. Because the thought of Keith's money in the young waiter's hands makes me feel a whole lot better.

I pull my phone from my bag, login to Spark—the dating app Keith and I matched on—and block his profile.

Sadly, the only *spark* tonight happened when I leaned over the centerpiece to swipe a slice of bread from the basket Keith was hoarding ("carb-loading," apparently) and I almost set fire to my sleeve.

Sipping on my expensive wine, I text my best friend and roommate, Aubrey.

> Another one bites the dust.

Was Keith with the hot bod but the crap name
actually a bald, beer-gutted catfish?

Oh, way worse.

Worse than the time I swallowed that
suppository?

I snort with laughter at the now-hilarious memory of Aubrey calling me in a panic after she bought some constipation medication at the pharmacy, swallowed two, then realized that the pills weren't intended for oral use.

I left work early to take her to the emergency room, where we were *laughed at* by the on-call doctor, who told us to go home and expect a rough night. Poor Aubs spent the next twelve hours on the bathroom floor, puking her guts out. Horrible at the time, but forever-fodder for the maid of honor speech I will one day give at her wedding.

Because all's well that ends well, and that on-call doctor ended up asking her out. The two of them are now engaged to be married.

Lucky for her, I've become good at maid-of-honor duties. I was maid of honor at my older sister Mindy's wedding two years ago, and for my cousin Daniella this past spring. Aubrey's wedding is the trifecta.

I'm practically Super Maid Of Honor at this point.

Or as my great-uncle Percival put it at Dani's reception: "Soon to be an old spinster if I don't lock a man down."

Which was charming. And not altogether inaccurate. Before I embarked on this slew of what have turned out to be very bad dates, I had pretty much zero dating experience to speak of.

> Put it this way… this man was the human equivalent of a suppository.

> What a waste of a pretty face.

> Assuming no second date then?

> I'd rather get kicked in the ribs by a horse again.

I wish I didn't mean this literally.

I put my phone down on the table and place my head in my hands, being careful not to smudge my eye makeup. Just because tonight's date was yet another evening down the drain doesn't mean that my mascara has to suffer.

Quit while you're ahead...

It's something I probably should have done years ago.

2

JAX

It's happening. It's actually happening.

"You're sure about this, Morris?" I say into the phone as I pace the sidewalk outside the Full Moon Bar & Bistro. It's chilly this evening, but I'm pretty sure that the goosebumps prickling my bare arms aren't due to the spring breeze, but more so what Morris just told me.

"Sure I'm sure." My mentor laughs jovially. "As of right now, you are officially a certified wilderness guide."

I stop pacing for a moment, clench and unclench my fist. My heart is galloping in my chest.

"You can start leading backcountry excursions as soon as you'd like," he continues. "Congratulations, Jax."

I'm not, by nature, a super smiley person, but the smile currently on my lips might split my face in two. Morris is the man in charge of the intensive course I've been taking through the Wilderness Guides of America. The guy might be in his late sixties, but he's fit as a fiddle and showing no signs of slowing down while leading people through their outdoor guide training.

The guide of guides, if you will.

And let me tell you, the training was no easy feat.

The past few months have been a grueling combination of classroom learning, mock excursions of increasing difficulty, first responder training, and exams. All meticulously done around my full-time shift work at the bar.

I'm relieved to hear that I've passed the intensive course with flying colors. I've never passed anything with flying colors before—but I worked damn hard to get here, and my hard work has apparently paid off.

"Thank you, Morris," I say quietly. "Guess I can give my resignation now."

I can hardly keep the nerves out of my voice. Because as excited as I am to have finally, *finally*, crossed this final hurdle, it also means that everything I've been working towards for so long is becoming... real.

Holy sh—

"You still planning on starting your own guiding outfit, leading excursions out of that cabin you bought?" Morris asks, apparently reading my mind.

I swallow. Keep my voice firm. "Yessir. Got my business license last week, and the cabin is currently under renovation to host guests starting this summer."

"Well, that all sounds great," my mentor says warmly.

Morris has been doing this job for forty years. Forty. And, though he must have had this same conversation a million times with a million candidates, he sounds... proud. Proud of *me*.

It's a new feeling—to have an older man talk to me with pride in his voice. My own father often uses a tone tinged with nothing short of disdain.

Disdain that's likely to be amplified tenfold when he learns about my new career path.

The thought makes me smile even wider.

"Do you have any bookings for the summer?"

"No. Haven't quite gotten that far yet," I admit.

"You'll probably want to start thinking about it soon," Morris cautions. "Get a website going, and a booking system setup. Do some marketing. Put together a social media presence."

"Hmm," I say noncommittally. Truth is, setting up a booking system and a website and everything sounds like a complete *nightmare*. Never mind social media. Which is why, until now, I'd shuffled all that business-y stuff to the bottom of my to-do list.

"Hey, Jax!" a high-pitched voice suddenly sings from behind my right shoulder.

I turn to face three girls waving at me as they waltz towards the front door of the bar. I know them well—they're regular Saturday nighters at Full Moon.

With my phone still pressed to my ear and Morris chatting about what my classmates are planning on doing with their new certifications, I nod at the girls and open the door for them. The first girl—pretty, with long black hair and olive skin—gives me a flirtatious look as she steps inside. "See you at the bar," she mouths.

I nod again as the door swings shut behind them. Inside the bar, the lights are dim and glowy, the atmosphere bustling. People seem to love this place, flocking here in droves every weekend...

I've been at Full Moon for years. People know me as a staple around here. Part of the furniture.

It's going to be a huge change when I leave this all behind. But I'm ready.

At least, I think I am.

Stepping into the unknown is something I do regularly as a wilderness enthusiast, but when I'm out there, on my own, I know I'm not going to fail. I'm confident. Self-assured in my survival skills.

Running a business, however? Dealing with people past a wink and a smile as I pour them a drink?

It's all new to me.

I've always wanted to live off-grid in a cabin in the woods. And while this just fuels my dad's "my son is a disappointment" fire, and my step-mom's upset that I won't find a woman to "settle down with ASAP" (living alone in the wilderness is not exactly conducive to a long-term relationship), I don't really care what they think.

Because being *out there*, in the wild, is the place I feel happiest. Most at peace.

I bought the cabin a few months back after years of saving, with the intention of turning it into both my new home, and my way of making money by leading guided excursions. Welcome people to the backcountry who want to change their lives, push their limits, and experience the nitty-gritty, exquisitely beautiful, sometimes difficult days in the Georgia wilderness.

As I get lost in these thoughts of my future workplace in nature, I look through the window of Full Moon and lazily scan my soon-to-be-ex-workplace in this concrete jungle.

My eyes land on a familiar brunette among the dining crowd.

It's hard *not* to recognize her, honestly. She's here every single Saturday night, always with a different guy, and always wearing a look of concern on her face, like she's not quite sure how she got here.

I've often wondered what her deal is. Why she always orders a bottle of Chilean red while she sits through dates she *clearly* doesn't want to be on, her foot tapping under the table (same table, every time) like she's mentally counting down the minutes until she can leave.

I know the feeling well. Usually because I'm counting down the minutes before I can leave the bar, too.

"Jax? All good over there?"

I give my head a quick shake and turn away from the window to resume my pacing. "Yup. Sorry, Morris. Just thinking about... my upcoming booming social media presence."

My mentor tuts good-naturedly. "You'll get there."

"Or, more likely, I can hire someone to get there for me," I mutter.

With what cash, I don't know. But I'm sure I can make something work. Maybe ask my little sister, who's somewhat of a TikTok star—whatever that means—to give me some tips.

"You'll need to think about the bigger picture too, Jax. How to sell this thing so people want to come to *you*. In fact, I'd suggest taking some friends or family on practice trips. Especially beginners who need a lot of guidance. The more experience you have—and the more natural and confident you appear as a guide—the more likely people are to book with you."

I'm nodding. Doing a whole lot of nodding and head bobbing.

But I have to admit, I'm overwhelmed. Probably in over my head.

It's not like I'm an outgoing people person with an active presence on social media. When it comes down to it, I'm content being alone. With my own thoughts and company.

Guiding is the best way I can think of to make money doing what I love, being where I love. Failing is not an option. I've sunk all of my savings into this cabin, and it's going to be my stepping stone to the life I've worked towards for a long time now.

I'm about to answer Morris—a joke to the effect of taking some of my more unwilling friends and family (AKA my sister

Maddie) to the middle of nowhere and leaving them there to fend for themselves like they're on *Survivor*— when the door to the bar flies open, and a blond man stalks onto the street, his face red as a beetroot.

I recognize him as the concerned brunette's date for the evening. And right now, he looks angry, his fists clenching.

What the hell?

I'm pretty good at reading people—serves me well as a bartender, let me tell you—and this guy strikes me as a man with some serious 'roid rage.

I immediately look into the bar, but there's no big commotion, no drama. So at least the guy wasn't getting himself into a fight.

My break is definitely coming to an end, so Morris and I say our goodbyes—with a promise from me to look into this whole website and booking system and social media fandango—and I cast one last glance at the angry guy on the street as I walk back into the bar.

He's standing on the sidewalk, clenching and unclenching his fists in clear agitation. But he's turned towards the street, probably waiting for his Uber or something. He doesn't seem to have any interest in coming back to Full Moon. Which means that he's not my problem.

As I make my way back behind the bar, I look over at the brunette to make sure she's okay, that the guy didn't take any of his anger out on her.

I'm not sure what I expected to see, but I'm surprised to see her smiling as she texts someone.

Another date, perhaps?

Yeah, I might be good at reading people, but I have to say that the concerned brunette with her parade of different men each week throws me for a bit of a loop. Which means that, on the bright side, tonight's shift is slightly less mundane than other nights.

I slip back behind the bar and nod at Dante, my fellow bartender. "Thanks for letting me take five. Everything good here on the floor?"

"All g, my man."

Guess I must have misread the situation outside, then. Maybe the guy was just red-faced from stepping out of the heat and into the cold, or something.

But again, not my problem.

With a shrug, I grab the next order and get back to work.

And that's when the front door swings open, and 'Roid Rage himself marches back inside.

3

HOLLY

"Hallie!"

The familiar, rude voice pulls my gaze off my phone screen and my relatively pleasant conversation about injuries-by-horse and there he is...

Keith is standing in front of me, his face glowing red like a beacon.

For such a nice establishment, this place has a real problem with pest control.

"Hello again, Keith." I give him a flat smile. "And for the fifteenth time, my name is Holly."

Instead of acknowledging this really, very simple fact, he leans towards me, getting into my personal space. I involuntarily shrink back.

"You don't get to call the shots, missy," he says, coating me in a cloud of his gross sour breath. On the bright side, "missy" is, at least, a change up from "Hallie."

"Pardon me?" I look at him with what I hope are unwavering eyes because I don't want to betray the fact that I'm quaking a little inside. Keith's a large dude, and he's angry right now. As little as I think of him, it's difficult not to be intimidated. He's purposefully leaning close to me, speaking quietly so as not to make a scene. Trying to both isolate and intimidate me.

"You think you're above everything with your high and mighty attitude, acting like you're better than me," he spits quietly, venom lacing his tongue.

I force myself to hold his gaze, though it's almost painful. Guys like this, who expect things from women and then use intimidation techniques when they don't get what they want, are the worst kind of men.

Why did I go on this date again?

Ah yes, that's right: *desperation.*

After ten straight terrible dates, I have decided that I hate dating with a passion. I hate the unknown of meeting someone new for dinner each week. Hate the cringey small talk bracketing awkward silences, the push-up bras and the heels that give you blisters.

But I'm in this situation because of my own sheer stupidity.

I'm almost thirty, I've spent the last few years of my life waiting for a relationship I now know will never happen, instead of putting myself out there. *And* on top of that, I've just been passed over for yet another promotion that I'm pretty damn sure I deserved.

Which led me to my New Year's resolution for this year.

I had to quit wasting time and get over my (apparently unrequited) feelings for my boss. Quit letting life pass me by. Quit being afraid to step out of my comfort zone.

Instead, I would seize the day, and go in search of my happily-ever-after.

Of course, the only way to achieve such a thing is to, you know, *date.*

So, I've thrown myself to the wolves, so to speak, of the modern dating scene for the first time in literal years.

Though, so far, it's less of a cool-and-trendy, cocktail-swilling at the bar scene, and more of a three-car pile-up, traffic accident scene. Complete with police cars, ambulances, and rescue helicopters.

But I have no idea how else to achieve my goal, short of sitting through all these dinner dates with men I meet online. Because unlike my sister, Mindy, I don't have any attractive male friends I can fall in love with. And unlike Aubrey, I certainly haven't ever had a doctor ask me out during a trip to the emergency room...

Although I do now have a habit of always wearing respectable underwear, just in case I ever get in a car wreck and my soulmate happens to be the surgeon who has to cut off my clothes before operating on me.

First impressions matter.

"I don't think I'm better than you," I tell Keith, though I am clearly the superior human in this situation. Though that doesn't stop my voice from betraying me with a tremor.

"Oh, yeah?" Keith moves closer still, and I want to gag at the mingled scents of musky cologne and alcohol-tinged breath.

I'm trying to think of what my next move should be, what my escape route might look like, when...

"Sorry I'm late. Traffic was terrible."

I jerk my head in the direction of the deep voice. Is Keith expecting someone? Brawn backup, perhaps?

Standing above us is a man I can only describe as *a tall drink of water.* Said in one of those old-fashioned western voices while tipping my imaginary hat and chewing on a blade of grass. Because *this* man is broad-shouldered and black-bearded and he's staring down at us with these intense slate-gray eyes that make my insides feel wobbly. He's dressed in all black: black jeans, black boots, black t-shirt.

He doesn't have the same obvious, pretty-boy good looks that Keith does, but he's handsome in a piercing eyes and rugged manly-man way that is infinitely more attractive in every single sense of the word.

This guy looks like he belongs in an ad for power tools. Or really big barbecues. Or... wolves. If there were such a thing as ads for wolves.

Keith pushes a stray lock of hair off his forehead and glares at the Wolf Man. "Who the hell are *you*?"

Not brawn backup, then.

"Jaxon." The guy says this like it's obvious. "And who might *you* be?"

Keith ignores his question. "Look, bro, we're kinda in the middle of—"

Jaxon—who I'm now realizing looks vaguely familiar—puts his hand on Keith's shoulder. Firmly. His expression remains mild, but his grip appears powerful. Commanding. In fact, I swear I see Keith wince a little.

"First off, I'm not your *bro*. Secondly, you were in the middle of nothing. In fact, your time was very much up. And as you have already caused enough of a scene this evening, I'm going to give you until the count of three to get the hell out of here and never bother this woman again." He gives Keith the full force of those mesmerizing eyes. "Understood?"

This Jaxon character makes for a rather imposing form, and not only is he at least four inches taller than Keith, he's buff in a way that makes him look like he'd come out on top in any street fight. There's a bit of a *West Side Story* vibe to him, without the random breaking out into song. Or gang membership. One would hope.

Keith, on the other hand, has the kind of muscular bulkiness that suggests he's seen the inside of too many gyms. The kind with smoothie bars and free tanning. And good ol' Keith seems to come to this realization as well, because he takes a step back.

"I have to get going, anyway," he says, sounding all business-like, but I don't miss the flicker of fear in his eyes. He recovers enough to smirk at Jaxon in this maddening, wink-wink-nudge-nudge, boys club kinda way. "She's all yours, buddy. But fair warning, she's not worth it."

Jaxon's mouth sets in a grim line for a moment that makes me somewhat fear for Keith's wretched life. Then, out of nowhere, he smiles, moves behind me, and sets a big hand on my upper back almost possessively. He smells as woodsy and manly and delicious as I thought he might.

"Not your buddy," Jaxon says, and then surprises me by giving Keith a conspiratorial wink. "And believe me, she's *definitely* worth it. In fact, I should be thanking you."

Keith blinks again like the idiot he is. "Why?"

"Your date with Holly was so terrible that it made *me* look good in comparison," Jaxon says smoothly. "I've been begging her to go out with me for weeks. And one dinner with you—just one single pasta course—made her decide to take a chance on me."

I tilt my head to look at the man in black, wondering for a moment if he's clinically insane, or if he has mistaken me for a different, much luckier Holly. And that's when I see the twinkle in those pretty eyes.

He's messing with him.

Suddenly eager to join in on the fun, I flash my own smile at Keith. "I texted Jaxon the second you left. Thank you for helping me find my *soulmate*." I say the word all breathy and reverentially, fluttering my eyelashes.

Beside me, I feel the vibration of Jaxon's deep, quiet chuckle.

Keith looks a little ill.

"There's a word for this," I continue, unable to help myself. "People who stand in for the actors before they come onstage. In fact, I think that's what they're called. Stand-ins."

"Or fluffers," Jaxon supplies with amusement.

I startle at Jaxon's unexpected input, then grin at him in thanks before turning to Keith solemnly. "Thank you for being my emotional fluffer, Keith. I'll be forever indebted to you."

"I'm not... I.... I'm not a FLUFFER!" Keith yells a bit too loudly before remembering that he's in a fancy restaurant and people can hear him. It's all I can do to keep a straight face.

Inside, I'm dying.

Dead.

Deceased.

Because this is too freaking good.

And then, Keith drops his voice a fraction. "I'm the main character."

"Sure you are," Jaxon says in this soothing, pitying tone that one might use to placate a petulant three-year-old.

Keith is not placated. He points from me to Jaxon. "Whatever this little circus is, I'm out!"

"Bye, Keith," I tell him, feeling genuinely happy for the first time in what feels like days as he flounces towards the exit.

As soon as the intricate oak front doors shut behind Keith (unfortunately not hitting him on the way out), I turn to Jaxon, eyes wide. "Um... Thank you for that."

"Don't mention it, *soulmate*." Jaxon throws me a wink and I go red.

He then gives me a quick once-over, like he's checking that I'm okay, and apparently satisfied with what he sees, he removes his big, warm hand from my back and sits in the chair opposite mine without being invited. He swipes a wine glass off the empty table next to us and begins filling it with my wine.

"Please, help yourself," I say dryly.

"Thank you," he replies with a smirk, totally unruffled as he takes a sip.

I assess him as he assesses the red wine, taking in his familiar-not-familiar features.

Who the hell *is* this guy?

"Nice company you keep," Jaxon adds.

Which is rude. Accurate, maybe. But still rude.

I choose to ignore his taunt, raise a brow at him. "Who are you and how did you know my name?"

"Like I said, I'm Jaxon. Jaxon Grainger. But you can call me Jax." Call-Me-Jax clocks my confused expression, then jerks a thumb towards the bar along the far wall. "Bartender. Usually found lurking in the back corner. And I know your name because I saw it on your credit card receipt."

Ah, the bartender. Makes sense that he looks familiar now.

I'm not quite sure why I've apparently chosen the Full Moon Bar & Bistro as my go-to date location. Maybe because they have deep-fried brie on the menu (which I obviously looked at online well before date number one). And once I started coming here, it simply never occurred to me to go somewhere else.

I like that I can eliminate an extra worry-factor every time I meet with someone new. I already know where the bathrooms are, what's on the menu, and what the staff wear so I don't accidentally dress in a way that I could be mistaken for one of the waitresses (this is based on date number four, which went downhill spectacularly fast after he started hitting on one of the *actual* waitresses right in front of me).

"Oh." I turn my head to see the rest of the bar staff watching us with unabashed stares. "Assuming it's not in your job description to come to the aid of customers on terrible dates?"

"I can honestly say that I'd never seen a *truly* terrible date until tonight." Jax lifts his gray eyes to meet mine. "At that point, it wasn't so much 'job description' as much as it was 'humanitarian obligation.'"

I should feel prickled by this, but something about Jax's mild expression—the way his tone is jokey but not mocking—makes me smile instead.

"Really?" I blink at him innocently. "I thought Keith was the poster-child for the perfect gentleman."

"That guy was for sure on the sex offender list."

I laugh at this, surprised by the sudden, unexpected turn this night has taken. Jaxon is... funny. Like, actually funny. And easy on the eyes. I'm not usually into guys with beards—Dylan was always clean-shaven and smooth-faced. But I gotta say, this guy's short, neatly-kept beard just adds to his sex-on-legs appearance. "You want me to draw up a little 'Wanted' sketch for you to tape to the doors so he never returns?"

Jax takes a glug of his—*my*—wine, then sets the glass down on the table. "Absolutely, I do. It's a fundamental part of my job to keep my patrons, both present and future, safe from creeps. Bartender with a cause, over here."

"My hero," I joke.

"What made you go out with that guy, anyway? Was it a blind date or something?"

"More like a dating app match gone wrong."

"And you matched with him because..."

"He had all his teeth and didn't send me dick pics?"

This draws a laugh from him—deep and throaty and slightly rough, like sandpaper—which, in turn, sets off an unexpected glow of pride, deep in my belly. It's nice to make someone laugh. Keith didn't think anything I said was funny.

23

"Wow. You're setting the bar high there, Holly. You might want to ask next week's date a few more questions about himself before agreeing to meet in person."

I tilt my head at him quizzically. "What makes you think I have a date next week?"

"Well, you're here every Saturday night. Always with a different guy. I figured you were a bit of a player." He winks at me as he says this, and the silence that follows this statement is very, very loud as I realize that the man sitting opposite me most likely *is* an actual badass certified player—takes one to know one, right?

Even if his assumption is very, very wrong.

I assess Wolf Man with objective eyes for the first time. He's my age, or maybe a little younger, AKA in the prime of his twenties. He's a freaking hot bartender at a gorgeous and trendy downtown restaurant.

Of course he's a player. Probably has a steady stream of waitresses and patrons lining up for a piece of the guy with the sexy beard and a penchant for saving damsels in distress from misogynistic a-holes.

Better to look like a fellow player than someone who's entirely desperate.

And so, I force out the creakiest, most alarming sound I've ever heard come from my own mouth. "You got me," I say through my forced laugh. "Big player over here."

Jax gives me a *look*. Like he isn't quite buying my player status now that he's actually talked to me.

Busted.

I throw my hands up, and for the second time this evening, find myself leveling the truth with a man sitting opposite me. *This red wine, I tell you!* "I'm lying. I'm not a player. I'm a woman on a hunt to find someone—find *the* one. Which is why I seem to be playing Russian Roulette every Saturday night, hoping I'm not going to be dining opposite the Hillside Strangler."

Jax is expressionless, his face like a lake of calm, neutral water. But unlike Keith's unresponsiveness, I don't get the sense this guy is flat-out ignoring me, but more... *reading* me.

His silent-but-calm demeanor seems to spur me on and I rest my head in my hands. "I figured I'd have to kiss a few frogs to find a prince. I'm not totally clueless. But I feel like I'm pretty much living in Frogland these days."

"The guy who just left was more of a toad than a frog," Jax supplies helpfully. Not.

"How was I supposed to know that? His stupid Spark profile said that he was looking for love."

"Which is code for: he's looking to get laid."

He's exactly right, of course. But I'm not about to admit that to him. "Well, why not *say* that?!"

"People lie."

I narrow my eyes at him. "You seem to know an awful lot about this topic."

He smirks. "I don't need to lie."

I bet you don't.

"Nor would I ever want to," he continues. "But some people are just assholes."

"Agreed. If only it was easier to spot said assholes before you meet them at a fancy restaurant."

I must sound more upset than I mean to, because when Jax speaks again, his tone is gentler. "It *is* easy if you know how to read people. Figure out their intentions before they make you believe the image of themselves that they're portraying on the internet."

I almost laugh out loud. Because if I couldn't figure out for so long that it wasn't going to happen with Dylan, I imagine that guessing the intentions of random men on the internet is probably not my forte, either.

"And how, exactly, would you propose I do that?" I tilt my head at Jax, skeptical of this sexy bartender who *doesn't need to lie* to get all the girls flocking to him.

He shrugs. "Lower the stakes. For the first date, go for coffee, or a walk somewhere public, or for a drink. That way it's less time consuming for you, easier to bail if the guy's a creep..." He nods at the receipt on the table. "And easier on your wallet."

"What makes you think that these men aren't wining and dining *me?*"

"Because I saw *your* name on the credit card receipt, remember?"

Oh, yeah...

Jax polishes off his glass of wine, and then stands. "I gotta get back to work." He's looking down at me with a strange expression that's somewhere between *a*mused and *be*mused. "You got a safe ride home?"

I wave my phone at him. "My Lyft awaits. And my driver has a five-star rating so I assume she's not the Hillside Strangler. Or on the sex offender list."

"Stay clear of unmarked white vans on your way outside and you should be fine."

I give him a little salute as I get to my feet. "Roger that."

"Oh, one more thing before you go..."

Without waiting for my response, he jogs off behind a couple of swinging black doors that must lead into the bistro's back of house. This would be the perfect time to escape Jax and his judgy stares, but I find myself waiting obediently, curiosity getting the best of me.

A few moments later, he reappears holding a pale blue box.

I blink at him. "What's that?"

"You always end your dates with cheesecake." He presses the box into my hands and looks at me kindly. Too kindly.

"That's... more than a little weird that you know that."

"I think the words you are looking for are 'thank you.'" He smiles like he's thoroughly amused.

"Oh, yes. Weird, but also thank you," I say, trying not to think about the fact that he's probably picturing me going home and sob-eating the cheesecake with a giant serving spoon while watching *Bridget Jones's Diary*. Which isn't my plan at all.

If anything, it'll be *He's Just Not That Into You*—AKA the story of my life.

"Good luck, Holly. It was nice meeting you."

"Likewise." I'm surprised to realize that I kind of mean it. "And thank you for saving me from Keith."

"His name was *Keith?*"

I nod. He sighs.

"Do me one favor, Holly?"

"Sure." I shrug. "I owe you one."

"Do better."

4

JAX

I stay out of other people's business, as a general rule. Keep my opinions and problems to myself and trust that those around me will do the same.

But sometimes, it gets to be more than a man can take, and you get to the point where you're obliged—forced, really—to step in. Save someone from a situation and/or from themself.

"What was *that*?" Dante—who does the opposite of staying out of other people's business, as a general rule—leans his elbows on the bar, looking at me with big bug eyes.

"Don't know what you're talking about." I shrug as I scan the next drink order and pour two pints of beer and a glass of Sauvignon Blanc.

When I started this shift a few hours ago, my plan was simply to get through it in relative peace and quiet, stop at home to pick up my dog and my things, and then head to the cabin for my weekend. Usually, if I can leave Atlanta by 2AM, I can get there sometime before dawn and watch the sunrise. In peace.

But unfortunately, the "peace and quiet" I was hoping for

on this shift has been totally derailed first by Morris's phone call, then by Holly-the-bad-dater, and now, by Dante's clearly incoming line of questioning.

Because, for some reason, he takes my non-committal response as a cue to keep talking.

"I've never seen you help a customer like that before."

"Sure you have," I reply. Which is true. I've kicked out many drunk and disorderly people—after food service finishes around 10PM, the bar stays open late on weekends and things can get rowdy. The second any idiot guy even thinks about putting his hands on a woman without her consent, I throw them out on their ass immediately.

But I can't say I've ever had to intervene while someone was on a freaking sit-down dinner date.

Dante's still staring at me like I've grown three heads. "You went right over there, kicked her date out, and sat down with her. And then, if that wasn't already totally unlike you, you brought her *cake*."

"Her date was a future star of *America's Most Wanted*." What I don't say is that seeing her over there—looking so vulnerable next to that huge, angry man—triggered something in me.

"But the cake," he repeats, going on like a broken record. "I've never, ever, in all the years I've worked here, seen you bring anyone cake…" Dante trails off, apparently painfully lost in thought. Then, he snaps his fingers—apparently having a lightbulb moment. "I get it. You're hitting that."

I raise a tired brow at him. "I'm most definitely not. And don't say 'hitting that.'"

"Well, I can't exactly say hitting *her*, can I? Because that would give things a bit of a dark turn."

I snort. "How about you don't say that either, then?"

29

Dante points at me, grinning like a fool. "You're totally hitting that."

"I'm about to hit *you* if you don't shut up."

"Is that why she's been coming here on all those dates? Trying to make you jealous?"

"That sounds like the plot of a bad rom com movie," I say as I get to work on a French Martini. My sister, Maddie, grew up addicted to those films, and I appear to have absorbed some of their fluffy, ridiculous plotlines by proxy.

"I'd watch it."

Dante cranes his neck to look at Holly's retreating figure and I follow his gaze as Holly steps outside and pulls her jacket on. Her petite frame appears small and slight as she shivers against the cold, even with the addition of those heels that she's wearing. It draws the sudden urge in me to run after her and check that she is, indeed, getting in a Lyft, and not an unmarked white van.

The woman seems to have zero survival instinct.

My jaw tenses at the memory of her staring down that drunken fool, a wide-eyed guppy as he closed in like a hungry shark.

I wanted nothing more than to punch *Keith* in the face when I saw him intimidate her like that. I saw his moves a mile off—he was keeping quiet to not make a scene, while he simultaneously made Holly feel like she was alone and out of options. I knew that song and dance by heart before I hit middle school, watching how my father behaved with my mom, and then his second wife.

The only thing that stopped me from swinging was the fact that the bistro is, at present, housing over a hundred patrons—including a large table of burly guys who look like they would be all too happy to get involved in a throwdown.

I wanted to teach the guy a lesson, not incite a riot.

"Does she know that you're still seeing Laurel?" Dante asks out of the corner of his mouth, as though Holly can somehow hear us from all the way outside the bistro.

"I'm *only* seeing Laurel," I say honestly with a roll of my eyes. The only dating I do is the casual kind, but I don't do the dating-multiple-women-at-the-same-time thing. I add a shot of Chambord and some pineapple juice to the ice-filled shaker in front of me. "Not that it even matters. I was just helping Holly out like any decent person would have."

"Holly... Hot name, too. Well, if you're not interested, do you mind if I go outside and have a quick chat with her? Show her what boyfriend material looks like?" He smooths his hands down his shirt, basically preening.

"Be my guest."

But somehow, I get the feeling that Dante wouldn't get too far with Holly. She surprised me—she's always so fashionably dressed and perfectly-put together... I wasn't expecting the sarcastic, self-deprecating humor, the quick-witted teasing, the awkward mannerisms.

I can't help but wonder what, exactly, a woman like that is looking for when she says she's looking for *the one*. Or why she's bothering to look at all.

"What're you guys talking about?" We look over to see Kara, one of the waitresses, standing in front of the bar with her hands on her hips.

"Just finishing the drink order for your table," I say swiftly, not wanting to dwell on the woman and her bad date anymore. I have other things to think about. "It'll be a minute."

"I have time." She catches my eye and winks flirtily.

I nod back. Dante, on the other hand, treats her to a full-faced grin, coupled with a strategic bicep flex as he leans forward on the counter. "Looking good, Kara," he drawls, all thoughts of Holly apparently forgotten.

My fellow bartender is a great guy, but sometimes I feel like his entire personality is chasing women. He's a good-looking dude. Suave and charming, too. And he's dated pretty much every female staff member in this restaurant... with the noticeable exception of Kara, who has made it clear from day one that she has eyes for nobody but me.

Which isn't ideal for her because I don't date coworkers. Or friends. Or friends of friends. Another general rule of mine. I only date women I'm not tied to personally or professionally and who are looking for the same thing as I am: no strings.

Strings are for puppets.

The one and only time I briefly dated one of the waitresses here, she spent the next few months cornering me in the stock room and tearfully telling me that she hoped I'd change my mind about wanting a serious relationship.

And as much as I hated to see her cry, I hadn't.

Don't get me wrong, it's not that I didn't think she was good enough for me. Not at all. In fact, most women I've dated have been way, way too good for me. It's just that I don't want to fall in love with anyone.

And, deep down, I know that they don't really want to fall in love with me, either.

I'm the temporary distraction, not the happily ever after.

So, now, I do everyone a favor by sticking to my rules and only dating women like Laurel—a flight attendant with no desire for anything to hold her in one place for long.

And speaking of Laurel...

I'm pretty sure she's in town next week, and while I'd like to see her, I should probably be working on some of the stuff Morris was talking about.

Although, Morris did say that I should get some experience leading beginners, and I'm fairly certain that Laurel hasn't been on a hike in the area. Or any area—she doesn't seem like the hiking type.

Maybe I could take her to the cabin for an adventurous date? That way, I could spend some time with her *and* get some of that wilderness guiding experience Morris was talking about. The thought calms some of the overwhelm I've been feeling since that phone conversation.

I strain the shaken vodka and Chambord mixture into a chilled martini glass and set it alongside the other drinks on the tray, and then add a shot of Patron to complete the order. "Here you go, Kara. That should be everything."

"Thanks, Jax." Kara smiles.

"Not gonna thank me?" Dante pouts.

It's Kara's turn to raise a perfectly groomed eyebrow at Dante. "What would I thank *you* for?"

"My compliment, of course," he says flirtily.

"Not sure it's much of a compliment. I *always* look good." Kara smirks, flips her hair, and picks up the tray of drinks before sashaying away, hips swinging.

"Yeah, you do!" Dante calls after her.

I elbow him. "Be cool, dude. And put your tongue back in your mouth."

"I think I might have a chance! Wanna see if she and Erin feel like getting drinks after work?"

"No."

"No" is my favorite complete sentence, and in my opinion, people don't utilize it enough.

Other people, that is. I have no problem saying no at any given time, for any given reason.

"Suit yourself," Dante says. "Maybe they'll want a menage a trois with me for the evening."

"Unlikely."

"You're such a pessimist," he responds, and for a moment,

the overwhelmed feeling that's been sitting in my chest since my call with Morris eases.

I like Dante, but sometimes, I really cannot wait to get out of here.

And maybe he's right. Maybe I can be pessimistic, and my solution is to stop being negative and simply take things step by step. One at a time.

I'll find some quiet time to talk to Orlagh, my manager, and give my resignation. I'll take Laurel for a hike or two to sharpen my guiding skills. And I'll ask my sister to point me in the right direction with marketing.

Before I know it, I'll be out of here and this place will be a distant memory...

Though a little part of me might miss seeing who the hell Holly turns up with on the next Saturday night.

5

HOLLY

Do better.

Jax's kinda mean but well-intended (I think) words are still ringing in my ears as I grab my keys and unlock the door of the bungalow Aubrey and I share.

We've been renting this place together for the past three years, but our lease is up in the summer and she's been talking about moving in with Alec, her ER Doctor in Shining Armor. Which makes sense—they're getting married soon.

I, meanwhile, will be striking out on my own. I won't be able to afford to pay the rent here on my own, and I don't want to live with a stranger, so I guess I can add "apartment hunting" to my to-do list before I turn thirty.

On the bright side, Aubrey has insisted that she will help me find a place when the time comes. And a cat. Because she's not a dog person and believes cats to have "nice smiles and soulful eyes."

I know. I wonder about her sanity, too.

"She's alive!" Aubrey squeals from where she's sitting on the living room floor.

I laugh as I walk into our cramped living room, which features heritage (read: old and long overdue a replacement) bay windows with busted seals that leak condensation and uneven thin-plank hardwood floors that are ideal for toe-stubbing. On the plus side though, our home also features a squashy, overstuffed old couch, a selection of Pottery Barn throw pillows and blankets (mine), and enough plants to reforest the Amazon (Aubrey's).

Aubrey's sitting with her spine straight and her legs crossed in front of her, which would look very zen if she wasn't surrounded by half-empty Chinese food containers. Her dirty blond hair is piled in a loose bun held with what looks like a zip tie, and she's wearing nothing but a flowy white tank top with a soy sauce stain on it and polka-dotted underwear. Her reading glasses are on, there's an open book in her lap, and soft classical music plays from the stereo.

"How's the studying?" I kick off my pointy-toed stiletto heels and flop onto the couch, swiping a container of veggie chow mein on my way down. I dig my chopsticks eagerly into the saucy deliciousness and twirl. "Mmmm," I mumble through a mouthful of noodles.

I'm starving. Despite the expensive dinner tonight, I barely touched my plate. Keith was a total appetite buzzkill.

"It sucks." Aubs looks at me solemnly. "Never become a lawyer."

I laugh. "I have no plans to ever do that in this lifetime, thank you very much."

Aubrey and I have been best friends since college, and we are the epitome of opposites attract. She—and I mean this in the nicest way possible—is a hot mess. She's never on time for anything, is booksmart but has the memory of a goldfish for any real-life engagements, and is constantly taking up and dropping new hobbies. But, she also has a heart of gold and treats everyone from the mailman to the homeless guy on the corner like her best friend. She has a wardrobe of floaty cotton and linen neutrals, but has no qualms leaving the house with unbrushed hair and mismatched flip-flops.

Me? I'm hard lines where she's soft edges. I have a perfectly organized Tupperware cabinet, a fastidiously-kept daily planner full of index tabs, and a wardrobe full of perfectly ironed dresses all hanging in a row. Where she's an extrovert, I hate talking to strangers (see, "I hate dating"), and I keep a quiver of self-deprecating-humor-laced arrows in my arsenal for when conversation becomes too personal or uncomfortable.

"Sooooo, about tonight..." Aubrey sets down her book, titled *The Bar Exam Is Easy.* Her eyes follow mine to the cover, and she snorts. "Spoiler alert, the title is wildly misleading. Once I pass, I may use my fancy new lawyer powers to sue."

"I think you'd win." I smile. "Wanna make a fake case for it?"

We do this sometimes. When one of us is trying to make an important decision, or we're mad at someone, or we simply disagree about something, we binge-watch *Suits,* then get dressed up in a couple of men's suit jackets Aubrey snagged for us at Goodwill, and debate, courtroom-style.

Each of us takes turns to convince the imaginary judge (Aubrey's stuffed flamingo, Pauly D) that we're right. Topics range from "Kiss, Marry, Kill: Mike Ross, Harvey Specter, Louis Litt" (Aubrey was squarely in the kill Louis camp, whereas I was all for offing Harvey... both of us wanted to marry Mike. Probably due to that scene with Meghan Markle in the filing room), to "should I get bangs?" (a resounding no), to "do you think what happened with Dylan is because I'm entirely deluded?" (I leaned yes, even after Aubs gave a tearful, wine-induced speech declaring that I was beautiful and special and Dylan was a grade-A idiot).

"Nope." Aubrey snaps her eggshell-blue fingernails in front of my face. "Stop trying to distract me and start telling me about your trainwreck of a date."

I poke at a mushroom with my chopsticks. "There's no more to say than what I texted you. It was a total off-the-rails disaster."

"Where's your phone?" Aubrey makes a gimme motion. "Let's forget Keith and go man-shopping."

I know my best friend is trying to help. That her heart is in the right place. But she and I have been "man-shopping" for me on Spark since my post-Christmas-party resolution, and we keep coming up empty.

What I'm looking for is straightforward enough:

1. He must be over 30 and under 45
2. He must have stable employment
3. He must want a family
4. He must be looking for a long-term commitment

I thought it was the perfect hit list to snipe an eligible bachelor... but here I am, just having spent an entire evening with *Keith*.

I used to think Dylan hit all those things on my list. He's 33, has stable employment as the manager of the Pinnacle, and he's always said he wants a family one day.

I *believed* he was looking for a long-term commitment with me, because at one point, Dylan wasn't only my boss... back in college, he was my *boyfriend*.

Dylan was the first guy who ever looked my way. I was a quiet, shy freshman, while he was a gregarious senior—and we were both majoring in Hospitality. I couldn't believe he gave me the time of day, but he seemed to appreciate my qualities of being responsible and hardworking, and liked that I wasn't into going out and partying.

We broke up when he graduated, Dylan tearfully citing a promise that "it just wasn't our time, but one day, we would find a way to be together, for real."

Fast forward a few years, and we end up working at the same hotel. I thought, at the time, it was fate.

But then, Dylan got promoted to manager, and it still wasn't "our time." But he was still sweet, still complimentary— still borderline flirtatious with me—enough for me to keep waiting.

Way too long.

Now, with hindsight, I don't know if it was ever going to be "our time." If I was ever going to be enough for him.

"Aubs, I think I've had enough Spark dates for this month." I pop the top button on my skirt to make room for more Chinese food I grab from the floor: spring rolls.

"Really?" Aubrey blinks at me through her glasses.

"No." I close my tired eyes. "The show must go on."

Aubrey, the eternal optimist, nods encouragingly. "You're doing great, honey. I'm proud of you. He's out there, we just gotta keep looking."

"Jaxon says I need to learn how to read people." Once again, I flash back to the bartender with the cute, boyish dimples and the straight-up manly, sexy confidence with which he intimidated Keith.

I close my eyes as the memory makes me smile.

There's a beat of silence.

And another.

And then, I realize what I've done. My eyes fly open to the sight of Aubrey staring at me, her eyes all big and buggy.

"And who is this *Jaxon* you speak of?"

I wave a spring roll at her. "Some bartender who helped me get rid of Keith."

"A bartender named Jaxon?" Audrey's tone is almost wicked.

"Ye-es."

"A bartender named Jaxon who kicked your date out of a restaurant and gave you dating advice."

"Jax was just helping me out."

At least, I think that's what he was doing...

"I'll bet he was." Aubrey's gray-green eyes are glittering maniacally as she sits on the couch next to me. Too close.

I shove a spring roll in my mouth so I can't respond.

She inches even closer, getting all up in my face. "And what did this *Jax* look like?"

I point at my mouth, indicating that I can't respond. She folds her arms. "I, quite literally, have all night."

For a moment, I consider lying to get her off my back, but there's no way I can keep this from her.

I swallow. "He was... good-looking."

"How good-looking?"

"Like, a normal amount."

"How good-looking, Holly? Don't think I missed that smile all over your face a minute ago."

I sigh. "Okay, fine. He was, like, crazy hot. In a mountain man kinda way."

"Ooh, like a lumberjack?"

"He looked like he would be very skilled at cutting wood," I confirm.

"And flinging you over his shoulder while running to save you from a rogue bear?" Aubrey clasps her hands in glee.

Correct.

I hold up a hand before my best friend's freight train of

enthusiasm can leave the station. "First off, aren't all bears rogue? Secondly, he's a bartender who basically flat-out confirmed that he's a player looking to have fun. Definitely *not* a dating prospect for me."

In fact, when I peered back inside while I waited an eternity for my Lyft, I could see him behind the bar, flirting up a storm with the pretty blond waitress.

"What, you don't like to *have fun?*"

I see Aubrey's bobbing eyebrows and smirking mouth and gleaming eyes, and I decide to blow right past it. "What I *don't* like is the thought of going on any more time-wasting dates with people who aren't ready to get married. I wasted enough of my time with Dylan. I need to find a man who wants to settle down with me. Not someone who still goes on spring break."

"Maybe he'll take you to the mountains for *Bears Gone Wild,* Montana edition. Have his way with you in a hammock."

"AUBREY!" I throw a spring roll at her and miss. She picks it off the floor, dusts it off, and pops it in her mouth with a devious grin. Before she can speak any more nonsense, I say, "Stop trying to live vicariously through your old and weathered single friend."

"I'm just *kidding.*"

"I know," I reply, softening slightly. Her heart is in the right place, even when her foot is in her mouth.

Aubrey sighs. "So, tell me. What did mountain-man-Jax say about reading people?"

"He basically said that I suck at figuring out what men *actually* want, despite what they may say in their dating profiles."

Aubrey pushes her glasses up onto her head and rubs her eyes. She does this when she's thinking, choosing her next words carefully.

"Holly," she says finally. "Have you considered that you might not have to go searching for the one right away, either? Maybe a fling with someone like this Jax guy is actually what you need right now. Take this pressure off yourself about the end goal and enjoy the journey. Enjoy flirting and dancing and kissing, even, and just seeing where it goes."

I almost laugh. "'Seeing where it goes' is not in the Dictionary of Holly."

Growing up, I was always the responsible one in my family. Mindy was funny and wild and had all the boys chasing her, while I was always planning for every eventuality in my life—to the relief of our parents, who were glad to have one daughter with a sensible life plan who didn't cause them sleepless nights.

My plan was to get my Hospitality degree, secure a job in my field, then get married. I scripted everything for myself, and when I met Dylan, he seemed to fill the right role in my script. So much so, that I didn't really consider anything else—whether I wanted to travel, or have adventures, or maybe even flirt and dance and kiss a little, as Aubrey said.

I loved Dylan, and I believed his promise that one day, we would be together. And when I first got my job at the Pinnacle, everything seemed to be going according to plan.

But now, the plan has gone very much awry, and I'm out here on the dating scene with my list of resolutions, trying to find an alternate plan at the last minute.

So Aubrey is incorrect. Now is not the time for self-discovery and fun. Now is the time for action.

"I don't want to see where it goes... I just need a new plan," I tell Aubrey with renewed vigor, the cogs of my mind turning back to something a certain sexy bartender said earlier tonight. I have a date lined up for next weekend—same place, same time —but maybe we *should* do a walk or a coffee, instead. Lower the stakes.

Or, at the very least, make it easier to run away if he starts monologuing about carb loading or anti-feminist propaganda.

Aubrey rolls her eyes. "You would say that."

"I would," I agree.

But I'm not wrong.

When at first you don't succeed... do better.

6

JAX

Orlagh took the news of my resignation well.

If you consider "taking it well" to be her throwing a (full) cup of coffee at the wall and yelling "Don't leave me with Dante to man the bar!"

However, slowly but surely, she's come around to the idea. I gave her six weeks' notice—plenty of time to find a replacement for me to train. And it allows me to get some of my affairs in order and to start tackling my list of to-do's.

Between my bartending shifts, I've been spending a lot of time at the cabin working on renovations, and it's really starting to come together. The next big job will be the front deck, and I have a feeling I won't be able to do it alone.

I've also (reluctantly) started looking into some PR and marketing companies, but honestly I have no idea where to start.

Which is why I'm finally carving out some time to get lunch this afternoon with my sister Maddie and her husband, in the hope that she might be able to help with some of this marketing and social media stuff.

And as for Morris's final piece of advice—getting more guiding experience? I did manage to take Laurel to the wilderness last week and, well...

I should have known that the excursion would not go well the moment I saw her pointy red manicure.

And I should have decided to call the whole thing off when she proceeded to don a life jacket, decorated with no less than six sets of bear bells, on top of her hiking gear.

"A life jacket?!" Maddie presses her lips together after I share this fun little tidbit. "*Please* don't tell me you were anywhere close to raging whitewater!"

I shake my head soberly. "Nope. Middle of the woods."

She snorts, and then eyes my forearms, which are currently sliced up with angry red scratches. "And are you going to tell us what happened, or am I just to believe you got mauled by a cougar?"

"There aren't any cougars in Georgia."

"Then tell me what happened," Maddie wheedles like she's seven years old again and begging me to play with her. Back then, she always insisted on using my GI Joes as her Barbie dolls' boyfriends—Ken didn't cut it, apparently.

Which is ironic, because she's now married to the human equivalent of a Ken doll.

Hockey Superstar Ken.

Maddie's husband, Sebastian, flashes me a very Ken-esque dimpled grin as he eyes the scratches. Battle wounds. "Maybe *Laurel* was the cougar."

We are currently seated on a nice patio in the warm spring sunshine, plates piled high with burgers and fries. A picture-perfect family get-together for a pitch I'm sure they have no idea is coming.

But I have to get through this explanation first. Which, yes, they are both going to laugh at me for, but I'm hoping this story will lend itself to said upcoming pitch...

Leaning back in my chair, I sigh. "Laurel is responsible for said mauling, yes."

"Ew!" Maddie yells, covering her ears. My dog, Rick, who was previously curled up at her feet, jumps up, gives her what I can only describe as a dirty look, and stalks over to flop down at my feet. He gives a dramatic groan and I lean down to rub his head. *I feel ya, buddy.* "That's disgusting, Jax."

While my sister looks straight-up offended, Seb looks almost impressed. "Not my thing, personally, but if that's what you're into, bro, I—"

I hold up my hands before Seb can finish that particular thought. "Calm down, everyone." I smirk. "She scratched the hell out of my arms because she was scared of falling into a ravine. Hence the hiking life jacket."

"Oh." Maddie smacks my arm. "Why on earth didn't you lead with that?!"

Seb frowns as he picks a piece of tomato off his sandwich and tosses it to Rick. "She was scared of falling... into a ravine?"

"Yup."

"But are there any ravines anywhere near—?"

"Nope."

Seb's frown deepens. He's from Western Canada—moved down here to play for Atlanta's NHL team, the Cyclones—and so he's very-well acquainted with the outdoors. "Are there any bodies of water, of any kind, that one could potentially fall into?"

"There's a stream by the trail."

"Well, that makes sense." My sister nods decisively. "Better safe than sorry. And if she can't swim, a life jacket is probably a good precaution."

Maddie isn't actually my sister, but my stepsister, and if her small stature, pale skin, green eyes and light brown hair are good indicators that we're not blood related—I'm tall, broad-shouldered, and have dark features—then her general hatred of the outdoors is the clincher. She's the worst hiker I've ever seen. Camping is like torture for her.

Which is why the proposition I've got for her today has to be delivered *delicately*, at best...

"The stream's about two inches deep."

"People can drown in only a couple of inches of water, you know!" Maddie retorts. "I read that somewhere recently."

"I think that's toddlers, love." Seb smiles at his wife affectionately.

"Still..." Maddie insists, then looks at me, eyes narrowed. "That doesn't explain the scratches."

"Laurel wanted me to carry her across the stream," I admit, my brain practically throbbing at the (literally) scarring memory.

"The two-inch-deep stream?" Seb says with amusement.

"That's right."

"Why?"

"In case she got carried off in a current and somehow plummeted into said non-existent ravine."

"Wow."

I nod. "So I picked her up and started to walk across the stream, and that's when we saw a little family of deer, and... Laurel lost the plot."

"Deer?" Maddie clarifies. "Like, *Bambi?*"

"The deer weren't the problem, exactly." I pick up a fry. Break it in half. "She was convinced that a bear would be along any minute to make a meal of the deer, and then, by proxy, us."

Seb bursts out laughing.

"She was so freaked out, she started screaming and dug her nails—freshly-manicured nails, mind you—into my arms, and well, *voila*." I gesture down at the scratches. "Let's just say that I shan't be seeing Laurel again anytime this century."

My brother-in-law only laughs harder. "Oh, I would have paid good money to see that!"

Meanwhile, Maddie tuts. "You're gonna need to put some hydrogen peroxide on those deep ones. But why on earth did you take her hiking in the first place? The wilderness is no place for a date." She shudders.

"That, I have now realized with startling clarity. I'm as scarred mentally as I am physically," I joke. "But at least now, I know that I will never, ever take someone I'm seeing to do anything outdoorsy again."

Maddie frowns. "I just meant that you shouldn't take any more girls who don't enjoy the outdoors. Your future wife will obviously have to be into all that weird nature stuff."

"Future wife?" I raise a brow at her, and she sticks her tongue out at me.

"Yeah, yeah, yeah," my sister grouches. "Marriage isn't for you and commitment sucks, and so on."

"Exactly." I point from her to Seb. "You two are an exception, of course. Because I would have happily married Seb myself."

He claps my shoulder with a grin. "Feeling's mutual, my man."

"Sometimes *I* feel like the third wheel with you two." Maddie pouts. "And honestly, Jax, I think you should think about dating someone who might actually be compatible with you, long term. You need more company than only Rick on all those multi-day trips you take to the middle of nowhere, even just for safety's sake." She glances down at my dog. "No offense, Rick."

"He takes plenty of offense," I say lightly as my mind, for

some reason, jumps back to that night a couple weeks ago when I helped that woman Holly in the bar...

She would spend every weekend searching for a soulmate with no luck, looking more and more downtrodden as the dates went by. Sounds way more miserable than flying solo to me. Though she hasn't been back to Full Moon for any more terrible dinner dates with 'roided up sociopaths, I have seen her drop by the bar to have a quick drink with a couple of different guys, so I can only hope that she's taken my advice and is lowering the stakes of her first dates. And that she hasn't, in fact, been chopped up into pieces by her Lyft driver, like she insinuated might happen.

"Well, my point stands," Maddie says decisively, sticking her fork into her pickle and dipping it into Seb's little pot of coffee cream before popping it into her mouth. *Has she lost her mind?* "You would do well to have someone with you who'd be able to dial 911 with her human fingers if one of you does, by chance, stumble upon one of these magical ravines."

"You sound like your mother with all that talk," I tell Maddie with a roll of my eyes. Her mom is my dad's second wife. Unluckily for her.

"Eek!" Her hand flies to her mouth. "You're right, I do. Gross. And I sincerely apologize."

"Apology accepted."

Maddie gives me a smile and a nod, and then glances quickly at Seb. Meanwhile, I shift in my seat, my stomach clenching.

I've indulged them with the Laurel story. We've pretty much wrapped up with lunch.

It's now or never.

"So, look—" I start, right as Maddie says, "We have—"

She presses her lips together and gives her head a shake. "Sorry. You go first."

I take a deep breath, weirdly nervous. I knew I'd have to tell them sometime, and I have the feeling I have to get this out now before I lose my nerve. "Actually, on the topic of me spending a ton of time in the backcountry alone, there is something I've been meaning to tell you guys..."

I shove my stubby fry in the pool of ketchup and swirl it around. As close as I am to Maddie, and as much as I like my new brother-in-law, there are some things I just don't like to share. Talking about myself doesn't come naturally, and when I try new things or set my mind to new endeavors, I prefer to keep my cards close to my chest. Let people think or assume that I have no ambitions outside of bartending and exploring the wilds.

I think, deep down, I'm scared of failure. The less people see you try, the less you can potentially fail. I'm sure it has something to do with the way my father brought me up, but honestly, that's a scab I prefer to leave alone. Picking at that particular personality trait of mine is not something I'm keen to do.

Right now, though, I don't have a choice. Part of making my dream a reality is telling the people closest to me about my plans. And, apparently, not being afraid to ask for help.

"What is it?" Maddie claps her hands.

"You know that cabin I bought a while back?"

"Yeah."

"Well, for the past few months, I've been renovating it." I shift in my seat again. "And I've also been working towards my certification for Wilderness Guides of America. So I can lead wilderness expeditions."

Maddie's eyes grow wide as dinner plates. "Wow, Jax. Good for you! When does it all start?"

"Well, it's already finished. I'm certified."

Her jaw drops while Seb claps me on the shoulder, looking

genuinely pleased. "That's awesome, man. I'd sign up for any course led by you."

"Thanks," I say, smiling back at him. I then turn to my sister, who's now opening and closing her mouth like a puffer fish. "Mads?" I ask gently. "What do you think?"

"I thought..." she starts. "I thought you were just bartending." Her flapping mouth finally settles down, stretches instead into a wide, beaming smile that puts me immediately at ease. "But *this* actually sounds like you, weird as I think you are for it."

Seb nods. "Seriously. This sounds perfect for you."

I laugh, both pleased and discomforted by their words. "You don't need to suck up to me anymore, I've already given you my blessing," I joke and Seb laughs, too. "It's not that big of a deal. Just something I'm trying out."

"No, this is a *huge* deal," Maddie says, raising her cup of tea like she's toasting me. "I'm so proud of you. You're gonna make the best guide ever."

"Hang on." Seb frowns. "What does this have to do with the cabin?"

I push my fingers through my hair. "Well, I'm renovating it so I can use it as the base for wilderness expeditions. Have guests group together there before we go out on longer hikes. Probably live out there myself, full-time. I've already given my resignation at Full Moon."

I could swear Maddie jerks back a little and Seb's face falls, but both of them recover quickly and Maddie leans towards me, placing her elbows on the table. "You're full of surprises today, aren't you? So when are you open for business?"

"Well, here's the thing..." I say slowly, wondering how on earth I should phrase this. I twirl the stubby fry around the ketchup with renewed fervor. "I have my certification now and everything's pretty much set to go, but my mentor says I should get more experience as a guide by taking people—particularly novices—out on some trips. He also says it's important for me to work on marketing my business. Build up my social media presence, say, on TikTok." I take a breath. "I was thinking that I could kill two birds with one stone..."

Seb chuckles. "Ahh. I see where this is going."

The guy catches on quickly. A lot quicker than Maddie, who is still smiling happily, totally unaware.

I raise my eyebrows at my sister. "So, I know you hate the great outdoors, but I'm hoping you can help me out..."

7

HOLLY

The Pinnacle Hotel is practically a landmark in downtown Atlanta. A heritage building that carries over one hundred years of history, preserved and pristinely cared for—to the point where it almost feels like it's stuck in the past.

It's meant to be quaint, charming. Romantic. But in the wrong light, it feels more like a relic. Something that used to be aspirational, but now, it's lost some of its shine. Gained a few mothballs.

Even the rumored resident ghost—a legend embraced by staff and guests alike about a portly man aptly nicknamed Peeping Tom who haunts the swimming pool changing rooms—has lost some of his spooky appeal since a real-life peeping tom was caught spying in there last month.

The thing is, I really do love the hotel. When I walked in here for my interview five years ago, I was immediately taken with the fact that the building seemed to tell a story. I fell in love with its old nooks and crannies and creepy folklore and eccentric regular guests, and I wanted to share that love with everyone who passed through the doors.

I get that Dylan, who is now the General Manager, wants to preserve its history and is reluctant to change too many things and update our processes —in fact, I admire his dedication to this. But I do think that there's living in the past, and there's preserving history in a fun way... one that brings the Pinnacle into the twenty-first century and puts it on the map as a must-book when visiting Atlanta.

The average age of our guests right now is frighteningly old. Like, getting to the stage that they could soon haunt the place, too.

So it's my opinion that if we want to bring in new customers, appeal to younger generations, we need to entice them by reaching them where they are—forget print ads in newspapers and magazines, we need a social media presence. Engage with potential guests and tell our story, in real-time.

That's not really my job title, though. As Dylan reminds me now in his gently coaxing, roundabout way as he peers at me through the tortoiseshell glasses I've always thought make him look like he should be modeling for Tom Ford or Armani.

"It's a nice idea, Holly." He makes a humming sound as he leans back in his chair, fingers steepled together. "But I don't think that's the image we want to portray here at Pinnacle. We want to show off that elevated experience, not drag our name through the mud."

"I understand," I reply, although I don't. Dylan is talking like I've suggested we bring in new guests with naked jello wrestling, when all I proposed was that we invite a couple of travel influencers to stay for a night or two—influencers whose social media is dedicated to visiting new cities and reviewing nice hotels. "I just noticed that we have a lot of midweek availability through April, so if we were to set up the influencers in a couple of our nicest suites, give them a fun and lively Atlanta itinerary, and have them promote a discount code valid

Monday to Thursday in their videos, stories and posts, we could probably fill those empty rooms pretty quickly."

"Well, you know I appreciate the initiative," Dylan replies with that lopsided smile of his that makes my knees a little weak. *Used to* make my knees a little weak. "Douglas has been hard at work putting together some ideas for the new billboard campaign and they look very promising. And he's finally gotten the Pinnacle Instagram account up and running, so do rest assured that I have been taking your thoughts on social media into account."

I'm not sure where to look, so I focus on the framed photo on Dylan's desk, the one at last year's Atlanta Hotel Awards, where he won a prize. He looks so happy in the photo—strong, yet determined—like he'd been willing his win into existence.

Dylan must sense that something he's said is bothering me, because his expression turns kind. His hazel eyes—perfectly almond-shaped and ringed with blond lashes—meet mine and he lowers his voice to that low, soothing decibel he always uses when he gives out compliments. "You're incredibly bright, Holly. Don't ever think I'm taking you or your ideas for granted."

I give a nod, lowering my face. "Thank you, Dylan."

Because honestly, there's nothing more to say. I was so excited, last fall, when Dylan decided that the hotel needed an official marketing department, and created the position of Marketing and Communications Coordinator.

I applied for it immediately. I know the Pinnacle and its clientele like the back of my hand, and for years, I've come to Dylan with countless ideas to fill more rooms. It felt like a job he'd created specifically for me, the promotion I'd been waiting for where I could truly shine... but in the end, Dylan ended up hiring Douglas—a seasoned marketing expert—externally for the position instead.

Which makes sense. While I have the practical experience, I have none of Douglas's marketing accolades. I got the sense that Dylan envisioned me for the role... but I guess it just *wasn't my time.*

So now, I need to respect his decision, even if the Instagram account Douglas has started feels a bit low-effort and impersonal.

"You know we need you in Guest Services," Dylan continues, his lips sliding into a smile. "We'd be lost without you out there," he adds with a wink.

He said the exact same thing when he told me he'd passed me over for the marketing job. Just a couple days before the second blow came at the company Christmas party that he'd also passed me over in an entirely different way.

"Better get back out there, then," I say, hoping my voice doesn't betray the fact I feel about four inches tall right now—and I shoot him the best smile I can muster, so he doesn't think I'm bitter.

"Thanks for stopping in. You know I'm always open to hearing your ideas." I nod and am about to leave when he says, "Oh, and Holly?"

"Yes?" I turn to look at him again, and his smile turns what I used to think was flirtatious.

"You look good today. I like you in that color."

I force my lips upwards. "Thank you."

I walk out of Dylan's office, stumbling a little over his compliment—*statement.* A few months ago, I would've thought he meant this to be sweet and sincere, but now I know it means nothing, has nothing to do with what we once were to each other. He probably talks like that to everyone, a morale boost or leadership technique.

Once I'm back out in the lobby, I scan the area to make sure that no guests are lurking, then quickly check my phone. Specifically, my DMs on Spark.

Trevor, my latest match, has sent me a picture of his pigs. Again.

That isn't a euphemism.

Because Trevor is a pig farmer, and while the photos are excessive, he seems nice and well-meaning. So maybe I can overlook the handlebar mustache—and the fact that he keeps calling me "young lady"—and instead ask him to meet for a walk in the park or for a drink?

I've been doing lots of these low-stakes, quick dates over the last couple weeks. And even though I haven't clicked with anyone yet, I have to give kudos to the rude, sexy bartender, because keeping things casual, initially, definitely *does* make things easier. On my mental health and on my wallet.

For example, I had zero in common with last Thursday's date, Malcolm, and a quick drink at Full Moon—during which I'm pretty sure said rude, sexy bartender watched me with a knowing smirk, winking at me when I caught his eye—was all it took for me to work out that we're not a match. Plus, I got my Saturday night back to do a Korean sheet face mask and watch *He's Just Not That Into You* for the five zillionth time. No more time wasted.

Instead of answering Trevor's message, I find myself flicking through the profiles of three guys boasting shirtless gym photos, two men holding up very large fish, and one particularly disturbing profile that proclaims the want of a woman with "nice big feet with straight toes."

That's when I get an alert that I have a new message from Emmett, 37, five miles away. My heart jumps a little.

Emmett is cute, with nice eyes and teeth that are almost too white. He sells insurance, likes jazz music, and fixes up vintage cars in his spare time. Which I'm sure is very interesting. But most importantly, he's a homeowner who dreams of filling said home with a family.

We've been messaging for a couple days, and the most suss thing he's said is that his favorite food is mashed potatoes. No spices, no particular flavor, no add-ins—not even cheese. Or salt. Just... mashed potatoes.

I open the message.

> Hello, Holly. How's your day going? Hope it's as radiant as you are!

Wow, he's... enthusiastic.

> It's been good. Doing my best to stay awake through the early morning shift and drinking lukewarm coffee by the bucketload over here.

> I actually find lukewarm coffee to be optimal for consuming. Not too hot, not too cold.

And also a fan of Goldilocks, apparently.

> Wish we could be drinking coffee together ;)

See, I don't have the ick at all. He's just being cute. This is his idea of flirty banter.

Before I lose my nerve—slash lose all hope of ever finding someone to fall in love with—I type out another message.

> Want to go for a walk this afternoon?

> It would be my pleasure.

8

JAX

I'm going to be an uncle.

Maddie is pregnant, and I'm going to be an uncle.

Not just an uncle... a *godfather*.

How in the hell am I going to be a godfather?

As I walk through the park in the direction of the bar—Rick trotting along in front of me, blissfully unaware of my current state of shock—I take deep breaths as I process this news.

I feel so unprepared. I don't think I've ever even *held* a baby before...

What if I drop the freaking thing?

I feel a bit nauseous at the thought. Well, that and probably also Seb and Maddie's entirely unnecessary, way-too-detailed recounting of their accidental baby making (Sebastian smugly used the words "super sperm," which really does not bear thinking about).

I'm excited for them, but also very shocked and vaguely terrified... which is probably why I reacted the way I did.

Helpful note to anyone receiving news that their one and

only sister is pregnant: probably best not to respond with, "Are you sure it's not just indigestion?"

Maddie seemed overjoyed by the news, which is good. It's not like the two of us had the warmest upbringing from which to draw inspiration on how to be a parent, but from what I understand, Seb comes from a relatively normal, loving family, so I'm sure he doesn't have the same qualms I do about potential fatherhood.

Rick and I are passing a playground and I stop for a moment to look at the mass of screaming children going wild. There's a flurry of activity orbiting the area as parents cheer for their offspring going down the slide or push their kids on the swings.

"Hello!" A voice speaks from somewhere below me, and I look down to see a little boy with a head full of black curls blinking up at me. "Can I pet your dog, mister?"

Rick loves kids, so his tail starts wagging a mile a minute, but I look in the direction of the kid's mom and dad for guidance. The mom nods encouragingly. "If it's okay with you. Jayden loves dogs, but we can't get him one because his sister is allergic. Breaks our hearts because he wants one so badly, but it's not possible."

"Oh, sure," I reply. "Go ahead, Jayden."

The kid gives me a huge toothy grin. "Cool, thanks!"

As Jayden bends to pet him, Rick very enthusiastically licks his nose, which makes him laugh and laugh as the mom and dad look on with matching smiles. The dad goes on to absentmindedly loop his arm around his wife's neck as they watch their son with glowing eyes.

I watch, too, but with something closer to trepidation as the pint-sized boy plays with my dog.

The scene seems so at odds with my own childhood. I mostly remember my dad being absent. He'd spend long days—

and nights—at the office. And when he *was* home, there was just yelling. Constant fighting.

Then one day, my mom left without me. And never came back.

When Maddie and her mother moved in with my dad and me a couple of years later, things were a little better. I was glad to finally have company in that big, empty house, and I loved my stepsister from the word go, but it's not like we became one big happy family. My dad still spent long nights at work, and Maddie's mother seemed sad a lot. Threw herself into sitting on boards for charities and spa weekends with her girlfriends.

A few years later, when I overheard my father on the phone talking dirty with his secretary (because he's a walking cliché, so of course it was his secretary), it made more sense why my stepmother was sad so much. Made more sense why my own mother left.

"You have kids?" Jayden's mom asks, snapping me out of my thoughts. It feels like an odd question to ask a stranger, until she gestures to the kids' playground nearby, and I realize that the only adults that hang out at such places are parents and creeps.

"No, I was just walking by," I say. The woman frowns, so I hurriedly add, "but I am going to be a godfather soon."

I remind myself that I'm supposed to be keeping this a secret, but I decide it's okay to tell her this because she doesn't know me or Maddie or Seb. Apparently, pregnancies aren't usually announced until they're about twelve weeks along. You learn something new every day.

And I clearly have a lot to learn if I'm going to be a good uncle-slash-godfather to this little creature. Which I obviously plan to be. Because as non-ideally as I first reacted to the news, Seb and Maddie still wanted me for the title.

Of course, I had to accept such an honor. And of course,

I'm going to do everything in my power to be there for the kiddo. Be nothing like my own father.

Hell, maybe I can take him—or her—hiking.

Jeez. *Her.*

What if it's a freaking girl?! When she's old enough to date, I'm going to want to kill every single guy that even looks at her.

"Oh, that's wonderful!" Jayden's mom exclaims, and I try to arrange my face into an appropriate expression of wonder. Because now, on top of being scared of dropping a baby that's not due to be born for months, I'm also terrified of said future baby growing up to date an asshole that I'm going to have to kill.

Wonderful, all round.

Jayden and Rick are now practically wrestling, my dog with his hind paws atop the little boy's chest as Jayden buries his face in Rick's fur, still laughing. I have to admit, it's a heart-warming sight.

The little family of three finally say their goodbyes, and I continue my walk around the park, smiling to myself.

As I look out across the park, I suddenly spot a familiar brunette in the distance. Is that...?

It's Holly. The not-a-player-but-just-a-terrible-dater. The woman I told, to her face, to literally "do better" a couple weeks ago.

I might feel a little bad about that.

And now, here she is, lurking by herself on a bench and looking like she's about to murder somebody.

My smile widens—I can't help but be intrigued by this girl.

And so, while I usually like to mind my own business, this is one thing that I'm going to have to go and investigate further.

9

HOLLY

Emmett and I agree to meet in Piedmont Park at 3:30PM because he has a rec league basketball game later this evening, which is nice, but it also doesn't give me time to go home and change after work.

Staid cream linen dress and cardigan combo, it is. Hopefully he's into really vanilla-looking wifey material.

I arrive five minutes early and duck into the pee-scented public bathrooms to fix my lipgloss and brush my hair. Then, I arrange myself on a park bench in what I hope looks like a friendly and approachable manner, with a touch of mystery and je ne sais quoi.

It's a beautiful afternoon and the air is warm on my face, thick with the grassy scent of early spring. I take off my cardi and stuff it in my purse, leaving me in just the strappy-shouldered dress. Which is cute, I think, if a little dressy for a walking date.

And I wait.

And wait.

And then, I wait some more.

4PM comes. I shoot him a message asking if he's on his way. No response.

Maybe he's stuck in traffic and can't text me? I reason, crossing and uncrossing my legs on the bench again.

It's getting hard to look effortlessly and casually cute while I'm borderline sweating in the sunshine. Not to mention one of my butt cheeks is going numb.

At 4:15PM, I check in again to ask if everything's okay. Still no response.

Oh, no. Maybe my phone has stopped receiving texts?

Just to be safe, I text Aubrey a smiley-face emoji. She responds almost immediately with an eggplant emoji.

Uncalled for.

But clearly, my texts are going through...

Finally, after an hour of waiting, I resign myself to the fact that he's not coming. And now, I'm hungry, cranky, my butt is sore from sitting on this stupid wooden bench for an hour, and for some reason—probably a combination of being hungry, cranky, and sore, along with the humiliation of being stood up and a dash of PMS—I feel tears forming in my eyes.

Annoyed, I blink them away. Then, I get up, shake myself off, and march over to the popsicle-wielding vendor cart a few steps away from me.

As soon as the strawberry lemonade freeze pop is in my hand, I'm tearing the wrapping off in a mildly feral manner.

When in doubt, consume sugar.

I've shoved the freeze pop in my mouth when someone behind me calls my name. "Holly?"

It's a man's voice. Has to be Emmett.

About. Freaking. Time.

And also... What terrible timing.

I remove the freeze pop from my mouth, lick my lips to make them seem somewhat glossy and not covered in pure

64

sugar, and plaster on what I hope is a blasé, easygoing, flirtatious expression before turning around to face him.

But when I whirl around, it's not Emmett standing in front of me with an apology locked and loaded. Instead, I'm face to face with a familiar, teasing grin.

"Thought it was you." Jax the Sexy Bartender smirks down at me. "Glad to see your Lyft driver didn't chop you up into tiny pieces."

I can't help but smile. I forgot he was funny. "Well, she was going to, but I bribed her with cheesecake so she said she'd chop up her next passenger instead."

"Thinking on your feet, I like it."

I have to laugh at this, hardly believing that I'm seeing him here. In broad daylight. Something about the Sexy Bartender seemed very nocturnal in my mind. Like he's a werewolf or something. But he's just as tall and handsome as I remember, dressed in all black again, but this time, he's accessorized with a baseball cap and a really cute dog that's pulling on his leash as he tries to get close to me.

Or, more likely, the popsicle.

"Who's your friend?" I ask, bending down to the little dog as he nuzzles my shins. "He's cute."

"This is Rick. He's a real ladies' man."

"Dogs do take after their owners, I've heard," I deadpan, now crouching with one hand stroking the dog, while I hold my popsicle out of his reach with the other. "Wait. You named your dog *Rick*?"

"Yup."

I examine the pup, who looks like he's a cross of about a hundred breeds. "Short for Richard?"

"Short for Rick Astley, actually."

I stare at him. "Rick Astley... the singer."

"That's the one."

"Like, one-hit-wonder, never going to give you up or let you down, Rick Astley."

"Exactly."

"Why?!" I exclaim.

A shrug. "He's a rescue. Wanted him to know he was in his forever home."

Well. I'll be damned, if that isn't the sweetest thing I've ever heard.

I give Rick Astley the Rescue Dog one last pet, then straighten to look at his owner, who's only slightly red-faced at this admission he just made. He's clearly a lot softer on the inside than his rugged, bearded exterior lets on.

And rugged, it really is.

His black t-shirt isn't tight, but it hugs his broad chest and strains over his biceps, one of which appears to be decorated with a large tattoo that's half-covered by the t-shirt sleeve so I can't work out what it is.

It's only then that I notice his bare forearms are covered with deep, red, angry scratches.

What on earth?

He looks like he's been dragged through a holly bush backwards. Twice.

Unfortunately for me, he catches me staring, and in an instant, his bashfulness is gone, and the smirk is back. "Trust me. You don't want to know."

"Hmm. Not so much a guard dog then?"

"Hell, I'm the one guarding *Rick*."

This makes me laugh.

"So what brings you to the park this afternoon all dressed up?" He changes the topic swiftly, folding his arms to hide the scratches. "Haven't seen you around Full Moon for the past couple weeks, so I assume you've been taking my advice on expanding your dates to other locations?"

66

I summon what I hope is a flippant smile. "Can't a girl spend an afternoon alone in the park for fun?"

"Not when she keeps glancing around like she's expecting someone to show up at any moment."

I blink at Jax. "How did you—"

"I saw you from across the park." His lips twist up a little as he nods towards my bum-numbing bench. "That's why we came over. Gotta say, you seemed more than a little lost in a place with literal maps and signs all around. I figured you were looking for *someone* rather than *something*."

I peer at him quizzically for a moment. "You really *do* read people."

"It's a skill."

"It's a touch creepy."

Jax bursts out a laugh and I can't help but notice the tendons in his neck as he throws his head back, his smile wide and genuine. I get the sudden sense that he doesn't laugh like this often, and it makes me feel somewhat warm that I elicited this reaction in him.

"Whatever you say, Holly," he says. "Guess I read this situation wrong."

I hesitate for a moment, chewing on my lower lip. And then, for some reason, I say, "Maybe not *all* wrong. I was expecting someone, a date actually... but I'm not anymore."

Jax's expression twitches slightly. "Damn. That sucks. But hey, it happens to the best of us."

"Has it ever happened to *you*?" I reply wryly.

"Well, no," he admits, and for some reason, his laughing expression doesn't irk me. In fact, it almost makes me want to laugh it off along with him. "Not to me, personally. But I see it happen all the time at the bar. People are assholes, remember?"

I trace my finger around my now-dripping popsicle, lick the strawberry flavor off my fingertip. It doesn't taste like much of anything. I'm frowning, going back once again—as I have so many times in the last hour—over my conversations with Emmett. "He seemed so interested... he was messaging me tons today. I just don't get it."

"I'll bet he has a girlfriend."

I snap my head up to look at Jax, sure I misheard. "What?"

"That behavior *screams* girlfriend to me." His expression suddenly darkens, but just as quickly, he shakes his head. Shakes it off. "All about the messaging, but then bails when it transitions into a real meet-up? He's shady, for sure."

I'm shaking my head over and over. "No way."

Jax's eyes meet mine again. "You know him better than I do."

Do I...?

It's not like Emmett and I met in person, not like we've even spoken on the phone. All I have are a couple surface-level details from our brief conversations over the last few days, and the info on his dating profile. And if Jax is right and he really *can* read people, he probably could've gleaned a lot more about the guy than I have.

"He probably got caught in traffic..." I try again, feebly.

Jax simply nods. Rick, as if sympathizing with me, gives my hand a lick. The fact that Jax is not calling me out almost makes everything feel worse.

I cough out a laugh that I hope sounds uplifting and positive, but actually sounds more like an indigestion hiccup. "I don't know why I'm upset," I say with a shrug. "Find a man who wrecks your lipstick, not your mascara, am I right?"

Jax smirks. "I always heard 'break her bed, not her heart.'"

The laugh this time is real, if still a touch teary. But when I see Jax's lips in a crooked grin, my traitorous stomach swoops dangerously.

"Charming," I mutter as I make a big show of rolling my

eyes while shooing away the pesky misplaced butterflies and positively raunchy mental images his words conjured.

"I like to think so." He throws me a teasing wink. "I'd better get going. Take it easy, Holly. Forget the ghoster and good luck with your next date. I hope he's your real Prince Charming and not another toad."

And with that, he saunters off, Rick Astley the dog trotting along at his side.

What a guy.

I don't realize I'm staring after him, lost in thought and mulling over his words, until something cold and wet trickles down my hand. I dump my melted popsicle in the nearest trash can and give my hands a wipe.

Now that I'm out of Jax's slightly mesmerizing presence, I'm thinking a bit more clearly.

And maybe I should take what he says with a grain of salt. After all, the guy has straight-up said that he's a player, so it would make sense that he assumes every other guy is exactly like him. He probably dates multiple women at once himself.

Maybe Emmett really *did* have a reasonable excuse for standing me up and Jax is just a big, hulking, tattooed pessimist who has no idea what he's talking about.

A pessimist with very strange scratches all over his arms. *What did he say about breaking beds...?*

Nope, Holly. We will not be going there.

As if on cue, my phone pings in my bag, making me jump. I check the screen to see a new message.

> This is Emmett's girlfriend. Whoever you are, stay the hell away from my boyfriend, you nasty little homewrecker!

Damn it.

10

JAX

I'm still thinking about Holly the bad dater when I arrive at Full Moon for my evening shift.

All I can hope is that she takes my advice and ditches that loser, whoever he is. Because if I know one thing, it's that there is no way in hell he was stuck in traffic...

But I can't dwell on the sassy, cute brunette and her slew of bad dates right now. The restaurant is due to open in fifteen minutes and I have work to do—both here, of course, and now also for my upcoming business.

Because alongside the big "we're pregnant!" news, Maddie also made some pretty compelling points. Obviously she's no longer an ideal guinea pig for me to practice my wilderness guiding with, but she said she would be glad to assist me with the marketing and social media stuff—from afar.

To be honest, she looked way too pleased to have a good excuse not to go out to the backcountry herself, and also to be honest, I have no idea how she's going to help if she's not actually out there to take pictures and videos... but I'm not the social media expert.

And anyways, before I do *any* of that, Maddie suggested that I get my booking system set up. You know, so that all the people she brings in through social media can actually *book a trip.*

My sister has a pretty decent amount of sass for a person who once came to me bawling because she was worried her Christmas cookies weren't "bringing enough holiday joy."

Needless to say, it looks like I still have a lot of work to do to get this damn business off the ground.

Not to mention I should also work out how to apologize to Maddie and Seb for referring to their future firstborn as "indigestion" and show them that I'm totally on board for this godfathering gig.

I should get them something. *Baby gifts are a thing, right?* I think as I whip off my t-shirt, shrug on a long sleeve, and head inside, Rick prancing at my feet.

Dante pokes his head up from behind the bar, where he's stocking the low fridges with mixers. "Hey, man. What's up?"

"Not much," I lie.

As Dante gives Rick some love, I do a quick mental count of the bottles stacked behind the bar. "Gonna get Rick set up in the front office, then I'll grab some vodka from the storage room. You need anything?"

"All good here. Just wondering who the hell is gonna keep this bar stocked once you abandon ship." He gives me a wink, ruffles Rick's head one last time, and then goes back to stocking, humming to himself.

I roll my eyes but tug at my sleeves, thankful that I brought a long-sleeve shirt for my shift. The goal is to make it through this evening with no intrusive questions or wild theories from my coworker, and I have a feeling he'd have a field day with the not-cougar-mauling on my arms.

After getting Rick settled down in his dog basket out in the front office—he's not allowed in the restaurant itself, but Orlagh, who sits in the office on Monday nights to order stock, loves to have his company for the evening—I grab the keys to the storage room and make my way across the restaurant towards it.

I'm walking past the front doors when they suddenly swing open.

Which startles me—we're not technically open yet and these doors should be locked—but before the doors open fully...

They shut.

Then open again.

What is this, a very strong wind?

They're on their way to shutting again when I reach for the handles and yank. Hard.

The doors fly open (definitely not the wind, then) and I poke my head out to see what the problem is. "Sorry, we're not open ye—Oh, it's *you*."

Standing in front of me is none other than Holly. She looks like she practically ran here, judging by the light sheen of sweat on her forehead and the disheveled hair. Her shiny pink lips are shinier than they were when I was talking to her in the park earlier, like she took a moment to reapply her lip gloss before opening the front doors.

And for some reason, this makes me smile. She's like an unfortunate romance movie heroine. A real life Hollywood starlet.

She laughs sheepishly as I look at her in confusion. "Yes. It's me. Hi."

"Can I... help you?" I frown as I assess her. She seems concerned (nothing new here), but it immediately raises my hackles. "Wait, did the guy finally show up and try something? Is that why you ran here?"

I'm peering past her into the street, ready to throw down,

when she puts a hand on my arm. "No, no. He most definitely did not show up."

I relax. "Oh. Okay. Let me guess, you have another date lined up here at the bar this evening." My lips slide into a smirk. It's just so easy—and enjoyable—to tease this woman. "Two in one day, even if the last guy was a no-show. That's some serious commitment."

"No. I'm, um..." Holly shifts awkwardly on her feet, then exhales. "I'm here to see *you*, actually."

"Oh?"

She opens her mouth. Stalls. Wrinkles her nose. Takes a deep breath.

"I think you're who I've been looking for."

I blink. "I'm sorry?"

"I think you're who I've been looking for," she repeats, with confidence. Her eyes are full of something that looks suspiciously like... hope.

Oh no.

Oh no, oh no.

"Holly," I start gently. Kindly. "That's very flattering and I appreciate it, but I'm not looking for any sort of rela—"

She suddenly dissolves into laughter.

What?

My frown only deepens as I stare at the woman cackling before me. She continues like that for a few more moments before wiping a tear from her eye. "Ohh, that's funny," she says happily. "No, no. I don't mean I want to date *you*."

She puts so much emphasis on the word *you*, I'm not sure if I should feel relieved or offended.

"Okay. That's, uh, good to hear."

She giggles as she pats me on the arm. "No offense or anything."

"None taken," I somewhat lie.

There's a silence.

"So..." I let the word hang in the air between us like a tightrope.

So what do you want, Holly?

"Right!" She snaps to attention. "I don't want to date you, but I do want you to help me find someone I actually want to date. Someone who wants to date me, too."

I scratch my temple as I look at her, trying to work out if she's serious. "You want *me* to help *you* find someone to date."

"Yes."

She *looks* serious. Hopeful, even, her shiny pink lips tipped upward as she stares at me.

I stare back at her quizzically, still trying to work this out. "Don't take this the wrong way, Holly, but I'm pretty sure we have different dating goals and... intensities."

"I know."

"So why are you looking for my help?" I glance her over. "Scratch that. What is so urgent that you would *run* all the way here to ask for my help?"

"You were right about Emmett! As unbelievable as that sounds. So even if I'm looking for a long-term commitment and you're looking for... I don't know, your next tawdry affair, you clearly have a talent that I am sorely lacking. So I need to know: what's your secret?"

I can't hold back a bark of a laugh. No less because who, in this day and age, can say *tawdry affair* with a straight face? "There is no 'secret.' I mean, I don't have, like, a strategy or outline for this sorta thing. Just stay clear of clowns like Keith and that loser who stood you up. You can do better than that."

"But *how?*" She tilts her head and smiles at me. "Someone recently told me that I can't read people."

"Now, who on earth would have said that?" I grin back.

"Oh, some jerk."

I snort with laughter. "Well, this jerk is very sorry."

"No, I think you were right on that point, too. But if you so choose to feel sorry, I know of a way you can make it up to me..."

I arch a brow at her and her cheeks pinken a little as she points at me.

"Stop that! I don't mean like *that*."

"Sure," I drawl.

"I'm serious," she protests. "I need someone to help me find better dates. Someone who can read people, because I'm obviously lacking in that department."

"You don't say."

"So... Can you help me?"

I stare at her, still a little confused. Why on earth would this woman want me—an almost-stranger with absolutely no long-term dating experience—to help her find the love of her life? "Don't you have friends who'd be better suited to help you?"

"You're my best hope."

"And you've gleaned that *how*, exactly?"

"Because you had Keith pegged in an instant. His profile said he was looking for love, but you knew immediately he was looking for *lovin'*, if you get my gist."

"I do. Unfortunately."

"And you knew Emmett had a girlfriend."

"Emmett?"

"The park-walk ghoster," she clarifies.

I frown. "I only knew those things because I know men like that," I say, silently correcting *men* in my mind to *one particular man*.

"Then help me avoid them! Help me find a man who wants the same things I do."

And for some reason—maybe the hydrogen peroxide

75

Maddie insisted on dousing my arms with has leaked into my brain—I find myself pausing. Find my gaze traveling over the girl with the cute dress and the messy hair and the *terrible* taste in men, and I see Maddie before she met Seb. I see their potential baby girl in two decades' time, wanting to find a good man.

I see all the women my father has hurt over the years. My mother included.

And so, I decide to humor her. Give Holly-the-bad-dater a hand with all her bad dates.

I raise a brow at Holly quizzically. "So, if I were to suggest that you stay for a drink right now, you'd say...?"

She puts her hands on her hips. "I'd say: are you offering to help me, or are you asking me out, Jax?"

This makes me laugh. Out of the corner of my eye, I see Dante, Kara and some of the other staff watching us from across the restaurant with undisguised interest. But I don't care. Because I've just decided that I like Holly and her blunt, abrupt mannerisms and weird ideas.

"And I'd say that I can't handle any more of your rejection for the moment." I chuckle, then gesture to the stools that line the bar. "Take a seat and we can get started with... weeding out all the toads."

11

HOLLY

"Sit," Jax says again as he comes up behind me, where I'm dithering in the middle of the restaurant. He points to a bar stool in the corner.

"Say please," I reply.

Why? Why would I say that?

And why does he smell so good? I still remember that smell from the night he saved me from Keith—that clean, woodsy, altogether manly smell that's nothing short of delicious. I mean, shouldn't he smell like spilled beer or something?

"Well, excuse me, ma'am. Where are my manners?" Jax laughs. I like that he laughs easily. There's something so nice about making an attractive man laugh. Not that Jax is an attractive man. Well, I mean, he *is*, objectively speaking. But I'm not personally attracted to him. Definitely not.

He doesn't fit any of the criteria I'm looking for.

"*Please* sit, Holly." He pulls out a barstool for me. Cocks an eyebrow. "Better?"

"Barely," I joke. But I sit. Obediently.

He walks around the bar, flips a dishcloth over one shoulder, and surveys me with squinty eyes that glow in the low, warm light of the restaurant. "What can I do you for?"

For some reason, his narrowed eyes make me nervous. They're a very intimidating color, sort of like a storm cloud before the rain. He's wearing a different shirt than the one he wore in the park, and this black, long-sleeved (and very arm-muscle-hugging) shirt makes the slate-gray color of his eyes even more pronounced.

"Um," I say. I'm parched, and what I want is a cranberry juice mixed with soda water. What I do, however, is flip my hair over my shoulder and say, "Scotch, neat."

I don't know if it's because I'm nervous, but my mouth has a mind of its own right now and it's going off script, clearly thinking I'm George Clooney or something. Who the hell orders scotch at 5PM on a Monday? Alcoholics and silver foxes, that's who.

I'm not even sure I've *had* scotch before.

Apparently, chasing down a man I barely know and asking him to help me find a boyfriend has brought out my spontaneous side, which I usually keep good and buried.

Jax raises his eyebrows a touch, but he doesn't say anything. Instead, he reaches for a bottle of amber liquid, pours a measure into a nearby glass, and places the glass on the bar with a flourish.

I eye it suspiciously. No ice cubes? Lemon and lime garnish? Not even a chilled glass?

He watches me watch my drink, a small smile playing on the corner of his lips as I sniff it suspiciously and wince.

But before either he or I can say anything, a peppy blond girl bounces up to us. I recognize her as the waitress Jax was talking to the night I came here with Keith. She's wearing a short black dress with white Keds and her hair is in one of those adorable high ponytails. She's even prettier up close.

"Um, sorry to interrupt..." she starts. Her expression suggests that she's anything but sorry.

"You're not interrupting," Jax says easily.

"Jax was just helping me with something totally not urgent," I add to let her know that I'm not encroaching on what may be her territory.

Jax smirks at me. "I'd hate to see what your drink of choice would be for an *urgent* issue."

"McDonald's vanilla milkshake, of course," I retort. "I like to save the hard stuff for when I'm in times of dire crisis. You know, job losses, natural disasters, celebrity deaths."

"I can see how that would be a smart avenue. You get fries to dip, too?"

"What do you think I am, an amateur?"

His eyes meet mine, and we share a smile. Hold eye contact for a beat too long before his gaze skates over my face, slowly and deliberately. When he speaks again, his voice has a husky quality that makes my knees a bit wobbly. "Anything but."

Whoa.

This guy's *good.* His dazzling stare would put Edward Cullen to shame. I need to ask him to give me some pointers.

"Are you Jax's sister or something?" The girl's voice pulls my attention away from Jax's hypnotizing eyes. I almost forgot she was here. "The one who's married to that hot hockey player?"

I shift on the leather barstool and cross my legs. "I *wish* I was married to a hot hockey player."

"Kara, this is my new friend Holly." Jax gestures between the waitress and me. "Holly, Kara."

I put my hand out and Kara takes it suspiciously. "You guys seem like you've known each other forever. Hence why I thought you were related."

I don't miss the emphasis on *related.*

She's into him. Definitely marking her territory.

She clearly doesn't know that she has nothing to worry about.

"No, no." I hold up my hands. "He's helping me with my Prince Charming."

Kara visibly relaxes. "Oh, that's great! Super great!"

I roll my eyes at her conspiratorially. "It will be, once I land him."

"Is he a friend of Jax's?" She looks over at the bartender flirtily. "Anyone I know?"

Jax casually picks up a glass and starts polishing it. "Holly, care to take this one?"

I flush red. "Oh, um... well, actually, I don't know who he is yet."

Kara blinks. Purses her pretty pink lips. "I don't get it."

"Well. I'm currently on a mission to find the perfect man."

Kara narrows her eyes, then grimaces awkwardly. Like she's pondering whether I'm a little unhinged and Jax is in grave danger.

"Hey, I think Orlagh's calling you." Jax nods at Kara. "Sounds like she's in the kitchen."

The waitress glances at her dainty white wristwatch. "Guess we're officially open, better go see what she wants."

"Nice to meet you," I say.

"Likewise," Kara lies.

She walks off, all wiggly hips and waggly ponytail. I sigh and flatten my hands on the bar in front of me. It's surprisingly clean and unsticky. Two points for Wolf Man.

"Looks like I saved you. Again." Jax grins.

"Your girl Kara thinks I'm Looney Tunes."

"Not my girl." He goes back to polishing glasses in that casual, flippant way that I've already come to recognize. I try

80

not to notice the way his big hands make quick work polishing the delicate stem of a wine glass.

"But she wants to be," I press.

A chuckle. "I thought you couldn't read people."

"No, but I see massive flashing billboards in front of me."

"Then you shouldn't have any problem learning how to spot massive flashing walking red flags," Jax says, pushing an order pad across the bar towards me. "Why don't you start by writing down everything you're looking for in a man, and we'll go from there."

I eagerly grab the pad of paper and tear off a piece. "Perfect." *I've got this one locked and loaded already!*

He goes on to toss me a pen, and I, of course, don't see it coming and miss it by about a foot. Reflexes of an arthritic grandma, apparently.

As I inelegantly slide off my stool and crouch for the pen, Jax calls down to me. "Oh, and Holly?"

"Yup?"

"This may come as a shock, but if your mission really is to find the 'perfect man,' you may be looking for a while. Because there's no such thing."

I leap to my feet and point his pen at him indignantly. "Oh yes, there is!"

He sighs the sigh of a very tired man. "Please don't tell me that you're one of those hopeless romantic types who thinks some shirtless Harlequin Hero is gonna ride up on his horse and whisk you away for a perfect happy ever after."

"Definitely not. But I *do* know that Henry Cavill exists, and if that's not perfection, I don't know what is."

"Hol," Jax says patiently. "That dude still has morning breath and gets smelly feet after a run. Because he's human."

"No, he's *Superman*." I slide back onto my stool, pen in

hand. "Maybe that should be the new first thing on my list: If you're not Superman, take a hike!"

Jax puts his arms on the bar and leans forward. "This is going to be a long night, isn't it?"

Once again, I try not to notice the way Jax's muscles pop as he leans forward on the bar, even through his long-sleeved shirt. The guy works out, there's no doubt about it. Probably all the mountain-slash-wolfy things he gets up to.

I'm clearly not the only one noticing this either. From across the restaurant, Kara's glare is sending absolute razor blades my way.

"Long night for you, maybe. Kara looks like she wants you *alllll night long*," I sing the last bit off-key.

"Don't change the subject, Lionel Ritchie." We smirk at each other, and I realize this is the most fun I've had with a man over a drink in a very long time.

"Why not go out with her?" I ask, plucking a tiny straw from a holder on the bar and swirling it through my (untouched) scotch.

"If I answer that, you have to answer a question for me. Deal?"

"Deal."

"I have three reasons."

"Hit me."

He holds up three fingers. Nice, long fingers. Big but not sausage-esque. "One, I'm not in the market for a relationship. Two, I don't date coworkers. And three, I'm leaving soon."

Oh. Points 1 and 2 seem valid.

Point 3 is... not what I was expecting.

I tilt my head. "Where are you going?"

"That's a second question."

"It is."

"I've quit my job here, just have a few weeks left of my notice period. Then, I'm headed to the wilderness."

Of course, he is. "Such an adventurous mountain man," I tease. Then, for some reason, I add, "That's cool, though. I wish I'd done something exciting like that when I was younger. Well. Not that, exactly. But like, gone on a cool adventure or something."

As soon as the words are out of my mouth, I realize how true they are. I might not be missing the "dancing and kissing and flirting" stuff Aubrey spoke about. But I maybe would have liked to go on an adventure. Do something wild and daring and totally uncharacteristic.

Instead, for all of my twenties, I've just been plain, old reliable Holly.

Jax can apparently read me a little *too* well, because he rolls his eyes and says, "What? You think you're old or something?"

"I'm almost thirty." I say this like it's a confession.

"So you're twenty-nine. Only two years older than me."

"Two years is a long time."

Jax rolls his eyes. "My turn now, and I get two questions, too." He holds up two fingers. "Question one. Why are you so intent on finding a partner?"

I freeze up for a moment as I try to figure out how to answer his question without telling him the exact truth. Which is that I've spent years wasting time on hoping for something with Dylan again, and in doing so, haven't put much—*any*—time into dating and therefore feel like I'm well on my way to becoming that old, withered spinster Uncle Percival spoke about so vividly.

I'd like Jax to believe that he's helping a regular, non-crazy, non-doomed-to-spinsterhood type of person.

So I swallow. Force what I hope is a calm, confident, breezy smile. "It's... time."

Jax's eyes skate over me again. "Okay."

Just that: *Okay.*

No demanding an explanation or laughing at me. He's simply giving me an out, without (showing) an ounce of judgment, and with (barely) any questions asked.

"Question two." He nods at my full glass. "Can I get you something to drink that you actually like?"

Busted.

12

HOLLY

"How is it almost midnight?" I groan as I check my phone screen in disbelief. Three cranberry juices later and I'm still here. On a barstool. Talking to Jax Grainger. My phone shows me no less than six messages from Aubrey, checking that I'm okay and haven't been kidnapped or joined a cult.

I send an *I'm fine, just out getting a drink - be home soon!* message to Aubrey and a response comes through almost immediately. I catch the words "hot" and "bartender" and "TELL ME." Quick as lightning, I flip my phone face-down on the bar, my cheeks reddening.

Jax watches me. "Everything okay?"

"I should go," I say a tad sheepishly.

"Big plans for the rest of the night?" he asks coyly.

I chuckle. "Well, according to my planner, after my date with Emmett, I was meant to go to the gym, get groceries, and reorganize my underwear drawer. Instead, I've been here for hours, shirking my responsibilities."

Jax laughs at that. He's currently straining simple syrup

into a glass bottle that contains multiple sprigs of fresh lavender, and I can't help but notice again how his big hands move so skillfully and deliberately as he works. He hasn't spilled a single drop.

The restaurant has been pretty quiet this evening, with a small but steady trickle of customers coming and going. Which means that we've had time to chat between Jax pouring me drinks and chopping limes and bringing me plates of french fries from the kitchen.

I'm surprised at how quickly time passed, how easy it was to sit here with him, shooting the breeze like... well, like George Clooney in an old-timey movie. Probably.

Jax puts down the bottle and nods towards the folded piece of paper in front of me—the one on which I wrote my four dating must-haves earlier. The one that I, at some point, folded into a neat square instead of showing him. "We haven't even gotten to the reason you came here in the first place."

He's right. We've mostly been chatting nonsense. Nothing deep or meaningful. For example, I asked him why he was a bartender earlier and he replied with: "I like measuring things."

Then, he promptly overpoured a shot and spilled liquor all over the bar. On purpose, I think, especially given his syrup-straining prowess. But I can't be sure.

Either way, it made me laugh.

I don't make friends easily. In fact, I can't remember the last time I made a new friend. My coworkers are great, but our friendship has never trickled outside the hotel's walls. And Aubrey basically adopted me as her pet introvert. But there's something about Jax's razor-sharp wit and silly banter that just clicks for me.

Although, maybe it's one-sided clicking, and over on his end of the bar, he's supremely bothered by the weird girl slurping cranberry juice who won't take a hint and leave.

I look at him sheepishly, my fingers pressing the edges of the folded piece of paper. "And yet, I still managed to take up your entire shift."

"Ah, it was a slow night. I was glad for the company." He swipes my empty glass off the bar and sets a new glass in front of me, which makes me feel good—I may be no expert on reading signals, but surely this means he's okay with me hanging out here.

If nothing else, at least my current state of desperation must be entertaining.

"Isn't there another bartender working?" I ask.

"Yup. I saw him sneak out the back with one of our waitresses, Ella."

"Sorry you got abandoned."

He laughs. "Believe me, you're way better company than he is. For one thing, you don't keep telling me that I'm hitting things that I'm not," he says cryptically. I frown and open my mouth to ask him what on earth goes on behind this bar on Monday nights when he glances at the clock. "Man, it really did get late fast. You got an early start in the morning?"

"No, I don't work until 2. Late shift."

He tilts his head at me, those slate eyes of his intent on mine once again. "I've just realized that I don't even know what *you* do for work."

I shrug. "I'm a magician."

Another easy smile lights up his face. "Should've guessed... you've got that sneaky Houdini look to you."

"I'll take that as a compliment."

"You should. Everyone knows that Houdini was the sexiest magician."

"Well, we all know that there were *so* many sexy magicians to beat out for that title. GQ couldn't keep up with the demand for magician cover models."

"Okay, okay. Before you go making too much fun of magicians, there's something you should know..." Jax wiggles his fingers at me in a disturbingly accurate magician impersonation. "I confess that I know how to make a mean balloon animal."

"You do?" I say with glee.

"Shh." Jax glances around the totally empty restaurant furtively. "Don't tell anyone. I can't have my sexy talents broadcast too loudly."

"The ladies do tend to love balloon animals." I smirk.

"Remind me to make you one, then." Jax eyes me flirtily, and a flush rises on my chest. He's way too charming for his own good, this one. And apparently, since I told him in no uncertain terms I don't want to date him, this does not exempt me from being flirted with.

"All magic aside, I actually work at the Pinnacle," I tell him.

"That cool old hotel over by North Ave?"

"That's the one."

"Is it really haunted?" Jax asks, pausing his stocking of some lemon wedges.

"Inconclusive."

He snorts a laugh. "What do you do there? Aside from ghostbusting and magic, of course."

"Guest services. You know—working the front desk, checking people in, making reservations... all that boring stuff."

I'm surprised to see his expression of interest. "You know much about bookings?"

Weird question, but I nod. "Oh, yeah. Basically an expert."

He nods slowly, seeming almost lost in thought. "Fancy."

"You should come by sometime. I'll book you in to make some balloon animals. Replace the piano player in the lounge with a mediocre magic show."

"I don't know." He grins. "We can't have all of your hotel guests falling in love with me."

And even though he says this as a joke (I think), he's actually right. A steady stream of elderly ladies frequent the Pinnacle for afternoon tea, and I have a feeling they'd go weak in the knees watching a handsome man entertain them.

"Doris *has* been single since her second husband died of old age. I'm sure she'd love to meet you."

"I'm down with an older lady. Gotta love that life experience." He twinkles at me cheekily.

I raise a brow at him. "You flirt in your sleep, don't you?"

"It's the only language I'm fluent in."

That checks out. I find myself tilting my head at him, curious about the Sexy Bartender who makes balloon animals and wants to fight off bears or whatever in the wilderness. The one I've asked to essentially be my dating coach without really knowing anything about his dating life.

"When was your last relationship?" I ask. "Or are you more of a perma-bachelor who has weekend-only flings?"

"C."

"Huh?"

"Option C," Jax says again.

I roll my eyes at him. "And what's option C, smartass?"

"I have one true love."

"Let me guess... yourself?"

He chuckles deeply. "Close, but not quite. Her name is Edna."

"Oh, so you *do* like older ladies."

"Born in 1973."

I gape at him for a moment while doing mental math until he adds, "Edna's the name of my van."

"Of course, it is. And of course you have a van. You look like the van type."

"I'll take that as a compliment." Jax smirks. "If you play your cards right, you can meet her sometime."

"I'd be honored," I say with a swift roll of my eyes. I'd be lying if I said I wasn't following about twenty-five "van life" Instagram accounts, but it's not like it would ever actually be the life for me. I slide my empty glass across the bar. "And now, I'm going for real this time. I might not work until the afternoon tomorrow, but it's way past my bedtime."

He nods, but then, he looks at me for a moment, like he's weighing something up in his mind.

"You got plans tomorrow before your shift?"

I smile dryly. "Nothing past the riveting list of things I was meant to do tonight. Why?"

"My shift isn't until 5pm tomorrow, so if you're free earlier, we could meet up to talk about your toad-kissing problem and what you're looking for in a non-amphibious partner." He taps the folded piece of paper by my hand.

"Well, there's a lovely visual. And I've already taken up your whole evening with my dating woes... are you sure that's how you want to spend tomorrow morning as well?"

A whisper of a smile crosses his lips. "To be honest, I think there might be something you can help me with, too."

"What is it?"

"I may be expecting some guests of my own."

I look at him, full-on confused. "Human guests? I thought you were headed out to the wilderness in the not-so-far future. So, unless you're expecting a pack of raccoons..."

He huffs out a laugh. "It's for a new venture of mine. I basically need to get a booking system set up." He's no longer making eye contact, instead focusing on putting some glasses through the dishwasher behind the bar.

"If I didn't know better, I'd say you were being a touch secretive, Jax Grainger." I place my hands on my hips.

"What're you planning on doing out there in the middle of nowhere? Starting a wolfpack cult?"

Jax snorts with laughter. "Something like that. But less cult, more adventure." He shrugs. "Basically, if I'm gonna sustain myself out there, I need guests."

Oh. Well that makes some sense. He's probably trying to Airbnb his place in the city or something while he lives in the middle of nowhere. "I'm sure I can help. Like I said, I am an expert with bookings and guest reservations. Unless you're trying to book something weird."

"What on earth would constitute a weird booking?"

"I don't know. Bookings to borrow kinky underwear? That's where I draw the line."

What? Why am I like this?

And who the hell borrows underwear of any kind, ever?!

Luckily, Jax just grins. "Kinky underwear, you say?"

"I don't know what you get up to in your spare time!" I wrinkle my nose at him. "All I'm saying is that if you want help with anything cult or lingerie related, I'm out."

"More of a granny-panties kinda girl then, Hollywood?" His cheeky grin widens.

"My underwear is none of your business."

"I'll take that as a yes."

I give him a flat look. "I'm no longer helping you with your weird booking venture."

A laugh. "Oh, come on. I need you, Holly. I'll even buy you lunch."

"Hmm. I do like lunch." I smile. "I guess that, as long as it's not a date, I'm in."

He laughs again. "Nah, I already told you—you're just good company... for an old woman."

13

JAX

Holly has to be the most... *unique* person I've met in a while. She's like a brain teaser puzzle that might look like it should be straightforward, but working it out requires a whole new way of thinking. And once you start trying to work it out, you don't want to stop.

She's weird, in a good way. And funny. I wasn't lying when I said she was good company—she's got this dry, self-deprecating humor that makes me feel strangely comfortable with her. We both use banter to deflect, and I kind of like that we're well-matched.

I don't usually warm to people so easily—or go out of my way to make friends—but something about Holly feels friend-like. I *want* to help her find what she's looking for. The fact that she might be able to help me get a booking system up and running is just an added bonus.

Though I'm still not exactly sure why she's so adamant about finding her forever person at *this* exact time in her life. The reason she gave me last night felt lacking, but I didn't want to pry.

It's not my business, I think as I go to meet her at our agreed-upon meeting spot at Oak Hill the following day. I show up three minutes after twelve, armed with a bag of tacos from Maria's Cantina—my favorite greasy dive Mexican place in the area—to find that she's pacing in circles.

"Hey, Hollywood," I greet her with a breezy grin. "Looking good today."

And she is. She's dressed in another sundress—navy, this time—with brown leather sandals and those signature pink glossy lips.

She jerks her head up, and something close to relief crosses her delicate features before she smirks at me. "Thought I was gonna be stood up for the second time in two days."

"I can't stand you up because this isn't a date, remember?"

Her smirk stretches into a smile. "This is true."

"Regardless, sorry I'm late. There was a huge line at Maria's," I explain, glancing down at the bag of delicious food. "You eaten there before?"

"Nope, but it smells amazing!"

We take a seat on the hill, the city skyline in front of us providing a great view. Holly thanks me for lunch as I unload the tacos al pastor, along with some fried fish, chicken, and chorizo options.

"This is already better than most of the actual dates I've been on recently," Holly says as she slips on her sunglasses and tilts her face towards the midday sun. Springtime in Atlanta is great—everything's coming alive and the weather isn't sweltering yet.

"Because I showed up?"

"And you haven't spent the last five minutes talking only about yourself, or your gym membership, or your pet pigs."

"I'm more of a dog guy," I deadpan. "Also goes back to my

point that you need to raise the bar a bit there, Hol. Sounds like it's practically rolling around on the floor."

"Why else do you think I asked for your help?"

"Oh, I don't know. Maybe my incredible prowess with women, my handsome good looks, my incorrigible charm..."

"Hmmm." Holly taps a finger to her chin before shaking her head. "No. Definitely the bar on the ground thing."

This makes me laugh. She's cute and definitely funny, which makes her a pretty great catch. If I didn't know she was looking for a long-term, husband-material type of commitment, I'd totally ask her out.

"Before we dive into my sad excuse for a dating life, I have to know... why on earth do you need a booking system? I was up half the night tossing and turning, wondering about it."

Flashes of Holly in bed at night dance through my mind, unbidden, but I quickly file them away. Give her a cheeky smile instead. "Piqued your interest, did it?"

"Absolutely. You don't strike me as the type to play mother hen and open your own B&B, or to host people in an Airbnb, so I can't imagine what you're up to." She shakes her head. "Or am I just to live in the dark and continue to assume it's something sordid?"

I have to laugh, but she has a point. I can't continue being so cagey with my plans, especially as she can probably help. There might also be a part of me that weirdly almost... *wants* her to know this dream of mine. For no real reason at all. "You know last night when I said I was leaving soon to go to the mountains?"

She nods. "I remember admiring this adventurous quality of yours, yes."

"Well, it's for my new job. Business, actually." I toss my fingers through my hair, almost nervous. "I'm starting a wilderness guiding outfit. I have a cabin a few hours northwest of here in the mountains and am renovating it to use it as a base for expeditions."

"Wow. That's awesome!" Her brown eyes sparkle with what looks to be genuine enthusiasm and excitement. "Are you going to offer, like, wilderness survival courses? Guided hikes? Oooh, team building exercises?! Have you seen *Pitch Perfect 2*, where Rebel Wilson gets stuck in the big cargo net?"

I have, actually. Maddie made me watch the first one while she was holed up on my couch last year, post-breakup with her ex-boyfriend and pre-Seb coming on the scene. I may or may not have watched the second one after she moved out.

And the third one.

"I'm thinking mostly guided hikes, to begin with," I tell her, stepping around her final question. "But the cabin has a big room that I've converted into a twelve-bed dorm so I have the space to eventually host bigger groups, too."

"This is so cool. I'd love to see it sometime. Or, at least, see pictures of it. Live vicariously through you and all your exciting adventures."

Her reaction to my news makes me feel strangely buoyant. It hasn't come very naturally—telling people about my business venture. But the more I do it, the more I believe in what I'm doing.

And for some reason, Holly's reaction seems to affect me more than most. Hearing that she thinks it's a good idea makes me feel more self-assured than I have in a while.

"Well, I hope the guests who eventually stay there will be as enthusiastic as you are."

"Let's get you some guests, then."

Holly proceeds to ask for my number so she can send me links to dynamic booking platforms that I can apparently set up myself and integrate with my website. A friend of a friend who specializes in web design is currently working on that for me as we speak.

These links, alone, would've been help enough, but Holly's not done yet.

As my phone pings with her texts, she rambles on, "You could also put it on vacation rental websites like Airbnb and VRBO and sync those calendars so you don't get double bookings. And you can offer the cabin as an 'experience'—that would be a great way to get some indirect business. I think there might even be a site dedicated to glamping. A cabin in the backcountry would totally count, I think."

I watch her excited expression and dancing eyes as she rattles off a ton of on-the-spot, stream-of-consciousness ideas. I can barely keep up. She's clearly very smart and knowledgeable, but it's her passion for the subject matter that seems so remarkable.

"How do you know all this stuff?" I ask when she finally tires herself out.

She shrugs, her lips in a lopsided grin. "Hospitality degree followed by years of work at the Pinnacle. I love coming up with ideas on how to fill rooms." Her bright and bubbly expression dims a little and she examines the half-eaten taco in her hand as she adds, "But I'm not an expert or anything."

"You sure sound like one to me," I tell her honestly. "That's already so helpful. I can't thank you enough."

"Sure you can. You're gonna help me stop going on dates with walking red flags."

"I'll do everything in my power," I say solemnly, crossing my heart, which makes her snort. I make a gimme motion. "No time like the present to get started. You got that hit list with you?"

She blinks at me, her deep brown eyes full of confusion. "My *what* list?"

"Hit list. The list you made last night with all the things you want in a man," I explain. "The one we never got around to talking about."

"Oh! That's a good name for it." She almost looks shy as she fishes the piece of paper out of her bag and hands it over to me. "Here it is. Everything I want in my ideal man."

14

HOLLY

I try not to cringe as Jax plucks the piece of paper out of my hand. "Over thirty... Stable job... Must want commitment and kids..." The corners of his lips tip up. "Okay. Now I can see why you didn't want to date me."

I laugh. "Told you it wasn't personal."

"Do you want my honest advice?"

"That *is* why I came to the bar to see you."

"Well, in that case..."

He crumples up the piece of paper and tosses it behind him.

"Hey!" I squawk.

Jax shakes his head. "Hate to break it to ya, but your hit list is trash, Hollywood."

"I beg to differ! That's my perfect-on-paper guy."

He grabs the paper he just threw and goes to smooth it out on the grass in front of him. "You're ridiculous."

"How is wanting those things ridiculous?" I challenge. "I think most single women looking for a partner would want similar things."

"I didn't say that wanting those things is ridiculous. I said that *you* are." He looks over at me and those strange gray eyes almost glow in the midday sunshine as he appears to study me. "You're that girl who's had her wedding planned since the eighth grade, aren't you?"

"No."

It was seventh grade. So joke's on him.

He smiles, like he actually heard my silent tack-on. "I get that you want to find someone suitable to settle down with, but you can't think that these four things are everything you need in your so-called 'perfect man.'"

I frown. "Well, I..."

But Jax isn't finished. "Like, take this whole 'wants to settle down and have kids' thing. Any scrub out there could *want* kids, but what does the potential future father of your potential future children look like for you? Because I'm assuming that, more than simply wanting kids, you'd want him to have qualities that would make a good father."

He doesn't wait for me to answer, just gestures towards my list again. "And you say you want a guy in his thirties or early forties. Trust me, I know a *ton* of a lot of forty-year-old men who are seriously not well adjusted. Hell, even some men in their fifties and sixties who have no concept of what it means to be in a good relationship." He says all of this dryly, but I could swear something heavy flashes behind his eyes. He looks away before I can identify it. "So, in reality, it's not age that's the issue, it's that you want a man who is emotionally mature, who is ready and willing for a relationship. Right?"

Jax is suddenly looking straight at me, those slate eyes boring into mine. It's all I can do to nod.

"Marrying someone means that you actually have to live with that person and enjoy their company. Be a team with them. Maybe eventually parent with them. So, what about personality? Values? Sense of humor?"

I take the paper, feeling like my head might either explode or float off towards the Atlanta skyline. Who's to know.

Because I'm seeing things with brand new eyes now. And once again, Jax Grainger is right.

But he's also not currently using dating apps to try and find himself a happily ever after.

"I guess I figured that if I set out with the minimum requirements, I'd be keeping my options open." I frown, thinking back over Keith and Emmett and a whole parade of other men who, quite frankly, sucked. "The dating pool is kinda bleak to begin with, and I didn't want to shrink it right off the bat."

"Quality over quantity, Holly. And to find the right *quality* man, you need to start swimming in the right pool," Jax replies thoughtfully, then points to my cell phone on the grass next to me. "Can I see your Spark profile?"

I obediently reach for my phone, but then pause, raising a quizzical brow at him. "You gonna toss my phone across the park, too?"

"Hopefully I won't have to." He grins. And for some reason, I unlock it, open my Spark app, and pass the phone to him.

He looks at the screen and winces. "Awh, Holly. Didn't I say to do better?"

"What's wrong with it?"

"*You're just one click away from finding your soulmate...*" he reads. When he looks up, his face is incredulous. "This is, quite literally, the worst dating profile bio I've ever seen."

"It's to the point," I reply, defensive. "Makes it clear what I'm looking for."

"It makes you look like a lunatic, is what it does."

My nostrils flare. "You're kind of rude. Has anyone ever told you that?"

"You wanted me to be honest, right?" He peers at me and I give a very, very small nod. "Look. Between the list of things you want in a partner and your dating app profile, all I've learned about you is that you... want a partner."

"What do you mean?"

He waves his hand towards my phone screen. "Where are *you* in all of this? I see a whole lot of 'wanting to settle down'—which, like I said, there's nothing wrong with wanting—but I don't see *Holly*, the person sitting in front of me."

My frown deepens. "Go on."

"Well, right now, I see a woman who's smart. Has a super funny and sarcastic sense of humor. Currently has a smudge of hot sauce on her chin." His eyes drop down to my mouth and my hand flies to my chin. He smirks. "Kinda uptight on the surface, but seems to have a deeper spontaneous side of her that is just aching to be shaken up. Try something new, if given the opportunity."

I'm weirdly flattered by this, despite him calling me uptight. Jax is apparently fond of doling out the tough love, but I'm here for it.

"Thank you. I think."

"I'm not done," Jax replies. "When I look at both your Spark profile and that hit list of yours, I see none of this. I see none of *you*."

I suck in a breath, almost scared of my next question. "What do you see?"

Jax meets my eyes shamelessly. "Desperation."

"Again, rude!"

"No. Again, honest. I'm not saying you *are* desperate, I'm saying you *look* desperate." His eyes are still burning into mine, but they're not sparking with their usual playfulness. He's being sincere. "No wonder you're not attracting guys you click with, or even like. You're not giving them anything *they* could possibly click with. You're like... fodder for all the creeps of the internet right now."

I want to be offended. Very offended.

And I want to tell Jax he's wrong. Very wrong.

But what I *know* is that I've been on so many terrible dates with said creeps of the internet that I was practically forced to come to him for help. And he hasn't been wrong yet.

Tough love, indeed.

I suck up my pride (what's left of it, at least), and look at the rude-but-apparently-well-meaning man in front of me. "So, what you're saying is that I'm not showing enough of myself and my personality in my profile, and I'm not looking for enough of *their* personality in my hit list?"

He nods. "Exactly. Goals and circumstances and external qualities only go so far for compatibility, and for chemistry. You have to dig deeper."

"Well, you could have said it like that. That would have been way nicer."

"*That* was to the point. Making it clear what I was talking about." He throws my own words back at me, and I have to chuckle. He continues more gently, "You're giving these guys nothing to connect with past 'wife me up and let me have your babies.' Which, honestly, probably has most reasonable guys running for the hills despite how hot you are, and all the *un*reasonable guys contacting you solely because they think you're hot and also desperate."

"Jax!"

He leans forward and wipes the sauce that I apparently did not remove from my chin with his thumb. His touch is gentle, but the pad of his thumb is rough, and the sensation against my skin makes me shiver.

"Am I wrong?" he asks.

I pause. Push away all bizarre shivers and thoughts of Jax calling me hot, and consider what he's said...

My parameters have been clear from the beginning. And yet, I've gone on dates with so many men who appeared, on Spark, to fit the bill of my ideal man, but not one of them has been in the least bit compatible with me in real life.

"Well, aside from all the 'hot' stuff..." I muse. "I guess you might have a tiny point. So, what do I do next?"

"You write a bio that tells people who *Holly* is," he says, a twinkle in his eye. "But first thing's first, we're gonna need to replace that picture on your profile."

"Not the picture, too?"

I look good in that picture, I think. It was taken at Mindy's wedding—I was dressed in a pale gold, shimmery floor-length dress with my hair in an updo. I'm clutching a bouquet and looking on at the vows being exchanged.

I'm not the most photogenic person in the world, but in this picture, my makeup looks great and my expression is pleasant. Neutral.

"You look like a bride."

I wave my taco at him. "I was Maid of Honor!"

"So? That doesn't tell me anything about *you*," he insists.

"But I look good in it."

"You always look good."

His sweet comment—said in such an off-the-cuff, almost *duh* kinda way—catches me off guard, and I find myself without a snappy response. I look at him, and quick as lightning, he whips out his phone. Snaps a shot.

"Hey!" I yell, indignant. "Nobody wants to see a pic of me with taco grease dripping off my face and talking with my mouth full."

He's not even listening. He's just smiling down at his phone screen.

"Ugh, delete it."

He ignores me, and instead, turns the phone around. "Look at this. Seriously, Holly, I'd totally swipe right on this if I was on Spark."

Timidly, I peek at the photo he's taken.

Wow. The woman in the picture has hot sauce dripping down her hand and her ponytail is more windswept than chic, but her eyes are shining and her mouth is laughing. It's not the most glamorous or smile-and-look-pretty photo in the world, but it looks like a snapshot of an actual moment in time. Like the photographer captured a candid of something real. Some*one* real who eats and breathes and laughs and loves.

"It's... good."

"Told you."

"Ah," I say, getting it now. "You buttered me up with that compliment so I'd look all sparkly and happy in the picture."

"You would think that." He raises a brow at me. "But was I right or was I right?"

"You were right," I admit, then meet his eyes. "In fact, you're damn good at this stuff. Remind me again why you're not in the market for a relationship yourself?"

"Well, for one, the whole moving to the wilderness thing. And for two... I don't want one."

"Ever?"

"Probably not. I'm not that guy." He gives me a smile that makes my heart a little stuttery. Weirdly. "But I am more than happy to help you find *your* perfect person."

15

HOLLY

Last Christmas, Dylan kissed me at our staff party. It was the first time we'd kissed since he kissed me goodbye after breaking up with me in college, and it made me think that this might finally be it. That he was telling me it was finally time for us to be together again, for real.

The party was taking place in an empty penthouse suite at the Pinnacle. Champagne flowed freely, someone had set up a karaoke machine, and it was the first time I'd seen Dylan let loose since he turned up half-drunk at my dorm room door one night in college, embarrassed he'd had a little too much to drink at his Choirboys Club social event.

That night at the Pinnacle staff party, almost a decade later, his cheeks were red as he belted out "I Kissed A Girl" by Katy Perry, his half-empty glass of sparkling wine sloshing over his hand as he gesticulated. The way he seemed to look right at me when he sang about kissing a girl, just to try it.

A little while later, I went out to the balcony for some fresh air, and he followed me. Told me I looked beautiful that night, that he couldn't keep his eyes off me...

And then, he kissed me.

It was the first time we'd kissed in years, and it felt familiar. Cozy.

After the kiss, he chucked my chin, told me I was cute, and walked inside. I'm not sure how the act of kissing led to my demotion from beautiful to cute, but I didn't think too much of it at the time. Because it was finally happening!

We could work together, and be together, and have our happily ever after.

My patience had paid off and my plan was finally back in motion.

The next morning, though, I came into work and was met with All-Business-Dylan. I figured he was putting on a front for our coworkers, trying to keep things hush-hush until we had a chance to talk about what happened.

I sought out a moment alone with him, and I was surprised when he simply smiled blandly at me and said, "good party last night, right?" He then made a comment about how drunk he'd been and how he didn't make a habit of having crazy nights like that.

I wasn't drunk the night before—a little tipsy off a couple glasses of wine maybe, but not drunk.

Did Dylan not remember our kiss? Or, even more mortifying, was I so out of practice he thought me a terrible kisser?

I opened my mouth, the words "about what happened" on my tongue, when Dylan snapped his briefcase shut and announced that he was off to meet with the hotel's owner about the new marketing hire he'd just made. A marketing hire who was not me.

And in that moment, I realized this was *not* our time.

Whatever that kiss meant to me, it clearly didn't mean the same to him, and I was sick of waiting for something that might never happen.

I needed to stop chasing the idea of Dylan and me being together for real, and start taking control of my own life.

Because I could only wait so long.

"All done for the day, Holly?" Dylan says now as he walks into the break room at the Pinnacle, clutching his briefcase in one hand and a coffee in the other.

I startle a little, snapped out of my thoughts, and quickly re-balance the laptop that's currently perched on my lap.

"Woah, there." Dylan laughs that deep, silky laugh I know so well. "Better not be our Pinnacle laptop you're playing around with!"

I laugh along with him. The joke is that the Guest Services staff only have one laptop between the four of us to use when one of us needs to work from home. So yes, breaking *the laptop* would be a problem. "It isn't, I brought my personal one." I shift a little on my chair. "And yes, I've just clocked out for the day. I'm finishing a little research I started on my break before I head home."

"Working above and beyond, Holly. Well done."

I look up at him, blush a little. "Oh, no. It's a... personal matter."

Dylan takes a sip of his coffee. "I understand." His hazel eyes then do a quick sweep of me. "Looking good today, by the way."

My blush deepens, but at that moment, my phone *pings* with a message from Jax.

So, any thoughts? Love it or hate it?

I smile as I finish up the email I'm writing to him with said thoughts.

It's been a few days since Jax and I met in the park for lunch, and we've been chatting quite a bit via text about his business and my dating profile. Which looks great now with my new photos and a bio that reads "looking for my perfect match." Apparently, this is better and "less desperate" than the whole *looking for a soulmate* thing. But it's still a work in progress.

Now, I've agreed to take a look at the website a designer is putting together for his business—complete with one of the booking systems I recommended—and offer him some feedback. I might not know much about site design, but I know a hell of a lot about what potential customers might be looking for to make a booking.

The site is just okay, in my opinion. I know it's only a beta version, but my main feedback is that it could be more immersive. Experiential.

I'm picturing a video of a gorgeous mountainscape on the homepage, photos of Jax leading expeditions, recommended itineraries that incorporate the senses... All alongside pictures of the accommodations, the flora and fauna, and meals cooked over an open fire. Or whatever it is he cooks on.

I'm so immersed in my email to Jax that I hardly notice Dylan taking a seat in the chair next to mine.

"What are you working on?" he asks.

I glance at him quickly. "I'm helping out a friend who's getting a website made."

"What's her site for?"

"It's for *his* new business," I correct.

"Oh."

I could swear there's a note of curiosity in Dylan's response, but he doesn't ask any further questions and I'm too distracted to elaborate. I send the email and then type a quick text to Jax.

> Sent you an email with all my thoughts. It's going to be great with some tweaking.

His reply is almost immediate.

> Anyone ever tell you you're a lifesaver?

> > All the time, actually. But I wouldn't mind hearing it again.

> Don't fish or I'll send you a really terrible voice note of me singing "Simply the Best."

> > Terrible for you, or for me?

> Both, most likely.

I laugh. Out of the corner of my eye, I noice Dylan looking at me again.

> You working today?

> > Just finished my shift. You?

> Nope. I spent the morning at the cabin to receive a furniture delivery, but I'm back in town now to do some shopping. I'm actually right near the Pinnacle at the moment.

> > What are you buying?

> A baby gift.

> Happen to know anything about what kids might want?

> > You are such a typical man. Who had a baby?

> Nobody. Yet.

> > Don't tell me this is a gift for someone you knocked up?

> > Are you going to be a father?!

My phone immediately rings and I answer it with a grin.

"Well?" I demand playfully. Next to me, Dylan is typing on his phone, but I don't miss the tilt of his head in my direction.

"You sound so appalled at the thought of my doing any sort of fathering duty," Jax replies, his tone equally teasing. "And in answer to your question, no. I'm not about to embark on a journey into fatherhood. My sister's pregnant."

"The one who's married to the hockey player?"

"You remember." I hear the warmth in his voice. "Yes. They asked me to be the baby's godfather."

"That's a big honor," I tell him. My sister and her husband chose his brother and his wife to be godparents to their twins. I am—*was*—only slightly bitter.

"Right. The thing is, I might've been so shocked about the news in the moment that I may not have acted all that happy about it..."

There's a sheepish note in his voice that makes me narrow my eyes. "Jax... what did you do?"

"Um. Well, I might've asked her initially if it wasn't just indigestion. And then, when she confirmed that she was, indeed, pregnant, I might've done a really bad Marlon Brando *The Godfather* impression."

"You dumb-dumb. That's the worst thing you could have done!"

"I know, I know. I panicked and totally screwed up." I can hear the anguish in Jax's deep, manly man voice. He's got to be one of the most... unexpected humans I've ever come across. "So, I clearly need to get them the best baby gift there ever was to show them how happy I actually am for them. How much I plan to step up and be there for them."

It's sweet. *Very* sweet. But I can't let him off the hook just yet. "You should know that I'm judging you."

"Oh, I know. I wouldn't expect anything less from you, Hollywood."

I can't stop the bubble of laughter that comes out of me. So loud that Dylan looks over again. I shrug apologetically and lower my voice. "What did you have in mind, then? It better be pretty darn special."

"I googled it and apparently cakes made of diapers are a thing? Do you think they'd like that?"

My silence must say everything, because he adds, "Come on, help me out here, Holly!"

I chuckle. "You, my friend, are beyond help. But if you're nearby, I could help you shop."

"Has anyone ever told you you're a lifesaver?" he says again and I laugh harder.

"You, not two minutes ago. And remember, I'm always happy to help... so long as no kinky underwear is involved."

That gets Dylan's attention. I just can't tell if it's negative or positive. Or if I should really care?

"You're the best, Granny Panties. I'll pick you up at the Pinnacle in five."

The line goes dead and I'm still smiling like an idiot when I realize that Dylan's head is swiveled all the way around and he's staring at me.

"Who was that?" he asks.

"A friend." My smile widens. Because it's true—already, Jax feels like a real friend. We've grown close in a relatively short amount of time, and I'm genuinely enjoying his presence in my life.

"The friend with the website?"

"Mmhmm," I reply, trying to decipher his clipped tone. He sounds almost bothered.

Could Dylan be... *jealous* right now?

Surely not. I chastise myself for even going there. He's probably just ruffled that I'm having inappropriate conversations about underwear at work. Which, I suppose, is fair enough.

I'm packing up my laptop and putting on my sweater when Raquel, my fellow Guest Services worker, pops her head into the break room. "Holly? There's someone at the front desk asking for you."

"A guest is asking for me?"

"Hey, Hollywood."

And suddenly, Jax himself is standing in the doorway behind Raquel. She peeks over her shoulder at him and her cheeks turn a shade of pink. "Thanks so much for bringing me here... Raquel, was it?"

My coworker—who I happen to know is happily married and therefore very much off the market—goes on to fully *giggle* before she heads back to the front desk.

"Wow," I say with a roll of my eyes. "Your charm really does know no bounds."

"What'd I tell you?" Jax says easily, eyes sparkling as he leans against the doorframe and looks down at me. "So, you ready to go?"

I hustle faster, collecting the rest of my things. "You said five. I assumed that was five *minutes* and not five *seconds*."

"Turns out I was closer to you than I expected."

"Ahem!"

A sudden throat clearing reminds me that Dylan Hanlin is still here. In the room with us.

Well, this is a first. I don't think I've ever forgotten his presence before.

"I'm Dylan," he says coolly, stepping forward to shake Jax's hand. "And you are?"

"The perfect man," Jax replies with a wink in my direction that makes me roll my eyes again, even as my cheeks get a bit warm. He steps forward to take Dylan's hand. "I'm kidding. I keep telling Holly that he doesn't exist and she won't believe me. But no, the name's Jax. Nice to meet you."

"Likewise." I wonder if I'm imagining the cool note in Dylan's voice, the way his eyes glide over Jax's broad shoulders and torso—much broader than his own, lean-on-the-side-of-skinny frame. "Nice of you to stop by for your friend, Holly."

Jax crosses his arms over his chest, and the look he gives Dylan makes me think that he noticed my boss's cool demeanor, too. "Yup."

The two men continue to stare at each other. I continue to gape like some totally bewildered goldfish. There's some sort of tension, pressure or something, building up in the room. I can't totally understand it.

In the end, I step forward, right in between them.

"Okay!" I clap my hands like I'm shooing chickens or something. Pigs, maybe. Trevor the pig farmer would be proud. "Well, Jax, shall we head out? You have some amends to make via baby gift."

Jax's eyes are on mine again and he smiles, and the tension seems to dissipate a little. "My lifesaver. See you around, man."

"Maybe you will."

Jax turns and I practically push him out the door, not daring to look back at Dylan.

An hour later, Jax and I have visited no less than four baby stores, and he has only become more perplexed as we looked at countless onesies, stuffed animals, and swaddling clothes. Not to mention the hundreds of cribs, and car seats, and strollers.

He's bought a couple of gorgeous board books—a wilderness ABC's book and *Guess How Much I Love You*—along with a cute onesie covered in whisks and spatulas (because his sister loves to bake), and inexplicably, he's also purchased a stuffed cougar. And yet, he keeps insisting that nothing is *right*. I'm genuinely impressed by his commitment to the task at hand. And mildly concerned for his sanity.

"What about one of these?" I call to him from a selection of high-end activity gyms, one of which has the prettiest woodland animal theme I've ever seen.

"I like it." He picks up the cloth structure and checks the price. "Two hundred and thirty dollars?! I mean, I want to find the perfect gift and money isn't an object, but... *sheesh*."

I laugh. "It's a known rule—the price always skyrockets when the word 'baby' or 'wedding' is attached to an item."

"Good thing I'm not having a baby or getting married anytime soon or I'd be bankrupt." He snorts, but it's goodnatured. I can't help but think that if he ever *does* decide he wants a serious relationship, he'd probably make good husband material for the woman who manages to change his mind.

He clearly cares about his sister and her unborn child. Cares in a way that's soft and sweet for such a rugged man.

The Wolf Man has a gooey center in there somewhere.

I watch as Jax wanders into the next aisle, picks up a box, realizes it's a breast pump, and hurriedly puts the box back on the shelf. He catches me watching him over the top of an arrangement of stuffed elephants and shrugs sheepishly. "Maybe not an ideal gift for a brother to give his sister?"

"Probably not."

He proceeds to glance over a selection of nipple creams, nursing pads, and breast milk bags. "I had no idea that having a baby required so much... *stuff*. My head's spinning with everything I've learned this afternoon."

"We're just getting started, Grainger."

He lets out a low whistle as he wanders further down the

next aisle. I'm still watching his broad, muscular back, a smile on my lips, when a nasal voice suddenly fills the air around me.

"Oh, my goodness. If it isn't Holly Greene!"

I spin around to see The Ghost of Mean Girls Past rushing my way, arms outstretched like she's going to sink her claws into me.

"Sabrina Wieler," I say feebly, the veritable deer caught in headlights.

She comes to a stop just ahead of me, all perfectly curled auburn hair, perfectly manicured fingernails, and perfectly made-up face. "McPherson, actually," she replies, faux-humbly. "Yes, Grant and I are married."

I look at her, not computing.

"Grant McPherson. Our starting quarterback." She says "our" like we're still seventeen and she's still a cheerleader fluttering her eyelashes at the jocks from her spot at the best table in the cafeteria.

"Right," I say weakly, suddenly feeling like no time has passed and I'm still the mousy girl reading a book in the corner at lunchtime. The shrinking violet to Sabrina's blossoming bouquet of prom queen roses.

She clearly misunderstands my staring at her in full nostalgia because she pats her round belly. "Two kids," she volunteers blithely. "Third on the way."

"Congratulations."

"How about you? Who's the lucky guy?" She seizes my left hand, tugging it towards her like I'm a freaking marionette. "No ring? Are you *divorced*?" She drops her voice, like "divorced" is a four-letter word, her eyes becoming beady and shrewd.

Sabrina Wieler has apparently not changed an iota since we went to high school, which is—thankfully—the last time I saw her. She was snotty and mean then, and she appears to be snotty and mean now.

"Oh, no, not divorced. Just plain old unwed," I say lightly, looking around uncomfortably. Jax is at the end of the next aisle, examining a tricycle. I pray he's not in earshot.

"Really?" Sabrina's blue eyes grow huge as her hands release mine and go back to cradling her baby bump. "So are you... in the family way? Without a husband?"

Her voice goes up an entire octave on the word *husband*—man, this woman has vocal range. I try not to cringe at her use of "in the family way" instead of being normal and saying "pregnant."

"No, I'm shopping for a friend."

"Oh."

Sabrina looks thoroughly disappointed by my non-pregnancy-out-of-wedlock. Would've probably made a great story for the group chat she surely has with all the populars from high school, all hanging on to their glory days.

"I still can't believe it. Holly Greene, in the flesh. Still Holly Greene." She laughs that nasally laugh of hers, her nostrils whistling. "What was your superlative in the yearbook? *Most likely to do nothing surprising with her life?*"

Either this woman has the memory of an elephant or she still reads our high school yearbook for fun. I'd bet money on the latter.

"Um, something like that."

"Crazy!" she practically shrieks. "Crazy how some things change. Because I'm more than surprised that *you're* single and childless, and *I'm* the boring, settled-down one."

More crazy how some people never *change...*

Before I can think of how to respond, there's a warm pressure on my back. A warm pressure, followed by an arm circling my shoulder and pulling me close. My shock factor only increases when lips brush the top of my head.

What in the—

"I don't know about you, but I'm pretty done with shopping."

That deep, familiar voice I've come to know so well—and that has come to save me not once but *thrice* now—automatically soothes my frazzled nerves.

"I'm thinking that we grab these receiving blankets and that Melissa and Doug peg puzzle with the farm animals, and then go get a cheese board and a bottle of chianti at that cute little Italian place behind the... oh, hi." Jax suddenly addresses Sabrina like he's seeing her for the first time. I notice the false, husky sweetness in his tone. "Sorry, hun. I didn't realize you were talking to someone. Didn't mean to interrupt."

My mouth hangs open as I look at Jax, who's currently gazing down at me like I hung the moon.

"I, uh—"

"I'm Jax." He offers Sabrina a firm handshake and a warm smile.

"Sabrina," she responds breathily, staring at him with starry eyes as she fluffs her hair with her other hand. He twinkles right back at her.

"This is Jax," I repeat dumbly, wondering what on earth is happening right now and wishing I had no part of it. "Sabrina and I went to high school together. And Jax is my fr—"

"Her boyfriend," Jax cuts me off swiftly, then rolls his eyes at Sabrina like they're best pals who like to gossip while they braid each other's freaking hair. "No matter what I do, I *cannot* get this one to put a label on things. All I wanna do is wife her up and put a baby in her, and she's all *no, I'm not ready, I have so much life to live, so many adventures to go on.*"

Sabrina nods along, like he's the pied piper and she's thoroughly enchanted by his utterly ridiculous pipe music.

I, meanwhile, am blushing head to toe at Jax's proclamation that he "wants to put a baby in me."

117

Which conjures up a lot of... images.

"She's so amazing, I'll take what I can get in this relationship." He cuddles me tighter, as if he can hear my thoughts. I must say, the woodsy, clean scent of his t-shirt is doing nothing to help with my current mental condition. "I'm just lucky that she's with me."

"Awh," Sabrina coos, looking at me totally differently now. Like having a hot boyfriend suddenly makes me a legitimate human being. "You two are so sweet together. Looks like you found a keeper, Holly Greene."

"Oh, yeah." I wave a hand, hoping it's not shaking. "I wanted to make the most of my twenties and live it up while I could."

"There's nothing like being able to grab dinner when we want without having to book a sitter. Spending our money and time on ourselves. Planning multi-day backpacking trips to the wilderness together..." Jax is still gazing down at me, those slate gray locked on mine so only I can see them dance. He's *really* laying it on thick.

Then, Sabrina lets out the biggest, honkiest whistle-snort. "Sorry. Sorry. I thought you said you two are planning on backpacking together. My hearing, I tell you. Went haywire with my first."

My spine stiffens. "You heard right."

She looks at me almost pityingly, then leans towards me. "Come on, Holly. You expect me to believe you're into, like, *hiking* now? You were never into all that nature stuff in school. You weren't, like, an outdoorsy girl or even an athletic girl." She snorts again. "Now, your sister Mindy, I could see it—she was always a wild card. A total riot."

I think she expects me to laugh along, but I can't bring myself to do it. Can't bring myself to fake it. Instead, I draw

118

inspiration from the warm pressure of Jax's arm around my shoulder, the way it clasped me tighter at Sabrina's laughter.

"I don't know what to tell you, Sabby," I say easily, using the nickname I specifically remember she used to hate. "Jax and I are going on a backpacking trip together."

"This spring. In the Appalachians," Jax adds smoothly.

"Three whole days."

"The Appa-*what?*" I squeak.

Sabrina finally seems to realize that no one is laughing with her and she settles down a bit. "Wait. Seriously?"

Next to me, Jax nods. I follow suit.

"That's—wow, Holly." Sabrina blinks at me, like she's something akin to impressed. "You really *are* different from how you were in high school."

"She's pretty incredible. And so much fun to be with." Jax smiles benignly. "Guess Holly *does* have a point when she tells me she wants to wait before marriage and babies." He pats my shoulder. "I should listen to you more, my love."

"You should," I say through a close-lipped grimace of a smile.

"Anyhow, we should go pay. That soft brie wont eat itself." He turns to look in Sabrina's direction once more. "Nice to meet you, Katrina. Good luck with your pregnancy."

With that, he steers me away from the woman in one seamless motion.

The second we're in the check-out line and out of earshot, I turn to him. "What happened back there? I think I blacked out."

"I think you agreed to come on a multi-day backpacking trip with me."

I give my head a shake. "Yeah, no. But thank you for saving me. Again. And also, what in the hell was all that? Receiving blankets? Melissa and Doug puzzle? Soft brie?"

"Told you that you taught me a few things this afternoon." That cheeky grin is back in place as he sets the items on the counter and the cashier begins to ring them up. I notice the way she assesses my empty ring finger, and then proceeds to shamelessly eye Jax up.

"I don't know whether to be impressed or terrified," I mutter as Jax pays and thanks the lady before grabbing the bags. "I appreciate the save, but that was quite an elaborate story. Don't get me wrong, the hiking in the Appalachians thing was a nice touch. And as for the marriage and babies spiel... well, I had no idea you were capable of that."

"They teach sex ed in the fifth grade, you know. I'm pretty confident that I know how to put a baby in you, Holly."

My body turns beet red and sizzles like it's been thrown on a barbecue. "I mean the effortless lying, you psycho!"

"Oh, that." His grin widens. "What can I say, I play a good boyfriend. And my cabin is close to the Appalachians, so there is actually a backpacking route up there that I'll be hiking this spring—with someone who's not you, don't worry—as one of the potential routes for my guiding business. That was a segue from the truth, rather than a total fallacy."

"Segue from the truth," I repeat with a snort as I will my heart to beat at a normal rhythm. "Who's the unlucky hiking companion then?"

He waves a hand. "No idea, but I'll figure it out. See where it goes."

A statement that was never in the Dictionary of Holly.

Past all of Jax's suggestive proclamations, I feel completely off. Something about my strange interaction with Dylan earlier today, and then, an hour later, being confronted with Sabrina... It feels like my past is closing in on me, reminding me of everything I am and everything I'm not. The person I might have wanted to be, and the person I've become...

120

Wow, Holly, you really are different from how you were in high school.

That Holly was never spontaneous or happy to just *see where it goes.* That Holly played by the rules, was always responsible. That Holly never knew how to step out of the confines of her world, the confines of her comfort zone.

I'm not sure I want to be that Holly anymore.

16

JAX

I've hung out with Holly a few times now. Spent literal hours talking with her and getting to know her.

But, I'm not going to lie, sometimes I still find her to be a puzzle I simply can't put together.

Like right now, for example.

We've just left the baby store and that awful Sabrina woman behind, and despite the (impressive, if a little unexpected) way she stood up for herself back there, she's got this pinched look on her face. Like she's deep in thought. As I fall into step beside her, I wonder if I went too far with the whole swooning boyfriend thing.

"I'm sorry if I crossed a million lines back there."

I don't add that I couldn't help myself. Hearing that woman talk down to Holly like she was somehow less than her because she hadn't found her person or had kids yet made me mad. Holly's awesome, and I hope she'll find someone soon who's worth the wait, but in the meantime, she's fine the way she is.

"Don't be sorry," she says, seeming surprised by my apology. "You were hilarious. Sabrina and her cronies are going to be chewing on this for months, I bet. Holly Greene—voted most likely to never do anything surprising—living the high life being wined and dined by her hot boyfriend."

"So you're not upset?"

She shakes her head. "No. I'm just... it's just..." She stops. Sighs. "Remember at the bar when you asked me why I was so intent on finding a partner now, at this time in my life?"

I remember. She didn't give me a proper answer.

Can't say I'm not still curious. Because I feel like something or someone hurt her, and I also feel she deserves to move on from that hurt and be happy, however that looks in the end.

"I do," I say, and then fall silent to give her space to speak, if she wants to.

"Well, it's because I spent the past few years head over heels for someone who didn't love me back. I thought he might, but I was wrong." She meets my eyes with calm intention. "I read the entire situation wrong, and I realized I'd wasted tons of time chasing something that was never going to happen, no matter how badly I wanted it to be real."

I pause for a moment, surprised. I wasn't sure what I expected, but it wasn't... this. It gives her whole manic desire to find a partner a little context. "I'm sorry."

She waves a hand. "It was my fault for being stupid. Put all my eggs in one basket, so to speak. I got so caught up in all things Dylan and all my feelings for him. I wasn't in any kind of headspace to go out and meet new people, and that's why I'm scrambling now."

"Wait." I stop walking. "Your boss, Dylan? That guy?"

I might've met him for precisely two seconds earlier today, but I got such a bad read off him. He seemed like one of those guys who's faking his whole personality—acting kind and sincere on the surface, but with a whole score of manipulative, calculated tactics underneath. I wouldn't trust the guy as far as I can throw him.

So, surely it can't be...

"The one and only." She turns her eyes heavenward. "I know, I know... I became such a cliché."

"At least you're not his secretary," I point out, trying to lighten the mood with my father's own dark story. "That would have been way more cliché."

She brightens a touch. "True."

"So you decided to go on all these dates to get over your feelings for him?"

She blows out a breath. "That was part of it. I also realized that I'm turning thirty this year and haven't achieved any of the things I hoped to have achieved by now. My sister's married with kids, my best friend's getting married... I guess I just felt like I was playing catch up. And so, I made a resolution: I had to quit wasting time on what-ifs with Dylan. Quit letting life pass me by. Quit being afraid to step out of my comfort zone."

"What else had you hoped to achieve by now?"

"I don't know." She chuckles dryly. "Cheese and wine with men who are dazzled by my company, weekends away hiking in the mountains... Or whatever story you spun back there."

She's clearly trying to make light of how she's feeling, but as she attempts a laugh, her eyes tear up at the corners instead. I have the urge to wrap my arm around her shoulder again, but I want to respect her space.

"It occurred to me after running into Sabrina that, although I do want to settle down with someone, if I was going to be single all these years, the least I could have done was made the most of it. Go on adventures. Climb the career ladder. Instead, I wasted my fun-loving twenties not having any fun and with nothing much to show for it. I stayed inside my comfort zone and always did what I was supposed to do."

I had no idea she felt this way—she seems so put together (in every area that's not dating) that I kind of figured finding her so-called Prince Charming was just the next step in her successful life plan.

"I—" I start.

"Anyhow!" She cuts in, her tone cheery and her cheeks tinging red with what looks like embarrassment. "Enough of this! I'm giving you a sob story you never asked for. Shall we hit up the next baby store?"

I shake my head. "No."

"No?"

"No," I repeat.

I think it's the first time I've said no to her. Funny, because I usually say it a lot, to everyone.

But after what she's just told me, there's something *way* more important we need to do right now than shopping.

Something *for* her.

"Come on, Hollywood." I reach out and use my thumbs to gently brush the tears that managed to escape from under her eyes. "There's somewhere else we need to be."

She blinks up at me, her brown eyes deep and inquisitive and actually really quite pretty. "Where are we going?"

"You'll see."

Half an hour later, Holly and I are sitting in Edna, turning off the highway.

And yes, she's using every opportunity she can to make some sort of joke about what she's calling my "infatuation with seniors." But I saw the expression on her face when she first saw Edna. She assessed the fully redone and painted siding, the plush seats, the old-timey radio I fixed up instead of replacing. The wonder in her eyes was clear as day.

As it should be. Edna's a freaking gem.

Holly's perked up a bit since our conversation outside the baby store, and I can tell she's curious about where I'm taking her. I myself am curious—excited, even—to see her reaction.

Which, it turns out, is a loud squeak of surprise. "Stone Mountain? I haven't been here in years!"

"Me neither," I admit.

Stone Mountain—popular with tourists and cityfolk looking for a day hike—is certainly not the first place I'd come to when I want to get in touch with nature. Way too crowded for my liking. But it was the closest place I could think of that would serve my purpose.

I pull into the lot, pay for parking, and climb out of the van.

Holly, however, hesitates before finally opening her door and addressing me without getting out of her seat. "What are we doing?"

"Hiking."

"To the top?" She looks alarmed. "I'm wearing a dress. And sandals."

"Well then, you'll look good doing it, Hollywood."

"But..."

I come around to her side of the van and hold out a hand towards her. "Come on, Hol. It's like, less than a mile. Suitable for all ages and fitness levels."

"Speak for yourself," she grumbles, glowering down at her outfit.

I laugh, but she's got a point. I wouldn't normally condone hiking in a dress (gives me Laurel flashbacks, if anything), but Stone Mountain is a short one and I have a feeling that Holly—with her spicy, determined nature—could make it up on pure stubbornness, alone. "Promise. You won't have any regrets."

And with that, we're off. Sandals and all.

It's an easy hike for an experienced hiker like myself, but I keep a slow, steady pace, checking on Holly often. Despite her initial protests about her fitness level and her footwear, she huffs and puffs forward like a steam train, never stopping for breaks or backing down. Even when the hiking trail eventually crosses smooth granite and her gripless sandals prove quite a bit more slippery than the sneakers I'm wearing. She refuses to accept the arm I proffer her, choosing to slip and slide as she scrambles forward.

Stubborn woman.

It brings a smile to my face and I can't help but think that Holly is so much stronger than she gives herself credit for. That she might often get overlooked because she's staying confined in a box that she doesn't belong in.

And maybe that's what's happened for her romantically, too. Dylan is kind of an idiot for letting her slip through his fingers, but after briefly meeting him, I sadly can't say that surprises me.

It only takes us a little over half an hour to reach the viewpoint, and when we get to the top, Holly bends over and puts her hands on her knees, catching her breath. It's a weekday afternoon, so it's pretty quiet up here compared to the droves that flock here on holidays and weekends, and I have to appreciate that there *is* a reason this hike is so popular.

It's beautiful up here.

I walk over to the edge, taking a moment to look around and soak in the view from our mountaintop vantage point. It's a clear day, and you can see for miles. Below us, the trees stretch out across the ground until they fade into the distant city.

Holly appears at my side. "Wow. It's gorgeous."

My eyes slide sideways towards her. Her face is red and wispy hairs are stuck to her sweaty forehead and honestly... she looks prettier than I've ever seen her. "It is," I agree, a soft smile on my lips as I drink in the enthusiastic, tired-but-happy expression on her face.

She catches me staring, and I quickly rearrange my features into a smirk as I turn towards the view.

"You're nice to hike with," I say. "The last person I took out hiking practically clawed the arms off me because she was afraid of getting eaten by a bear."

Holly throws her head back and laughs. I like her laugh. It's bubbly and sweet, but with an undertone of straight cackle. "I was wondering how you got those scratches!"

"Do me a favor and when you meet your so-called 'perfect man,' don't cut him to pieces while he's trying to help you escape a non-existent predator."

"Noted." She grins, then puts her hands on her hips. "Now, I'm sure you didn't take me up here just to see me almost fall flat on my face."

"No. Not *just* for that." I wink at her, and then gesture out to the glimmering Atlanta skyline. "I brought you here for this."

"For the beautiful view?"

"For perspective," I reply. "We started all the way down there, and then you did the hard thing—pushed yourself beyond where you thought you could go—and now, you're up here. And you can see the city in a whole new light. From a whole new vantage point."

"That's true." She looks almost wistful. "I never make a point of getting out of the city on my days off." She shakes her head. "Yet another thing I should have done more."

"But that's the thing. Maybe you're looking at it wrong. Maybe you didn't waste your time or miss out on all the 'shoulds.' Maybe you learned something through a hard situation that's brought you to where and who you are today. Made you stronger, or more resilient, or more *right* for the person who does come along and loves you back."

She stares at me, her brown eyes flickering as she takes in what I'm saying.

Then, her eyes become shrewd, almost challenging, and I like to see that fire in her. "How do you know so much about this stuff? Are you like some sort of secret relationship guru on top of your bartending and wilderness guiding?"

"Nope."

I'm just a guy who grew up watching the person he once idolized treat women like total dirt and make them feel worthless.

But of course, I don't tell Holly that. We're here for *her*, not for me.

We share a smile, and then she says, "So what do you suggest I do next, Mr. Dating Coach?"

"I prefer 'O Wise One.'"

"Nope."

"Worth a try." I stare out at the horizon for a few moments, taking in the way the afternoon light reflects off the buildings so that Atlanta seems aglow. It really *is* a beautiful city. And I'm happy I got to take Holly here, that I—and moreso, that *she*— could see how strong and capable she really is.

And then... it comes to me.

"I think we need to revisit that terrible hit list of yours."

She tilts her head at me. "Add more things to it?"

"No, we're going to throw it out altogether for now." When I look at her, she's frowning at me in full concern. "And replace it with your quit list."

17

HOLLY

"My quit list?" I wrinkle my nose, taking this in.

I'm still sticky and out of breath from the uphill slog and fairly rattled that I almost cried earlier as I admitted how hopeless I felt. But I'm mostly blown away by how unbelievably kind and considerate Jax the Bartender is turning out to be. And—*fine*—wise as well.

He's... so much more than just a bartender.

"I think we've been looking at this all wrong," he continues, his slate eyes sparkling like the cityscape ahead of us. "Our perspective has been wrong. We've been focusing on your hit list when we should have been focusing on the things you wanted to *quit* doing. AKA your..."

"Quit list," I fill in the blank.

"Right. Because the thing is, once you start focusing on your quit list—on yourself and all the things you want to do for *you*—an actual hit list will come naturally from there. One that's more than the external factors you listed. One that will lead you to a man who's truly ideal for you."

He's standing there, smiling at me like he's discovered the answers to life's secrets. And meanwhile, I'm staring back blankly, feeling more lost than ever.

He seems to sense this because he asks, "What were the three things you wanted to quit again? Those resolutions of yours?"

I frown. "I want to quit wasting my time on someone who would never love me back, quit letting my life pass me by, and quit being afraid to step out of my comfort zone."

"Exactly." He takes a breath. "Can I be honest for a moment, Holly?"

"Like you've done anything else." I pull a face to show him I'm teasing, then cock my head. "Go on."

"In the short time I've known you, you sat through an entire meal with Keith when you didn't want to be there, you made excuses for that guy who stood you up, and you apologized for taking up my time after I already agreed to help you. Plus, you've helped *me* way more with my website and bookings system, anyway." He tilts his head. "And *just now*, you let Sabrina insult you when you could have bid her goodbye and walked away."

I wince a little, but not so much from Jax's words as from the fact that he's right. Again. I force out a laugh. "So you decided to take me up a mountain so you could list all my shortcomings while I'm tired and out of breath?"

He doesn't answer my question. Instead, he says, "Look, you want to get over your feelings for Dylan, right? I think, in order to fully move on from him and find your perfect match, you need to focus on the other two things on your quit list. Go after what you want in other areas of your life, and put yourself in situations out of your comfort zone that aren't to do with dating."

What he's saying is making some sense... maybe.

"I think you spend all your time focused on what other people want, instead of what YOU want. And you try to give other people a version of you that you think they'll like, instead of just being yourself."

"I'm not sure I want you to be honest anymore," I say, my cheeks warming a little under his scrutiny.

He simply shrugs. "I'd apologize, but I'm not sorry for telling you that you're underestimating yourself. That being *you* is the best thing you can be."

I chew on my lip as I study the distant skyline, soaking in this new perspective.

"So what do *you* want, Holly? Forget everything and everyone else." He pauses. "Deep down, what do *you* actually desire?"

It's a question that hits me. Hard.

I've always been the responsible one. Never done anything unpredictable. Nothing surprising. I've never really let myself consider what I want, what I might desire for myself. I've always simply gone along with the next logical step, with everyone's expectations of me—and my expectations for myself. Always deferred to what seemed to be right, instead of what *felt* right.

And seeing Sabrina's face earlier, how shocked she was that I was doing something she didn't expect...

For that brief moment in time, I wanted it to be true. I wanted to be *that girl* who lived her life big and wild and would take off on a whim on multi-day excursions to the middle of nowhere.

It lit a fire in me. A fire that's still burning beneath the surface, like embers waiting for the right gust of wind.

I set my jaw. Turn back to Jax and look him dead in the eye.

"I... I want sparks. Fireworks. Adventures." I swallow. "Romance that makes me feel like I'm on a rollercoaster, but with someone safe next to me, holding my hand." I say this all in a burst, then press my lips together, surprised by my own admission.

Jax smiles, like I somehow gave him the right answer. And I realize it really is the right answer for me. That *is* what I want.

"That's it, Hol. You need to find someone to *complement* you, not *complete* you. You're already a whole person all on your own, but to find your equal partner, you first need to pursue who *you* are and what *you* want in life. Find what brings you joy and makes you happy, and then find a person to share all that with you and even add to it." I grin. "And in the process, you'll be checking off all the items on your Quit List."

I nod slowly. It's not like I've never heard this before—I've watched many a romcom, read many a romance novel with a similar concept about loving and knowing yourself first. But having Jax say this to me so point blank... well, it *is* a new perspective. I feel it so strongly, feel so inspired in this moment. And I don't want to lose it.

So, before I can think about it, I say the one thing that I know, in my gut, *feels* right.

"I need to go on that backpacking trip with you."

The words hang between us and Jax looks surprised. I, myself, can hardly believe it. But it's true.

I *need* to do this.

Because the flutters in my stomach right now were activated by Jax's earlier mention of a multi-day backpacking trip— flutters that are way stronger than any I've had with my dates thus far. And, as much as I want to find a partner, the idea of getting lost in an adventure in the process is so unexpectedly appealing.

And maybe it really *is* time that I start chasing—start identifying—the things I want... in more areas than just dating, like Jax said.

I *want* to do this. A wilderness hiking adventure sounds... fun. Exciting. Exactly what I need, but have no idea how to do it myself.

But Jax knows.

And Jax is already doing a multi-day hike this spring and apparently he has yet to find someone to go with him.

Biting my lip, I try to find a downside to seizing the day with this idea. Come up short.

"*You* want to come on the backpacking trip in the Appalachians," Jax finally says.

"I do."

His jaw is working as he thinks it through. "It's not going to be for the faint of heart."

"I know." For some reason, his hesitation is only adding fuel to my fire versus burning it out. Until I consider something and falter a little, my smile slipping off my face. "You don't think I can do it?"

"Of course you can," he responds immediately with a firm nod of his head. "It's not that at all. I'm just..."

He trails off, seemingly still lost in thought.

I paste my smile back on. "Look, we're friends now, right?"

"Right?"

"And friends help each other out."

"They do." Jax narrows his eyes, looking at me like he's trying to read a book in Mandarin.

"You said you'd be hiking a route out in the Appa—whatever they're called—with someone who isn't me. But what if it *is* me?"

Jax's face becomes impassive. And then, after a moment of hesitation, he begins to nod.

"It's actually kind of funny you're suggesting this," he says slowly. "My plan *was* to find a novice hiker to take out there—my mentor recommended I get more practical guiding experience before actually opening for business. I expected to ask one of my sister's friends or someone at work, but..."

"See!" I exclaim. "It's perfect!"

"It's going to be grueling," he cautions. "Think blisters and no bathroom facilities and dehydrated food."

"Exactly! It's an adventure. You'd have a hiking buddy, I'd be pushed out of my comfort zone."

My heart is literally pounding with excitement. I can't believe how much I'm looking forward to this.

And not gonna lie, the mental image of Jax out there leading me in the wilderness is downright sexy. Surely all women would go crazy to see this guy chopping wood and bushwhacking and scaling peaks and... whatever it is, exactly, that wilderness guides do.

Which gives me another idea. "And in the process, what if I work on some of that immersive content that I was talking about for your website? Maybe take some photos for your social media..."

I trail off as some of my bravado fades. I'm probably getting ahead of myself. This sounds like a no-brainer to me, but what if Jax has the same reaction Dylan usually has? Doesn't want me getting in the way with all my grand ideas?

But instead of responding right away, like Dylan would, Jax is silent for a moment. Thoughtful.

And then, finally, a smile spreads across his face. "You've got yourself a deal, Hollywood."

"Pleasure doing business, Mr. Bartender... or should I say, Mr. Wilderness Guide."

When our hands meet, his feels big and warm around mine, and a tingle travels down my arm.

Safe and dangerous, all at once.

Then, a flicker suddenly crosses Jax's face. "Hang on, I just need to check... you're not deathly afraid of ravines, are you? Because if you are, I will need to rescind my agreement."

Random.

I give him a puzzled look. "I am afraid of many things, but ravines have never made it onto the list, no."

He looks weirdly relieved by my response.

My hand is still clasped in his when my phone buzzes in my purse, jolting me out of the moment.

I drop his hand, shake off those dumb tingles that one should not feel when shaking the hand of a man who is helping you find a man who is not him, and grab my phone.

> Wanna come over for sushi and board games tonight?

> Bring Aubrey, if you like, so we have four.

> But make sure you tell her that she has to play properly this time and can't go giving away her wheat to solve world hunger.

I snort a laugh at this. When Mindy says "board games," she means honoring the long-standing tradition in our family of playing Settlers of Catan. Which is probably a tradition in many families, but the Greenes play with the Traders & Barbarians expansion pack, and we add our own layers of bribery, extortion, blackmail, and bartering.

Apparently, natural resources bring out the worst in us.

Mindy's husband, Luke, has embraced the competitive chaos with open arms, but Greene Family Game Night is *not* for the faint of heart, and Aubrey, quite frankly, sucks at it. She's too much into peace and love to make a good barbarian.

"A new Spark match?" Jax asks from beside me.

"Nah, it's my sister." I turn to look at him, and then, a slow smile spreads over my face. Unlike Aubrey, Jax seems to have no problem doling out tough love and hard truths. A barbarian in the making, really. "Hey, you have plans for this evening?"

18

HOLLY

Mindy and Luke have a really nice townhouse in a really nice suburb that looks really normal and nice from the outside.

But then, you open the door and are immediately swept off your feet by both a tornado and a hurricane.

That tornado and hurricane being Sage and Sawyer, my adorable—but very noisy and destructive—niece and nephew.

"Aghhhhhhhhhh!!!!!!!!"

Sawyer is screaming at the top of his lungs when I push open the front door. Behind him, Sage is bashing him over the head with a plastic toy Paw Patrol cell phone that keeps exclaiming "Chase is on the case!" with every blow.

"No, no, no, no, no." Mindy comes skidding into the hallway in her sock feet. She swoops down to wrangle the cell phone out of Sage's clutches while simultaneously rubbing Sawyer's head. "Gentle hands, honey, remember? We don't hit our brother. Or Mommy. Or anyone."

Sage laughs like this is the funniest thing in the world.

"Hi, Hol," Mindy says to me as she scoops up a still-bawling Sawyer and places him on her hip. "Just another fun evening at Casa Donovan. Hope you brought earpl..."

Mindy's mouth falls open when she spots the huge hunk of man hovering in the doorway behind me. Her eyes light up like a slot machine hitting the jackpot. "Who is *this?*"

"Mindy, this is my friend Jax. Jax, my sister Mindy... and her mini sociopaths."

As I say this, I make a gimme motion, and Mindy dutifully plops Sawyer into my arms. I cuddle him close, inhaling that delicious baby scent he still has. At sixteen months, the twins are growing fast, and it makes me want to slow time right down to keep them this tiny and delicious-smelling for longer.

"Nice to meet you, Mindy," Jax says warmly, extending his hand. "Thank you for having me."

She takes his hand and pumps it up and down enthusiastically, her eyes still starry. "Holly told me she was bringing a friend, but none of her other friends look anything like *you.*"

"Shut up, Min."

"No. Look at this man. Why is he your friend and not something way more exciting?" She says this in a stage whisper he can obviously still hear, and then adds, at equally non-subtle whisper volume, "Don't you want to climb him like a tree?"

As if.

Hot as he is, I will certainly not be doing any climbing of any kind on Jax. In fact, on the way here, he helpfully suggested that I update the bio on my Spark profile to read, "looking for sparks, fireworks, and someone to hold my hand on my next adventure."

Which, I have to admit, has a less intense, much snappier vibe to it.

"Shut *up*, Mindy."

My sister is all brash confidence and zero filter, which is the *worst* combination to be around for the embarrassment factor.

"Oh, are you gay?" Mindy asks Jax, then looks at me again. "That would explain it, because if I were you, Hol, I'd be all over that like white on rice."

"You can't just ask people that," I say through clenched teeth. "And for the record, no, he's not. Not that it would matter if he was, because he's my *friend*."

Mindy gives me squinty eyes. "Either way, we will be talking about this later."

"We brought wine," Jax cuts in swiftly, proffering a nice bottle of chablis and looking very much like he's trying not to laugh.

"I love you already," Mindy tells him as she accepts the bottle, thankfully stopping with her ridiculous Spanish Inquisition into our platonic relationship for the moment. Once you get to know her, you realize she's got a heart of gold, but she can be a lot to take at first. "Come in, both of you."

As we move into the foyer, Sage pauses her maniacal cackling for a moment to stare up at Jax with big googly eyes. A little piece of drool spills out the side of her open mouth. A little obvious, but I can't say I blame her—Jax is hot.

"Up," she commands him, holding her chubby little arms up like she's about to begin a miniature sun salutation.

Jax's eyes pop, his forehead puckering as he looks from Sage, to me, to Mindy, to Sage again. Mindy shrugs. "She really likes men. You can pick her up."

"Uhh," Jax says.

"You don't have to," I tell him.

"I just don't want to drop her."

"Don't be crazy." Mindy picks up Sage and practically throws her at Jax. The little girl's arms immediately loop around his neck, and his big hand cradles her back at the same time, holding her firmly in place. "See?"

Jax doesn't respond. He's gazing down at Sage—who's got her dad's dark brown eyes and her mom's sandy-colored hair—like she's a strange, magical creature. "Hi, Sage," he says softly. "I'm Jax."

In response, Sage grabs his nose. Twists it, hard.

"Ouch," Jax mumbles.

Mindy beams. "Wow, she really likes you."

We follow Mindy—me happily bouncing Sawyer on my hip, Jax gingerly holding onto Sage for dear life—through the hallway and into the kitchen at the back of the house. It's my favorite room because of the accordion doors that run the length of the room, letting in copious amounts of fresh air and natural light.

Mindy's husband Luke is standing by the counter, emptying bags of kettle chips into bowls. He's one of the good ones—a man who loves to laugh and isn't above clowning around, but who is also a great husband and father, and loves my sister something fierce.

When he looks up, the corners of his eyes crinkle as he smiles. "Hey, Holly. Good to see you."

He then catches sight of Jax, and his eyebrows practically hit his hairline. But luckily, he's a little more subtle than his wife, and so he merely wipes his hands on a towel, then strolls over to introduce himself.

Watching Jax attempt to shake hands with my brother-in-law while holding onto Sage like she's about to break into a million pieces at any moment is perhaps the most precious thing I've seen in years.

He says he's not great with kids, but I have the feeling it's because he has no experience with them. If he treats his future godchild with anywhere near as much reverence as he's currently treating my niece, I'm sure he will be totally fine. More than fine.

I smile at the sight, thinking that this bartender—with all his rough edges—is nothing like the man you first think he is.

I plop Sawyer in his exersaucer and then relieve Jax of Sage so he can shake hands and chat properly. I'm sitting down with the second twin on a playmat when Mindy sidles up next to me and pokes me in the side. "Who is he? Seriously."

"Just a new, um, hiking friend."

"Hiking? Since when are you into hiking?"

"Since now."

Mindy peers at me like a curious owl, all ruffled feathers. "Are you feeling a little feverish?"

"No, I feel great." Spurred on by her surprise, I add, "We are going to the Appalachians for a three day hiking trip later this spring."

My sister's eyes almost bug out of her head. "You do realize that hiking in the backcountry is a different type of exercise than walking the length of the Mall of Georgia with an iced coffee?"

It's not an entirely uncalled-for caution, given my entirely non-outdoorsy history.

"I hiked up Stone Mountain with him today. In sandals," I tell her proudly, peeking over at Jax, who's now deep in conversation with Luke as they pour wine into glasses.

Mindy must see something on my face because her grin practically splits her face in two. "Are you doing this stuff coz you're into him? Is he looking for one of those real outdoorsy girls with the year-round tans and penchants for zip-off cargo pants and waterproof river shoes?"

"No!" I can't help but laugh. "I'm doing it because I *want* to. I wanted a change, wanted to try something new."

The look of admiration on my sister's face is everything. "That's awesome, Holly. Good for you. Sounds like a real adventure."

She's always encouraged me to throw caution to the wind, to be more spontaneous... but I suspect that, up until this point, she didn't actually believe I had it in me.

She then raises a brow, glancing over her shoulder towards the two men. "But I don't understand why you'd rather sample life in the backcountry than that hottie in our kitchen right now."

I roll my eyes. "I don't want to 'sample' anyone, as you so eloquently put it. On top of trying new hobbies, I still want to find a long term partner, and Jax, lovely as he is, is not looking for a relationship. He told me so himself."

Mindy waves her hand airily. "That could change at any minute."

Not always.

But I don't get a word in edgewise because Mindy is still going. "Luke's older brother Liam insisted that he was never getting married or settling down, but then, he fell so hard for his now-wife that he practically broke his face in two." She grins. "Literally. He quite literally fainted when he proposed to Annie. They ended up in the ER so he could get his eye stitched up."

Of course he did.

"Why do all of these love stories seem to involve the ER?" I grouch, thinking of Aubrey. "I need to find myself a hot doctor to stitch me up and fall in love with me."

"Well, if that's what you want, can't you filter by profession on that dating app you're obsessed with?"

My eyes widen as I reach for my phone. "Mindy, you're a genius!"

But then, I pause, my eyes flickering over to Jax. And I think of what he and I just spoke about on the mountain.

Because now, thanks to his coaching, I'm not sure if what I *thought* I wanted in a man is what I actually want.

Or at least, I'm seeing what I want with a new perspective —that while finding a doctor in his thirties who wants to settle down and have a family is a nice thought, I also need to make sure that I'm considering much more than these external qualities—superlatives, really—when thinking about my romantic future.

It does make me wonder about Jax, though. He's made it clear that he doesn't want a romantic relationship, but he doesn't seem to be the callous player I first thought he was. He's honest and funny and charming and obviously good with kids (after some time with them). He has a great personality and has so many qualities I like, and we do get along really well...

"Luke's brother changed his mind?" I ask her.

"When he met the right person." Mindy winks at me knowingly. "The right person can change everything. Luke and I are a prime example of that, too."

She's not wrong. From what I know, those two were both wilder than wild before they found each other. And while some people never change (ahem, Sabrina), others might just need to find the right person to see things differently.

I'm chewing this over in my mind when Jax walks over with a glass of wine in each hand for us. "Here we go."

Mindy takes the glass, then looks at him with the scariest eyes I've ever seen. "So, Jax, you got a girlfriend? Wife? Long list of ex-lovers?"

I feel my entire face flush bright red. "You don't have to answer that. Mindy is insane."

Jax laughs easily. "None of the above."

"Well, what are you waiting for?" Mindy smirks.

But he takes it in stride. "I'm more into keeping things casual. I don't see myself ever getting into a long-term relationship or marriage. I mean, it works for other people obviously. But it's not for me."

He says this with strength, certainty. Confidence in what *he* wants.

And just like that, I realize that Mindy's not the one being insane. I am.

I'm trying to change some things in *my* life, but that doesn't mean that Jax is suddenly going to change and become a potential romantic prospect for me. He's helping me, and that's all.

My hit list may not be watertight, but I have to face the literal facts: Jax doesn't want marriage, or kids, or even to settle down, anytime in his future. And I'm not going to make the same mistake of developing feelings for a guy who can never love me back the way I want to be loved, all because I'm being dumb enough to think that the other person might change their mind.

This journey is about *me*. Finding what I want. Focusing on my plan, my quit list... and not the hot guy helping me execute said quit list.

Quit while you're ahead, Holly.

The only way I'll stay ahead with Jax is to remember that he's my dating coach, and keep said dating coach firmly in the friend zone.

With a determined nod to myself, I open Spark on my phone and click onto my profile—complete with my cute, new, taco-wielding profile pic and adventure-loving bio. And then, I type 'doctor' in the search bar.

19

JAX

Over the next couple of weeks, I don't see Holly much. I split most of my time between my shifts at the bar and driving to and from my cabin, where the renovations are coming along, slowly but surely.

Thanks to my website—which is now live, but still lacking good imagery and video content—I've had *some* interest, which is great. But I need to have somewhere for these people to sleep before I can start opening up bookings.

One thing at a time.

Either way, I'm feeling positive one bright Thursday afternoon as my brother-in-law Sebastian, his teammate Aaron and I finish building a large deck around the premises while Rick the dog naps under a towering Georgia pine. The sun is shining, my shirt's off, and I'm covered in sweat, muscles pleasantly sore from the hard work.

"This is looking amazing," I say as we put the final touches on the railings. "Thanks again, guys."

"It's nothin'," Aaron says before taking a swig of blue

Gatorade. "Honestly, building decks would have been my chosen career if hockey hadn't worked out."

"No way would hockey have not worked out for you." I laugh. Aaron Marino is a stellar NHL right winger—has been for years. "But lucky for me, you have the carpentry skills, too."

"Well, that's just genetics," he says with a one-shoulder shrug.

I'm pretty handy, and I've handled a lot of the renovations myself, but building a huge deck is not the easiest to do alone. So, I asked Seb if he could help me on a couple of his days off. You know, trying to get better at asking for help and all that.

Luckily for me, he readily agreed (and lucky for Dante, who I also considered asking, but then I figured he'd freak out if he broke a nail... or a sweat). Seb then went on to enlist Aaron, whose family literally owns a company specializing in decks.

Turns out the guy is a freaking deck connoisseur, and the results of his vision—and all of our gruntwork—are way better than I could have imagined.

I can already picture people sitting out here on Adirondack chairs at dusk or sipping beer under the sparkling fairy lights after a long day spent hiking. I could install a little bar out here, get a few big barbecues set up for cookouts. Add a firepit.

"Genetics or not, this was a huge help," I say as I look out towards the expansive view.

"What can I say? I'm good with my hands." Aaron smirks.

"Would Tessa agree?" Seb asks with a snort.

"Unequivocally."

Seb laughs and looks over at me, putting on a dumb hockey announcer's voice. "In his spare time, Aaron Marino likes hot redheads, building decks, crocheting, and... Scrabble!"

"Words with Friends," Aaron corrects, not looking in the least bit bashful about it, either.

"Wish I was good with words," I say. "Maybe I should try it. Pad out my vocabulary."

"What, find a word to use other than 'no' every once in a while?" Seb ribs me.

"Hey, I said yes to being your kid's godfather, didn't I?" I shoot back. The pregnancy isn't public knowledge yet, but Seb has filled his teammates in.

"Grudgingly as all hell." My brother-in-law laughs good-naturedly. But I shoot him a thankful smile for being so understanding about my initial reaction to the news.

The morning after the full-day excursion of shopping, hiking, and sister-visiting with Holly (crazy that we ended up spending the whole day and evening together without meaning to), I turned up at Seb and Maddie's apartment wearing a t-shirt with a quote from *The Godfather* movie. I went on to hold out the huge bag of baby gear I purchased the day before, along with a heartfelt apology and a picture of me holding baby Sage to illustrate the fact that I was, in fact, capable of being cool with a baby.

They laughed in my face. Mostly because they knew that I wasn't trying to be rude or seem unsupportive the day they told me, but that I needed time to process and get my head around the new, unexpected—but very welcome—responsibility.

Honestly, Maddie was much, much more interested in who-the-hell's baby I was holding in the picture and I ended up having to answer about a billion and one questions about Holly.

Nosy as can be, my sister.

"So *he's* the one who beat me out for the title," Aaron says cheekily, elbowing Seb in the ribs.

"Listen," he argues back, sounding all reasonable and father-like already. "If I'd made you godfather, I also would've had to ask Mal, and Colton, and Dallas, and Jake, and Triple freaking J." He winces. "Jeez, imagine that moron wielding a baby..."

The two of them break into laughter at the mental image of a team of hockey players vying for pole position as godfather, but it gives me pause for thought. Maddie and Seb *did* have a lot of options for the title—Seb has two brothers as well. And yet, they chose *me*.

I'm determined not to fail them. Or the baby.

I'm going to have a successful business. One to be proud of. I'll take the little nugget hiking and camping, teach him or her to fish and tie knots and realize that they can be anyone they want to be. Do anything they put their mind to.

The morning of my *Godfather* apology, I asked Maddie and Seb whether they still wanted me to be the godparent of their child given that I intend to live in the middle of nowhere and therefore might have to raise the kid in the wilderness. Both Maddie and Seb laughed and said that, if it ever came to that, they might like the idea of their child growing up like *Tarzan*. At which point the conversation *totally* got away from me as Maddie went on to swoon over Brendan Fraser in the live-action movie.

At that moment, my phone buzzes. I smile when I see who the message is from.

Mini-golf date tonight.

My smile grows. Ever since Holly updated her profile to show more of who she is (i.e. toned down the psychotic "marry me" vibes), and is dating her way, on her terms, she seems to be having more fun. We've been texting to debrief after each date, and one night, she even stopped into the bar to tell me about how she'd just been for ice cream with a guy who groaned "mmm" after every overtly sexual lick of his cone, and so she pretended she was going to the bathroom and booked it out of there.

I'm so proud of how far she's come.

> Who's the lucky guy? New or a second date?

> New guy—a cute podiatrist. Wish me luck.

"Podiatrist?" I wonder aloud, frowning at my phone screen.

"Foot doctor," Seb and Aaron say in tandem. When I look up at them, Seb shrugs. "What? Hockey players have gross feet."

I raise my brows. "Noted."

> Foot luck.

> That was the worst joke ever.

> I'm practicing my dad jokes for my future godfathering duties.

> Better keep practicing.

> Will do. Didn't know you were a mini-golf fan?

> No idea if I am, but it sounded fun and I wanted to try it.

> That's what I like to hear! Knock 'em dead.

> You think this is an appropriate outfit for mini-golf?

She proceeds to send a selfie, taken in the mirror of what looks like an extremely tidy bedroom.

I smile at the silly expression she's making at the mirror, all cross-eyed and pursed-lipped. She's wearing a short, baby-blue jumpsuit thing with white sneakers, and her hair is in a messy bun.

She looks... Well, let's say that podiatrist, whoever he is, *is* a lucky guy.

And in my opinion—limited mini-golf knowledge notwithstanding—she probably looks more fancy than one might normally look to play a game where you swing a club. But Holly always looks fancy, and it suits her. She should wear what she wants to wear.

> Do you feel good wearing it?

I guess I do.

> Then I think it's perfect.

I'll call you to let you know how it goes.

> Hoping it's a hole in one ;)

Oh my gosh, stop it.

> Are we still on for tomorrow?

Absolutely. Looking forward to it. I think.

This makes me chuckle. Her dates have been going well lately, but we still have the other items on that quit list of hers to work on, and I've thought of the perfect activity to get her out of her comfort zone and into adventure mode.

Just like she's hoping to do on our hike.

It's very... convenient how that all worked out. I can't say exactly why I was so hesitant when she first proposed that *she* be the one to do the multi-day trip with me. After all, I do need to practice my guiding with a novice hiker. And if she can take immersive whats-its for my social media (or whatever), all the better.

It's probably just because she screams "city girl." *Holly-wood.* Maybe a part of me is reliving the whole Laurel situation. But at the same time, Holly surprised me when we climbed Stone Mountain. She has so much grit, so much determination.

And though I do prefer to hike alone, I have a feeling she won't be a bad person to hike with. I might actually... enjoy myself. Enjoy spending those days with her.

I file those thoughts away—they're not important or relevant right now.

But before I put my phone away, I'm finding myself scrolling back through our conversation so I can look at her selfie again.

There really is something about her. Maybe it's the glimmer in her eyes, the hint of sarcastic, self-deprecating humor and wit lurking right below the surface. That, and her zest for adventure; the confidence she seems to be gaining by the day, while remaining unafraid to make fun of both herself and, well, me.

I type out another text.

> Remember to bring a bathing suit, by the way.

What? Why?

Should I bring sunscreen, too?

> Probably yes. Unless you want to burn like a lobster.

Should I be scared?

> Nah, not scared. Worried, at worst.

You're the worst.

> See you in the morning!

At that moment, a pinecone hits me in the face, ricocheting off my forehead with no small amount of force.

"What are you grinning at over there?" Seb asks.

"Oh, I know that smile." Aaron points at me like he's accusing me of murder. "That's the exact smile Seb started wearing when he and Maddie started sending each other all those NSFW texts."

"That, I didn't need to know," I say dryly. "And nothing. I'm texting a friend."

"That Holly girl again?" Seb pries, and before I can answer, he turns to Aaron with a triumphant expression. "He says they're just friends but he's taking her hiking. To the *back-country*."

"Ooh, the backcountry," Aaron says like he's ten years old, and the two of them snort with laughter. "Is she hot? Are you into her?"

"I'm only taking Holly because Maddie was too busy being knocked up to come with me." I elbow Seb as I say this, and he laughs. "We're going on a multi-day hike to build up my guiding experience, and she'll be helping me with social media content and all that stuff, too." I gesture towards the deck we're sitting on. "You know, so I can run a business and make money. We can't all be pro athletes, can we?"

"You guys gonna get all cozy in one tent?" Seb winks, totally ignoring my attempt at a subject change. "Try not to get *too* cozy. Or on second thought, do. Baby Slater could do with a cousin."

"Yeah, hold that fantasy. No coziness will be happening. Period. And she will have her own tent, thank you very much."

A tent that I will be staying well away from. Because, well, maybe I like her. Maybe a little too much.

But I also know what she's searching for and it ain't me.

153

I'm the temporary distraction, not the happy ever after, remember?

And Holly needs no distractions right now. She's a woman on a mission.

We're friends. With no benefits. Each of us have our own, entirely unromantic reasons for going on this trip together. End of story.

I've done these types of trips a million times—always solo—and I have a pretty good idea of the route I want us to take. It needs to be a bit of a challenge, something that will occasionally put Holly's perseverance to the test but will still allow her to enjoy her time out there.

I hope.

But, just in case, I might make sure she has short nails before we leave.

20

JAX

The next morning, bright and early, I'm pulling up outside a small, well-kept bungalow with whitewashed stucco, a cherry-red front door, and a front lawn that looks like it's been mowed with perfect precision.

It's all very groomed and proper... until you see the front door mat, which proclaims *Hang on, I'm probably not wearing pants.*

I hover on the doorstep for a moment before I ring the doorbell. Holly never did call me after her date last night, and I wonder if it's because she was out late or because my cell service was patchy on the drive home from the cabin.

I'm curious how it all went... only in my capacity as "dating coach"—as she calls it—of course.

Professional all-around over here. Even if Seb and Aaron did get me a bit rattled yesterday with their cozy-tent talk.

But they're wrong. This is just... taking a new friend on new adventures. A friend who is currently on a Spark-wide search for a man who is the polar opposite of me. That's all. Ain't nothing wrong with making a new friend.

Even if said friend is crazy hot and also the exact right amount of crazy.

Suddenly, the door opens, and a familiar voice draws me from my thoughts. "There's a boat strapped to the top of your van."

I look up to see Holly standing in front of me, frowning as she looks over my shoulder. No good morning, no hello, just straight down to what she's thinking. I kinda like it.

She's wearing a loose black sundress that falls to her mid thigh and has these sexy little straps on the shoulders. Her hair is in a neat French braid down her back, and when I sneak a glance at her lips, I note with a smile that they're bubblegum pink and glossy once again.

"You're really not wearing pants," I reply, instead of addressing her observation. "Your mat doesn't lie."

She quirks her head questioningly, and then, she glances down at the door mat. "Oh, that's Aubrey's. My roommate. She hates pants."

"I'm sorry to hear that. What did pants do to her, if I may ask?"

"You may, but don't say I didn't warn you..."

"This sounds raunchy."

"I wish. She feels like her pants judge her when she wears them."

"Have you recommended she get a pair with a better personality?"

Holly laughs. "Well, that's only part of the problem. They also make her lady parts feel restricted. Like they're in lady part jail." She clocks my expression and her grin widens. "Wish you hadn't asked now?"

"I do." I laugh, a sudden sense of calm washing over me as I realize that spending the day with Holly is going to be just fine.

"And that'll teach me to ask questions related to a woman's choice of clothing, which I will obviously never, ever do again."

"If only all men had that outlook." She sighs. "And now that you know all about Aubrey's relationship with her wardrobe full of unworn slacks and jeans, are you going to tell me why Edna is wearing a boat as a hat?"

"We're going kayaking."

Holly's jaw drops. "Today?"

"No, next week."

"Shut up." She gives me squinty eyes. "What I mean is... I've never been kayaking."

"I seem to recall a certain someone telling me that they were looking for adventure."

"I did say that, didn't I?"

"You did. And didn't you update your bio to say that you're looking for someone to have adventures with?"

"Maybe." She draws out the word.

"Ergo, you need to be going on adventures yourself in order to have someone join you on your future ones."

Holly narrows her eyes at me slightly, but then acquiesces. "Okay, okay. Should I get changed?"

"You have a bathing suit with you?"

"Under my dress."

I try not to dwell on anything *under her dress* as I shoot her what I hope is a carefree smile. "Then, nah. I like what you're wearing."

"I guess pants *are* overrated."

"I couldn't agree more, Hollywood."

21

HOLLY

That grin of his is starting to feel like a jolt of electricity to the stomach.

Obviously, Jax loves to crank up his flirty charm to make me blush—it might as well be his favorite freaking song on the radio. Ridiculous man.

I just wish that I didn't get warm all over when he looked me up and down slowly, his eyes lingering on my legs for a hint of a moment too long. *I like what you're wearing.*

Clearly, I need to get my head on straight.

"So?" Jax asks from the driver's seat of his van—sorry, *Edna* —his eyes moving sideways to meet mine before turning back to the road. He's wearing a light gray t-shirt today so the tattoos on his bicep peek out below the sleeve. I think it might be the first time I've seen him in something that's not black.

Gray works for him as well as black does... but I genuinely think this guy could dress up like a Teletubby and I'd think it was sexy.

My body doesn't seem to understand that Jax is my dating coach and not a potential date. It must be because we talk about my love life so much—it puts me in that headspace when I'm around him.

"So, what?"

"How was your date with Foot Man?"

"*Ian* was very nice. Kind. Carried a decent conversation," I reply. Which is true. My mini-golfing date with Ian the podiatrist wasn't as awkward as some of my other dates. I was able to talk to him without feeling itchy all over, or like my skin was too small for me. We didn't have that relaxed, easy banter and laughs like I do with Jax, but still. By all accounts, it was a solid enough first date.

Jax doesn't say anything, so for some reason, I add, "He has a summer home in Savannah."

I don't know why I say this. It's not like that's why I liked him. I liked him because he seemed like a reasonably good human being who didn't ogle my chest when he asked me about myself. And sure, there may not have been many—if any—sparks and fireworks between us. But that might come about on a second date, I'm sure.

If he asks me out again, that is. Last night, we parted ways with a simple "good night"—no further plans were made.

"He sounds fancy." He glances my way. "Able to support and provide for a family."

I shrug a shoulder. "I guess so."

"So did you beat him at mini golf?"

"Yeah. Twice, actually."

"Were you good at it?"

I laugh. "Horrible. But he was even more horrible. We had such a laugh about it."

"I don't buy it. He was probably letting you win."

Once again, Jax is insanely intuitive—I had a feeling that Ian was letting me win a couple times last night. "Well, that's kinda sweet, right? Gentlemanly?"

Jax's lips form into a smile. "I wouldn't have let you win."

"I wouldn't expect anything less from you," I say archly. And I really wouldn't. With Jax, I would have had to push myself. Get competitive. Fight for it. Like I did during board game night with Luke and Mindy last week.

It sounds... fun. We should go mini golfing together sometime. *Friends do that, right?*

"Come on, Holly, I know you don't want the pity W. It's sexist. You wanna win fair and square, or lose fair and square. Well, unless you're playing Catan. You were like a freaking bloodhound during that game. Ruthless."

Glad of the subject change away from Ian, I laugh. "When I find my man, I'm going to have to ease them into meeting Game Night Holly."

"Nah, if they can't handle her, they're not a keeper."

I turn away so he doesn't see the blush spread over my face. Truth is, I had way more fun than I probably should've had that night with Jax, Mindy, and Luke. We ended up playing best of three, and the last match came down to Luke and me, locked in a head-to-head. I swear Jax was building roads to get in the way of my path, just for the hell of it. Just to test me, make me sweat.

Though of course, it was hard to pay attention to winning when the laughter and conversation flowed so easily, Mindy and Luke snuggled close together on the couch, Jax with an arm draped loosely on the back of my chair.

It was cozy. Maybe too cozy.

The last couple of weeks put me back on track with my goals. I dove right back onto Spark with the intention to keep up my dates as I work on my quit list with Jax. And I have to admit, I've had a lot more fun. Even if a large part of that fun has been calling Jax after dates (especially after the bad ones) and laughing about them.

"I'm sure Ian could handle Game Night Holly," I say to the window, and it fogs up with my breath.

I draw a doodle heart in the fog, then hurriedly wipe it away.

Because I'm not so sure I'm right.

In my mind, kayaking didn't sound all that bad.

I was nervous, sure. I always get nervous for new things.

But on the drive to Sweetwater Creek State Park, I kind of pictured doing some leisurely laps in a tandem kayak together—gliding around on still, glassy water, and then sitting at the beach in the sunshine and eating a picnic.

I didn't consider the fact that Wolf Man was the one taking me on this adventure. Because here I am, wading into less than calm water with the bottom of my dress bunched into one hand, my pretty new shoes abandoned on the shore behind me. I'm walking slowly and steadily, trying not to think too hard about the fact that my bare feet are currently squelching into mud on the lake floor with every step, and there's only one seat in that stupid boat—which I'm pretty sure is meant for me.

I hike my dress up further around my thighs, then turn to look at Jax, who's walking just behind me. It's a small comfort to know that he's close enough to catch me if a sudden freak current were to try and sweep me away.

Well... I hope he'd save me first and not the kayak.

"What now?"

He pats a hand on the red boat. "Get in."

I blink at him, then at the boat. "How?!"

"By using your legs."

"I hate you," I tell him.

He laughs. "Don't worry, Hollywood, you got this. I won't let you fall."

I don't know why, but I believe him. I hike my dress up even more and gingerly place one foot into the kayak. I notice Jax grasping onto the sides of the kayak to keep it steady, and I try to do the same.

But as I push up on my other foot, the kayak rocks precariously and I almost go ass over teakettle into the water. Somehow though, Jax keeps his promise and manages to both steady the shaking boat, and hold my hand as I sit without losing my balance.

I stretch my feet as far as they'll go in front of me and smooth down my dress.

"Feeling good?"

I nod. The boat is small and my legs are cramped, but I feel okay. "Yup."

"Wanna take your dress off before you start?"

"Are you being pervy or asking a legitimate question?"

"Both," he says innocently.

I snort a laugh. "What would the reason be for taking it off?"

"In case you tip over."

"Tip over?!" I squeak. "You never said anything about tipping over!"

"Because I knew you wouldn't get in the boat if I did."

"Seriously, I hate you."

"You can do this, Holly."

Deep down, I know I can. The last few months, whenever I've tried to step out of my comfort zone, I've always gotten flustered. But when I push myself to do it, I end up appreciating it. Feeling proud of myself.

And Jax hasn't steered me wrong yet.

"You can swim, right?"

I gulp. "Right."

"And I'll give you a life jacket. Worst that could happen is that you get a bit wet. No big deal."

He's so annoyingly casual and assured about everything.

But I must say... It is motivating.

"Hold the boat steady again?" I ask, and with a sigh, I lift my butt so I can wriggle my dress off.

The lilac bikini I'm wearing underneath isn't anything fancy. It's pretty plain and modestly cut, but the visible appreciation in Jax's slate eyes makes my stomach burn.

Clearly, he reacts to me, too. And this makes me feel good— even if it *is* just plain old surface-level attraction, it feels nice to be on the receiving end of it.

I remind myself that Jax is a man, and he probably has this reaction seeing any female with a pulse in a bathing suit.

But the odd thing is, in the little while I've known him, I've never actually seen or heard about him going out with anyone. Whatever his so-called casual dating life looks like, he keeps those cards pretty close to his chest and away from our conversations—although I guess that makes sense, because *my* dating life is the source of this unlikely friendship between us, not *his*.

Our eyes catch for a moment, but he quickly looks away. Grabs the life jacket currently slung over his shoulder and passes it to me.

A couple of clicks later, my life jacket is secured and Jax is handing me a paddle. He pushes me into deeper water and...

Everything goes okay.

From his position standing shin-deep in the shallows, Jax gives me advice on how to sit and position my body. How to hold the paddle. How to use it.

Learning on the job, he calls it.

Foolish, I call it.

But, it's effective. In mere minutes, I've picked up a rhythm moving my arms and am guiding the paddle through the water left, then right, then left again. The repetitive motion helps me relax. So much so that I begin to enjoy the moment. The smell of the dense foliage around the water, the call of birds echoing through the trees, and the feel of the sun and wind on my face.

As choppy as the water seemed from back on the shore, it's actually not bad now that I'm in control of the boat. Jax said that this area of Sweetwater Creek is actually a reservoir, so I don't need to worry about moving water or currents, but I do spot a patch of disturbed-looking water to my left, where it looks like the river apparently flows in.

I make a mental note to avoid that area, and stick my paddle in deeper, trying to turn the boat around so I can point myself in the direction of stiller waters.

"Yes, Holly!"

Jax's voice carries over the wind from somewhere behind me as I'm turning the boat. I go to look at him, but in doing so, jerk my paddle further downwards, which sends the boat teetering.

"Woah," I say as the kayak rocks and I try to regain my balance.

But, it's too late. I'm drifting towards the moving, choppy water *way* too fast, and while I know that Jax is yelling instructions from the shore, I can't hear anything.

In fact, everything goes totally silent... until a wave hits the side of the boat, and it tips over. I'm thrown into the water, and suddenly, everything is deafening.

Ooh, frick, it's cold!

It's still March—definitely not what I would consider swimming season. I'm thankful for the life jacket (though I am a decent swimmer) because, as quickly as I'm plunged into the reservoir, I pop up at the surface, bobbing like a cork as I splutter and cough out the water that went up my nose.

Gross.

I wipe the water and mascara out of my eyes, and ardently hope that I don't get pink eye or something—there seem to be a lot of ducks and geese that frequent this area.

Then, I bob around to face the shore, and quickly discover that Jax is... gone.

Gone!

What the hell? Did he see me tip over and think, "ah, this is a good time to go get a slurpee" or something?

Not that I need his help, but still.

Frustrated, I eye the upside-down red kayak bobbing a few feet from me and calculate my next move. I'm not sure whether I should leave the thing here, swim to shore and wait for Jax to appear again, or if I should try to flip the thing over. Making a snap decision, I swim over to the boat and place my hands under it.

Out of nowhere, there's a sudden warm body at my back. Two strong, tanned arms appear on either side of me, flipping the boat upright in one smooth motion.

"Nice tip."

I turn to see Jax treading water behind me, trying (and failing) to hide his smile. His hair is all tousled and wet, and the beads of water on his eyelashes glimmer in the sun. He looks better than ever... while I'm sure I look like a startled raccoon.

"You doing okay there, Hol?"

"Never better," I say as I push a chunk of wet, ropey hair off my forehead. "Just got too hot and decided to go for a cooling swim."

He laughs. "You know you're not allowed to swim in the reservoir, right?"

"Why?" I freeze, a sudden very unwelcome thought hitting me. "Are there alligators?"

"Don't freak out," Jax says slowly. Carefully. Which, of

165

course, means *yes, there are alligators in here,* and I should, very much, freak out.

But I know that freaking out won't help, so I put on my big girl panties and nod. "Tell me what to do."

The approval that glimmers in Jax's eyes is almost worth the imminent threat of an alligator biting off my toes. Almost.

"I'm going to get the paddle and I'll get in the kayak first. Then, I'm going to help pull you in."

"Okay."

He swims a few feet to retrieve the bobbing paddle, his strong arms slicing through the water in such a way that I wonder if he might be part dolphin in addition to part wolf. He comes back to the kayak, and in one smooth motion, pushes himself up out of the water and swings his body lithely into the boat. For such a big guy, he moves very smoothly.

Unlike me. Because what Jax does next is reach down, grab me by the shoulders of my life jacket, and haul me out of the water like I'm the catch of the freaking day.

"Oof!" I flop-roll like a codfish into the kayak.

Into his *lap,* to be exact.

And if I managed to stay calm before, I am certainly not calm now.

This boat was already tiny with one of us in here. With two, it's positively claustrophobic.

"Nice one, Holly. You did great."

"Mmmmrh," I mutter incoherently from my position, awkwardly flopped against him, my life jacket pressed up and almost cutting off my esophagus.

He parts his legs so I kind of slide down between them, sitting between his thick thighs with my back against his chest. Bare chest. Because obviously, he took his t-shirt off before swimming out here. Thank goodness for this life jack—

"Now, I need you to take off your life jacket." Jax's deep

voice cuts into my spiraling thoughts. "Unclip it and slide it off. I'll secure it to the ropes on the back."

"What?" I crane my head to look at him, which is also a mistake, because now, his lips are inches away from mine.

"If you're scared of falling in again, don't worry. I won't let that happen."

Wasn't even on my mind until he said it, but okay.

"I just don't have the space to paddle right now, so if you take it off, you can lean back against me properly and I'll put my arms around you to paddle us back to shore," he explains.

Holy mother of pearl. I should have taken my chances with the alligators because this feels infinitely more dangerous than a stupid sharp-toothed amphibian hunting me down.

"Okay," I say. I can hardly argue with his impeccable logic.

My heart decides that this is the moment to start cantering in my chest. Apparently, the imminent thrill of Jax's torso against mine is greater than plunging out of a kayak into freezing waters.

And yes, I know that this is Atlanta and the water is cool, at best, and ergo, I'm being dramatic. But I'm kind of freaking out right now.

I unclip the lifevest and hand it to Jax, who secures it, and then goes on to wrap a big arm around me. His rough hand grazes over the skin of my stomach as he pulls me flush against him, my bare back against his bare chest, with only the strap of my freaking bikini top separating us. "Just like that, good girl."

Goosebumps break out all over me and my heart picks up speed to a gallop. I can only hope and pray that Jax thinks this is all adrenaline from my fall.

His body is hot and hard, and I feel the thud of his heart against my back as he reaches around me and picks up the paddle, effectively pinning me in place.

"Doin' okay, Hollywood?"

I swallow thickly. "Yup."

"I'll have you back to shore in no time. Trust me."

I *do* trust him, I realize.

The four minutes it takes for Jax to paddle us back to shore feels like an eternity of exquisite torture. His skin scorches mine, and his chest rises and falls smoothly with each breath he takes, while each breath *I* take feels shallow and rough, filling my senses with his smell.

I bite my lip so hard I taste blood. Try to think of the most unsexy things I can. Ingrown hairs. Period cramps. Congealed bacon grease. Being trapped here with Keith right now instead of Jax.

Nothing works. So I resign myself to defeat, leaning my head back against Jax's chest and letting out a long, shaky breath.

I almost jolt in surprise when I hear Jax's breath hitch. Just slightly. Just for a moment.

Almost like he... might be feeling this, too?

Is this what sparks and fireworks are meant to feel like?

Impossible, I tell myself.

When we get to shore, I spring up like a Jack-in-the-Box and throw myself out of the kayak so fast, I almost faceplant in the shallows. And while I'm stumbling around like a drunken flamingo, Jax pulls the boat out of the water effortlessly.

He goes on to grin at me, like we didn't just share skin and breath and heartbeats and heat for what were potentially the longest minutes of my life. "I'd say, overall, that wasn't a bad first time."

"Avoided the alligators, at least." My voice is surprisingly non-shaky. *Mental high-five.*

Jax grabs a couple of towels from his backpack and passes one to me. I wrap it around myself and can't help but breathe in the delicious scent of his laundry detergent. The towel smells like him, and it's making my knees a little weak.

"How do you feel about calling it a day and getting some coffee to warm up?" he asks me.

"Perfect." I grab my own bag, and dig out my dress—Jax must've folded it and placed it in here for me—and my cell phone.

The screen lights up suddenly and I see that I have a message from Ian.

Ian. The man I enjoyed, who took me on a perfectly enjoyable mini golf date. The man who made me smile and chuckle, even if they weren't full-fledged laughs. The man who told me within five minutes of meeting me that he can't wait to get married, but he's been holding out for the right woman.

Yes. I should be thinking about Ian. Not the tattooed mountain man with the ridiculously high core temperature.

Shaking all memories of Jax's hot skin from my mind, I open the message.

Hi, Miss Holly. How about a second date?

22

JAX

"You sure you want another one of those things?"

My sister narrows her eyes at me. Playfully, but still not in a way that I'd mess with. "You sure you want to ask me that?"

"I am not," I say as I get to work making her another lemonade with extra lemon juice, topped with whipped cream and chocolate syrup.

And in case you're wondering... no, that is not on our menu.

But what the pregnant lady wants, the pregnant lady gets.

It's a busy Saturday night at Full Moon, and Maddie's hanging out at the bar, drinking her weird sweet n' sour lemonades and watching the TV screens behind my head. Seb is playing an away game in Dallas tonight, and Maddie insisted that *all* of the bar's TVs show the game.

The Cyclones are losing 5-3, and this seems to be making Maddie's mood more sour than her lemonade.

I, on the other hand, feel strangely sour for an entirely different reason. Namely, a certain *situation* that is currently taking place at the other end of the restaurant.

"After this one, I'm cutting you off," I joke as I put a straw in Chocolate Lemonade Number Three and slide it across the bar to Maddie, glancing over her shoulder as I do.

"You wouldn't dare." She takes a long sip, winces, then sighs happily. "I have no idea why this tastes so good. Non-pregnant me would be horrified."

"Mmm," I say distractedly, now trying to see past a veritable bouffant of hair at table three that's blocking my view of the booth behind.

A booth. She's never sat anywhere but at table seventeen on her dinner dates.

"What do you keep looking at?" Maddie asks, craning her neck around. "Is Margot Robbie sitting back there or something?"

"No, no, don't look," I tell her. "It's nothing, just a friend on a date. I'm curious to see how it's going, is all."

"Liar," Maddie says, sticking her finger in the mountain of whipped cream atop her drink and then licking it off. "Is it Holly?"

Ugh. Her and Seb tell each other everything.

I nod.

She twists around again, then looks back at me with a brow raised. "You never told me she's drop-dead gorgeous."

"Didn't seem relevant," I reply.

But it *is* relevant. Because tonight, Holly is wearing a short, dark red dress with a low neckline that shows a tantalizing hint of cleavage, coupled with strappy high-heeled sandals, and gold hoop earrings. There's a red scarf tied in her hair, and her lips are the same glossy bubblegum pink as ever.

She looks good. Damn good.

But maybe not quite as good as she did the other day when she sat on my lap in that kayak, her head lolling against my chest. All I could think about for that whole paddle was how I hoped my heart wasn't beating so loud and fast she could hear it.

Ever since that afternoon, when I close my eyes to sleep, all I see is her in that purple bikini. But it's more than just her (admittedly incredibly sexy) body. It's those brown eyes dancing with a mixture of contempt and mischief as she verbally spars with me. Her crazily messed-up wet hair and cheeks dripping with black mascara after she tipped over in the kayak and then immediately tried to solve the problem and right the boat.

She's way more comfortable outside of her comfort zone than I think she realizes. A fighter.

And right now, as I watch another guy lean close to her as he laughs at something she's said, I wonder if he sees this about Holly, too. If he's giving her enough credit for the person she is.

"You're totally jealous right now," Maddie tells me, a delighted smile on her face.

"It's not like that," I reply. Which is true.

Because, yes. I like Holly. A lot. That much is clear to me— I'm not in *complete* denial of how I feel when I'm around her.

And yes, if things were different, I'd ask her out. Pursue something with her.

But I know that what I can offer her is so much less than what she's looking for, and she deserves to find what she's looking for. I'll help her do it. I promised I'd help her do it.

I just don't think Foot Man is the right guy for her.

Maddie sucks another sip of her gross lemonade through her straw. "I've never seen you jealous before."

"I'm not jealous, Mads. I'm... helping her out." I'm also distracted. Because over Maddie's shoulder and behind the voluminous hair at table three, Foot Man has suddenly leaned in close to Holly and is whispering in her ear. Holly's chin is tilted up as she listens, a small smile on her pink lips. I clear my throat. "I'm observing her date so I can offer her pointers later."

At this, Maddie chokes on her drink, hacking and coughing. Alarmed, I reach out to pat her back. But luckily (unluckily for me), she recovers quickly. "I'm sorry. Did you say that *you* are giving her dating pointers?"

"That's right."

"And she thought *you*," she pauses long enough to gesture vaguely towards me before continuing, "were qualified to do such a thing. You, one of the most commitment-phobic people I've ever met."

"I'm not commitment-phobic."

Maddie ignores me, wiggling her straw around her glass so the liquid is stirred up into a whirlpool. "I've never known you to go out of your way to help someone before. Let alone help them with their *dating problems*."

"Why does everyone keep saying I never help people?" I grouch, my mind flying back to the night I met Holly and Dante's shock at my stepping in.

"Because you mostly avoid people."

All I can do is shrug. "Not at work. Listening to peoples' woes is basically part of a bartender's job description."

"Doubt that you're supposed to be jealous when they're on dates with other people, though." She widens her eyes at me. "I'm not sure it's a good look on you, Jax."

"Just for *that*, I'm cutting you off." I whip the half-drunk lemonade away from her and dump it down the sink, smirking in satisfaction at her outraged expression.

"You total jerk—"

"Hi!"

Holly is suddenly standing at Maddie's shoulder, shooting me a little wave. She looks from me, to my sister, and back again, and makes an apologetic face. "Sorry if I'm interrupting."

"Hello." Maddie's smile is impossibly bright as she turns to greet Holly. "You are most definitely not interrupting. Holly, right?"

Holly beams back at her. "Correct. I'm a friend of Jax's. He didn't tell me he was expecting company while he was working tonight, but he never tells me anything about his love life." Her eyes shift to me as she says this and she waggles her brows.

"That's because there's nothing to tell," I reply. "Holly, this is my *sister*, Maddie."

"Oh!" she squeaks. "Sorry about that. Nice to meet you, Maddie. Are you the one married to the famous hockey player, then?"

"The best hockey player in the whole NHL," Maddie says proudly, nodding up at the TV behind the bar. "He's playing right now, in fact."

"I hope he's winning." Holly sparkles. "I hear congratulations are in order, too."

"Thank you," my sister says, cradling her belly as she shoots me a curious look, clearly wondering how close I am with Holly that I would share this news with her. "Seb and I are pretty excited. All the more because we got this guy to say *yes* to being the godfather."

"He'll make a great one, I'm sure of it." Holly says this with so much confidence, I feel it in my core. I can't help but smile at her.

"So," Holly says as she settles onto the barstool next to Maddie's. "Tell me about these hockey players. There's so many books featuring hockey players these days—I keep hearing about how hot they are, but I know nothing about hockey."

Maddie turns on her stool. "First of all, the rumors are true. Trust me." She winks. Horrifyingly. "And also, don't worry about not knowing the sport. When I first started working for the Cyclones, I knew *nothing*—"

"What happened to Foot Man?" I interrupt swiftly, unable to help myself. I'm much more interested in hearing how Holly's date went than listening to Maddie waxing eloquent about Hockey Superstar Ken, even though he is pretty great.

I go on to set a cranberry and soda on the bar in front of Holly, almost as a reflex, and Maddie arches a brow at me questioningly.

"Work emergency," Holly explains, nodding towards the now-vacant booth. She then picks up her drink. "Thank you. I'm so thirsty."

"What kind of work emergency could a foot doctor possibly have on a Saturday night?"

"I don't know," she says, pulling a face. "Frostbite? A severed toe?"

"Could have to tend to a hockey player," Maddie offers. "They have really gross feet, you know."

"So I've heard." My eyes are still on Holly, trying to gauge what she's feeling right now. A *foot emergency* kind of sounds like a brush off. "How did the date go?"

She rolls her eyes. "Right now is not the time to stop being brutally honest with me. Yes, it was probably a fake excuse." She rattles her ice around in her cup. "Which is actually... okay."

I nod slowly, my eyes still sweeping over her face as she examines her now-empty glass. For a second, I almost forget my sister's presence, until she suddenly clambers off her barstool.

"I need to pee! Too many lemonades for me. Be right back."

I'm not sure if Maddie timed her bathroom break on purpose—or if nature really was calling—but either way, I'm grateful to have a moment alone with Holly.

"She seems nice."

I can't help but chuckle as I grab the next order and start working on a dry gin martini. "Maddie's my favorite family member by a long shot. She plays the role of annoying little sister a little too well sometimes, but I love her to death."

"You guys have any more siblings?" Holly blinks. "I've just realized I know nothing about your family."

"Nah, it's only the two of us. We're actually step-siblings— her mom is married to my dad."

"Cool. Are you all close?"

"Not really. My dad's kind of a jackass." I don't know why I'm telling her this. "Mad's mom isn't the warmest person on earth either, but being married to my dad does not help, I'm sure."

"That's too bad." Holly looks at me, biting into her full bottom lip with her teeth. "But at least you and Maddie are tight?"

"Super tight. But enough about me, tell me what happened on your date," I say as I ring up an order on my computer for a cheesecake delivery to be made to the bar.

Holly sighs. "Well, to be honest, I think he made the excuse because we ran out of things to talk about by the time our main courses arrived. He was probably just trying to wrap things up easily and smoothly, for both our sakes." With this, she shrugs. "I'm not too sure where to go from here. Maybe I need to come up with more interesting conversation topics?"

"I doubt that's the problem. What did you talk about before the conversation ran dry?"

"I dunno, a variety of things. My work. His work. Our families. Math."

"Two orders of cheesecake?" Kara suddenly appears by the bar holding two plates with huge slices of peanut butter chocolate cheesecake.

"Thanks, Kara," I say, right as Holly exclaims, "You got me cheesecake? That's so thoughtful!"

Kara's smile fixes in place. "He's a thoughtful guy," she mutters as she sets a plate in front of Holly.

I indicate the vacated stool with a purse still slung over the back of it. "The other one's for Maddie. Thanks again."

"Sure." Kara shoots a slightly sour look at Holly before stalking away.

"That girl really doesn't like me," Holly observes as she digs her fork into her slice. She shoves a huge bite in her mouth. "Mmm, so good."

"She likes you just fine," I tell her. "So you and Foot Guy talked about math?!"

"*Ian* likes math-based riddles and games."

"Sounds riveting."

"Hey, no hating on math nerds."

"I wouldn't dream of it."

"Hating on them or stopping?"

"You'll never know."

"You're insufferable." Holly rolls her eyes at me. "It's nice that he has a hobby. And he's... *nice*. Checks all those boxes from my original hit list."

"But?" I prompt.

She sighs, drawing patterns in her cake with her fork. "You were right. Those things only take you so far. And I think..." She takes a deep breath, then lets it out slowly. "I think I like Ian as a person, but I don't *feel* anything when I'm with him. Or anything close to something."

"Shooting for fireworks, right?" I hold up my hand, and she rolls her eyes again before high-fiving it. But I see the little smile threatening to break free from her lips. "Hey, in all seriousness, I'm proud of you. You're focusing on what you actually want."

"Trying to, at least." She ducks her head, but not before I see on her face that she's warring with herself.

"Your sister seems so happy." Holly peeks up from behind a curtain of dark hair. "Head over heels for her man. I want to feel like that."

"Well, you'll be pleased to know that those two started out getting drunkenly hitched in Vegas as a revenge plot to get back at Maddie's cheating ex."

"What?!" Holly's eyes go huge.

"It's true," Maddie says, popping up out of nowhere. She claps her hands as she hops back onto her stool. "Oh, yay! Cheesecake."

"How on earth did that end up happening?" Holly asks her.

"It's a long story involving a very diabolical scheme. But we just... fell in love somewhere along the way."

Holly laughs incredulously. "Wild."

"How about you?" Maddie grins wickedly. "You have a cheating ex and want revenge? Because I'm sure Jax would marry you."

"I do not, but thanks for the thought," Holly replies with a laugh. "And from what I gather, Jax would never marry anyone, for any reason. He's anti-marriage."

She's smiling, joking around, but I find myself wanting to tell her that that's not quite accurate. In fact, since Seb and Maddie got together, I've seen how marriage can almost be a good thing. Can take a totally screwed-up situation and create something beautiful, instead of the opposite.

"He's an idiot," Maddie declares. "So, Jax said you were on a date tonight?"

"Yup, but I don't think there'll be a third date. He wasn't my guy."

For some reason completely unbeknownst to myself, I cut in. "Holly's looking for something long term. Someone who's ready to settle down, but who will also challenge her. Someone who makes her laugh and goes on adventures with her and makes her feel butterflies."

Maddie gives me a strange, slightly unnerving look. It's a long look that stretches for several uncomfortable seconds before Holly pipes up. "Jax has been helping me out. I was kind of a hopeless case, wasted way too long on a guy it wasn't going anywhere with."

"Oof, I know the feeling. That cheating ex of mine was like that—it wasn't going anywhere, though I didn't see it at the time. He even broke up with me on TV."

Holly looks positively outraged. As I was too, at the time. "He *what*? That's awful! And I thought drunkenly kissing my boss at a work party and then having him pretend it never happened was bad."

I just about drop the glass I'm holding. "Wait, what did you say?"

Holly blinks at me. "What?"

"You two *kissed*?" I ask. "When?"

In my periphery, I see Maddie giving me the side eye. I can almost picture her thinking the word "jealous" all smugly. But I'm not, I'm... confused.

"Well, many times," Holly replies, which does nothing to lessen my confusion. "But the particular time I'm talking about happened last Christmas, you know, before I put my list of resolutions into motion."

Didn't she say her crush on Dylan was completely one sided?

Maddie waves a hand, impatient. "Who cares when? The point is, some men suck and some don't."

I ignore her, looking straight at Holly. "What am I missing here?"

"Well, I didn't think it was relevant to tell you before,

179

because I'm meant to be moving on, but Dylan and I used to date back in college."

I can almost feel the ice traveling through my veins at this revelation. *What the actual hell.*

"I thought you said you read the situation wrong," I say, calmly as I can.

"Yeah," she replies with a shrug. "I must have. I was so excited after we kissed again, thought that we might have a real second chance at being together. But I was wrong. The next morning, he acted like it never happened, and I realized that kiss meant something different to me than to him."

I study her face, so sincere—like this is somehow all *her* fault when to me, it sounds like he very much led her on. For *years.* While in a position of power as her boss.

I'm completely floored. To the point where I have no idea what to say.

Maddie, meanwhile, smiles. It's not a smile I like.

"I have an idea!" she exclaims as she turns to Holly. "We should set you up with Aaron."

"Aaron?" Holly asks.

"Like Seb's teammate?" I choke out at the same time.

"Who else?" Maddie shimmies excitedly. "Holly, you'll love him. He's really hot, but a total sweetheart who would never kiss you then pretend it never happened."

"With a hobby of picking up redheads," I mutter before I can stop myself.

"Nope." She looks at me, her expression all too innocent. "He's turned over a new leaf. Keeps telling Seb that he wants what we have."

Holly seems to be mulling this over. "Hot, you say." She peeks at me, for some reason, before her gaze shoots back to Maddie. "Like, sparks and fireworks hot?"

"Definitely." Maddie nods. "The guy's got hella charisma and charm."

Holly bites her lip tentatively as she stares up at the screen behind the bar, where the game is still playing. "Which one is he?"

The Cyclones have just scored to equalize—5-5. The camera pans over the guys bumping fists and man-hugging, and Maddie exclaims "that one!" as it zooms over Aaron's (admittedly very handsome, but for some reason, currently very irritating) face.

"Wow," Holly says solemnly.

"Wow, indeed," my sister agrees. "Are you up for it?"

Holly seems to consider this. Her eyes flicker to me for a moment, and we hold each other's gaze for a heated moment before I look away and flash her a quick thumbs up.

A thumbs up. Like some cheesy sidekick cheering her on.

Because as strangely uncomfortable as the idea of Holly dating Aaron might make me—so much so that I kinda feel like my skin is itching—I know that, for her sake, this is worth a shot. Encouraging her to go on a date with someone who's fun but also kind, and isn't the poster child for her initial hit list, is exactly what I should be doing right now.

"Aaron's a great guy," I say truthfully. "Good personality, but won't be intimidating or too in-your-face."

As well as the fact that he's rich and famous and has women literally throwing their underwear at him.

"But, he is under thirty," I can't resist adding with a teasing grin.

She matches my grin, then turns to Maddie again. "I'll do it. If he's up for it, of course."

"No way he wouldn't be," Maddie assures her.

"I'm gonna look him up!" Holly digs her phone out of her

purse, and as her fingers fly over the screen, I pull a face at Maddie.

"What're you doing?" I mouth.

She imitates flicking a lighter. "Lighting a fire under your ass," she mouths back.

AKA trying to show that I'm jealous.

I love my sister, love everything about her—including what a schemer she is—and I somewhat appreciate all her devious effort to push me towards Holly. But unlike me, she has no idea how to read a situation, and she's got this all wrong.

I'm not jealous. I'm happy for Holly.

Like I said... Aaron is a great guy.

23

HOLLY

"What in the absolute frick is going on right now?!"

Aubrey's squawk is nicely timed as, down on the ice, a guy throws another punch and he and his opponent tumble down, elbows and fists flying.

"No idea," I mutter as I shove a fistful of popcorn in my mouth. I try not to wince as a guy's head bounces off the ice. "But jeez louise, this sport is violent."

"I kinda like it."

"Thought you were a pacifist." I smirk. Twenty minutes at a single hockey game, sitting on a hard plastic seat and breathing in cold, metallic air tinged with the scent of stale beer and overcooked hot dogs, and Aubrey's throwing all her values out the window, apparently.

Although, in her floor-length cream maxi dress and fluffy beige jacket, she's hilariously out of place among the sea of crimson jerseys in the RGM arena. Like she meant to attend a rodeo to eye up some buff cowboys, but somehow ended up spectating this frozen bloodbath instead.

I, meanwhile, am sporting an Atlanta Cyclones hoodie I

borrowed from Jax and am trying very hard not to focus on the fact that, like his towel, it smells just like him. The sweatshirt is about six sizes too big, so it kind of feels like I'm wrapped up in a Jax-scented blanket.

"I *am* a pacifist." She puckers her lips. "Unless hot, rugged, athletic men are ice-wrestling like this. Then I'm all for a good smack of violence."

This makes me laugh so hard, I almost choke on a popcorn kernel. Which earns me a dirty look from the fan seated next to me. Apparently, ice fights are no laughing matter and require more of a very loud heckling response towards the opposing team's fighters.

"Jax warned me that might happen." I grin.

On the ice, the refs are finally trying to intervene and break up the fight. I can make out the appearance of a Cyclones player involved in the tousle—dark hair and eyes, face radiating anger. It reminds me once again to thank Jax for scoring us these unreal seats that give us a very nice close up of the action. Perks of being an in-law of the star of the team, I guess.

I grab my phone, snap a picture of the scene, and send it to Jax with a text reading "thanks for getting us ringside seats to the fight." He unfortunately had to work tonight and couldn't come with us. The guy's pretty damn busy between his remaining bar shifts and all of the prep work he's doing to get his business open. Makes it all the nicer how much time he's been spending helping me.

"What's Aaron's jersey number again?" Aubrey asks.

"22." I spot him talking to a teammate as they both watch the fight from a few feet away. It's so odd—two guys get in a tussle, and everyone else just kinda politely waits until they're done sorting out their differences.

"I still can't believe you scored a date with him." Aubrey shakes her blond waves.

"It's not really a date. It's more of a... general invitation to introduce myself later."

After tonight's game, a bunch of the players are hitting up a fancy bar in downtown Atlanta. Illusion, it's called.

I know it's fancy, because I looked it up. And when I say I looked it up, I mean that I spent multiple hours this week stalking Google so that I know what the dress code is, what drink I want to order, where to park when I arrive and how to pay for said parking, and where to find their bathrooms.

I'm fully out of my comfort zone here—turning up at a bar to "introduce myself" to an athletic celebrity... but I'm glad for it, in a weird way. I feel jittery and mildly anxious instead of the whole mere-moments-from-a-full-conniption-and-panic-attack that I would have once felt. This feels a little bit adventurous.

Which is progress.

But that doesn't mean I'm also not super, duper happy that Aubrey is coming with me.

It was her idea to take Jax up on his ticket offer and come to the game first. That way, if all else fails, conversation wise, I can ask Aaron a few questions about hockey later.

"A date with an athlete. Talk about living the dream," Aubrey practically swoons. I can almost see the stars coming from her eyes.

I laugh. "Don't you have a fiancé? Guy called Alec?"

"Doesn't mean I can't live vicariously through my old and weathered single friend!" She exclaims oh-so-dramatically and I roll my eyes as she reaches for her phone. "But speaking of Alec, I should probably check in with him. Saturday nights are always busy in the ER."

She grins as she types up a quick text to her fiancé. Meanwhile, I let my eyes linger again on number 22, Aaron Marino. Star right winger with a dazzling, white smile.

"So," Aubrey says after putting her phone away. "We have any intel on this guy?"

"Jax says he's a bit nerdy." I tilt my head, checking my phone absentmindedly. "He likes playing Scrabble and crocheting, of all things."

"Sexy."

"I think so."

"Does *Jax* think so, too?"

I blink at her. "What does Jax have to do with sexy crocheting?"

Aubrey raises a thick, perfectly groomed brow at me. "You have a freaking meet-and-greet with a superstar athlete. A smoking hot one, to boot. And you're here, at his game, and you've done nothing but talk about Jax and check your phone to see if he's texted you."

I frown. "That's... not *entirely* true."

"Fine. You've also eaten some popcorn."

Touché.

"I *am* excited to meet Aaron," I insist. "But Jax is the one who set this up, for goodness sakes."

"And how does that make you feel?" Aubrey says in her best psychiatrist voice.

I pause.

Because sure, my body has certain... reactions whenever Jax is around. But there's no way to avoid that—the guy's got an insanely magnetic presence. And I have fun with him; I laugh more with him than with pretty much anyone else, and he gets my way of communicating perfectly. I feel comfortable with him, yet when he's close, I feel almost... electric.

During my date with Ian the other night, I kept stealing glances at Jax across the bar. I couldn't help myself. And I wondered if, maybe, he was glancing at me too. I could only think about the day in the kayak when I was sitting in his lap

186

and my heart was beating so fast and my skin felt fuzzy and warm wherever it met his.

Sparks. That really was the only way to describe it.

And in fact, when Ian made up his whole foot emergency excuse, I felt excited... because it meant I got to go hang out with Jax again.

But then, his sister Maddie suggested this blind date with Aaron, and Jax was enthusiastic as a freaking Dallas Cowboys cheerleader about the idea. And I felt like a freaking idiot for once again almost forgetting the mission I'm meant to be on.

Aaron is handsome and successful, and from our short text exchanges so far, I can tell Jax and Maddie are right when they say he's a great guy. So, tonight I'm going to go out in search of those sparks with a guy who's not my dating coach.

That's what I want: sparks, romance, and commitment.

And while Jax might be able to give me the first of these, the other two simply aren't on the table with him.

"It makes me feel no way at all," I conclude, facing Aubrey. "Jax and I are just friends."

The arena suddenly explodes in a cacophony of whoops and cheers. A sea of crimson rises up all around us, and I stand alongside everyone else, fully confused. I glance over to Aubrey to see if she has a clue what's going on.

She simply smirks back at me. "Well, would you look at that. Your new boyfriend scored and you totally missed it."

24

HOLLY

It's really dark in here. Dark, and loud.

More of a nightclub or lounge than a bar.

I haven't been to a nightclub since... Well, ever. My one and only dalliance into the glittering Atlanta nightlife was back during my senior year of college, when I went out with some friends from my major. We were celebrating the end of our theses, and we went to a place called Maze. Which was, quite literally, a maze.

Whoever thought this would be a good layout for a bunch of drunk people must've been very drunk themselves. Because within five minutes, I was totally lost and running around in circles like a lab rat. About an hour later, I finally made it to an exit, which led to a very sketchy back alley. My heels got coated in garbage juice as I tried to orientate myself and find my way to the main road.

Finally, a very nice drug dealer pointed me in the right direction. And he didn't even seem too upset that I didn't want to buy any of his drugs.

After that night, when I did go out, I stuck to regular bars and restaurants. And always made sure to look places up online before going.

But I must say that tonight is going much, much better so far.

Illusion consists of a big, open room with a dance floor in the middle, a bar that runs the length of the back wall, and an elevated, roped-off VIP section to the left. The music is upbeat and fun, and the flashing lights are making me feel more excited than disoriented.

"Ahh, I love it here!" Aubrey squeals in my ear. "We should go out more!"

"Let's get a drink," I yell back. Aubrey offered to drive, and I could use a splash of liquid courage.

We make our way towards the bar, threading through throngs of bodies moving on the dance floor with our pinkies linked so we don't lose each other.

Once we reach our destination, I smooth out the black minidress I changed into in the car (which was no small feat of gymnastics, let me tell you) and fall in line behind a crowd of people vying for the bartender's attention. While we wait, I survey the room for someone who looks like Aaron.

"They're up there!" Aubrey points—very subtly—to the VIP area, where there is, indeed, a cluster of hulking hockey players. More than a few very attractive women are swarming them, flipping their long hair and flashing flirty, furtive glances every which way.

Frick. Why didn't I arrange to meet Aaron for coffee or something? One on one, in a quiet place that has clinking silverware and Parisian cafe music for background noise, rather than thumping bass and tons of yelling.

"Maybe this wasn't such a great idea." I frown.

"Nonsense," Aubrey tuts.

I look up in the direction of the hockey crowd again and

find myself making direct eye contact with Aaron himself. I'm gratified to see his lips slide into a smile of recognition, and he beckons like he wants us to come join them. It's actually a rather sexy sort of moment—the type of thing you see in a movie when the hero and the heroine make eye contact across a crowded room.

Of course, it's not like everything around us fades or time slows down or anything. But I feel like this is a promising start to my search for sparks.

I nod back and hold up one finger to indicate that I'll be there soon, adrenaline surging through my veins.

This *is* a good idea, and it's happening.

I'm stepping right out of my comfort zone. *Jesus, take the wheel.*

"What can I get for you?" The bartender pops up suddenly, grinning. She's tiny, with bright purple hair and three nose piercings.

"Um, a tonic water and... a Long Island Iced Tea."

"Sure thing."

Aubrey looks startled. "Long Island Iced Tea? Really?"

"Sorry, did you not want tonic water? I can order you something else—"

"No, you just tend to order vodka cranberries if you're drinking a cocktail. I've never seen you divert from the usual."

I shrug as I fork over a whopping thirty dollars. "Tonight's all about trying new things."

The bartender sets a tall glass of brown liquid in front of me and I take a big sip. Try not to gag.

"What is this?!"

Aubrey laughs. "Like, straight liquor."

Good grief.

Well, here goes nothing. I take another gulp, then nod my

head towards the velvet ropes surrounding the VIP area. "Shall we?"

Aubrey doesn't need to be told twice. She wriggles out of her little beige jacket and swings it over her shoulder jauntily before we stroll over to the VIP area.

I try my best to look confident. Like we belong.

All we've got to do is walk in like we're meant to be there, and it'll be—

"Woah, there." A big, meaty hand shoots out in front of me, blocking my path.

I glance up at the bouncer, all confidence leaving my body in one fell swoop. "Sorry!" I squeak, like a mouse who's been caught stealing cheese.

He looks me up and down and shakes his head, like he's already decided my fate. "You have a VIP pass?"

"Well, no, I—"

"She's here to see Aaron Marino!" Aubrey declares boldly.

The meaty-handed bouncer—who also has a meaty neck—laughs so hard, a vein pops on his forehead. "Her and every other woman in this bar."

"No, she knows him," Aubrey insists.

I nod along—the silent encourager—while sucking on my straw. The more I drink this cocktail, the better it tastes.

"That's what they all say." The bouncer moves to stand in front of us, blocking our path. "I'm going to have to ask you to move along, ladies."

I'm about to wholeheartedly agree with this man and scurry away when it suddenly dawns on me that I *do*, in fact, know Aaron (sort of) and I *am* here to see him (actually).

"I'll just call him and tell him to come down and get us!" I say loudly.

This surprises the bouncer for a moment, but he quickly recovers. Shakes his head again like he thinks I'm trying to pull the wool over his eyes. "You go ahead, then." He folds his arms. "I'll wait."

I unzip my purse, hands shaking slightly. I've texted with Aaron, of course, I have his phone number. But I somehow feel like this bouncer is somehow gonna call my bluff.

I'm pulling out my phone when a deep voice says, "Hey, Lenny, you can let them up. They're with me."

Lenny the Meathead turns to face Aaron, who's now standing on the stairs ahead of us. He's dressed in a blue button-down shirt that strains across his very wide chest, and he's smiling directly at me, those pearly white teeth flashing while his green eyes sparkle.

I have to say, he really *is* a good looking man.

And now, the seemingly unflappable bouncer is very flapped. "Oh, Mr. Marino. I'm sorry, I—"

Aaron holds up his hands. "Please, call me Aaron. And we're all good." Then, he smiles right at me again. "Hi, Holly."

"Hi!" My voice is no less of a squeak than it was a moment ago.

Lenny dutifully moves aside and opens the rope barrier for Aubrey and me.

"Thank you," I tell him.

Aubrey is less polite, throwing him an "I told you so" as we glide past him and follow Aaron into the VIP area.

Upstairs, there's a large, semi-circular banquette couch that curves around a low table loaded with ice buckets and half-empty bottles and glasses. One of the hockey players seated on the couch—devastatingly handsome with his piercing eyes and tousled brown hair, by the way—grins at us in what can only be described as a "panty melting" sort of way.

And no, my panties are not melted. But I can totally see that this is the effect he's going for... and that it probably usually works.

Wow. Jax really *has* taught me some things.

"Leave for two seconds and you come back with an angel and a devil on your shoulders," the handsome man says, running his hand through his hair roguishly.

It takes me a second to realize that he's referring to Aubrey and me as the angel and devil, respectively. I get the comparison, at first glance. Aubrey, with her blond waves and long cream dress, is a striking contrast to me, all in black with my dark hair straightened and chic.

It's funny, because of the two of us, Aubrey is definitely the devilish one. Guess looks can be deceiving.

"Going to introduce me, Aaron?"

"Calm your ass down, Dallas." Aaron rolls his eyes. "You act like you've never seen a beautiful woman before. This is Holly, and her friend—"

"Aubrey," she fills in, and Aaron shakes her hand.

"Appropriately angelic name," Dallas volunteers.

"You're not as charming as you think you are," my friend replies, to which he laughs raucously.

"I like you already," he says with a wink. "Come sit down."

I look at Aubrey, who shrugs blithely, then goes to sit beside the flirty flirt on the couch. Probably to put him in his place and take him down a peg or two.

Aaron, meanwhile, scrubs a hand over his face. "You'll have to excuse Dallas. I think he might've been raised in a barn."

"Aubrey's not as angelic as she looks. She'll keep him in line."

"Good." Aaron's eyes twinkle. "But Dallas is dead wrong about the devilish, by the way. You look stunning tonight. Even more beautiful in person."

I know it's a line, but he delivers it well, and I'm not *not* here for it. "Thank you."

"Can I get you a drink, Holly?"

193

I wiggle my half-empty glass at him. "I'm all set."

He gestures towards a couple of tall stools at a bar-height table for two in the corner and he even pulls my stool out for me in a semi-joking way. As I hop up onto it, I find myself smiling.

This is actually pretty fun.

"Are Maddie and her husband here tonight?" I ask as I look around the crowd of hockey players.

"Nah," Aaron says with a shake of his head. "They don't get out much anymore. Seems to happen to all the guys who partner up and settle down."

I don't miss the slightly wistful note in his voice. Sounds like Maddie was right when she said that Aaron was looking for something more than flirtations and partying.

"As fun as clubs can be, nothing beats a wild night at home playing Scrabble in front of the fireplace in your pajamas, am I right?"

"Exactly!" Aaron beams.

I smile back at him before taking another sip of my drink. And yes, I'm aware that I'm fully taking unfair advantage of the fact that I know this man loves Scrabble.

But at that moment, I get a flash back to what Jax said on Stone Mountain... that I try to give people a version of me that I think they'll like.

It's literally what I just did. Because I am, myself, pretty indifferent to Scrabble.

I make another resolution—that for the rest of tonight, I won't do such a thing again. I will be myself. Exactly who I am.

For the next little while, Aaron and I chat easily. I ask him a few questions about hockey, he asks me about my job. I tell him about how I know Jax (leaving out the dating coach part, of course), and he tells me how lovely Jax's cabin is—how the renovations are almost done and he thinks it's going to do great.

It's a nice conversation. Aaron is warm and friendly with a killer smile. But I have to say, the vibe between us seems more friendly than flirtatious. The chemistry simply doesn't seem to be there.

About halfway through his story about building the deck at Jax's hideaway, his eyes drift to a point just behind me. Again.

I try to ignore it, figuring he's probably checking on one of his guys or something. "I can't wait to get out there and see it for myself. I'll be going with Jax soon for this big backpacking trip he has planned. And in return, I'll be taking some pictures for his website."

I run a finger around the rim of my glass, waiting for Aaron's response. Maybe a question about the backpacking trip or something.

Instead, he utters a non-committal, "Oh, cool."

Yup. He definitely sounds distracted, and now, I have to take a look for myself.

I peek over my shoulder and see that someone new has entered the VIP area—a girl with long, copper-colored hair and a silver dress. She's talking with a group of guys, her hand resting on one of their arms.

"Who's that?" I ask, curiosity getting the best of me.

Aaron startles a little, and he gives me an apologetic smile. "Olivia Griswold. Jake Griswold's sister."

"Is he your teammate?"

"My best friend and teammate." Aaron nods. "He's a defenseman."

This means absolutely nothing to me, but I tilt my head, more curious than bothered by the fact that he's currently ogling another woman. "So are you and Olivia... a thing? Or were you?"

His dark eyes snap back to meet mine. "Jeez, no. Never. That girl hates my guts."

195

"Why?"

He shakes his head. "Long story."

At that moment, Olivia glances over at us, and she and Aaron share a look that's loaded with so much tension, you'd need a chainsaw to cut through it.

Jeez. Talk about sparks flying.

But then, Olivia's eyes narrow, glittering and alight as she flips Aaron the bird and turns away. Aaron, meanwhile, rolls his eyes at her back. But the look in his eyes is undeniable...

"You're into her," I say. It's not a guess, it's a statement of fact.

Aaron shakes his head staunchly—a man in denial. "No way. It would never happen."

"I get it," I tell him gently. "It sucks to have feelings that aren't reciprocated."

Of course I get it. I've been in that exact situation, know how that story goes all too well. Intense sparks that will never lead anywhere real... that's exactly how I feel about Jax.

I mean Dylan.

Frick.

How much alcohol was in this stupid cocktail?

Aaron looks almost regretful as he studies me. "I'm sorry, Holly. You seem like a really nice person, and I've just gone and screwed this up, haven't I?"

I laugh. "No, not at all. We can be friends and have another drink together, what do you say? You can even tell me about Olivia, if you like."

"Wow, that makes me sound like a total mess." His lips slide into a smile. "But, deal. What can I get for you?"

I ask for another Long Island Iced Tea—because, clearly, my alcohol-addled mind needs more alcohol right now. As he flags down one of the waitstaff to place our order, I slip my phone out of my bag.

Another bust, he's totally into someone else.

The reply comes through much quicker than I expected—
it's bound to be a busy Saturday night at Full Moon.

I'm sorry, Holly.

It's okay. I'm actually having fun!

And I am. It wasn't quite the fireworks I was hoping for
with Aaron—especially given his whole hot hockey player
prowess—but the man's heart is clearly elsewhere. And I can't
exactly blame him for that.

My second cocktail arrives, and I drain half of it in a couple
of gulps.

25

HOLLY

I finish my second Long Island Iced Tea in record time, and I am soon feeling the effects of these "straight liquor" cocktails.

Across the table from me, Aaron—who's had a few drinks too, I'm guessing—is laughing uproariously along with me at our own patheticness.

He told me about how Olivia hates him, but he can't bring himself to hate her.

I, in turn, told him all about my Dylan saga. I also maybe briefly mentioned that I'm now fighting feelings I shouldn't be having for someone else.

Namely... a certain bartender who must not be named.

Is this my lot in life? To only like men who are totally unavailable and not into me?

Because my date with Aaron is by far the best date I've been on yet... and he's in love with someone else.

At some point, we rejoin the big group on the couch, and I'm feeling warm inside as I loll my head on Aubrey's shoulder. She's texting Alec, who's about to come off his shift in the ER. "Are you ready to go?" she asks.

I shake my head against her shoulder. "No, I'm having fun. You go ahead, though. I'll take a Lyft home later."

"I don't know—"

"I'm fine," I insist. Because it's true. I'm buzzed, but not drunk. And I never stay out late, or hardly ever go out in the first place. I want to seize the day, keep having fun. "Aaron will make sure I get home safe, won't you?"

Aaron crosses his finger over his heart. "Solemnly swear."

"Okayyy," Aubrey says slowly, looking hesitant as she tucks a strand of blonde hair behind her ear.

I sit up and give her a little shove. "Go see your lover boy!"

Dallas nods at her, his green eyes suddenly sincere and all hints of roguish flirting extinguished. "We'll take good care of your girl, I promise."

These hockey players are so sweet, I tell you. Way sweeter than those violent outbursts on the ice earlier would have suggested.

This must be what Mindy felt like back before she settled down and had kids. She used to go out partying every weekend, surrounded by guys and living her best life.

I have to admit, it feels nice to be in this role, even if it is for one night.

Aubrey eventually acquiesces, saying she'll text me every fifteen minutes to check in with me.

Once she leaves, I order a third cocktail. Not sure why. Must be because I'm having such a nice time, not worrying about impressing a date or the way I'm coming across.

I'm just being myself. No more lies about being super into Scrabble or loving all things crochet. I'm being Holly Greene. Well, a tipsily-more-sociable-people-person version of Holly Greene.

In fact, I am feeling so tipsily sociable that, whenever

Dallas suggests we all hit the dance floor down below, I'm one of the first to get to my feet.

A group of us, including Aaron, Dallas, someone bizarrely named Triple J, and a couple of the girls, make our way out of the VIP section and towards the dance floor. Right before we get there, though, I nod at Aaron. "Need to pee, I'll meet you in a minute."

Never thought I'd be telling a star athlete my bladder status, but here I am.

He glances around the bar quickly—he has the advantage of height above this hectic crowd of people. "Want me to come with you?"

I shake my head and yell above the music, "I'm good, I already know where the bathrooms are."

"See you on the dance floor, then!" Aaron gives me an aye-aye-captain sort of salute with a lopsided grin that makes him look even more dashing, and then, he disappears into the throng of people near the dance floor, following his hockey guys.

I turn on my heel, take a few steps...

And run straight into a tall man's lean chest.

I look up at his face and my jaw drops.

"Dylan?!" I squeak.

Oh, for goodness sake. Of all of the things to happen right now...

Dylan blinks down at me. "Holly."

His hands are clasping my upper arms to steady me, and I suddenly notice how cold they are. I hurriedly push away from him and end up stumbling a little—more so from the sticky floor gripping onto my heels than from the alcohol. "Fancy seeing you here!"

It's only then that I realize he's wearing a suit. And he's with a whole group of suit-looking types. All very professional looking. Which I'd imagine is a bit odd for a bar, but how would I know? They're also all very sober looking in comparison to, well... me.

"What are you doing here?" Dylan asks, a strange look flitting across his face. "I didn't know you liked to go out on weekends."

"I'm here with some new friends!" I turn around to point in the direction of where Aaron just disappeared, but the hockey players have been swallowed by the crowd on the dance floor, so I ultimately look like I'm pointing at imaginary friends.

"Right." Dylan appears mildly concerned, his blond brows drawing into a frown. "Don't you have a shift tomorrow?"

"Not until later in the day," I reply, some of my alcohol-soaked bravado wearing off.

"And you're sure this is the most.... responsible choice on a work night." His eyes do a quick sweep down my body. He now seems even more concerned and my shoulders arc instinctively.

Dylan has this way of making me feel a little small at times. I used to brush it off as him trying to hold back from flirting or showing his feelings for me in front of our coworkers—although he did also have a habit back in college of dismissing me. At the time I chalked it up to him being older, more worldly and experienced.

And maybe, once upon a time, I would have believed that his current concern was grounded in whether I would wake up unwell tomorrow and wouldn't want to go to work.

But right now? It kind of feels like an attempt to clip my wings. I don't want to shrink. I want to soar.

So, I step further away from him, choosing not to respond to his comment. "I better go, I need to pee. Don't know why I told you that. Need to go to the restroom to pee. Uh, I mean, I need to go to the restroom."

With that, I leg it to said restrooms, where I lock myself in a stall and collect my thoughts.

How completely bizarre that Dylan's here right now. But also... *so what?*

It's not illegal to be at the same club as your boss, and it isn't illegal to go out the night before a shift at work (unless you're a surgeon or pilot or something). And if Dylan thinks I'm here all on my own and I have no friends... Well, that just makes me look brave, doesn't it? Confident.

With a decisive nod, I finish up in the stall and stride out to the sinks.

"Love your dress," says a girl reapplying her lipstick in front of the mirror.

"Thank you, I love it, too!" I declare. Because I do.

Back out in the darkness of the club, I purposely walk in the other direction and do a full lap of the perimeter so I can avoid Dylan and his suity friends. *Phew,* no sign of them.

I eventually spot the hockey guys dancing up a storm in the middle of the dance floor, and I smile as I start to walk over.

Until I feel a hand on my arm.

Cold fingers, to be exact.

They stroke over my bare skin as the word "Holly" silkily comes from Dylan's mouth again. "Can we talk?"

His touch feels overly familiar, a tad flirty. I move out of his reach. "Um, I dunno, I kinda need to get back to my friends—"

Dylan laughs. "You're cute."

That damn word again.

"I'm not lying. They're over there." I point towards the dance floor—this time right at Aaron and Dallas and the crew—and then look at Dylan triumphantly. Like it's a win that my friends aren't in my head, but are real flesh and blood people.

Dylan only laughs harder. "Holly. Those are professional hockey players."

Frustration starts to bloom in my stomach. "I know. They're the Cyclones."

"Are you trying to make me jealous, Hol?" He takes a step closer, his breath misting over my face as he talks. One of his hands has found its way to my back and I feel the cool pressure through my dress. "Because you know, it might just be worki—"

At that exact moment, I'm suddenly airborne, my body being pulled sideways as one huge hand locks itself on my hip.

A huge, very warm hand.

"There you are, Holly! I've been looking for you everywhere!"

The familiar, much deeper voice fills me with so much relief, I'm almost surprised. The big, warm hands are now circling my waist and I find myself pressed up against none other than Jax's chest.

"Jax, what are you doing here?!" I exclaim. He's whisked me—half-carried me, really—to the middle of the dance floor and he places me back down on my feet gently. But his hands remain on my hips.

Jax, of course, doesn't answer my question. Instead, he looks down at me, his gray eyes almost hard. "You didn't tell me that creep Dylan was here."

"I didn't know until I ran into him a few moments ago." I crane my head around just in time to catch a flash of Dylan's shocked face before the crowd of dancing people swallows us up.

"I don't trust that guy," he grumbles, following my eyeline. But then, he faces me again and his rigid body relaxes slightly. "But I'm glad I found you."

"I am, too," I reply as I become very, very aware of our proximity. We're basically pressed together in the midst of so many sweaty bodies, and his woodsy smell is once again engulfing me. His gray eyes hold me captive as I ask, "So, really. Why are you here?"

"I came the second I was done with my shift." His hands

tighten protectively on my back as someone to our left busts out an over-eager dance move, jostling us. Next to the rest of the club-goers in their fancy shirts, he stands out in his black t-shirt and black jeans... in a good way. "When you said it was a bust, I thought you could use the company."

"That's sweet." Really sweet. And thoughtful, too.

Speaking of thoughtful...

I lean in closer so I don't have to scream over the noise. "We better go tell Aaron where I am. He promised Aubrey he'd look after me."

Jax puts his lips to my ear. "All good, I already talked to him. He knows you're with me."

You're with me.

Those three little words, coupled with the tickle of his warm breath on my neck, send a shockwave through my body.

I turn my head to search for Aaron, and sure enough, he's looking our way. Offers me a grin and a salute, before turning his attention back to the very sexy strawberry-blond he's currently dancing with.

A distraction from Olivia, perhaps.

"Do you want me to take you home?" Jax asks. And he means this as taking me to my house and dropping me off there before he goes back to his own house. Obviously.

But I shake my head. And keeping with my resolutions, I tell him what I really want, at this moment.

"I want you to dance with me."

A flicker passes through his eyes, but he slowly nods. "Okay, Holly. Let's dance."

And then, he begins to move. His hands begin to move, too, trailing up my spine as he moves his body in time with mine.

He can dance.

Jaxon Grainger, the tattooed, barbed-mouthed bartender can freaking dance.

And I am here for it.

Boldly, I circle my hands around his neck and rest my head against his chest, breathing in his addictive smell as I move my hips in time with his. We're pressed close together, our movements sweaty and slow, his hands moving lazily along my back, my shoulders, my arms, my hips. And though his touch is light, almost careful, it sends a fire licking through me.

I breathe in shakily, totally lost in this moment. Totally powerless to the insane heat gathering low in my stomach as I begin to move my hands along his shoulders. I marvel at the feeling of the corded muscles tensing below my touch.

He shudders slightly, and I suddenly feel a burning need to kiss him.

Because those fireworks and sparks I've been craving for so long? They're currently exploding, crackling all over my body. And I don't want to fight it tonight. Can't fight it.

Drunk more on Jax than on liquor at this point, I tilt my head up. Meet his eyes. His pupils are dilated, black inking into the glittering slate gray surrounding them.

He then reaches a hand up, tucks a strand of hair behind my ear, and his fingertips set my skin alight. My breath catches as our eyes lock and time slows right down. I start to move towards him...

And the music screeches to a stop. The lights come on, flooding the dance floor.

"That's it for tonight, folks!" The DJ calls into his mic. "You don't have to go home, but you can't stay here."

There's a mix of drunken cheers and boos as the crowded dance floor begins to slowly empty, and I close my eyes for a moment, dazed and confused.

I can't believe I almost just did that.

When I open them again, Jax is looking at me with an

almost pained expression. "I'd better take you home, Holly." His voice is pure gravel.

I want to protest.

Want to rewind thirty seconds and live suspended in that moment forever.

But instead, I nod, trying to ignore the tension still pumping through my veins.

He smiles at me, and my eyes linger on his lips for a moment too long.

If I'd kissed him, would he have kissed me back?

I'm not sure I want to know the answer. Or know why I'm asking myself this question in the first place.

26

JAX

What in the hell was I thinking?

As I gently maneuver Holly through the crowds and out of the bar, the only conclusion I can come to is that, clearly, I wasn't. At all.

Because I'm pretty sure that the number one thing you *shouldn't* do when helping someone find their perfect match is to *almost kiss them*, especially when they're technically still on a date with someone else.

Even if said date was making out with another woman on the dance floor at the time.

Everything in me wants to chalk it up to good, old-fashioned lust. Holly's a ten, and in that short black dress, she's a freaking eleven.

But I know better than to lie to myself like that. Before I even got her text earlier tonight, I was already feeling something foreign to me, loud and clear: *jealousy*.

My sister was freaking right. I was jealous. Jealous that Holly was out with Aaron. Jealous at the thought of them talking together, laughing together. *Very* jealous at the thought of him touching her or dancing with her.

I wanted to be that guy tonight.

When she told me that things weren't going to work out with him, I felt almost relieved. Felt like I had to see her. So I got off my shift as early as I could and came straight to Illusion. Searched the place for her.

And then, I saw her speaking with that asshole boss of hers, and my jealousy turned into an almost righteous anger that throbbed through my veins.

The moment he put his hand on her back, I wanted to rip his arm clean off.

That guy has such nerve for ever stringing her along. Keeping her a secret when she deserves to be put on a pedestal.

Because based on what Holly's told me and on what I saw tonight, Dylan is exactly the type of guy I first sensed him to be. The type of guy who sees women as disposable and not worthy of respect. The type of guy she should stay far, far away from.

And the thing is, I don't think Holly knows that that situation was far from being *her* fault.

I interrupted before I could even think about what I was doing, literally swooping Holly away from the man. But I was gratified to see that she was glad I was there. Everything about her body language—about the look in her eyes—told me clearly that she wanted to be in my arms, and not his.

So much so that when she asked me to dance, I couldn't say no. And when she pressed her body against mine, I couldn't help but move with her, lose myself in that moment...

"I can get a cab," Holly says when we finally get outside. It's a total mess out here. Groups of people are lining the sidewalks, talking, laughing, and scrambling to get rides.

No way am I going to leave her to fend for herself.

"Yeah, no." I put a gentle hand on her elbow and steer her

left towards a side street where I've illegally parked Edna. I'm sure I have a ticket by now, but it's worth it. "Aaron and the guys promised Aubrey you'd get home safe, and Aaron passed the baton to me. So, I am going to make sure I see you right to your door."

She crosses her arms. "Okay. But on one condition."

"What's that?"

"McDonald's drive-thru on the way home. My treat."

"You need a crisis vanilla milkshake?" I ask, wondering if she's feeling upset or out of sorts after seeing Dylan.

"No, I'm happy right now." She smiles and our eyes catch, and a surge of energy soars through my body.

Soon enough, it's 3AM and we're sitting on the front doorstep of her bungalow—right on top of Aubrey's "I'm Probably Not Wearing Pants" mat, Holly with my fleece jacket slung over her shoulders. She needed it way more than me. I tend to run hot. A couple of little red boxes sit in our laps as we eat chicken nuggets and give ourselves chocolate milk mustaches. When Holly leaned over me at the drive-thru and ordered a Kids Happy Meal, I wanted to laugh, but as she peeked back at me over her bare shoulder and asked me what I was getting, all I could say was, "Make that two."

It was a good choice. The little Pokemon toys that came with the meals have fallen over on the step next to us, lying on top of each other like they're tangled up in a serious make-out session.

And here we are, laughing and laughing as we talk about everything and nothing, until we lapse into a comfortable silence and look up at the stars.

I don't remember the last time I felt this peaceful and content.

Probably my last solo backpacking trip.

I don't usually feel this relaxed in the city, but maybe it's because this neighborhood is quiet, dark, and still. It feels like we've got the whole city to ourselves. Or maybe it's because Holly's just rested her head on my shoulder, yawning into her hand as she does. It's a gesture that feels familiar. Easy.

Like she's done it a million times and will do it a million more.

"Bedtime?" I say as I smile down at her sleepy form.

"I don't really want this night to end," she confesses, sitting up. "But yes, I should probably go to sleep. Wanna make sure I'm well-rested for our wilderness excursion."

I snort as I rise to my feet and hold out a hand to her. "That's over a week away."

I honestly can't believe it's coming up so soon. My last shift at Full Moon is the morning of the day we leave—a brunch shift —and then Holly and I will be on our way to the cabin. We'll be starting the hiking route I've mapped out for us the following day.

"I'm excited for it," she says, and I can hear the sincerity in her voice. "I can't wait to get away for a few days. Escape the city. Get some time off work and enjoy myself."

My brow crinkles as this reminds me of Dylan again. I hate that she'll be seeing him tomorrow— well, later today.

"Listen, Holly..." I start, though I'm not sure what I want to say. Maybe tell her that she's doing the right thing moving on from that guy.

But she's on her feet now, yawning and stretching and she clearly didn't hear me. One of her hands is still in mine, and for some reason, I don't let go.

"I enjoyed myself tonight," she says. "A lot."

"The hockey game or the bar?"

"This," she replies softly. "With you."

Instead of responding, I wrap my arms around her, drawing

her into my chest so I can hug her. She buries her face in my shirt, and I feel her breath through the fabric, tickling my skin.

"I enjoyed this, too," I say in a voice barely above a gruff whisper. I'm trying to appear calm and composed, though I'm sure she can feel my heart attempting to beat right out of my chest.

She moves her head back to look at me, her eyes dark and half-closed. "Hey, Jax?"

"Yeah?"

Her teeth sink into her bottom lip for a moment before she says, "I wish the music in the club hadn't stopped when it did."

Me too.

The thought is completely undeniable. Though it should probably be denied.

Perhaps against my better instincts, I lean down and place a soft kiss on her forehead. She shivers as my lips graze her skin and then stills, staying tightly wrapped in my arms.

Eventually—too soon—she opens her eyes and steps out of my embrace, disappearing into the house with a final smile my way. I leave her front doorstep with my hands in my pockets and a whole mess of thoughts and feelings that I have no idea what to do with.

27

JAX

Before last week, I can't remember the last time I ate McDonald's.

But I'd be lying if I said I haven't found myself back there again since that night with Holly.

No less than twice, I might add.

And I might have to go a third time today to get one of Holly's crisis milkshakes, because I have my last shift at Full Moon this morning. Right after that, Holly and I are heading to the cabin so we can go on a damned multi-day—and night—hike together.

Which gives me approximately three more hours to get my head together, while simultaneously wondering where *her* head is at.

I wish the music in the club hadn't stopped when it did...

So much for me never taking anyone I'm romantically involved with to the wilderness again. Because like it or not, I have feelings that are most definitely romantic for Holly. That much is crystal clear to me.

What's not clear to me is what she feels—or doesn't.

But we're not romantically involved with each other, a little voice in my head reminds me. Maybe she moved towards me the other night because she was tipsy and having fun. Maybe, at that moment, she was looking for a "temporary distraction" after the non-starter of a date with Aaron and a run-in with Dylan.

It doesn't help that I haven't seen Holly since that night. We've been texting back and forth a lot, coordinating details for our trip and talking about some social media accounts she was kind enough to set up for me. But nothing feels different between us, far as I can tell via text. I'm left wondering if I should have just kissed her on her front doorstep, while she was in my arms, or if I'm reading too much into something that doesn't have any business being read.

This is all in the back of my mind as I power through the Saturday brunch service—which mostly consists of mimosas and Irish coffees on my end.

Before I know it, I'm clocking out of the job I've held for the past four years for the last time.

"Jax!" Orlagh's voice is thick as she locks the restaurant's front door behind the last brunch customer. "I can't believe it's finally time. We're going to miss you around here."

"Nah, what you're really gonna miss is Rick's company on Monday nights," I joke, embarrassed that, under the surface, I'm actually beginning to feel a little emotional.

Because it's all starting to feel very real. All *becoming* very real.

"Good riddance, is what I say!" Dante says cheerfully, whacking me on the back. Below his breath, for my ears only, he adds, "With you gone, maybe Kara will finally go out with me."

"I hope so," I tell him honestly. Then, I grin. "For your sake, obviously. Not hers."

Dante laughs. A couple of the waitresses go on to gather some champagne flutes from behind the bar, and Kara passes them around.

"To Jax," she says softly. "We really will miss you."

"I'll, um, miss you guys, too."

And as I hold my glass up to them, I realize it's true.

As much as I want to leave, Full Moon has been a huge part of my life the last few years. It's what I told Holly on Stone Mountain all those weeks ago—maybe time is what's needed to bring you to where you need to be. And my time here at the bar has put me in the exact spot I'm in today—with the cabin of my dreams, launching my own business, and about to go on my very first hike as a certified guide.

Funny how things go.

We drink our champagne, and then, a round of hugs is thrust upon me. Which I return with as much enthusiasm as I can, though I'm not a hugger. These people have been a great work family, and it really is the end of an era.

Orlagh squeezes me super tight before swatting my arm. "I'll be sure to book this motley crew in for a teambuilding wilderness excursion."

I chuckle warmly. "I would like that very much."

Kara hugs me last. I go to give her a quick, platonic pat on the back, but she wraps her arms around my shoulders and pulls me close. "Now that we don't work together, maybe we could hang out sometime?"

I offer Kara what I hope is a kind smile. "I don't think so. You're great, but—"

"It's *her,* isn't it?" Disappointment passes over the waitress's features. "Holly?"

I open my mouth to say no, it's not anyone but me, myself and I, but nothing comes out.

Because now that I don't work with her, I should have no problem going out with Kara. She doesn't seem eager to settle down and get into anything serious, and if we're no longer coworkers, I won't be breaking my dating rules to take her out. She's nice looking, and has a fun personality. I'm sure we'd have a good time together.

But the problem isn't that I *can't*. The problem is that I *don't want to*.

I haven't wanted to go out with anyone for a while now. The only woman I think about is the one I can't freaking have.

Holly wants long-term. She wants love and commitment. And I, above all else, want her to be happy. Even if the thought of her finding happiness with someone else is starting to give me a stomachache.

So when I try to say no, it's not Holly.... I can't.

I swallow, and the word "yes" leaves my mouth.

Kara nods, like she expected my answer. "Lucky her."

I couldn't disagree more with her statement, but I also know that I can't dwell on that right now. Because despite that unfortunate "yes," Holly and I are *not* together, and that's how things have to be.

This is my time to do or die. My chance to get my business off the ground and running successfully. I can't fail.

Won't fail.

I've put my money, my time, and my energy into this dream, and it cannot come to nothing. And even though I'm now entering this experience with feelings I cannot be feeling for the woman I'm taking with me, I will do everything I can to keep this hiking trip streamlined and productive.

Professional.

We're just going to drive up to the cabin, do a little three day hike while capturing content for social media and the website, and then we're gonna get the hell outta Dodge. And I absolutely will *not* do something dumb like try to kiss her.

That's the plan. And that's what's gonna happen.

28

HOLLY

Some people say that absence makes the heart grow fonder. This week, my lived experience has been more absence makes the heart go haywire.

Because I am freaking the hell out right now. I'm T-minus twenty minutes from taking off for a few days—and nights—in the wilderness with Jax Grainger. The man who I pretty much gave full invitation to kiss me... and in response to my brazenness, he kissed me goodnight on the forehead in the most platonic way imaginable—like he was tucking a little child into bed.

Awesome.

"I've got you in a King Suite for three nights, breakfast included," I tell Mr. and Mrs. Goldberg, an elderly couple who stay at the Pinnacle about three times a year. They live down in Pensacola, spending their golden retirement years on the beach soaking up the Florida sunshine, but their daughter lives here in the city. She has a long-haired cat—who Mr. Goldberg is unfortunately highly allergic to—so the couple stays with us instead of with her when they visit.

"Thank you, Holly," Mr. Goldberg says. "And does the suite have—?"

"A jacuzzi?" I nod. "Sure does, as you requested."

Mr. Goldberg winks—yes, *winks*—at me. "Wonderful. Mrs. G and I love to take a jacuzzi bath when we're here."

He doesn't actually come right out and *say* that they jump in the tub together, but it's heavily implied. And while it's sweet that they still clearly love each other in a way that they want to express physically, it also isn't what I want to be picturing right now in my already fragile mental state.

"Well, you enjoy that," I reply woodenly.

"Oh, we will." He taps his keycard on the reception desk jauntily. "We're going for dinner with Catherine tonight, but we will see you in the morning, I'm sure."

"I'm afraid I won't be here after this afternoon. I'm taking a few days off."

"Lovely, dear," Mrs. Goldberg twinkles. "Going anywhere nice?"

"The Appalachians," I say with a smile.

Even so, my stomach fills with a heady mixture of nerves, anxiety, and butterflies for the millionth time. The day is finally here, and I hope to all hell that I didn't bite off more than I can chew. That I wasn't completely out to lunch when I practically insisted Jax bring me on this adventure.

All those weeks ago—when I proudly and very bold-facedly lied to Sabrina about being into the great outdoors—I never would have guessed that I'd end up here... about to leave for my first multi-day backpacking trip.

With a man who I may or may not have *completely* misguided feelings for.

On the bright side, Jax *has* been incredibly helpful over the last week, texting me often about what to pack. And I've been relieved that, over text at least, things have seemed normal between us.

Probably because nothing actually *happened*, I remind myself. The night at the club, Jax probably thought I was being silly, and was dancing with me to humor me. I'm sure he has no idea how much I wanted to kiss him.

Definitely has no idea that, when I woke up the next morning in the cold, hungover light of day, I wanted to kiss him even more.

Still do.

I hope things feel normal between us in person, too.

I ended up borrowing a backpack from Luke's brother Liam, who's recently come back from his own backpacking adventure with his wife in South America (seriously—who knew so many people were into this backpacking thing?! Though it sounds like *his* type of backpacking wasn't so much outhouses and hiking boots and hand sanitizer as it was long bus rides and hotel rooms in various colorful cities).

Jax assured me that he has the sleeping and cooking gear out there already, but he made sure to tell me what clothing and personal items I'd need. His packing list was super detailed and helpful, which will be a great resource to share with guests when the time comes.

At that moment, Raquel, who's just finished checking a guest in, suddenly pipes up, "Get this, Mrs. G. She's off on a backcountry hiking trip with this, like, insanely hot mountain man."

"Oh, my days!" the elderly woman exclaims, fanning herself with a brochure for the CDC Museum. "That sounds very exciting. Is this mountain man your beau?"

"No, no," I say with a swift shake of my head. "Just a hiking buddy."

Raquel snorts. "A hiking buddy with a body one could write sonnets about."

"You wanna go in my place?" I give what I hope looks like a casual, devil-may-care eye roll.

"Definitely!"

Mrs. G reaches out a wrinkled hand laden with gold rings and pats my forearm none-too-gently. "If I was your age, I would certainly make the most of this hiking buddy of yours. Live while you're still young and all that. What are the youths calling it these days... benefitting friends?"

"I believe the term you're looking for is 'friends with benefits,'" Raquel volunteers helpfully. Not.

"All that time alone in the woods together." Mr. Goldberg tuts. "You're bound to do some kind of hanky panky."

My stomach clenches at the thought of doing any type of hanky *or* panky with Jax. Even the idea of being physically close to him makes my face flood with heat. That brush of his lips to my forehead last week was enough to elicit full-body shivers, so I can hardly imagine what actually kissing him would be like...

Like freefalling, I imagine.

I clear my throat quickly. "No, it's not like that with us."

Although as I say these words, I recognize the longing behind them. It's all too familiar. Longing for something—for someone—I can't have. The last thing I need to do is put myself through that again.

I'd be an idiot to develop feelings for Jax, but honestly, I'd kind of also be an idiot not to. Because it's not just sexual attraction; he's also an awesome guy. The type of person who eats Happy Meals with you in the middle of the night and laughs with you till your ribs hurt. The type who's there to catch you when you fall... but instead of picking you up, he teaches you how to get up yourself. Makes you braver. Stronger.

And so, I clearly need to separate these things out—my physical pull to him, and my entirely *friendly, non-physical* relationship with him—or these next few days are going to be very, very difficult to get through.

Talk about a whole new spin on getting myself out of my comfort zone.

"Oh, look, there he is now!" Raquel points out the front window of the hotel, and our elderly guests spin around in time to catch a glimpse of Jax, sitting in Edna's driver's seat and talking to one of our valets.

And despite my very clear, very concise logic, my stomach erupts with enough butterflies to fill a whole habitat.

"Oh, my!" Mrs. G exclaims. "Oh my, oh my, oh my. That boy is positively *delicious.*"

She's not the only one looking—Jax has caught the eye of more than a few elderly patrons milling around the lobby. The place is quickly becoming *Cougar Town.*

"He's early!" I hiss-whisper to Raquel, running my hands over my pressed work pants and blouse. "I'm not ready!"

I mean this in so many more ways than one.

Raquel takes in my frazzled expression and winks at me. "Girl, you better get ready, because that man is coming for you."

Whew. Did it suddenly get very, very hot in here?

29

JAX

Pulling up to a historic landmark five-star hotel in an old, beat-up van with a mutt dog hanging out the passenger window is certainly one way to make an entrance.

And despite the skeptical once-over a valet in a navy blue uniform gives me as I drive up to the front doors, I roll down my window.

"Are you staying at our establishment, sir?" he sniffs.

"Here to pick up one of your employees. Holly Greene."

The guy's expression becomes marginally more friendly at the mention of Holly's name. "Oh. Okay, you can park in the staff lot around the side."

"Thanks, man." I crank my window back up—no such thing as electric windows in a van from the 1970s—then park in the staff lot next to a douchey powder blue Lexus that has to be Dylan's.

Resisting the urge to encourage Rick to lift a leg on the car, I clip on my dog's leash and we head for the foyer of the hotel.

It's a warm afternoon, and my light gray t-shirt and dark jeans look conspicuous as all hell amongst all the hotel guests dressed in designer finery. As I wait, I find myself shifting from foot to foot in anticipation, almost nervous to see Holly again.

Luckily, I'm only standing there flamingoing awkwardly for a second before Holly pops out of a door to the side of the lobby.

"Hi!" she exclaims a little too brightly, waving. She's still in her work clothes: dark-gray dress pants with a button-down baby-pink shirt and heels.

I like her in pants.

Dresses, too.

Damn, I like her in everything.

"Hi," I reply, pretending that the last time I saw her, I wasn't kissing her on the forehead like some awkward pre-teen kid who didn't have the nerve to bite the bullet and kiss the girl for real. "Are you ready?"

"Born ready." She says this while making a little finger gun at me. She then looks down at her hand like she's disgusted with it and its uncoolness. "Just gotta get changed. Give me five minutes?"

"Sure thing." I take a seat on one of the silk couches, commanding Rick to lie down so he doesn't jump up and leave paw prints all over the pristine furnishings or something. I shift uncomfortably on the fabric seat, but still feel jittery, so I reach for one of those magazines no one ever reads that always sit on coffee tables.

Hmm. *Ducks Unlimited?*

Sounds riveting.

"Jax, right?"

I look up from my thrilling read to see Holly's coworker smiling at me. Rachel, maybe?

"That's right." I follow her eye line to the magazine in my hand and give her a wry look. "Was just brushing up on my knowledge of mallards. Real fascinating stuff."

Her smile widens. "I've read that one about sixteen times, it's been sitting there for years. I'm pretty much an expert on blue-winged teals by now."

"Impressive," I reply, and she laughs.

"Not sure if you remember me, I'm Raquel. We met briefly a couple of weeks ago when you stopped by to pick Holly up from work."

"I remember."

Raquel goes on to perch on the sofa closest to me. "I can't believe you're taking my girl hiking. She's a changed woman since she met you, I swear." She looks behind her, like she's checking for eavesdroppers, then lowers her voice anyway. "You've definitely helped her get over that awful Dylan thing, that's for sure. It's nice to see her happy again."

This makes my heart clench a little. I play it off with a shrug. "Awh, I haven't done much. It's all Holly."

"Either way, you've done a good thing." She pats my arm affectionately. "She really likes you, you know."

My brows shoot up. "Did she tell you that?"

"She didn't have to. It's written all over her face."

I'm not so sure about this statement, or about what exactly Raquel means by it. But I don't have time to question it, because Holly suddenly reappears from the side door. "I'm here, I'm here!"

Rick makes an excited little snort and I stand to greet her... then do a double take.

Because Holly is wearing a freaking sports bra and matching spandex shorts.

She looks like she's about to appear in an 80s music video or something. And while I'm not going to dwell on why I suddenly find throwback workout fashion a huge turn-on, I *am* very much going to dwell on the fact that her tiny little outfit is absolutely going to lead to a full-body sunburn. Not to mention make Holly a very tasty meal for the mosquitoes.

"What in the hell are you wearing?" I demand, forgetting all about my vow to never comment on women's clothing again.

She glances down at her body, then back up at me, her expression confused. "Hiking gear."

"I don't know what you think hiking gear looks like, but I can tell you it's certainly not that."

"It's Lululemon!"

"Lulu what now?"

Holly rolls her eyes, and I nod towards the backpack slung on her back. "I hope you've packed some proper clothing in there."

"If you mean more hiking gear, then yes, I have."

"Unbelievable," I mutter. "Didn't I send you a packing list?"

"Yes, and I followed it to a T." She kicks out her foot and I am relieved to see that she's sporting what look to be sturdy hiking boots, at least.

I can't help but smile to myself. I was nervous about how things would go with Holly after last week's forehead-kiss situation, but as always, we're leaning right back into our groove. A comfortable, familiar groove that I enjoy way more than I ever would've expected.

And so, I lean in even more, heaving a sigh. "I have some spare flannels you can borrow."

"This is fine," she says, lifting one bare shoulder.

"You're going to freeze!"

"It's, like, seventy-five degrees outside."

"Not where we're going, it's not."

Raquel, who's watching us with undisguised interest, her head swiveling in each of our directions as Holly and I volley back and forth, suddenly bursts out laughing. "Oh, I would pay money to be a fly on the wall for this. You kids have fun."

"Thanks," Holly says as she hugs her friend, who stealthily winks at me.

I relieve Holly of her backpack and sling it over my shoulder. It's heavy, which I think is a good sign. Hopefully there are some sensible layers of clothing lurking within.

We're turning to leave when Dylan comes waltzing out of the elevator, sweeping into the foyer like he's the lord of the manor. His face twists in disapproval when he sees me. Twists further at the sight of Rick, which bugs me much more—I definitely just saw a pair of pedigree poodles prance by without receiving any hate.

Dylan strides over to us in a few long strides. "Hello," he says tersely.

I know he's remembering me dancing with Holly at Illusion last week. And I know it bothers him, so I decide to be an asshole and smile at him warmly. Rub some salt in the wound.

"Hey, bro," I say in a friendly, almost jovial tone. He looks like the sort of guy who takes great offense to being called *bro*. "Willan, was it?"

More like Villain.

"Dylan." His eyes flicker with contempt and I keep on smiling at him.

Holly suddenly steps forward between us. "My shift just ended, and I left the reports on your desk that you asked for. We're heading out now."

"Yes. Probably best we don't linger in the lobby while not dressed appropriately." Dylan's voice is stiff, even as his eyes do a slow sweep up Holly's body. I suddenly want to cover her up for entirely different reasons. "Where are you off to?"

"Taking Hol backpacking for a few days. We're driving out to my cabin to spend some quality alone time out there." I let my voice linger suggestively on the words *alone time*, and watch as old Dyl barely disguises a wince. I shoot him a wink. "But don't worry, I'll bring her back in one piece. Promise."

Dylan's cheeks turn an unhealthy puce. He clears his throat. "Right."

Meanwhile, Holly sticks a finger into my side. "Let's *go*, Jax. Bye, Dylan. Bye, Raq."

I give a jaunty wave to Raquel while Holly quite literally pushes me towards the hotel's doors.

"Yes, lovely to see you again, *Raquel*," I say pointedly as I'm manhandled—no, *womanhandled*—out of the place.

As soon as we're outside and around the corner of the hotel, Holly turns to me and places her hands on her hips. Her pink lips are pursed and she looks... bemused. "What was *that* all about?"

"What do you mean?"

She sighs impatiently. "You know what I mean. Wanna tell me why every interaction between you and Dylan is like a shoot-em-up showdown in an old western movie?"

I don't, really. But I know Holly can handle herself, know she should hear this, so I level with her.

"Your boy Dylan is jealous."

"I highly doubt that," she replies.

I pop open the van's back door and place Holly's backpack beside mine, then help Rick up so he can get cozy in his dog bed. He usually rides shotgun, but that's Holly's seat for this trip. "Look, Hol, don't you think it's weird that he's your ex-boyfriend, yet he compliments you every chance he gets? That he refused to promote you into an opportunity you would *shine* in? That he freaking kissed you at a work party and then pretended nothing happened?"

"Of course I do. But I guess I thought, up until the morning after that kiss, that this was all playing a part of our love story. I believed he was my Prince Charming, waiting for the right time for us to be together." She screws up her face. "As I now know was very stupid."

"Not stupid." I push my fingers through my hair. "Thing is, I don't think you read anything wrong with Dylan. I think he kept you waiting on purpose."

"What are you saying?"

"I'm saying that you're good at reading people, Hol. Better than you think you are. You just... were made to doubt yourself."

She considers this for a few moments, seeming more thoughtful than sad. "I wondered that a few times. But I trusted him. We had a history together. He was my first love—and when he broke up with me back when he graduated college, he said it was because it wasn't our time and promised that we'd be together when the time was right."

Wow. He's even more slimy than I thought. Stooping as low as he needed to to get what he wanted.

It's all too uncomfortably familiar. A story I've seen play out before, with no happy ending for anyone involved.

"He did you very wrong," I reply. "I have no idea what his end goal was, but I know he's manipulative and strategic, and he figured out how to get you in his clutches and keep you there."

"Just out of reach." She bites the inside of her cheek as she peers back towards the hotel doors. "So all those times that he *seemed* to be flirting with me..."

"He probably was," I finish for her.

"I bet he kissed me for a reason, too," she says, her eyes flickering with indignance. "Basically kept me on the back-burner like a good little responsible back-up plan to use when and how he saw fit."

I follow her gaze back towards the hotel as I choose my next words carefully, not wanting to add insult to injury for her. "I think the guy has a classic case of wanting what he can't have. He strung you along, and now that he thinks he can't have you —now that he thinks he might be losing you—he wants you more than he did before. Pathetic, when you think about it."

"Super pathetic." I expect Holly to follow this up with something sassy, or even go into denial, but instead, her eyes cloud over in thought. "Hmm." She turns to face me. "But how did you see all of this in him without even knowing him?"

I give her a smile I hope is somewhat bright. "I knew someone like that once."

Holly nods once, seemingly still lost in thought as I open the passenger door for her.

"Jax?" she asks quietly, making no move to get into the van.

"Yeah?"

"Thanks."

When my eyes meet hers, I nod at her. "No problem, Hollywood. What am I here for but brutal honesty?"

She laughs at that, the sound light and bubbling as the creek by my cabin, and my heart squeezes in my chest. "I don't know—maybe your incredible prowess with women, your handsome good looks, your incorrigible charm..."

I snort. "Watch your mouth, Hollywood. You're gonna inflate my head with my own words if you're not careful."

She's still laughing as she climbs into the van (while I try not to look at her butt—yeah, who am I kidding? As I totally check out her butt), and I get into the driver's seat and stick the key in the ignition.

Here we go—just me, Holly, and a whole lot of open road and alone time stretching out before us.

What could possibly go wrong?

30

HOLLY

The three hour drive to Jax's cabin is fairly uneventful.
And I say *fairly* because I spend a large portion of the drive
shifting positions, due to the fact that Rick the dog decided he
had no interest in his dog bed and wanted to spend the whole
drive sitting shotgun on my lap, tongue lolling sloppily out of
his mouth.

So much for my nice new Lululemon gear.

"Sorry, Hol," Jax says apologetically after Rick lets out a
large sneeze. "You sure you're okay with him sitting on you like
that?"

"Absolutely," I reply, wrapping my arms tight around Rick.
"I'm great."

And I really am. Because after my conversation with Jax
earlier, everything in me *knows* I made the right choice by
moving on from Dylan.

I feel relief, I feel understood. And even more than that, I
feel... *validation.*

Validation that maybe all this so-called wasted time
wasn't *entirely* on me and my own idiocy. That it wasn't all

my fault that Dylan kept me strung along on a false promise.

I find I'm actually grateful for that kiss we shared at the Christmas party because it ultimately forced my hand to move on in the first place.

Better late than never.

For the first time in a long time, I'm stepping out of the box I've put myself in—the box that dictated that I had to always be responsible and always follow the plan.

It's totally liberating, because what I care about right now isn't what Dylan—or anyone else—thinks, but what I think.

And here with Jax, about to embark on a new adventure, I can finally focus on my own worth. Where *I* am and how *I* view myself.

It's a lesson I needed to learn, and as difficult as it was—it all brought me to this moment.

A moment in time where I'm exactly where I want to be.

"Is this it?" I exclaim as Edna pulls off the dirt road and into a little clearing. Rick starts whining with excitement.

In front of us is a gorgeous little log cabin surrounded by towering Georgia pines. They create a beautiful silhouette against the rapidly darkening evening sky.

It's *stunning.*

"We're here," Jax confirms, his eyes skating over my face. "Welcome to the basecamp for Grainger Guides."

"Love the name." I smile at him.

"It's a work in progress," he replies easily. "Maybe you can help me workshop it."

Jax turns off the van and hops out, going around the back to unload our backpacks. Rick immediately dashes into the clearing and starts running in circles, and I get out after him and stretch my back, looking down at my now-dirty outfit.

Earlier today, I worried things might be tense between Jax

and I after what happened last week. Thought there might be some awkwardness given that I basically said I wanted to kiss the guy, and he went on to give me a chaste *forehead peck*. But everything feels totally fine.

Well, aside from the fact that I couldn't stop thinking about how his forearms looked as he rested one over the steering wheel on the highway (hot. They looked hot. And bonus, those scratches seem to have healed up marvelously).

"This is so, so much better than you made it out to be," I tell him as I look around in wonder. The log cabin is at the far end of the clearing. It's got a sloping roof with a chimney, and a huge wraparound deck that's just begging you to pull up a chair and read a good book.

"I haven't even given you the tour yet."

"Well, what are you waiting for?"

He smirks at me, but I sense a flash of hesitation in his expression. "Guess it's now or never."

It's funny. As confident and relaxed as Jax generally is, he seems more reserved than usual while giving me the grand tour. I can't help but wonder if it's because it's odd for him to have me out here in this place.

He leads me through a kitchen and living area, a small room he plans to make his bedroom, and another, much bigger space that he tells me will be the bunkroom for guests (it's also where I will be sleeping tonight, apparently).

When we step out onto the large back deck he built with Aaron and his brother-in-law, I have to catch my breath. It's topped with cozy furniture that Jax assembled himself and multiple strings of solar-powered lights that are beginning to glow against the indigo-streaked sky as night officially falls upon us.

"Jax, this is amazing! People are going to go nuts for this."

"Wouldn't say that yet. You haven't seen the outhouse."

"Lead the way," I reply, my voice full of false enthusiasm for all things outdoor-toilet.

We walk off the deck and he leads me around the corner to another surprise: along the back wall of the cabin, Jax has rigged up an outdoor shower that uses water heated by the sun.

"Can't say I've ever showered in the wild before," I say with a laugh. The thought doesn't actually sound all that bad. In fact, it sounds kind of... fun. Freeing. You can just *bare* all to the surrounding trees.

"It can be a lot of fun," he tells me, confirming my thoughts, and I feel my cheeks heat. I wonder how many dates he's taken up here. If they've used this shower, too.

I don't really like the thought.

"Feel free to use it whenever you like," he says with a teasing little wink.

"Maybe I'll try it out tonight." My words come out more sultry than I intend, and I catch a flare of what looks like heat in Jax's slate eyes before he looks away. "Let's go check out the outhouse!" I add, and let me tell you, if there's one way to dampen a spark of heat, it's an outdoor toilet.

We walk to the edge of the clearing and he shows me a little hut-type building that's made of the same wood as the log cabin. It almost looks like a secluded shed. We don't go inside, and I don't care to peek—unlike the outdoor shower, the thought of using the outhouse does not have me jumping with joy.

"I know it's not glamorous," Jax says, his slate eyes somberly intent on my face. Spark-snuffing managed, apparently. "But it's part of the experience."

"People will want an authentic experience," I reassure him. "It will be part of your brand."

He laughs. "That's one way to spin it."

We make our way back towards the cabin. The sky is

getting darker and darker, but the lights on the deck shine bright. The forest around us is quiet, but not an empty sort of quiet. I can hear the gentle sound of birds flying to their nests for the night, the rustle of wind through the leaves. I feel very much at ease.

"So what do you think, Hollywood?" Jax asks as we climb the steps onto the deck. "Is it gonna make it to the hall of fame?"

"If it were up to me, yes. Absolutely."

He smirks, but then, his smile becomes almost gentle. He reaches a hand out towards me, but then lets it drop. "Hey, by the way, I'm sorry if what I said earlier today came out wrong."

I frown at him. "What do you mean?"

"Like the Dylan stuff."

Oh. Right. Almost forgot that all happened today.

"That's okay, Jax."

He shakes his head. "No, I want to be better at the brutal honesty thing. It's just my opinion, my own read of the situation—"

"No," I tell him, cutting him off firmly. He seems surprised —as am I—and he stays silent for me to continue. "What you said made a lot of sense. If anything, I feel... happy."

Jax raises a brow. "You do?"

"Yup," I reply. And I mean it. It's been a good day. "Doesn't hurt my mood that it's so awesome here!"

He half-turns away from me, his forehead creasing into a frown as he gazes out into the darkness off the deck. "You're the first person to come here and look at this place through the lens of a guest. I'll admit I'm... nervous that, if you don't like it, it's a sign of things to come." He gives me a wry look. "No pressure."

A weight lifts off me as I realize his hesitation earlier wasn't due to me being here in his wilderness world, but more that he was worried about what I was going to think.

"It's perfect," I tell him with full sincerity.

"I want to make this work so badly." The intensity on his face makes my heart feel soft and mushy. I love how important this is to him. Love that, for something so important, he values my opinion so highly. "I've put everything into it."

"It *will* work," I say confidently. "We'll get a ton of footage over the next few days and get your website and Instagram looking so beautiful, nobody will be able to resist booking with you."

Because it is perfect here. For being so far off the beaten track, the cabin definitely looks comfortable. It has everything you could need. The ideal base for backcountry adventures.

In fact, being here with Jax and seeing it all firsthand makes the whole thing seem so much more real.

This is going to soon be his life. He'll be living out here, wild and free and totally committed to his dream.

"I like your optimism," he tells me with a smile like sunshine.

And I like it when you smile, I think as our eyes catch.

"I believe in you," I reply, my heart picking up speed.

"You're one of a kind, Holly Greene. You know that?"

We stand there, staring at each other for a few moments before he gives his head a shake. "Enough talk, more action—I better get started chopping wood for the fire."

And then, he whips off his shirt.

It's seriously breathtaking here.

And I'm not just talking about the scenery.

I take a cooling sip of water as I lean against the wooden exterior wall of the cabin and watch Jax chop wood. Watch the corded muscles in his arms tense and contract in the dim evening light. The beads of sweat dance down his broad, bare chest with abandon. The clench of his jaw as he swings that freaking ax with military precision.

And don't get me started on those shoulders. Jax's shoulders put all other shoulders to shame. These are Wagyu steak shoulders, while everyone else's are minced chuck.

I didn't even know that I noticed things like shoulders until now.

Why on earth did I ever think men below thirty were a dealbreaker for me? This man is in his physical prime, and then some. Twenty minutes of watching him chop wood and get the fire going and I still haven't adjusted to the spectacular view.

Dragging my eyes away from Jax, I force myself to instead focus on the navy blue sky, with stars beginning to glitter above the tops of the Georgia pines.

"Wieners okay?" Jax calls to me, jarring me from my thoughts.

"Sorry?!" I sputter.

He laughs. "For supper. My plan was to roast wieners over the fire. That work for you?"

I gulp as he uses his shirt to wipe the sweat from his brow. "Yup. Wieners are... good."

"Great. I'm almost done here, then we can get started on cooking."

"Perfect, I was... uh..." *Standing here staring at you for the past goodness knows how long?* "Grabbing my camera! Wanted to snap a nighttime shot of the deck with the lights glowing."

I dash into the cabin and grab my camera, and then take a few frames of the twinkling deck. I also take a surreptitious shot of shirtless Jax in front of the fire, swinging that ax to split the last pieces of wood. This one will be perfect for Instagram, because in my opinion, Jax is the face of this company, and while his experience and gentle but firm persona will draw people to book with him, his face and physique won't hurt either. That much, I'm sure of.

Jax gets the fire going even stronger, and I set up camp chairs in front of the crackling flames. Rick is happily dozing in his own chair, face angled towards the warmth. I wrap myself up in one of Jax's flannel coats. Because yes, he was right—it's freezing out here at night. And yes, it smells as woodsy and delicious as he does and I can't stop inhaling his scent as it surrounds me like an embrace.

As we sit by the blazing fire and cook hot dogs, which we then eat right off the roasting sticks like barbarians (a story I fully plan on recounting at the next Greene Family Game Night—Mindy will be proud), I quickly grow warm and full and sleepy and content.

Beyond the flames, we're shrouded in total darkness, and beyond the fire's crackle, engulfed in so much silence.

I tilt my head backwards so I can take in the stars again, sprinkled like salt above the towering trees. "I feel like we're the only two people in the universe right now."

"The backcountry has a habit of doing that to you."

"I can't believe you come out here on your own," I say with a shake of my head. "I'd be petrified of getting brutally murdered."

I really would. The expansive darkness and the lack of power and cell phone service would have me curled up in a ball and praying for morning to come.

Yet somehow, having Jax with me, I've never felt safer.

"You've seen one too many horror movies," he tells me. "There's nobody here but us."

"Still," I press. "Isn't it nicer to be out here with people?"

The look he gives me is loaded. "Depends on who's with me."

"Hopefully the guests pass your litmus test," I say, swallowing thickly.

"Hopefully." He smiles softly at the fire. "But in the meantime, I'm glad *you're* here, Hollywood."

"I'm glad I'm here, too. I think we've pretty successfully blasted through my quit list. Now, I just need to work on feeling sparks and chemistry with the men I'm dating."

Like I feel every time I'm with you.

The thought sends a thrill through me, and I stand from my chair and walk towards the fire, holding out my hands to warm them so that I look busy. So the telltale red blush on my face can be passed off as a glow from the fire. Or something.

In my peripheral, I see Jax stand, too. He moves to my side and stands still, a looming presence over me until I finally turn to look at him.

The intensity in his eyes would almost be frightening if it wasn't so darn... sexy.

He smiles, and it's like a defibrillator shock to the chest, jolting me to life.

I face him full on, staring up at him so my eyes can travel his face. "What're you thinking?"

His lips crack into a small smirk, and his eyes seem to linger on *my* lips. "I'm trying to be better with the whole brutal honesty thing, remember?"

"And I told you, I like when you're honest with me."

"Okay, Hollywood. You know what I think?"

"No, but I'm pretty sure you're about to tell me." I attempt a laugh, but my voice cracks.

He moves closer. So close that I can smell the salt on his skin, feel the heat radiating off of him. "I think that, up until now, you've only ever dated boys. And that right now, you're wondering what it would feel like to actually be kissed by a man."

His statement catches me totally off guard. "Excuse me?"

"You wanted Dylan for years, Holly. And he's still a boy. Peter Pan. He might be over thirty and he has a good job and all that crap... but he never grew up. I think now you're seeing that for yourself, and realizing you want a man, not a boy."

"Okay, fine. Maybe Dylan's a bit of a man-child, I'll give you that. But before him, I..." I trail off but have nothing to offer, because like I said, my dating experience is limited and boring. But I feel derailed by Jax's words and I'm currently scrambling. I attempt a flippant smile. "You think you're more of a man than everyone who came before you?"

"Yes." His voice is grave with no trace of its usual humor. "I do. And more than that, I don't think anyone's ever kissed you properly before."

The gall of this makes me simmer with indignancy. "Dylan was a very good kisser, thank you very much."

Although I'm not sure that he was. The last time we kissed, it felt sloppy. Rushed. Like I was a dirty little secret, and not a moment to be cherished.

Jax's slate stare stays steady. "*Dylan* is a moron who didn't take the time to learn you, to know you, to work you out. To figure out what makes you tick. What makes you squirm. What makes you sigh with pleasure."

I put my hands on my hips. "And what makes you think you're the expert on what makes me *sigh with pl—*"

In return, he reaches out one large hand and skims his knuckles against the side of my face before cupping it with his palm, his calluses dragging against my sensitive skin.

"I'm just saying, Holly. If *I* ever were to kiss you...." He tilts my chin in his big hand so that my eyes are forced to meet his rapidly darkening gaze. "I'd make damn sure I did it properly."

My heart is pounding in my chest, my rational thoughts thick and hazy with desire. I thought I was desperate to kiss him at the club that night, but that feeling pales in comparison to this one, here and now, in front of the fire with nobody around for miles.

It's me and him. Him and me.

And I know I've got to do it. Seize the day, no regrets.

I keep my eyes locked on his as I whisper, "So, kiss me."

31

JAX

I'm not sure what I'm doing right now, but I'm also not sure I'm capable of stopping.

Everything in me is absolutely aching to kiss her so thoroughly that she forgets Dylan's name.

Hell, until she forgets her own name.

At this point, our chemistry is absolutely undeniable. Electric, even. I know kissing her would be incredible, that I'd kiss the living daylights out of her until the earth shatters beneath her.

But I'm also aware that underneath all those crazy feels are actual feel*ings* that are developing at an almost alarming rate.

In a few short weeks of knowing her, Holly Greene has become the first person I think about when I wake up in the morning, the laughter that keeps me going through my day, and the person I crave when I go to bed at night alone.

In most circumstances, that would mean kissing her is a good idea. But in this case, it's all the more reason *not* to kiss her.

I can't be the guy who gives her everything she wants. Everything she deserves.

The last guy that kissed Holly did it with entirely dishonorable intentions, and she got hurt. And I'll be damned if I'm ever going to do anything that could potentially hurt her.

Dylan may not have been her Prince Charming in the end, but I'm no damn prince either.

"I'm not sure that's a good idea," I say as levelly as I can for a man whose pulse is currently in double time.

"I think it is," Holly says with a little frown. "You might actually have a point about the men—I mean *boys*—I've dated, and so I clearly need the experience kissing men. For all I know, I could be a terrible kisser. Maybe you could give me some tips. Some changes I could make to be better."

"You don't need to change a damn thing," I practically growl. "Any guy would be lucky to even get the chance to kiss you, just the way you already are."

"So, why not kiss me and show me what I should look for in a kiss?"

Lord, give me strength.

My eyes travel over Holly's face—the set of her jaw, her brown eyes that sparkle orange in the firelight, her lips that are parted. She seems determined, seems set on what she wants.

She doesn't look like a woman who's bluffing.

"I can tell you what you're looking for," I reply, resisting every natural instinct in me to *show* her. "You want to find a man who kisses you like he's going to move heaven and earth for you. Bring down the sun, moon and stars. You deserve to be kissed like that, and you shouldn't settle for less."

Holly looks at me, her face a question mark, and I worry I've said the wrong thing for a moment, until she suddenly smiles and says, "Have *you* ever kissed anyone like that?"

Her question catches me off guard.

"No," I admit.

But a minute ago, I was sure thinking about it.

"And you think it would be like that for us?" The heated look in her eyes is doing things to me that it really shouldn't.

I can't help but reach out and put my hands on her arms, and she shudders as I hold her in place like I'm simultaneously trying to pull her towards me and keep her just out of reach.

"Damn right it would," I reply. Because if I know one thing for sure right now, it's exactly that. That if I kissed her, I'd be all in. I'd be unable to kiss her as *just* her so-called "dating coach," an experiment, a practice run. "Like I said, I'd do it properly."

Her breath hitches at my words, goes ragged, and her dark eyes are burning in the light of the fire in a way that's almost my undoing. I'm still hanging on—barely—by the last shred of self-control that I have.

I've spent most of my adult life avoiding situations like this. Avoiding *feelings* like this. I grew up with such a twisted idea of what love looks like—that it hurts, no matter if you stay or leave. There's no winning.

And right now, look where developing feelings has led me. Because all I want to do is kiss her, and I'll be damned if I do, damned if I don't.

"Then it's what I want," she says decisively. "I want you to show me what a proper kiss can be like. How it feels to be with a man, like you say."

Well, I'll be damned.

32

HOLLY

"I... can't."

His eyes are full of longing, his voice gruff, and his hands are searing my skin. The entire world is spinning and all I can see is Jax. The anchor at the center of it all, grounding me. Holding me steady with that gaze of his, carefully trained on my face in a way that suggests blinking would unravel this spell.

If I'm fire, he's gasoline. And the blaze of heat and color that lights up my darkness is simultaneously casting new shadows.

He's everything I thought I didn't want and everything I'm desperate for, all at once. My longing for him has become physical, almost primal, a need coiled deep in my belly so tightly that it's making me crazy. Never have I ever wanted someone so badly.

Never have I ever been more petrified of stepping out of my comfort zone.

But if something doesn't happen right here, right now, I'm gonna lose my damned mind.

"Why not?" I demand.

"Because I... just, no. Okay? I can't." As he says this, his hands tighten on my hips.

"But you want to," I challenge.

His eyes lift heavenward, like he's exasperated, but I don't miss the flicker of something that looks akin to lust.

Ha. He's a victim of his own great teaching skills, because right now, I'm reading him like a book.

I just don't know why he's holding back.

"Fine," I say with a pout. I'm not above playing dirty. "Guess I'm going to have to find someone else to practice with."

The flare of jealousy in his eyes is unmistakable. "Who?"

I tap my jeans pocket, where I have my phone. "The first hot guy on Spark who makes my heart pound." I look at him and shrug casually. "Or maybe Aaron would be up for some no-strings kissing."

"No." He looks outraged at the suggestion, his fingertips digging into my hips now in a way that I hope he never lets go. "Absolutely not."

I smile at him sweetly. "Then who?"

"Holly," he says my name almost like a warning, and I'm beginning to think that maybe I *did* read this all wrong.

Maybe he's not burning to kiss me the same way I'm burning for him. Maybe he's trying to tell me that I'm going too far, pushing past his role as my dating coach.

Disappointment fills me as I step out of his embrace and turn to leave. Where I'm going, I have no idea, but I'm not going to stand here and simmer in humiliation.

I start to walk away, but I've barely taken a step before Jax lets out a long exhale...

Mutters two little words:

"*Screw it.*"

His hand is suddenly on my arm, and his fingers dig

roughly into my bare skin as he spins me around and pulls me towards him in one swift motion.

Then, his mouth is on mine.

His kiss is hot and forceful and so damn intense that my legs shake like they're struggling to hold me up. Jax must sense this because his hand slides around to my lower back, pulling my body flush against his as he kisses me more deeply.

I whimper, and he nips at my bottom lip in response.

My arms circle his neck and drag him down close to me, my brain completely devoid of any thoughts except an insistent *more, more, more!* My hands twist into his thick dark hair, and the groan that comes from his throat is so unbelievably sexy, I feel like I might pass out.

There's nothing gentle about the way this man kisses, and when his tongue skims my bottom lip, I can't help but moan. Every inch of my body feels like it's on fire and burning oh-so-good.

Jax clearly likes what he hears—what he tastes—because he makes a noise deep in his chest and his other hand slides along the side of my body and up to my face, skimming my cheekbone with the callused pads of his fingers.

I love the way he touches me confidently, skillfully, like he's not afraid I'm going to break. Gentle and rough, all at once. He tugs on my hair, tilting my face towards his as he begins to move forward. He's still kissing me as he walks, backing me up until I'm pressed up against a huge, broad, knotted tree trunk, and the length of his huge, broad body is against mine. My hands scrape at his back for purchase as I cling to him for dear life.

Jax breaks the kiss, looking into my eyes for one searing moment before he moves to press a line of hot, open-mouthed kisses down my neck. When his mouth moves over my pulse, I suck in a breath.

246

"Holly," he hisses in my ear almost desperately, his teeth grazing my earlobe before his mouth is back on mine.

Everything stops. The forest around us stills. The world ceases to turn as I lose myself entirely in this man's powerful, all-consuming kiss. Come alive under his purposeful, confident touch.

It's sexy and rough and sweet and tender and explosive fireworks and toe-curlingly romantic, all at once. Forget getting him out of my system, all I want now is to do this forever. Never, ever come up for air.

Because he was right.

I have never in my twenty-nine years been kissed like this. It's all the sparks and fireworks I've ever wanted and so much more—I'm already an addict. He's still freaking kissing me and I'm already desperate for my next fix.

He's ruining me for everyone else. And I'm happily letting him.

33

HOLLY

When I wake up the next morning, the first thing I notice is the stunning dawn light pouring through the windows of the cabin's bunkroom. Shortly thereafter, I notice the heavy weight on my chest...

Rick the dog has apparently deemed my breasts the perfect pillow on which to sleep.

"Morning, Ricky," I murmur as I rub behind his ears. He makes a contented noise and snuggles closer to me. I cuddle him for a few minutes before gently placing him on the ground next to my sleeping bag. "Come on, boy, time to get up. I'm sure your dad is already out and about doing foresty things without us."

Your dad.

AKA The Mountain Man Dog Daddy of all Mountain Man Dog Daddies.

And, also AKA, the world's best kisser.

My experience may be limited, but there is absolutely *no way* any other man on Earth can kiss better than Jax kissed me last night. I don't think it's even scientifically possible.

My whole body feels alive at even a flickering thought of that kiss. And to be honest, while a part of me thought (hoped) that kissing Jax would rid me of my ever-growing attraction for him, I was sorely mistaken. I don't even know how I'm going to survive the next few days alone with him without doing it again.

Thinking about how Jax's eyes blazed, how his rough hands felt against my skin, how my name sounded on his lips as he kissed me is, well... not conducive to quelling those feelings.

More like pouring gasoline on them, really.

But what if now, in the light of day, Jax thinks he made a mistake honoring my request? What if things are different between us, or worse, what if he pretends it never happened? Pretends that we didn't share that insane, head-spinning, thrill-inducing kiss...

I roll about in my tumble of sleeping bag and sit up with a sigh. Dwelling on these what-ifs—and on sexy thoughts about Jax and his extremely sexy mouth—is not going to help me. I need to focus on the day ahead. And there are a couple of time-sensitive issues I have to deal with.

First, today we start our backpacking trip, and I have to admit, I'm nervous. A multi-night hike sounds quite daunting now that it's upon me. I have a feeling that Mindy was right when she said this wouldn't be like walking the Mall of Georgia for exercise.

And then secondly...

I have to pee. Badly.

I held out on using the outhouse last night before bed, which was a mistake because I woke up twice in the night bursting to pee, but couldn't fathom the thought of creeping outside alone in the dark to relieve myself. So I kept holding it. And I'm kind of regretting that decision.

I shuffle out of my sleeping bag and shove my feet into my

flip-flops before throwing on Jax's flannel over my pajamas—which consist of a white tank top and pink short-shorts with hearts printed all over the butt.

No time to worry about getting dressed, or even tending to my bedhead. Nature calls.

Outside, there's no immediate sign of Jax, but the fire is going again and there's a tin kettle sitting on a grate above it, so he must be around here somewhere. It's a crisp but pretty morning, the weak early morning sun doing little to fend off the chill of the mountain air. What strikes me, though, is how still everything feels. Peaceful.

Well, as peaceful as one can feel when their bladder is this full.

I trudge towards the outhouse, the morning dew on the grass dampening my bare legs.

When I arrive at my destination, I rap on the wooden door with my knuckles. "Jax?" I call cautiously.

There's no answer, and so I duck inside. I've been cautioned that, when we go on the big hike later, the woods will be my bathroom and this outhouse will apparently feel like luxury in comparison.

Lovely.

A couple of breath-holding moments later, I'm running out of the outhouse, feeling weirdly accomplished. Now *that* was definitely out of my comfort zone, but I'm glad to have made it through my first pee in the wilderness. It honestly wasn't as bad as I expected.

As I stroll back to the cabin, it occurs to me that I should probably shower. Especially if we won't be anywhere near bathing facilities for at least the next three days.

Would the solar-heated shower bags even be warm at this time of the morning? I should probably check before grabbing my little portable shower caddie.

I turn the corner towards the back of the cabin...

And am greeted by the sight of Jax's butt.

Literally.

Jaxon Grainger is standing ten feet in front of me, under the water of the open air shower. And he's naked.

And wet.

And did I mention naked?

My brain doesn't even know what to do with this information. All of my thoughts basically turn into a mush of wet paper mache as a swell of the *Hallelujah Chorus* sung by a choir of angels blasts through my mind in an impressive crescendo.

I stand there, frozen on the spot, as my eyes go everywhere and nowhere all at once. They take in the water sluicing off of Jax's muscular back in rivulets, the way his forearms and biceps flex as he washes his hair. I notice how strong and muscular his thighs are; the jagged scar bisecting his right shoulder blade and cutting into the edge of the tattooed artwork that decorates the area.

And let's not forget that butt.

It's a good butt. A very good butt.

A coherent thought finally runs through my mind: Jax Grainger is *all* man.

And whew, what a mighty fine man, at that.

Just when I thought I couldn't possibly be more attracted to him...

I stare at him in a bit of a trance for another moment or ten, until Rick trots up next to me and barks, snapping me out of my reverie. I suddenly realize I'm standing here, ogling my dating coach like a wolf closing in on a particularly juicy steak.

"Shh, Rick!" I hiss frantically while slowly, carefully, starting to back away.

Rick wags his little tail and barks louder.

"No, no, no. Please no," I beg. To no avail.

Jax begins to turn his head towards the noise, so I do the only thing I can possibly think to do in this situation...

I run away.

As fast as my flapping, flip-flopped feet will carry me.

I race back to the cabin, change into my clothes for the day (sans shower), and then sprint like Usain Bolt to the edge of the clearing and make my way through the trees towards the stream below.

I think I prefer to take my chances against a rogue bear than find out if Jax saw me staring at his naked self.

Sitting by the creek, I dangle my feet into the cool water (which, quite frankly, does nothing to cool me off). And while I know that I should probably be feeling embarrassed and awkward right now, I can't help but simply feel awestruck as I take in the glorious view of the sun climbing over the treetops and hilly peaks on the horizon.

I wait until I am one thousand percent sure that Jax is done showering and fully clothed. Then, I put on my best casual stance and stroll back to the cabin like I've done nothing more this morning than take a peaceful wander around the forest.

Outside the cabin, there's a pile of gear that Jax is meticulously moving into two backpacks laying on the ground next to him.

When he hears me coming, he looks up. Shoots me a lopsided grin. "Morning, Holly."

"Good morning." I try my best to smile and look normal, and not like a woman who has seen him butt-naked. No pun needed because *literally*.

"You go for a morning walk?"

"Went down to the stream. Just wanted to—"

"Take in the view?" he finishes for me, his grin widening as his eyes lock onto mine.

"Something like that," I reply, sure that my face is burning scarlet right now.

"You never know what you might come across in the wilderness." He shrugs easily, but I catch a glimpse of his teasing smile.

At the same time though, I feel strangely relieved. This banter and teasing feels normal—or at least normal for us. He's not acting awkward or weird about last night. Or about the fact that he most *definitely* knows that I saw him naked.

I fold my arms, playing it cool. "Very true. In fact, I believe I may have come across a Sasquatch this morning."

This makes him laugh. "A Sasquatch, you say?"

"Apparently they're real. Not even at your cabin for twenty-four hours and I've already seen a wilderness legend. I'm impressed."

"Well. If you think that's impressive, wait until you see the view you'll be waking up to tomorrow morning."

He says this so pointedly, so flirtily, that my cool slips and is replaced by a veritable, hot flusterfest. I swallow thickly, convinced that there's a sudden shortage of oxygen in this heavily treed, pollution-free, uninhabited pocket of nature. "What will I see tomorrow morning?"

The glint in his eyes is now positively wicked. "The camp spot I've selected for us tonight. There are mountain views for miles. What did you think I meant?"

Jerk.

"That," I croak. "Obviously."

He laughs, but when his eyes catch mine, there's a new heat in them. A heat that tells me that, even though we're fine and nothing's weird between us—even though we're "back to normal"—he's thinking about last night as much as I am.

"I'm almost done packing our backpacks, so I'm ready to go

when you are—adventure awaits," he says, not taking his eyes off me.

I don't reply, just keep my eyes steadily fixed on him. All I want to do is kiss him again. Scratch that—I *need* to kiss him again.

At that moment, it hits me.

For so long, I've been so focused on not wasting any more time, been focused on the destination rather than the journey. But out here, in the mountains with Jax, we have nothing *but* time. No matter what happens, one thing's for certain, and that's that we get to spend the next three days here alone together.

And I plan on enjoying every moment of our adventure.

"Born ready," I finally reply, which earns me a dimpled smile.

With that, we're off.

Rick leads the way, Jax is close behind him, and I bring up the rear—while focusing all my efforts on trying not to stare at another rear as I go.

34

HOLLY

The hike is grueling.

Jax wasn't messing around when he said that it was going to be a challenge.

This is technically, according to Jax, one of the "easier" routes. But with the length of ground we're covering, the rough terrain, the progressive incline, and the backpack strapped to my shoulders, this feels a whole lot more in the department of "extremely hard."

By the time we stop at a viewpoint for a water and snack break, I'm sweaty, panting, and my muscles are aching. I take a seat on a nice, smooth rock and attempt to catch my breath.

"You're doing great, Holly," Jax says as he helps me unclip my backpack and maneuver it to the ground. He takes off his own pack, then unscrews the lid from a metal water canteen and passes it to me. "Handling it like a pro."

"How many more miles are we covering today?" I ask through a gasp before chugging water. Until I remember the peeing-in-the-woods situation and slow down my gulps.

"Four down, three to go." His eyes rake up and down my body. "How're you holding up? Sore anywhere?"

"I'm fine," I say squeakily. Truth is, my feet are already sore, but I can't bring myself to tell him that I might be getting blisters due to the fact that I did not actually wear the hiking boots he purchased for me around my house to break them in.

And yet... *I'm happy.* Truly happy.

The sun is shining down warm on my face, the birds are singing in the trees, and the air is becoming progressively crisper and cooler—fresher, if that's even possible—as we gain elevation and leave the forest behind. I'm exhausted, feel like I'm about to pass out from over-sweating (if that's a word), and would love a relaxing bubble bath right about now, but I'm also really enjoying myself.

It doesn't hurt that Jax has been by my side the entire way.

"Let me know. Prevention is the best medicine and I've got the first aid kit for a reason." He tells me as he links his fingers behind his head and lifts his arms, stretching out his shoulders.

They must be aching—his backpack weighs probably three times mine. I'm sure he's given me all the light stuff while he carries pots, pans, tents, food, water, and goodness knows what else. And the man has barely broken a sweat.

As he lays back, turning his face towards the sun, I can't help but notice that, from this vantage point, his bicep tattoo is on full display—a detailed, beautiful mountain-scape surrounded by pine trees stretching into an inky night sky sprinkled with stars.

The mountains are as much a part of him as he is a part of them.

It's so clear that he belongs here, and I have not a single doubt in my mind that his business will be a roaring success. He's been nothing but patient, kind and informative about the area as we've hiked this morning.

Professional to the nth degree... if you don't count all the flirty, smirky remarks about the shower incident, and his lingering eyes whenever I use the hem of my shirt to wipe my brow.

As I'm doing right now.

His silver gaze on my body makes me flush even more.

"Hot?" he asks roughly.

"Very," I respond, then shake my head. "I can't believe we have three more miles to cover."

"It'll be over before you know it."

"Maybe leave me here to sleep on my rock," I joke. "Come back for me in three days' time."

"Don't make me carry you." His words sound like the most delicious threat ever, and my cheeks heat at even the thought of him slinging me over his shoulder and marching off.

"I won't," I tell him, puffing out my chest with mock bravado. "I've got this. I'll crawl there if I have to, but either way, I'm doing this."

He leans down and tucks a stray, damp lock of hair behind my ear. "That's my girl."

His words are like the equivalent of shotgunning six cans of Red Bull, because if I wanted to prove that I could do this before, I *certainly* want to now. Anything to get him to look at me again with that smoldering gray stare and refer to me as *his*.

I jump to my feet and Rick prances around my ankles in circles. "Let's get back to it."

Jax's lips slide into a smile. "And in case you need more motivation, I have a little surprise for you when we get to camp."

"Ooh, what is it?"

"Wouldn't be a surprise if I told you now, would it?"

"Spoilsport."

"Three more miles, Hollywood."

I'm not going to lie, with every step of those three miles, the pack on my back feels heavier and more cumbersome, the boots on my feet rub more, and my breaths become shorter and shallower. But I grit my teeth in determination, and Jax gently encourages me every (literal) step of the way.

At one point, we cross a rocky section of ground with a shallow stream of water, and Jax extends his hand to me like he's the Prince Freaking Charming of the Backcountry. I place my hand in his, trusting him completely as he guides me from rock to rock, helping me find firm footing every time I teeter.

Meanwhile, he's like a mountain goat, easily picking out a route without so much as a wobble, his thumb tenderly brushing over the edge of my hand as we go, like he's silently reassuring me that I've got this. That he's got me.

We cover another mile or two before I begin to tire. Though it was cold last night and chilly again this morning, the blaze of the sun at full height in the sky makes for sweaty, uncomfortable hiking, especially as we're on an exposed path without the shade of trees for relief.

One foot in front of the other... one foot in front of the other...

I'm trudging, my gaze on my throbbing feet, my concentration on the sound of the blood rushing in my ears, when Rick lets out an excited bark.

Startled, I look up, half-expecting to see a bear charging towards us. Instead, I'm greeted with the most welcome sight of all time.

What I thought was the rush of blood pounding in my head is actually rushing water. Because on our right is a gorgeous waterfall cascading down into a rock pool.

"Wanna go look?" Jax asks, nodding at a snakey little trail that forks off our route and leads down to the water—which, I imagine, is cool and fresh and would feel like a godsend on my sore feet.

I don't need to be asked twice. "Yes!"

We ditch our backpacks and pick our way down the side trail, Jax holding my hand for balance when I need it.

Rick reaches the bottom first and goes straight to lap up some water. Jax and I reach the bottom shortly after, and I jump up on a rock at the edge of the pool and turn my face upwards, reveling in the delicate mist dotting my cheeks.

It feels like sweet relief, and all I want to do right now is plunge headfirst into the beckoning crystal clear waters. I'm sticky and hot, and my feet and muscles ache. A dip would be the best thing ever.

"Are you thinking what I'm thinking?" I ask as I gaze out at the pool the same way one might look upon an oasis in a desert.

Jax clearly has the same idea, because when I turn to him, he's already stripping off his shorts and shirt. Clad only in his boxer briefs, he throws me a look that practically screams, "I dare you, Holly."

Then, he starts to run. Dives into the pool in one, smooth motion.

The icy water splashes me as he plummets below the surface. When he pops up a couple of seconds later, he's grinning. "Come on, Hollywood! Whatcha waiting for?"

Good freaking question.

I don't have a bathing suit, but the sports bra I'm wearing under my tank top and my spandex shorts will have to do.

Without giving myself time to think, I take off my socks and boots, shed my tank top, and then take a running jump.

Splash!

I plunge into the freezing water and it feels like pure bliss— a shock to the system in the best way.

"Wooo!" I yell when I surface and the sound echoes around

the area. We haven't seen anyone else all day, and I'm surprisingly okay with it. I'm not thinking about being murdered in the wilderness anymore. It feels like we're in our own little world—just the two of us and Rick.

Jax swims over to me and we make our way to the waterfall. I follow his lead ducking beneath the heavy spray and it's like a very aggressive massage. I stay under the flow for a few minutes, head bent forward as the water pounds on my back.

Then, an arm circles around me and pulls me gently backward behind the waterfall.

And there we are... Jax and me, pressed against each other in a narrow gap between falling whitewater and a rockface.

"Hi." Jax is looking down at me almost tenderly as he splays one hand on my lower back to keep me anchored to him. He uses his other hand to push my wet hair out of my face. "Having fun?"

"The most fun," I tell him. "And you?"

"Definitely," he replies decisively. His hair is all tousled and damp and there are droplets of water clinging to his dark eyelashes. "I'm about to be a full-time guide, but believe it or not, this is my first time going on this sort of a hike with anyone."

"Really?" I blink at him. "I know you often go to the backcountry alone, but I figured you had some hiking buddies you would meet with sometimes."

"There are people I hike with from time to time. And I've even taken Maddie camping before, though she hates it." He laughs. "I'll be hiking with many people soon because of my business, but when it comes to these big, multi-day trips for pleasure, I've always preferred to go alone."

"You never wanted company?"

"No," he says as his eyes fix on mine. "I didn't know if I'd be into it."

My breath hitches. "And?"

"And what?"

"Are you into it?"

"Oh, believe me, I'm into it." His eyes darken as his hands tighten on my back.

The crash of the waterfall isn't a match for how loud my heart is beating right now. We're both half underwater, pressed against the smooth rocks under the waterfall. There's only inches separating his lips from mine.

"Hey Jax?" I whisper shakily.

"Yes, Hollywood?"

"I...." I trail off, unsure how to form my thoughts into coherent words.

"Tell me what you want, Holly." His voice is rougher than sandpaper as he moves his hands to my face, his eyes dark and heavy-lidded. His calloused fingers slide below my chin to cup the edge of my throat and his big thumbs skim over my cheekbones. A bolt of heat rockets through my core and my pulse jumps erratically under his touch.

"I think I want another lesson," I manage to choke out.

"And who do you want that lesson from?"

"You," I practically whimper.

"Good girl," he says with a smile, and then, his lips meet mine.

They're cold from the water, but his mouth is searing hot, and I tangle my hands in his hair and get lost in him. Lost in the sensation of his body heat in contrast to the chill that envelopes us. Lost in the sound of his breathing—raw and shallow—above the pounding waterfall. Lost in the way he tastes cool and sweet and so perfect that I never, ever want to stop kissing him.

My body melts against his as he kisses me slowly, languidly, *thoroughly,* until I feel warmed from the inside out, and my legs tremble beneath me. He moves his hands from my face, dragging them down the sides of my body until they slide under my thighs and he lifts me. My legs wrap around his middle and he's holding my weight.

He breaks the kiss for a moment, pulling back just far enough to look into my eyes, an expression of total wonder on his face. He goes on to press one short, soft kiss to my lips. Two. His hands tighten on my thighs and his mouth moves over mine again, picking up the tempo of the kiss and sending it from hot to scalding.

Freefalling, indeed... but with a parachute to catch me.

Safe and dangerous, all at once.

After the blissful kiss under the waterfall, Jax and I drag ourselves out of the water and lay in the sun to dry off for a while. My head rests on his chest and his arm is draped loosely around me, his fingertips drawing lazy circles on my arm and giving me shivers.

Neither of us say much, but it's a comfortable, companionable, silence. We don't have to speak to be in sync, and I love it.

Too soon, the sun is dipping low in the sky, smoothing along the horizon, and we're on our way again.

I walk with a sense of peace and gratitude as we hike the last mile. What an amazing experience, and what a perfect person to share it with. I feel privileged that Jax let me into this part of his world.

Eventually, a small trail forks off to the left and Jax nods towards it. "Our site is just up there. You did it, Holly."

Another few feet and we pop out in the most spectacular clearing.

"Woah." My breath catches as I take in the lush scenery.

We're standing at the edge of a meadow full of wildflowers, the mountain landscape kissed pink by the rapidly setting sun. The gentle breeze is cool on my (probably) sunburned face (despite the six coats of sunscreen Jax insisted I apply). Somewhere in the distance, there's the sound of running water.

It's like a freaking screensaver.

"This is beautiful, Jax."

I tear my eyes away from the view to look at him, and I find that he's watching me. "I'm glad you like it. You want your surprise now or after we set up camp?"

I ponder this for a moment. Then, I remember that I'm trying to take things one step at a time. Enjoy the journey without sprinting for the destination.

"Later," I tell him, and the corners of his eyes crinkle as he smiles.

We make surprisingly short work of setting up camp, pitching our two tents a few feet from each other. I was a little worried about sleeping on the ground, but it turns out that Jax also brought these cool mats that inflate to provide some semblance of comfort.

He unpacks the cooking supplies from his backpack—with a caution that the dehydrated mac n' cheese we're having for dinner is "well, edible"—before he takes out an insulated drink container and passes it to me.

"What is this?" I ask, twisting off the lid.

"Try it."

I take a small sip of the thick, white liquid... and turn to Jax in total wonder. "What the—?"

"I wanted to be prepared in case you hated hiking and were in crisis mode."

This freaking man, I tell you.

"How in the hecking heck did you get a McDonald's milkshake up here?!"

He grins. "Let's just say it required some forward thinking, a Yeti, and a lot of ice."

"That's..." *Probably the sweetest thing anyone has ever done for me.* "Wow. Thank you, Jax. You're pretty amazing, you know that?"

I wrap my arms around him in a fierce hug, and he immediately pulls me closer, holding me tight against him.

"Anytime, Hollywood," he says into my hair as I bury my face against his chest and breathe him in. I can't get enough of this kind, wonderful, completely unexpected man who has turned my life upside down.

"I'm so glad you brought me on this hike."

"You're always welcome to join me. Always."

As he pulls back to look at me, I can tell by the expression on his face that everything in him means it. He's enjoying every moment of this adventure together as much as I am.

35

JAX

"Oh, my gosh, Jax! Look!"

Holly clutches my arm, but instead of looking at where she's telling me to look, I instead peek down at her.

After three days in the backcountry, her cheeks are red and wind-burned, her lips—devoid of their usual pink gloss—are chapped and dry, and (most of) her hair is arranged in a sloppy braid (the rest of it is flyaway wisps framing her head like a halo).

And dammit, she's never been so beautiful as she is right now.

She catches my stare and puts her hands on her hips. "What?"

"Just curious whether you think you're spying another Sasquatch, Hol."

She narrows her eyes at me. "I hope not. One was quite enough, thank you very much."

"Glad to hear it," I say with a wink, and enjoy the way her cheeks redden as a result.

It's hard to believe that the sun is now setting on our last full day of hiking. Tomorrow, we pack up and head back to the cabin.

I find I'm almost homesick. Which isn't unusual—I tend to feel this way every time I'm leaving the backcountry. This is something else.

Before Holly, I'd head out into the wilderness on my own and feel like nothing was missing. I was content alone. Now that I'm out here with her, everything feels more vibrant, bright, and beautiful.

It's been a wonderful few days. The two of us have fallen into the most natural, easy rhythm that's both comfortable and exciting at once. Seeing a route I've walked so many times through Holly's fresh eyes has renewed my excitement for what's to come with guiding, while giving me a whole new appreciation for this beautiful part of the world. We've talked, laughed, cuddled and bantered together for three full days, and each morning, I wake up in my tent beyond excited to see her, to tackle the day together.

It's undeniable that I'm falling for Holly. Hard and fast. No point in fighting it—it's happening with a force I could never resist. Would never *want* to resist.

I don't remember the last time I felt this good. And looking at her now, in the dim glow of the early sunset, with her eyes sparkling and her body language relaxed... she's giving off an overall sparkle of warmth and happiness that confirms she's loving this as much as I am.

Tomorrow, we go back to reality, but I don't want to think about that right now. Don't want to think that whatever this is between us could ever stop. If I know one thing for sure, it's that, for me, this is so much more than just "kissing practice."

Not that she needed any practice in the first place. Because kissing her (which I can confirm, we've been doing *plenty* of over the past few days) is unlike kissing anyone else. In fact, I don't know how I'll ever desire to kiss anyone else.

But what this all is for *her*, I'm not sure. For now, I want to focus on what's left of today. Focus on being with her and feeling like we're in our own world with nobody around for miles.

"Seriously, Jax, look! People!"

Holly's words shake me from my unbelievably gooey thoughts and I whip my head up to look where she's pointing.

Sure enough, there are a couple of hikers in the distance, coming our way. The first humans we've seen since we arrived in the wilderness.

Rick, currently on a rope leash attached to my backpack, makes a sudden and unexpected low growl in his throat.

"Shh," I caution him. It's so unlike him to growl, I'm surprised. From what I can see from here, the hikers don't appear to be a threat. Rick ignores me and growls again. "Rick Astley, stop that!"

He does not stop that.

Holly frowns down at Rick, then turns worried brown eyes on me. "Should we be concerned?"

"I mean, it's highly unlikely that they're anything other than fellow backpackers." I squint into the distance. "They probably just spooked Rick or something. I'm sure it's fine."

Of course, that's when the screaming starts.

"Help!" one of them bellows, waving their arms as the other chants, "SOS! SOS! SOS!"

They don't slow their pace, now heading our way and picking up speed.

"They're in trouble." Holly's hand tightens on my arm and Rick growls again. "What should we do?!"

My first instinct is that they're running from something,

and I take a moment, take a deep breath, and think about our best move.

Being out in the wilderness on my own so often, I've come across my fair share of precarious situations. In those cases, time has always slowed around me as I channeled my inner calm. Now, I'm gratified to find that I'm calm as always as I step slightly in front of Holly and Rick.

While a part of me wants to walk out to meet (and maybe help) the pair running towards us, I don't want to leave Holly alone. Besides, Rick is still acting like Michael Myers and Freddie Kruger are coming at us—I don't think he'd take well to me striding over to a pair of horror-movie serial killers. So I cup my hands by my mouth as I call out to them, "Are you hurt?"

At this point, they're close enough that I can make out their forms. It's two men who—judging by the way they're running—don't *appear* to be injured. Physically, at least.

But they're also wearing... helmets? And they're holding large objects I can't quite see yet, but they glint and shine in the setting sun.

What in the absolute hell?

"Save us!" one of them shouts.

Well. That's ominous.

Though I can't actually see anything chasing the men, I quickly unhook a couple of bear sprays from the back of my pack and pass one bottle to Holly, while grabbing the other for myself.

"Remember how to use this?" I ask as I step fully in front of her, shielding her from... exactly what, I'm not sure. The two helmet-wearing maniacs themselves? A charging bear? An *actual* sasquatch?

"I think so." Holly's voice is a little shaky.

"Remove the safety clip, check for wind direction..." My

voice is quiet but firm as I recite the steps I taught her before we left the cabin.

That's when I notice that the helmets the men are wearing are of the Viking variety. Complete with big-ass horns.

Not only that, but I can make out what the men are carrying now: swords.

Swords!

Rick growls again, and all I can think is that I've brought this beautiful, incredible woman to the mountains to *die at the hands of madmen.*

Then, one of them stops. Halting in his tracks so suddenly that the other one almost barrels right into him, like some kind of second-rate *Bugs Bunny* cartoon.

"Wait up, Phil," the first one says. "I don't think that's Don and Steve."

Don and Steve?

The Viking men have stopped about forty feet in front of us, and they peer at us curiously. Like *we* are the ones who are out of place out here, without Viking merch.

"We come in peace!" the bigger man yells, raising his sword above his head like he's an actual Viking surrendering a battle. *Good grief,* he's wearing a chainmail vest. I feel like we've hiked straight off the Earth and into *The Twilight Zone.* "Please don't set your dog on us," he says as they both walk forward at a normal pace this time.

I'm beyond baffled, and also a little irked, because they just scared the absolute hell out of all of us and haven't given an explanation as to why they're in the middle of nowhere in full-fledged HBO-drama-level costume.

"Mind telling us what the hell's going on?" I say, my voice low and commanding. My finger's still on the trigger of the bear spray. I'm not yet convinced that these men aren't insane and I'll be damned if I let Holly get in even a second of danger.

"I'm Phil," Viking One says, then jerks a thumb at his buddy. They're still standing an awkward distance away from us. "This here's John. We were roleplaying a battle in the forest —Vikings versus King Harold's army—and we got horribly lost. Don't suppose you've stumbled upon a couple of guys dressed like the Enemy English?"

I blink, totally taken aback. "You were WHAT?"

Behind me, I hear a snuffling noise. I whirl around, worried that Holly's crying or frightened. But she's...

Doubled over, snorting with laughter.

"You were about to spray a couple of rogue LARPers," she cackles, hands on her knees. Rick, apparently no longer seeing these goons as a threat, cheerfully licks Holly's hand.

"Why isn't anybody speaking English right now?!"

"They're, like, roleplayers," Holly explains. "It's a whole thing. People dress up as characters and they might reenact historical events, like battles or whatever. Sometimes, it's fantasy based. One of my colleagues is super into it."

Dumbfounded does not even begin to cover what I'm feeling right now.

I turn back to look at Phil and John—AKA Tweedledee and Tweedledum—as they approach us slowly. Only then do I get the pleasure of noticing that Johnny Boy is wearing what appears to be very tight spandex leggings beneath his too-short chainmail.

"You're out here... playing a game?" I narrow my eyes at them.

"Yes." Phil nods nervously, tapping on his sword. "See? Plastic."

"What in the actual fu—"

"Nice to meet you guys!" Holly pops her head out from behind me. "I'm Holly and this is Jax. Sorry you're lost. You seem like you're a long way from home."

"A long way from sanity, more like," I mutter as I collect Holly's bear spray along with mine and tuck them into my backpack's side pocket. The men are in *full* dress-up gear, aside from their New Balance shoes, and they don't appear to have anything with them in the way of survival supplies. Or supplies of any kind.

After a very confusing few minutes of conversation with Phil and John the Vikings, we finally determine that they entered a trailhead miles from here this morning and lost their way. They apparently weren't aware that they wouldn't have cell service, and therefore, Google Maps (not very authentic Viking-like in my opinion, but what do I know). They've been wandering around for hours without food or water, looking for their buddies—the "Enemy English."

"You guys are never going to make it back to the trailhead before nightfall," I tell them, still incredulous about this Viking-themed turn of events. Dusk is already falling, and they have about five hours of walking to do, minimum, to get back.

"We really *are* gonna die," John says glumly, hanging his head so the long, stringy wool hair attached to his Viking helmet falls in his face.

"Don't say that," Holly comforts the man, patting his back awkwardly. "There's got to be something we can do, some way to get you out. Right, Jax?"

She turns to me expectantly and I consider our options. I have an emergency beacon, but a helicopter rescue for a couple of lost Vikings probably isn't in the cards. And while part of me wants to give them both a granola bar and a flashlight and send them on their merry LARPing way, I know that isn't the right thing to do.

"You'll have to camp with us tonight," I say, and I could swear that Holly's gaze flickers towards me. It makes me wonder whether she's enjoyed our time alone as much as I have. "We're going to set up camp in a clearing about a half mile down the trail. We have some extra supplies because some people actually *like* to come to the backcountry prepared."

"Thank you!" Phil exclaims, completely missing my sarcasm. Or he's grateful enough not to care. "Thank you to both you and your wife for your generosity!"

My... *wife*.

I look at Holly, the word snagging in my brain.

My entire life, I've never met anyone I wanted to spend time with past a couple of casual dates. Until now. These past few days, it's been fun not to be a lone wolf out here in the wilderness, but part of a pair. Gifted with a partner in crime for whom I'd fight to the death. I'd defend her with my life from any and all Viking threats. And *that word* doesn't feel so uncomfortable, so foreign, anymore.

As I'm looking at Holly, she looks at me. Her eyes are sparkling, and her expression spurs me on as I put an arm around her, happy to pretend, happy to fall further into this wonderful groove we've made for ourselves over the last couple days.

Holly leans into my embrace. "My husband is a generous man."

Husband.

Nope. That word doesn't feel so bad either.

And that's how the four of us—plus Rick—end up trudging to the spot I've marked on the map for camp tonight. The whole way, Holly chats amiably with the pair of Vikings, even as her hand is loosely intertwined with mine. She seems so at ease in her skin out here. Has taken to the wilderness like a duck to water.

Well, maybe something more graceful than an ordinary duck. A *blue-winged teal* to water.

At our base for the night, the group goes to find firewood in the surrounding forest while I stay back and assess our gear. There's a creek for water nearby and I have enough filtration tablets for tonight, as well as a couple of extra meals. And as for the...

Well, crap.

I didn't think about the sleeping situation.

I'm frowning, looking down at the tent bags, when Holly and her Viking friends return, arms full of wood. Holly must sense what I'm struggling with because she looks at me with a question in her eyes.

"Oh, isn't that lucky!" John chirps all excitedly, chainmail clink-clanking. "You and the missus brought two tents!"

We *do* have two tents, each designed for one person. We also only have two sleeping bags and two ground mats. It gets cold here at night, and Tweedledee and Tweedledum don't look to be wearing much more than their chainmail.

I'm unsure what the protocol is here—we completed a module during the course that focused on emergency how to's when coming across an individual or group that isn't prepared for the conditions. But that particular lesson did not include pretend Vikings in dad sneakers.

Holly lifts her head towards me, and when our eyes meet, I realize that everything is going to be okay. Everything will be fine because I have this woman here with me.

"Isn't that lucky," she repeats with a twinkling grin.

I have to smile back at her, because tonight, I'm clearly the lucky one. I'm going to get to hold her all night, just as I've wanted to do for a long time now.

And if there was ever a silver lining to coming across two lost idiots in the woods, this is it.

"So, Phil." I turn to the burly Viking with the first smile I've sent his way. "I hope you don't mind spooning..."

273

36

JAX

Dinner is a quick affair and it consists of two bags of dehydrated chili split into four portions, to which I add the rest of my pepperoni stick snacks for extra protein. Holly, the Vikings and I end up chatting—they aren't the worst, it turns out—around the fire until nightfall, when the temperature drops and our LARPing friends start to shiver.

As unlucky as I feel that we came across *them*, Phil and John are genuinely lucky that they found *us*. Tonight is much colder than the previous nights we've spent on the trail. They would have been frozen if they'd stayed out in the elements.

Soon enough, we're bidding good night to an exhausted pair of Vikings.

And let me tell you, they create quite the show as they try to cram their huge bodies into one tiny tent, tripping and falling over one another.

Holly and I watch them for a moment, bemused, before walking across the clearing to our own tent. We stand outside it, looking at each other in the darkness. Holly seems almost shy, tucking a strand of hair behind her ear as she assesses the one tent we're going to be sharing.

"Let's get you inside before you freeze." I unzip the tent and turn back to her. "You sure you're okay with this? I can sleep—"

"Where?" she asks with a teasing laugh. "Outside? Even Rick would be cold out here."

I snort, unable to keep myself from teasing her back. "I'd find a way to keep warm."

"I have no doubt you would. You're basically a man-shaped hot water bottle. Which, now that I think of it, sounds like something Aubs would totally buy on Amazon."

I have to laugh at that. "Whatever makes you comfortable, Hol. You want me outside, I'll sleep outside. You want me in there with you, I'll do that. You want me to go join Tweedledum and Tweedledee, I will... yeah, I will not be doing that," I correct myself as my mind paints a horrifying picture of my being squished between two snoring Vikings.

Holly just smiles. "*You* make me comfortable." Her eyes dart sideways to the tent at the other end of the clearing, and yup, right on cue, I'm hearing snores. She lowers her voice anyway. "With those weirdos, I need you in the tent with me for personal safety reasons. Obviously."

"Obviously," I repeat with a smirk, then give her hip a little slap. "Now get your cute butt in the tent before we both freeze to death."

She giggles as she ducks inside with Rick hot on her heels. I give her a minute to change into her pajamas and do one last check around the campsite before she gives me the all-clear to come in.

It's at that point that I attempt to enter the tent.

Attempt being the operative word.

There is, quite literally, not a shred of extra space in here. Meaning that Holly and I are, indeed, going to have to spoon.

Holly's already turned on her side, facing the wall of the tent, while Rick is curled up at her feet. I quickly change into a clean set of base layers—I usually sleep in boxer briefs, but of course, tonight is not the night for that.

Soon as I'm ready, I lay down behind Holly and pull the unzipped sleeping bag over us like a blanket. I insisted that she use the camping pad seeing as we won't both fit on it, and I make myself comfortable on the ground. Luckily, the campsite has thick grass and bush.

"You all right?" I ask her in a whisper.

"More than all right. Surprisingly comfortable, actually. What about you?"

I loop my arms behind my head, staring up at the ceiling of the tent. "Very all right. And very comfortable." I pause for a beat. "I actually can't believe this is our last night."

She takes a moment to answer. "I'm not sure I'm ready for this adventure to end."

"Me neither," I say.

Maybe it doesn't have to.

"It can be the first of many," I add decisively. I have no idea what it means, I just know that it's what I want. Badly.

Because now that I've had her out here with me, the thought of returning here alone, without her, feels... *strange.*

At that moment, she shivers. I instinctively turn, wrap my arm around her, and pull her body flush against mine.

Holly gives a little chuckle, and I feel it move through her body. "Wonder if Phil and John are this close right now."

I snort, nuzzling my nose against her hair. "It's cozy in there, I imagine."

"Not as cozy as it is in here," she murmurs sleepily.

I can't help but let my lips brush the top of her head and

276

she curls her hand around mine and pulls our entwined hands to her chest. I feel her heartbeat beneath my palm, thumping in a steady, soothing rhythm, like she's already half asleep.

"Sweet dreams, Holly," I say softly.

"How could I have anything but sweet dreams when I'm with you?" she whispers back, and I smile into the darkness as we fall asleep together, our bodies curled around each other, my hand splayed over her heart.

37

HOLLY

When I first went on this adventure, I had no idea what to expect. I was a total novice, a fish out of water, and coming here took a real leap of faith—both in myself and in Jax as my guide. The leap paid off. Three days in and I already feel stronger and more resilient in so many ways. I've laughed hysterically as we sparred back and forth, I've cried as I've remedied painful blisters, and I've woken up each morning filled with gratitude that I get to experience this. And I get to do it all with him. I've learned so much about my mountain man guide, and about who I am as a person when my everyday life is stripped away.

And it turns out, I'm a wild woman of the forest. Fully embracing every second of it.

I am cavewoman, hear me roar!

And just when I thought this trip couldn't have any more highlights, I'm waking up this morning in Jax Grainger's strong arms.

The way he held me last night, the way he cuddled me close and let me use all of his body heat when I shivered with cold, all while he pressed his hand to my heart and whispered into my hair, was nothing short of... well, perfect.

Because that kind of intimacy? It can only be real. Not practice, or coaching, or experience.

It's genuine closeness. Connection. And I'm pretty damn sure he feels it, too.

I mean, the way he looked at me yesterday when Phil mistook us for a married couple... *wow*.

Instead of correcting him, Jax's stormy gray eyes were laced with something that almost seemed like longing. Then, he smiled and put his arm around me, like us being married was the most natural thing in the world.

I'm not going to lie, I liked it. More than liked it, in fact.

Funny how, with every man who checked all my boxes, I rarely made it past the first date. But with Jax—the man I didn't want to date because he checked none of them—I want nothing more than to continue this togetherness of ours.

Because I feel more at home out here in the unknown with him than I have for a very long time. Feel more *myself*.

I plan to enjoy all the time I have with him. Enjoy the rest of this incredible experience to its fullest.

At that moment, Jax stirs a little behind me, pulling his arm from around me so he can stretch. I follow his arm's movement, rolling onto my back in the very cramped space so I can look at him.

And, frick. If I thought the man was gorgeous whilst hiking up a mountain, or soaking wet in a rock pool, or wearing all-black while bartending... seeing sleepy Jax with his slate eyes lazily half-shut and his hair tousled is really something else.

"Morning, Hollywood," he murmurs. "Sleep well?"

"Best sleep ever."

"Me too." He wraps his arm around me again to cuddle me

close. I love hearing his voice thick with sleep like this. We lay there, still and calm for a few minutes, in total peace and quiet.

Until my stomach lets out a thunderous gurgle-growl that would put a pride of lions to *shame*.

Rick even lifts his head and stares directly at me in a rather judgy way.

Jax sits up and smiles down at me. "A little hungry, Hollywood?"

My cheeks are fire-engine red. "Don't know what you're talking about," I say, my voice rising on the last word to cover yet another growl. "Maybe it was Phil and John."

"Ah, yes. Of course. The Viking-bros are growling at us, all the way from across the campsite."

"Probably their morning ritual. Viking battle cries at dawn and all that."

I must sound absolutely bananas right now.

Truth is, I actually am quite hungry and could do with a banana.

Jax laughs, running a hand through his bed-tousled hair. "Uh-huh, we'll go with that. On an unrelated note, did I mention that our current location puts us about two and a half miles from the cabin?"

I blink up at him, noisy stomach be damned. "We're that close to being done?"

He nods. "I planned the route so we'd loop back to base early on the last day of hiking. It should make packing out easier and more enjoyable. And make it easier to get a good breakfast."

"You really did think of everything."

His eyes dance across my face. "And here's what I'm thinking right now: why don't we forget the nasty powdered eggs that were on the menu for this morning, leave The

LARPing twins with some water, the last of our trail mix, and a map, and get the hell out of here."

I raise a brow at him and he laughs.

"Relax, Hollywood, I'm joking. We'll make sure Phil and John can get home safe, and then hightail it back to the cabin and drive to the nearest town so I can buy you a proper breakfast." His smile widens. "Assuming you can hang tight that long?"

"Absolutely, I can." I nod. "I've faced my fair share of obstacles over the last couple days. I think I can make it through the hunger pangs for a big waffle payoff."

Jax looks at me with an expression that makes my toes curl and my stomach fill with butterflies. "That's my girl."

And so, after helping John and Phil assume their Viking gear again, Jax makes sure to go over the map slowly and carefully, providing clear, concise instructions until the two insist that they know just where they're going.

As we wave them goodbye, we pack up our campsite and head out on the trail for the last time. Our packs are lighter now that we have less food, and the trail is downhill, so we get a really good pace going.

"You were actually super nice to the Vikings this morning," I call back to Jax. I'm leading the way today while he walks a couple of steps behind me. "Very helpful and professional, Mr. Guide."

It's a cloudy day, and the air is cool and humid as a foggy blanket, the ground slick with morning dew. I'm kind of glad it's not sunny. It would be harder to leave this gorgeous nature behind if the sun was beaming down and making everything golden and perfect.

"I don't know if giving them dehydrated eggs and a map they can't read counts as nice. Or helpful," Jax responds and I laugh. He doesn't give himself enough credit.

Maybe he'll finally give credit where credit's due when his business is up and booming and he has a billion five star reviews.

Which probably isn't too far off.

In contrast, I'm not looking forward to going back to my job whatsoever. I can't conjure up any excitement for it, and I honestly haven't given it a second's thought since I got to the cabin a few days ago.

"So, now that your practice guiding session with me is over, what's next? Are you going to start taking bookings?"

The path is just wide enough for him to fall into step next to me. "First off, I need to get all the videos and pictures you've been taking up on my site so I can attract said bookings. Maybe go back to the cabin after dropping you home seeing as I have to wrap up a few small, last-minute things for guests. Have to rent out my place in the city, too. Set up satellite internet at the cabin. Basically a big, long, boring to-do list. I'll be back and forth from Atlanta a lot while I get that done."

He glances my way and I keep my face carefully neutral. "Satellite internet?"

"Yeah. It's the best way to get online in remote locations, according to Google." He grins. "Never needed it or wanted it before, but I have to get online to manage my bookings."

"Makes sense." I nod, and I'm glad to hear this. If he has internet, it means that we can keep in touch when he's out at the cabin. You know, in case I want to tell him about any more of my bad dates...

Who am I kidding? There isn't anyone else I want to date. Not even a little bit.

I only want to be with Jax. But hearing him talk like this— about a to-do list that he'll start tackling later *today* because we'll soon be back in the city—makes everything seem all too real.

His business will be off the ground soon. I'll be seeing him a whole lot less.

But does that have to mean anything?

Old Holly would've said *yes*, it absolutely means something. She would've felt the need to "be responsible," focus on the fact that our being together isn't logical. It can't go according to any sort of plan I've ever had for my life.

But after these last days in the wilderness, I'm not sure I feel that way anymore.

Because I like this man.

Like him very, very much.

And maybe we don't have all the answers right now. But maybe we don't need to, either.

Maybe we can *see where it goes.*

I take Jax's hand almost shyly. "Let's log on when we get to breakfast and see if anyone's made an inquiry."

"Right this second, I'm way more interested in bacon and eggs than bookings."

I have to agree with him. Though a huge part of me doesn't want to leave this magical adventure with Jax, another, greedier part of me (probably my growling stomach, honestly) is unreasonably excited for a fresh, hot meal.

Visions of bacon dance through my mind as I prance ahead of Jax down the trail, Rick by my side. We're so close to that big breakfast now, I can practically smell it.

"I want waffles! With whipped cream and maple syrup," I sing, feeling wild and free and a touch delirious.

"For me, it's a double stack of chocolate chip pancakes. And bottomless coffee, of course."

"Mmm. I can't wait for coffee. And avocado toast with scrambled eggs, and a huge frosted cinnamon bun, and a strawberry-banana smoothie, and—"

What happens next seems to happen in slow motion.

My foot lands on a damp rock... slips right off of it... and rolls sideways, making a strange, stomach-curling ripping sound.

A terrible bolt of pain shoots through my ankle and I yelp as I fall to the ground.

"Ouch!" I clutch my ankle with both hands, pain radiating through my body.

Jax is by my side in a nanosecond, kneeling down beside me and gently moving my hands away so he can cradle my foot. Meanwhile, I'm trying not to cry. The pain is sharp, acute at my ankle, while the rest of me now feels numb.

"It's okay, Holly, everything's going to be okay." Jax's voice is low and comforting. Steady. "I know it hurts, but we need to determine how bad the injury is. Can you stay with me for that?"

Our eyes meet—mine full of tears, his calm and level. I'm worried that if I open my mouth, I'll cry for real, so I nod my head once.

"Okay. First, I'm going to take your backpack off. Is that all right?"

I nod again and he unclips the strap at my chest before slipping his hands under the shoulders of the bag and easing it off me.

"I'm going to rest your foot on top of your bag. It's important to keep it elevated. Okay?"

"Okay," I whimper, then wince as he lifts my foot and props it up on my backpack.

"Now, this part might hurt. I'm going to unlace your boot because I need to check for swelling. I'll be as gentle as possible, but tell me if the pain is unbearable. Can you do that for me?"

"Yeah." My voice is more tearful than I'd like. "I'm so sorry, I should have looked where I was—"

"Don't you dare be sorry for anything. It was an accident, and I'm here to look after you. So first, I'm going to see what we're working with and then I'll go from there. One thing at a time, all right?"

"All right," I agree. Through the haze of shock and pain, I'm once again so glad that Jax is here, taking control of this situation.

His fingers work the laces of my boot and he manages to slip it off along with my (rather gross by now, I'm sure) hiking sock. With every move he makes, he checks in with me, letting me know what he's doing, then asking how I am and if I'm okay.

Finally, Jax asks if I can move my ankle. I try, but it's agony.

He takes another look at the injury before saying, "Well, the good news is that I'm pretty sure it's not broken."

"W-what's the bad news?" I ask shakily, my foot still cradled in his big hands.

"It looks like a pretty nasty sprain. We're gonna get you out of here, and we'll go to the nearest walk-in clinic to have a professional assess you."

"How do you always know exactly what to do?" I ask thickly.

His lips tip up at the corners. "I don't. But I'll always do everything in my power to take care of you and keep you safe."

He retrieves the first aid kit from his backpack and gives me some painkillers and a canteen of water while he gets to work bandaging my foot. It's only as he does this that I notice his hands shaking slightly. He's not as unruffled as his cool, competent exterior suggests. It makes me warm to this incredible, caring, sarcastic-but-tenderhearted man all the more.

Once my foot is skillfully wrapped, he packs our stuff and goes on to sling his backpack over one of his broad shoulders, and mine over his other.

"Ready?" he asks.

"Yup. I might need some help stand—*Ooh!*"

I'm suddenly airborne as Jax sweeps me into his arms in one effortless motion. One big hand beneath my thighs, the other behind my back. My head falls against his chest, and I hear his heartbeat as he starts walking again.

"I can do this!" I all but flap my arms at him. "Seriously. You can't carry me *and* all our stuff!"

"I can and I will," he says decisively before turning his slate eyes on me. "And no, you can't do anything about it."

I open my mouth to retort, but he has a point. I really, literally, cannot do anything about the fact that this Mountain Man has me bundled up in his arms, pressed up tight against his chest.

And perhaps more importantly, I really don't *want* to do anything about it.

So I oblige, wrapping arms behind his neck and trying to keep my bandaged ankle somewhat elevated even as Jax strides down the trail, practically whistling.

I've never felt more cared for, or safe, in my life.

And it occurs to me, as he walks out of the wilderness with me cradled in his arms, that no time I spend with this man is wasted time. I'll take every minute I can get with him. Even if those minutes bracket periods of time that he gets to be out here, living his dream.

Because today, "seeing where it goes" has been officially added to the Dictionary of Holly.

38

JAX

This freaking doctor is giving Holly the eyes.

And yes, I know that he's *supposed* to be checking over her, but surely, smiling at her like that isn't part of the job description. I have to clench my fists by my sides as it takes everything in me not to let my inner caveman out of his cage. You know, the one who'd grab Dr. Love here by the lab coat and hurl him across the room for putting his hands on her... aka for doing his job.

I'm feeling a little unhinged right now.

I'm not sure it's a feeling I like.

I can't believe Holly got hurt. I was meant to be looking after her, leading her, guiding her. Instead, I was distracted. Remembering how I held her in my arms as I slept, and joking around with her about freaking breakfast, and thinking about how much *I'd* like to make her breakfast in the morning. I wasn't looking at where she was stepping.

"A moderate sprain," Dr. Love proclaims, giving Holly a little pat on the leg that is, if I'm being entirely honest, nothing more than a professional, friendly gesture. However, right now, his gestures are making my unreasonable self feel all kinds of things.

Because I'm the one who said I'd never do anything to hurt her, and he's here making her all better.

"So, where were the two of you hiking?" the doctor asks as he writes something on a prescription pad. He refers to "the two of us," but he's very clearly looking at Holly.

She shrugs as she gingerly shifts on the table. "The Appalachians entry trail. We just came out of a three day back-packing trip in the area."

"Three days, huh?" His eyes barely glance at me. "Only the two of you?"

"Well, us and a couple Vikings." Holly gives me a private smile that makes my heart thump. She goes on to explain, "Jax is starting a guiding outfit to take people out there."

"Oh, so this guy's your guide." Dr. Love nods. "That explains it."

Excuse me? I raise a brow at the doctor and am about to ask him what he means by that, exactly, when he steps closer to Holly, resting his hip against the table next to her. He goes on to tell her about the myriad of "secret" hiking trails he knows in the area before moving on to recommendations for all things crutches and ice and elevation.

As he speaks with Holly, his green eyes locked on her face, I can't help but notice that the guy's got that clean-cut, prep school sort of look that Holly used to like, complete with a perfectly groomed, blond mustache that (even I have to admit) is pretty impressive. He appears to be in his late thirties, and judging by the photo of him holding a toddler on the screen-saver of his computer, Dr. Love here likes kids.

Holly is alert, smiling, and nodding, her face turned towards him. Even though her hair is in a messy braid and her face is bare of makeup, she looks more beautiful than ever—

her inner confidence shining through so that she's almost glowing.

Dr. Love clearly sees it too, and he's like a moth to a heat lamp.

This guy is definitely more along the lines of what she was looking for. Finding someone like *him* was always part of her plan.

And my plan was always to be alone.

But plans can change, can't they? Because every time I consider the Vikings' comments about Holly being my *wife*, I'm aware that, for the first time, the thought of love—of forever—could be exactly what I want.

I don't know what to do with my feelings about this. How to sort through them.

Especially when Dr. Love is staring at my girl like he wants nothing more than to whisk her away for a passionate weekend of trail exploring and mustache grooming.

At that moment, Holly turns her head away from the doctor to look at me, and her expression changes from carefully paying attention to soft and sweet. Happy. Her cheeks color and her eyes crinkle at the corners and I suddenly *know* that she feels what I'm feeling, too.

And while I may have no idea how to be everything she wants and needs, I'm going to try my damndest.

After we're done at the doctor's office—and have picked up a better bandage and some painkillers from the pharmacy next door—I carefully help Holly back into the van. Dr. Love sent us off with a wink (in Holly's direction) and a gentle reminder that she makes sure she has someone with her ("a roommate or best friend, perhaps?") to help her get around and monitor her over the coming week or two while her ankle heals.

Of course, I very adamantly insisted that *I* would be doing the helping and monitoring.

"How're you doing?" I ask Holly now, reaching over her to fasten her seatbelt, though of course she can do it herself. All I want to do right now is take care of her. Keep her safe.

"I'm good," she tells me, pink tinting her cheeks at how close we are right now.

"Ready to head home?"

She shakes her head. "I believe I was promised a breakfast date."

I blink at her. This amazing, nutty woman, I tell you. "You... still want to go for breakfast after all that?"

She gives me a little nod, her expression almost bashful. "I was looking forward to a date with you."

"Then a breakfast date, you shall have," I reply. Because I'll give her anything she wants. Happily.

My favorite little diner is only a five-minute drive from the clinic. I've stopped here numerous times for breakfast after being at the cabin, and the food is good (if calorie-laden and greasy), the coffee strong and piping hot. There's also a nice shady area to park so Rick can hang out happily in Edna, enjoying the morning breeze through the van's cracked open windows as he eats his own breakfast.

But as I carry Holly into the bright, retro interiors of the diner, my feet practically stick to the syrupy floors and I falter. The food might be tasty, but this place is a total dive. Not exactly romantic first date type stuff.

"I, uh..." I look at Holly, perplexed. "The waffles are great here, but it's not exactly fancy. We can go somewhere else—"

"Don't you dare!" she declares with a grin. "Put me down

in the nearest booth and order me all the waffles. This is perfect!"

She's *perfect*.

Everything I never knew I wanted. Everything I never knew I *needed*.

I deposit Holly as gently as possible in a cozy booth in the back corner, and the waitress soon comes over with a pot of steaming coffee.

"Well, lookie here. You two have clearly been through the wars and lived to tell the tale!" chirps the plump older lady with smile lines and a name tag that reads Cheryl. "Better get you caffeinated, and quick!"

"Yes, please!" Holly holds out a mug for the woman to fill. She takes a sip of what must be scalding liquid, and then sighs with happiness while simultaneously wincing in pain. "Ahhhhh—ah! Hot! But also, mmmm... that's better."

She's so damn cute—and so, so much more.

I slide her the cream and sugar, and thank Cheryl as she fills my cup.

As Holly dumps creamer in her coffee, we place an order for enough breakfast to feed a small family. Of horses.

What can I say, my girl's hungry and in need of a good meal.

"I'll get that right over to the kitchen. Y'all sit tight and enjoy that coffee in the meantime." With another jaunty wink, Cheryl stalks off.

Meanwhile, Holly clasps her fingers tightly around her coffee mug, seeming concerned. It takes everything in me not to unclasp them and intertwine them with mine. "Listen, Jax, I'm sorry again."

"What on earth do you have to be sorry for, Hollywood?"

She swallows thickly, staring into her coffee. "For not paying attention, for getting injured... it's such an unfortunate end to a pretty amazing trip." She glances at me quickly. "Right?"

Now, I can't resist reaching for her hands, unclasping them from her mug to hold them in mine. Pressing a kiss to the top of her right hand. "It was beyond amazing. And you were amazing, Hol, the whole time. One of the strongest, bravest people I've ever met. You have nothing to apologize for. Nothing."

She smiles at me tentatively. "Well, you sure seemed to know what you were doing out there. You're going to be a great wilderness guide." Her eyes sparkle slightly as she nods towards my backpack on the vinyl seat next to me. "Speaking of, you should plug your phone in and we can see if any bookings came through while we were gone."

"You should plug *yours* in and let your loved ones know that you're safe and in one piece." I glance at her foot. "Ish."

She screws up her face, like she's thinking about this (and maybe not loving the thought?) Then, she shakes her head. "Nah, I'll do that later when I'm home."

She doesn't want our time together to end either, I think as I almost reluctantly plug in my phone and load the backend of my site.

"I doubt anything's come through yet," I say as the page loads slowly. "But with the stuff you captured out there? No question that the bookings will be pouring in once that footage is live and..."

I trail off.

Stare at my screen.

"Holly, I think there's a booking on here."

"What did I tell you?" she sings. "Grainger Guides is officially open for business. When's it for?"

"Hopefully not too soon," I say lightly. "Still gotta get a privacy screen for the outdoor shower before any guests come my way." I smirk at her. "You know, to reduce Sasquatch sightings."

She throws a little pot of creamer at me.

"It's for..." I look back at my phone and note the dates. Swallow. "Next week."

Seven days away. I'm not ready.

And more than that, Holly's injured. Can I really leave her to finish all my prep work at the cabin?

How the hell am I going to do this?

"Here we go." Cheryl suddenly appears back at our table with her arms full of plates. "Two orders of pancakes with a side of bacon to get you started, and your eggs and waffles will be out shortly."

"Thanks," I say distractedly, my mind still on the problem at hand.

"Out on the Appalachian trails, were you?" Cheryl asks after setting down the plates. Hikers and campers often come through here, and our current, bedraggled, sight-for-sore-eyes state is nothing new to her, I'm sure. But she's eyeing us with curious interest.

"We were," Holly says enthusiastically, and then launches into a spiel about me and my cabin and Grainger Guides and the first booking that's come in. Seriously, it's like she's been reciting the elevator pitch for years.

It strikes me, once again, what a natural she is with all this marketing stuff... aside from one very current, very obvious problem.

"I'm not sure you sitting there with an injured foot is the best advertisement for my business," I say with a wry smile.

"Nonsense, honeypie!" Cheryl pats my shoulder as she refills my mug. "This little lady's face is glowing like she just had the best few days of her life."

She shoots me a wink and I can feel the red creeping up my neck as I look at Holly.

She *does* look happy—which could be the painkillers kicking in—but somehow, I know it's not. Somehow I know it's... *us.* This life-changing trip we went on together that progressed from friendship to kissing to so much more.

And at this moment, I realize with startling clarity that I already know how I'm going to do this. Because, when it comes to Holly, I no longer want to be the temporary distraction.

I can't bear even the hint of a thought of another man with Holly.

Another man holding her, kissing her, touching her...

It makes me want to lose my damned mind.

I want to be the real deal for her.

Everything else comes second.

39

HOLLY

Lying on my couch with my foot propped up was kinda fun. For about a day.

It's been five days now, and let me tell you, it is no longer all that fun. On the evening of my homecoming, I took a scalding shower while sitting on a stool, changed into my comfiest sweats, and then Jax spent the evening with Aubrey and me, binge-watching the first season of *Suits*.

Jax had never seen it before, and so to make sure that it was an entirely authentic viewing experience for him, Aubs and I made sure to repeat all of Harvey Specter's cheesiest one-liners in mock-deep voices while we consumed a steady supply of Godiva truffles and Sugarfina champagne bears. Aubrey was in charge of refreshments, and her idea of "crisis snacks" is significantly more boujee than mine.

Not that I had any complaints.

"Hello, Ms. Broken Ankle," Aubrey says now as she swans into our living room in another of her tank-top-and-polka-dot-panties combos and plops down on the floor next to the couch.

She tears open a pack of seaweed crisps. "How you holding up?"

I shift on my elbows, trying to get comfortable. My body feels restless after all this time spent on the couch. Especially given that I was hiking and walking for three whole days prior to this injury. "I'm surviving. And for the last time, Aubs, it's not broken, just sprained."

"Potato, tomato," Aubrey says with a breezy wave of her hand as she crunches into a crisp, her eyes on the TV. I paused my show a little while ago for a bathroom break, and so Aubrey is watching the TV Sleep Mode screensaver.

"To answer your question, my ankle is feeling quite a bit better," I tell her. "Would hate to know what a 'severe' sprain feels like, though." I wince. "But I've been diligent, been sticking with the regime of rest, ice, compression, and elevation that the doctor prescribed."

"Not to mention those handy painkillers."

I laugh. "True."

"Then again," she continues thoughtfully, "maybe you missed a beat there."

I narrow my eyes at her. "Missed a beat, how?"

"With the doctor who attended to you. Sounds like he was pretty nice looking." She catches my stare and shrugs innocently. "Well, not for me or you *obviously*. You've got your Mountain Man dream babe to literally wait on you hand and foot. But I have loads of single friends who would probably throw themselves down mountains just to go out with a handsome doctor. Could've been a prime opportunity for a matchmaking scheme."

I have to laugh at that, rolling my eyes. Aubs is right—the doctor *was* very handsome. But honestly, I didn't even care. My days of wanting my very own ER doctor moment a la Aubrey and Alec are over, because I seem to only have eyes for one man.

Said Mountain Man who carried me through my doorway five days ago, then deposited me on this very couch—kinda like a groom carrying his bride over the threshold. Only said bride hadn't showered in three days, was wearing a very sexy (not) walking boot, and had twigs in her hair.

It's only a sprain, but Jax has been treating me like I broke all the bones in my body or something.

For three full days, he only left my bungalow to sleep, shower, and grab fresh clothes at his house. And to show said house to potential renters. As my dedicated sexy nurse (his words, not mine), he tuned in to my every need, getting me ice packs from the freezer, bringing me blankets when he insisted I looked cold, and ordering all my favorite takeout foods.

At the end of each evening, he also carried me to bed like I might shatter into a million pieces if I so much as took a step—my protests that I was totally fine to hop-shuffle there myself fell on deaf ears.

Turns out, Jaxon Grainger is extremely stubborn when it comes to taking care of people. Which is yet another totally unexpected, totally incredible green flag quality to add to his impressive repertoire.

"Considering switching careers already, Aubs?" I ask her as I steal a seaweed crisp from her baggie. "Sick of this whole law business?"

"No... Well, *yeah*, I'm sick of it." She rolls her eyes dramatically. "But I could do some matchmaking on the side. A type of glam, young Judge Judy type who's out to reunite the young and soon-to-be loved up."

"Now there's a show I'd watch," I reply.

"Speaking of, what are we thinking for tonight? More *Suits*, or are we all *Suited* out for now?"

297

Before I can say or do anything—like yank the TV remote out of her reach—she's clicking a button, the TV screensaver disappears, and the show I'd been watching is on full display.

She gives me an incredulous look. "*Man vs. Wild?* Really, Holly?"

"I'm bored," I say in an attempt to justify my choice of televised entertainment.

"You'd watch *He's Just Not That Into You* for the millionth time if you were bored," Aubrey says with a dismissive wave of her hand. "You're watching that and fantasizing about your mountain man. Mentally pasting his face on top of Bear Grylls's while he does all kinds of daring mountain-y things, and then drooling like a slobbery baby over it." She waggles her eyebrows at me. "Not that I blame you."

"That description is both detailed and disturbing in equal measures. And for the record, I am *not* doing that."

Also for the record... I totally am.

I haven't heard from Jax since he tucked me in on the couch and kissed me goodbye yesterday. Which makes sense—the cabin doesn't have phone service or internet (yet)—but even so, I find myself checking my phone every two minutes, in case he calls. It's probably overkill on my part—he's only been out of the city for one night—but I know this was the right call.

As helpful and attentive and amazing as Jax has been, I've also been acutely aware that he's spending all this time in Atlanta with me, instead of at his cabin prepping for his first booking to arrive. *Tomorrow*, according to that inquiry he showed me at the diner.

And that's why I put my foot down and insisted he go. He seemed hesitant as he left, checking in on me once, twice, thrice more before he walked out the door, but it had to be done.

After all, that privacy screen for his outdoor shower ain't going to install itself. I don't love the thought of any rogue guests having Sasquatch sightings—that sight is for me and me only from now on.

I'm already counting down the days until he's back in the city for a visit.

Then again, maybe this is a feeling I'll have to get used to.

I'll just be excited for Jax from my sofa two hundred miles away, cheering him on while trying not to miss him too much.

"I'm simply educating myself on all things wilderness," I insist.

Aubrey throws a champagne gummy bear at me. "You're a terrible liar, but I still love you."

She then takes advantage of my propped-injured-foot situation and turns off Bear scaling a frozen mountain in favor of Meghan Markle looking impossibly perfect in a variety of pencil skirts.

"Aah, that's better." She sighs happily.

I roll my eyes at my best friend just as my phone pings with an iMessage.

The veritable Riverdance my heart performs in my chest when I see his name on my screen is almost embarrassing. *Finally!*

Hello from the cabin - which now has internet!

Welcome back to this century :)

It's been a minute. Is Taylor Swift still famous? Justin and Hailey still married?

The fact that you know who Justin and Hailey are is very… interesting.

My brother-in-law is Canadian. I can speak it almost fluently now.

Oh yes, a very important bilingual skill to have.

Right up there with Spanish, French, and
Mandarin, I think ;)

I snort with laughter.

Rick says hi, by the way. He misses you.

A photo of the little dog accompanies the text. Rick has one paw up, like he's waving.

Tell Rick I miss him, too.

I send a little heart emoji, but of course, it doesn't quite cover what I'm feeling right now. Which is more along the lines of: *I miss you like a weirdly huge amount so much please come home asap and stat, please and thank you.*

Aubrey turns her attention from the TV to look at me. "Is that him?"

I nod. "He just got internet at the cabin."

"Now you can keep in touch. Although, I don't understand why you didn't go back out there with him. You obviously wanted to."

"For one, there's the whole 'I have a job to get back to tomorrow.' And for two..." I gesture to my foot. "I think I'm better off here right now."

As much as I like it better there.

The thought surprises me, but it's true. For that glorious few days in nature, I got to be part of Jax's world. I felt good there.

I expected to miss *him*, of course. Miss his steady presence and his easygoing conversation and the feel of his arm around me when we watch TV together.

What I wasn't expecting was how much I would miss it out in the wilderness.

> Have any more bookings come in yet?

Too many. A ton of booking requests, lots of interest. I haven't been able to keep up. And it's all thanks to you and your amazing videos.

> I'm so happy to hear that.

And I am. Of course I am. Though it's a bit of a double-edged sword, I'm glad to hear that the work I've been doing has paid off.

Over the past few days of my being homebound, I've made the most of it by uploading the pictures and videos I took on our hike to Jax's company socials.

It's been... *fun.* Energizing. I've loved having the chance to be creative and dig right in to *showing* just how amazing Jax and his business are. I switched on my best marketing brain and came up with good captions, researched niche hashtags that would reach the right audience, and even put together a highlight reel that I pinned to his Instagram. I also uploaded it to his website as the background to the homepage and it looks excellent, if I do say so myself.

I was almost upset when I finished all the things on my marketing to-do list because I enjoyed it so much.

In comparison, fortunately (or maybe unfortunately), I've been cleared to go back to work tomorrow. Not only do I feel stuck and unfulfilled there, but Dylan has been messaging me to tell me I'll be doing back-office work until my foot is better for "aesthetic reasons."

Quite frankly, I'm a bit annoyed at myself that it took me this long to realize what an absolute douchewad that man is.

I put my phone to the side and clamber to my feet clumsily. "I might go to bed," I tell Aubrey. For some reason, I'm no longer in the mood for raunchy TV office romance and *somebody* turned off my Bear Grylls fest. "No offense to you or *Suits*, but I'm pretty tired."

"Okay, Hol." My roommate gives me a hug. "Big day tomorrow, hey? Back to business."

"Ugh. Could not be less excited for it."

Although I'll be glad to see Raquel and catch up with any Peeping Tom ghost drama that happened while I was away, overall, I could not be less excited to be back in the swing of things.

Back in the city with a bandaged ankle and my job at the hotel, while Jax is back where he belongs in the wilderness, getting ever increasing reasons to stay out longer. As nice as it was to be wild and free for a little while—and I've loved living out my quit list—real life still comes with some responsibilities. And working for Dylan Hanlin is sadly one of mine.

Back to good ol' reliable, responsible Holly.

40

JAX

I frown at my phone, rereading Holly's messages and feeling totally unsure what to think. Something feels off.

It's probably my fault for chickening out and telling her that Rick misses her instead of being upfront and confessing that it's *me* who misses her.

A lot more than I would have ever imagined I was capable of missing anyone. I thought I'd feel better after I got the satellite internet installed and I could text her, but if anything, texting with her has just sharpened my current feelings of aloneness.

Coming up to the cabin knowing that I wouldn't be able to contact her for two days didn't sit right with me, but when she encouraged me to go, I went.

I knew I had things to do. It was only sensible.

And now, I'm standing in the middle of the cabin's living room, which features plenty of plushy furniture and nature-themed local artwork hanging on the walls. I turn in a circle as I take in the fully-stocked kitchen, and the open door to the dormitory bedroom which now features twelve perfectly made-up beds.

The lit-up patio is perfectly visible through the double doors at the end of the room.

I'm looking at my dream incarnate. Years of planning, followed by months of hard work to make it happen, and finally the doors to Grainger Guides will officially open tomorrow to welcome the first guests.

I wasn't sure about the name, but Holly convinced me to keep it. Said it rolled off the tongue nicely and centered me as the face of the company.

Which is a strange thing to consider—I've never thought of myself as the face of anything, but here we are.

"What do you think, Rick?" I ask my dog, who retreated to the living room's shaggy rug after his photo shoot and now appears to be sleeping, clearly not thinking about anything at all.

I should feel elated. Full of excitement. And I am excited... but something's missing.

Some*one*'s missing, to be exact.

Because out here in the center of everything that used to be more than enough for me, there's a Holly-shaped hole that I can't fill with my own company. Being alone with my thoughts no longer feels like blissful silence, but echoing loudness.

I miss her presence—her laughter filling this cabin, her smile lighting up the evening darkness—and this feels like an incomplete moment without her by my side, soaking it in with me.

When she was here, she fit. I wanted to share everything with her that I previously wanted to keep for myself.

And over the past couple of days, as I've worked on stocking my gear room, adding the screen to the shower, and cleaning and tidying and putting final touches on everything, all I could think about was her.

I keep wondering if she's okay, how she's doing, how she's feeling about going back to work tomorrow...

All I want to do is be there for her.

I shouldn't have left her.

I should have stayed, kept taking care of her.

For so long, I rejected the thought of any kind of romantic relationship, not only because of my upbringing, but because I'd convinced myself that my lifestyle wasn't conducive to love. That I couldn't fit a relationship around the plans for my life.

But now, everything I used to think has been flipped. For so long, all I wanted was to escape the city, but right now, all I want to do is tell Holly face to face that *I'm* the one who misses her.

Show her that I'm serious about making this work. That I don't want to just fit a relationship around my life plans, but have my life plans fit around *her.*

Us at the center, together.

Before I can think too much, I'm grabbing my keys and whistling for Rick.

"Come on, boy. We're going home to Atlanta tonight."

41

HOLLY

I can't sleep.

After leaving Aubrey to watch *Suits* alone, I don't know how long I spend tossing and turning in bed, wrestling with thoughts of work and Jax and *responsibilities*, but it's pitch dark outside when my phone lights up on my nightstand.

> You still awake?

I rub the sleep from my eyes, wondering why on earth he's texting so late. He should be fast asleep by now so that he's fresh to welcome his guests tomorrow.

> Yeah. Laying in bed, thinking. What are you up to?

> Also thinking.

> What's on your mind?

> You.

> What's on yours?

> You.

My heart picks up speed when I see the little bubbles pop up in response.

> I was lying when I said Rick missed you earlier.

> Well, not lying, coz I'm sure he does miss you. But I miss you more.

A little lump forms in my throat as I stare at my phone screen in the darkness.

> I miss you, too. It's stupid, but I kind of wish you could be here right now.

A crack of light suddenly illuminates the room, and I look up to see that my door is being pushed open.

"Aubs?" I murmur in confusion.

"It's me." That gravelly, deep, familiar voice fills the room and my heart feels whole all at once. "I, uh... might have made use of the spare key under your pants doormat. Which is not that wise, by the way. Makes it real easy for someone to break in."

"Jax! You're here?!" I ignore his extremely valid point as I half-sit in bed, attempting to smooth my hair as I take in the welcome sight of him. He's illuminated by the light in the hall, and he's got his phone in one hand and Rick tucked up in his other.

I'm not entirely sure I'm not dreaming right now.

"Wait. What are you *doing* here?"

"Like I said, Rick missed you. Begged me to come say hi, in fact. He was pretty relentless, so I eventually gave in." Jax is close enough to me now that I can see his eyes roaming all over my face, like he's drinking me in.

307

When he meets my eyes, his expression turns a little bashful. But even in the dark room, I see the shadows under his eyes. See how tired he looks. "You drove three hours back to the city in the middle of the night because Rick begged you to?"

"Sure, let's go with that."

Rick jumps out of Jax's arms and curls up next to me, nuzzling his head into my arm. Meanwhile, his Mountain Man Daddy gives me the softest, dopiest look before he kicks off his shoes, takes off his shirt, and slips into bed next to me.

It's the first time we've shared a bed (or tent or sleeping bag) since the camping trip, and yet, it feels so familiar. Like something we've done a million times before and will do a million times more.

He wraps his arms around me, cradling me to his chest, as he continues, "Let's go with that and not that I was so happy to talk to you again. That when you texted me, it made me miss you so much that I had to come see you tonight. Even if it was just to quickly say good night."

I swallow the lump in my throat as I relax in his arms, not quite believing that he's come all this way for the sole purpose of saying good night to me.

"I'm glad," I tell him. "Even though I feel bad that you're going to be insanely exhausted tomorrow."

"That sounds like a then problem, not a now problem," he replies sleepily, but I can hear the smile in his voice.

"Mmm, what's a now problem, then?"

"Maybe that I've been up at the cabin since yesterday morning, and the whole time I was out there, all I could think about was doing this."

He half-sits, takes my chin, and kisses me.

In an instant, my world lights up.

He kisses me with an intensity that I can feel everywhere—a resolved intention that makes it hard to catch my breath.

Our kisses have ranged from hot and fiery to slow and steamy, all of them equally spark-and-firework filled, but this one is new. This one is achingly tender.

He caresses my face, strokes my hair, moves his lips against mine over and over, like he's communicating something he can't put into words. Like he truly cherishes me, like he never wants to let me go.

This feels like... *love.*

"Thank you, Holly," he whispers against my lips.

I peer at him through the darkness. "For what?"

"For believing in me when I could barely believe in myself."

"I'd bet on you with my last dollar, Jaxon Grainger." I say this with conviction because I mean it with everything in me.

He blows out a breath. Closes his eyes for a moment before saying, "I'm not great with feelings, but I need you to know that you mean the world to me, Holly."

I cover his hand with mine. He seems to have something to say and I want to give him space to speak, like he's done for me so many times before.

"My mom left when I was young, and it kinda broke my heart," he says in a rush before taking a deep breath. Slowing down. "Back then, I didn't really understand it, didn't get why she left. Thought it might've been because of me. Kids always think it's about them, right?"

He gives a dry chuckle and I pull his hand to my heart, overcome for the little boy he's describing. The heartbreak he must have experienced, so young.

"When I got older, I found out that my dad had cheated on her. A lot. And my heart broke again—this time, for all the people he had hurt. For my mom, who he drove away, and for what I lost in the process. I think it gave me such a skewed view of relationships, so that I purposefully stayed away from them. I never wanted to catch feelings. Risk hurting anyone or being hurt."

"I understand," I tell him. Because I do, in a way. I think a part of why I held onto the idea of Dylan for so long was because I didn't want to risk being hurt. Didn't want to risk putting myself out there and catching feelings, so I stuck with the "safe" option. Didn't step out of my comfort zone.

Jax, meanwhile, simply decided to guard his heart and remain alone. My own heart breaks for him, for all the grief and hurt he's been through.

"I've been functioning on the premise of being okay with brokenness for so long, I got a bit jaded in the process. But then, I met you. You've changed everything." He laughs softly and shakes his head. "I spent all this time helping you tackle your quit list, but it turns out, I can't quit you, Holly. And what's more, I don't think I want to. I *know* I don't want to. I want to be here for you, through everything."

I can't help but wonder when anyone last took care of him. He's spent all this time taking care of me, helping me, advising me—but who's been taking care of Jax? "I want to be here for you, too. If you'll let me."

He inhales sharply. "I will."

"Will you stay with me tonight?"

His arms tighten around me, holding me closer in response. Everything I want and need, and somehow more.

42

JAX

The next morning, I wake up happy and at peace with Holly in my arms once again.

Funny how I used to always say no, but all she makes me want to do is say yes to her. Anything she wants, ever, I'm there.

She sighs contentedly as she rolls over and places a hand on my chest.

But then, that happy sigh turns into a whole lot of swearing.

"Jax!" She shakes my arm.

"Mmpf?" I respond sleepily. After spending the last couple of days working my butt off to get the cabin ready—plus the late drive last night and staying up with Holly—I'm feeling more than a little sleep-deprived.

This is what we get for kissing all night instead of sleeping.

She shakes harder. "Jax, wake up! It's after 9!"

She pushes the comforter off of us and rolls out of bed about as elegantly as she rolled into my lap in that kayak all those weeks ago now. The memory still makes me smile.

"I need to shower. I can't go to work with my hair like this."

I lazily open one eye and survey her. "Morning, sunshine. And I say leave it—I like your hair like that, all messed up from my hands."

She flushes red, then flicks my forehead. Hard. "Usually, that would be a very exciting thing to hear. The type of thing that would have me throwing myself back into bed next to you. But today is the grand opening of Grainger Guides, and if you don't get that magnificent butt of yours up and out of bed, you're going to be late."

"Magnificent, huh?" My second eye pops open. "And, nah, they're not coming till way later, so I was thinking I'd spend my morning buying you coffee and driving you to work. I also want to visit my sister before heading out."

"Oh!" she says, looking pleased. "I'll take all the time I can get with you."

I reach over and give her a cheeky grin as I flick her forehead. "Good. Now, why don't you go get your own magnificent butt into that shower, then?"

"Deal." She plants a quick kiss on my mouth before hobbling off.

Meanwhile, I stretch out in her bed, wholly glad that I decided to come back here last night.

I feel amazing. I get to wake up with Holly on the day my business officially opens, and in a few days, when the booking is over, I plan to come straight back to her and do this all over again.

For the first time in a very long time, something deep inside me feels accomplished. Feels unafraid of failure.

And I have Holly to thank for this change.

Life is good, though a little bittersweet as I have to say goodbye to her for another few days.

Half an hour later, Holly's back in one of her sundresses with her trademark shiny pink lips and we're pulling up outside

The Pinnacle. I hold her takeout latte as I help her out of Edna, making sure to take lots of care with her injured foot.

When we turn around, Dylan is standing outside the hotel doors, watching us with an expression as dark as midnight. His chin is down, and he's glowering at us under hooded eyes, looking not unlike a cartoon vampire.

I shoot him a little wink, then turn my back on the clown and wrap my arms around Holly. Dylan can watch us all he wants, but I'm not going to let him and his beady gaze ruin my goodbye with my girl.

"I'll text you when I get up there," I promise Holly as I squeeze her shoulders. Breathe in her smell.

"I wish I could come with you," she replies.

"Me too." I press my lips to hers, and our kiss is sparky and hot and sweet and full of promise for what's to come.

When she finally pulls back, her eyes are glowing. "I'll miss you."

I press my forehead to hers. "Same."

"Well, well, well. This looks cozy."

I swear, the man's voice is somehow as beady and snakey as he looks. *Here I was, hoping I wouldn't have to talk to this jerk.*

I turn around, annoyed. "Hi, Willan."

"Dylan," he corrects crisply. "Nice to see you two are together now. Very *cute*."

He looks directly at Holly as he says this, and I'm surprised to see her wince. It's a small flash of an expression that passes over her face in an instant, but it's a wince nonetheless.

Together.

Is that what's tripping her up?

We're definitely together, in my mind, but we haven't discussed labels yet. Nor have we discussed if she has any potential lingering feelings for this moron—but I reject that notion pretty swiftly.

Holly has lived out her quit list and moved on.

With me.

End of story.

I put an arm around her and pin Dylan with a glare. "Damn right, we're together."

Her eyes are bright. "Yeah, we are," she echoes.

Dylan smirks. "I suppose I should be saying that I'm happy for you. But if I may ask, how does that work, practically speaking?" He tilts his head towards me. "Don't you live in a hut or in your van by the river or something?"

"He's a wilderness guide," Holly practically hisses, like she's a feisty little dragon. I dig it.

I love how far she's come, how much confidence she's gained in herself.

"How aspirational," Dylan says dryly, his tone dripping with sarcasm. "I'm sure having a girlfriend three hours away in the city is good for both business and pleasure."

"We're just seeing where it goes. Not that it's any of your business," Holly says with an upward tilt of her chin.

I'm proud of how she's standing up for herself—for *us*—but something doesn't feel right about that sentiment when it comes to what we have. This is so much more than just *seeing where it goes*.

"We're going to make it work," I add, shrugging off his "aspirational" insult. When he comes at me, it's laughable. It's when he comes at Holly that I want to knock him out.

As if he hears this, he turns to her with a dangerous smile and claps his hands like she's a chicken. "Holly, now that you've finished saying goodbye to your *boyfriend* here, you better get inside. Raquel is having an issue with one of the room blocks for the Herman-Schultz wedding next month."

"I—" Holly starts to protest, and Dylan's lips thin as he wags a finger at her.

"Your shift started one minute ago, Holly. Not setting a great example, being late for work after a vacation, is it."

My fists clench by my sides and I'm a second away from giving the guy a piece of my mind about the fact that Holly is *injured* and he's acting like a *jackass*, when Holly gives me a little shake of her head. As if to say that it's not worth it. And she's right—*he's* not worth it.

She gives me a final kiss goodbye and then heads towards the front door on her crutches, and I watch her leave, making sure she gets inside safely. Our goodbye was a little dampened by the presence of *Willan* but I couldn't be more proud of my girl and the way she stood up for herself.

Meanwhile, Dylan is making no move to leave.

He just stands there, peering at me, and I, in turn, ignore him completely.

It's only once Holly's safely inside and I'm about to get back into Edna that he finally speaks.

"Guess we're not too different, you and me."

I glance back at him, my glare cold as ice. "Excuse me?"

"We're the same," he says with ill-concealed delight as he fixes me with razor-sharp eyes. "I didn't see it before, but I do now. And when she realizes that she's always going to play second fiddle to a bunch of trees and rocks, she'll remember where she really belongs."

"I have no idea what you're talking about. Holly is my priority."

"Yet here you are, saying goodbye to her." His smile turns into a full blown Chucky-esque grin. "What you don't under-stand, Jax, is that this whole new-fangled hiking and camping and broken-ankle adventures and being late for work thing is not who Holly is. I *know* Holly. And most importantly, I know what she really wants. I *have* what she really wants. So she can enjoy slumming it on this little... *detour* right now, but we both know she'll be back on course soon."

"You don't know a thing, Dylan," I tell him.

And then I leave, before I have to listen to one more word out of this idiot's mouth.

43

JAX

My jaw clenches almost painfully as I drive towards Seb and Maddie's apartment building, and though I'm trying with everything in me to not let Dylan's venomous words affect me, I keep catching on one thing he said:

I have what she really wants.

What a guy.

A guy who fills Holly's original hit list, but he's all wrong for her. She doesn't want him or need him—I know this as well as I know my own name. But still, something's niggling at me.

Holly is my priority and I want nothing more than to make it work with her. But it's not like I have any personal experience with committed relationships—I've always guarded my heart, and giving it to someone is a whole new experience. Of course, I've seen Seb and Maddie's relationship, but when push comes to shove, I'm not sure *I* can be that person for someone.

What if my heart isn't enough for her when I'm gone so much?

I can't bear to think that Holly might feel like a second fiddle to my guiding lifestyle. It's not like I can drive to her place every night when I have guests staying with me at the cabin.

It seems exceedingly ironic that I've always been content as a lone wolf, that I've spent years saving up to execute this plan so I can uproot my life in Atlanta and pursue a solo life in the wilderness. And now, it's coming to fruition at the exact moment that I meet someone I *want* to put down roots for. Want to change my forever-solo ways for.

My hands tighten on Edna's steering wheel at the thought of Dylan getting to see her every day, while I miss her.

I'm jealous, and my sister was right—it's *not* a good look on me.

When I get to Maddie's apartment, the door flies open before I can even knock. "You're here!"

I wrap my sister in a hug. "Missed you, Mads. Where's Seb?"

"He's showering; just got back from practice. Coffee?"

"Definitely." More caffeine sounds perfect right now.

We've barely seen each other lately with everything going on, and I want my sister to know that I'm here for her, whatever she needs, whenever she needs it. Because all I want is to be that guy for all the people I love, whatever Willan may think.

After Maddie fixes a cup of coffee for me and a peppermint tea for herself, we go outside and sit on the balcony, drinking in the morning sunshine. Of course, there's also the blaring traffic noise from below—their place is in the heart of downtown, near the RGM arena that's home to the Cyclones. It reminds me again why I love the wilderness: the peace, the quiet, the lack of beeping horns.

"You guys thinking of moving after the baby gets here?"

She shakes her head. "No. Or not right away, anyhow. We thought about it, but then, we realized that not everything has to change at once. We're lucky to have such a spacious apartment, and we can see how we feel as the baby gets bigger."

I take a drink of coffee. "That's a good way to look at it."

She laughs. "Mom lost it when I told her. You should've heard." She puts on a high-pitched voice as she continues, *"An apartment in the city is no place for a baby, Madelyn! That baby will be roaming the streets and addicted to meth before you know it!"*

Her impression is so uncanny, I can't help but laugh. "Meanwhile, my dad will probably buy the baby books on how to make their first million by the time they're out of diapers."

"Along with a tiny pint-sized suit and briefcase." She then taps her fingers on her mug as she peers at me curiously. "Have you talked to your dad lately?"

"I do my best never to talk to him, if I can help it." I pull a face. "You know, the majority of my hesitation to be your kid's godfather was because of him."

She rolls her eyes. "As if you're anything like your father, Jax. You'll be a *way* better godfather to my baby than your dad was a father to us."

And suddenly—despite the coffee—I feel tired. Weighed down with the thoughts that have occupied my mind since running into Dylan. I don't know if it's the exhaustion or the stress from my first booking arriving later today, but my deepest fears are creeping back into the corners of my mind, gathering like cobwebs. Which may be why I find myself saying, "I'm scared of failing. Of letting you and the baby down. Of not being the right choice for this kid's godfather."

My throat feels tight as I frown down into my coffee.

Maddie, meanwhile, laughs. *Laughs.*

"Newsflash, Jax: you'll screw up sometimes, sure. We all do, it's inevitable. The important thing is not whether you fail or succeed, it's what you do with both your failures and successes. How you let them shape you." She places a gentle hand on my arm so I have to look up at her. "And you're nothing like your father, because unlike him, you have a moral compass. You care about people other than yourself, put other people's needs before yours, where your dad was always selfish."

"I *am* selfish," I say quietly. "I'm chasing my dreams instead of staying here in Atlanta to be here for you and my godchild."

And I'm potentially asking way too much of Holly to enter into a relationship where I can't physically put her first all the time.

"But of course you should! You should chase your own dreams, because that's what your niece or nephew is going to see in you. What will inspire them to chase *their* own dreams."

"I just... I want to always show up for the people that matter to me," I say gruffly.

"Listen, being there for someone doesn't mean being physically present 24/7," Maddie says with a wave of her arm. "Look at Seb—traveling is part of his job, he's gone all the time. But that doesn't mean he isn't there for me. Because being there for someone is showing up when it matters. And that, you always do."

My frown deepens. I can't bring myself to look my sister in the eyes.

"Even if you don't see that in yourself, you're good, Jax." She puts her hand on my arm and squeezes. "You're worthy of being loved and of loving other people. You're enough, exactly as you are."

I have no idea what to say as my mind tumbles back to the moment my six-year-old self watched his mother walk out the door and never come back. How that little boy internalized that she left because he wasn't enough to make her stay.

That, despite how much he loved her, she didn't love him enough.

And then, on the flipside, I spent the rest of my childhood watching Maddie's mom—my stepmom—stay, year after year, affair after affair, even though there was clearly no real love between her and my father.

My childhood gave me a warped view of love. Made it look and feel like something ugly. Dangerous. Something that hurt and was better avoided.

And I avoided it for so long because I felt, deep down, like I was either never going to be enough for someone, or that I'd fail that person and make them unhappy if they stayed with me.

A let down.

But I meant what I said to Holly last night—she's changed my perspective. On everything. While I had my heart locked up and was scared to fail in case it led to a broken heart, she's been willing to put herself out there and fail, time and time again. She's been so much braver than me, all along. Trying and failing, and trying again.

And maybe that's what love is meant to look like—something that you keep trying for. Keep working on. Keep committing to, in the good times and in the bad.

My fears are no longer going to keep me from trying. From putting myself out there for the woman who means the world to me. Because in the end, if it comes down to it, my heart breaking for Holly is still preferable to having an unbroken heart that never got to experience beating for her.

That's the kind of love I want, and the kind of love I have with Holly. Selfless. Putting the other person first.

What I saw growing up wasn't love.

Love gives, not takes. Builds, not destroys. Adds, not takes away.

Someone to complement you, not complete you.

I meet my sister's eyes. Clock her knowing expression.

"What are you smirking about?"

"You love her, don't you?"

"What?" I say again, like an idiot.

"Holly. You love her."

I blink. "How did you kn—?"

"Because that conversation *obviously* wasn't just about the baby, you dumb dumb." Maddie cuts me off with a gleeful grin. "I think everything you're scared of in terms of 'failing' with the baby and me, you feel tenfold when it comes to Holly because you're head over heels in love with her."

"We're just..."

I stop dead in my tracks. I can't finish my sentence because I don't have any other words to finish it with that aren't a lie.

"Yes. I'm in love with her," I say instead, a little dazed. The words sound foreign to my ears, but they sound right.

They fit.

"I knew it!" Maddie cheers.

I'm half-elated, half-terrified. Fully invested. Holly is the love of my life, plain and simple. And I'm going to do everything in my power to show her that, to make sure she knows this truth to her core.

"So what in the hell do I do now?"

"Simple." My sister gives me a *duh* look. "You show up for her when it matters most."

44

HOLLY

The Pinnacle is the same as ever: shiny at first glance, but perfectly worn around the edges when you look closer.

Nothing ever changes here—although, I see we have a new issue of *Ducks Unlimited* magazine, which I'm sure Raquel is pleased about.

But other than some fresh poultry, it's the same people, same decor, same old-fashioned analog marketing tactics (we got new printed brochures when I was away, courtesy of Douglas, I imagine), and same horrible boss.

I'm actually stunned that I didn't see Dylan's true colors earlier. I can't believe all the things he just said to Jax about me playing second fiddle to a bunch of trees, or whatever idiotic statement it was.

Jax always puts me first. I see it, and I feel it, with the sort of clarity I never had with Dylan. It's a feeling I ached to have for so long and never did, whereas Jax has been there for me from day one.

The terrible date at the bar with Keith.

The baby store showdown with Sabrina.

My kayaking fail.

Dylan, that night at the club.

My ankle on the trail.

Showing up last night when I missed him. This man has done nothing but take care of me since I met him. And of course I'm grateful beyond belief.

But who's taking care of Jax?

That small voice in my head repeats the same question I asked myself last night.

I saw the stricken look on his face as Dylan let his verbal assault fly, and I am furious that he then sent me inside so I couldn't have another moment with Jax before he left. Now, all I want is to assure him that everything my boss said was a lie. Dead wrong.

Come to think of it, I'm also furious with myself for listening to Dylan and actually going inside.

One minute late. Please. I've worked countless extra hours, gone above and beyond for years, yet here he is, griping at me over sixty seconds.

In a fit of defiance, I set my bag down on the reception counter and slip my phone out of the side pocket, fully intent on sending Jax a message to let him know that Dylan was totally out of line and clearly a little insane.

Unfortunately, the voice that used to give me heart palpitations interrupts me.

"I hope you had a very nice vacation, Holly," Dylan says in a way that suggests he hopes I had the opposite.

"The best," I tell him, opening my text thread with Jax.

"Back to reality now, so time to turn your devices off." He looks smug as a Cheshire Cat as he waltzes behind the reception desk, where I'm hovering, and grabs my phone right out of my hand. He then turns it off and tosses it back in my purse. He shakes his head, affecting his most businesslike voice. "Tsk tsk... texting at work. What has gotten into you? Now, please help Mrs. Shanahan over there with whatever she needs."

One of our regulars is, indeed, walking across the lobby towards us.

"Okay, Dylan," I respond as calmly as I can, resisting a deep urge to say *aye-aye captain* and give him a sarcastic salute. I paste on my best professional smile instead, but Mrs. Shanahan simply gives me a wave as she passes the reception desk on her way to our games room.

"He's in fine form today," Raquel whispers as Dylan's office door slams behind us.

I roll my eyes at my friend. "I'll say."

Because damn him telling me what to do.

And for taking my phone out of my hand like I'm in high school or something.

I really don't know how I've been doing this every day. For years, I've been working for him. Hanging on to some pipe dream that I now realize I never *actually* wanted.

Truth is, as wonderful as the Pinnacle is, I don't think I want to be here anymore. My heart isn't in it—it's three hours away, in a freaking log cabin with an outhouse.

And the fact that I'm not on my way there with Jax right now feels plain wrong. I have this sense in my gut, like I'm finally reading situations clearly. Or perhaps Peeping Tom the pervy ghost is haunting me.

Dylan's office door creaks open again and I wince instinctively.

"Holly? Now that you've assisted Mrs. Shanahan... A word?"

I look around to see Dylan leaning out of his office door, crooking his pointer finger at me.

"Okay, boss." I wearily get to my feet and grab my crutches.

325

I have no idea what he wants as I follow him into his office, but I also don't really care.

"Please, sit down." He gestures to the chair opposite his desk and I sink into it. He doesn't seem particularly pleased—I missed a week of work after my sprain, but I took unpaid leave for that.

"So-o," he draws the syllable out as he steeples his fingers on his desk and rests his chin on them, peering at me. "Aside from that rocky start this morning, you know that I value you as an employee. And you may have noticed that Douglas hasn't been around since you got back."

I hadn't, actually. Not that I wasn't paying attention to my surroundings, but Douglas worked in a side office and he never seemed to come out. Never interacted with us staff members. I always assumed he was holed up in there, being antisocial.

"I'll level with you, Holly. He didn't work out."

I keep my face carefully neutral. "I'm sorry to hear that."

"The promotion is yours. Congratulations. You're our new marketing manager."

Dylan says this like it's a gift. Like I'll jump up and down with joy, overwhelmed with gratitude. A few short weeks ago, I would have.

But right now, I just feel... *annoyed.*

Bothered by the fact that Dylan's lips are all wet from where he keeps licking them. Bothered by his smug expression. Bothered by how weirdly pointy his hands look with his chin resting in them.

And beneath all that, I'm bothered that, once again, I was a second option to him. Something on the backburner for when his first plan didn't work out.

I can't believe I ever had feelings for someone like this. Now that I've fallen for someone like Jax, it is amazing to know what I've been missing all this time.

"Nah," I hear myself saying, sounding exactly like Jax with his casual nonchalance. "I'll pass."

"W-what?" Dylan splutters, his face falling.

"Pass."

"Why?!" he demands.

I smile sweetly. "It's just not the right time."

"Excuse me?"

His questions are getting repetitive. But luckily, I have only correct answers for him.

"You heard me. It's not the right time. I don't want the promotion. And on second thought, I don't want to work for you in any capacity. I quit."

Dylan scoffs. "You're being ridiculous."

"No," I say with a smile, remembering how Jax called my hit list ridiculous. "The only ridiculous thing I did was wait *way* too long for you to choose me, when you were never going to. So now, I quit. I'm done."

"What're you gonna do?" Dylan demands.

I shrug, feeling about a thousand pounds lighter. "I'll see where it goes."

"This is not like you, Holly."

Another smile plays on my lips. Because Dylan never knew me, not really. "Yes, it is actually. It's exactly like me."

"Is it that guy, Jax? The tattooed van-man?" He sniffs. 'You're really choosing *that man* instead of me?"

I shake my head. "No, Dylan. I'm choosing myself."

Find someone to complement you, not complete you.

All this time, I was waiting for some Prince Charming coded fairytale to come along and save me. But Jax taught me how to save myself. How to stand on my own two feet and fight for what I want. Grab life and all it has to offer.

I want a partner, not a savior.

And I want that partner to be Jax. No matter how that

looks, I choose to be with him, because I've already chosen myself.

So, with that, I turn on my heel and strut right out of Dylan's office and right out of his life like the badass that I always hoped I could be.

Outside the hotel, I take a deep breath, waiting for the impending dread to hit me when I realize what I've done. How irresponsible I've been.

It doesn't come. Because I made the right decision for *me*.

Regardless of what else happens, of what may come, I get to live in that knowledge.

Happily, I begin to crutch forward on the cobbled sidewalk, but of course, I end up tripping over a wobbly piece of rock.

I lose my balance, begin to fall...

And a pair of strong arms come around me, pulling me up against a very broad chest.

"Jax!" I squeal in delight, wobble-turning fully to throw my arms around him. "How many times are you going to have to save me?"

He laughs, a deep rumble moving through his chest. "You're the one who's saved *me*, Holly." He pulls back a little so he can look into my eyes, his gray eyes glittering. "I realized I couldn't leave today without first telling you that... I love you. I'm in love with everything that makes you who you are, Holly Greene."

"I love you, too," I reply, tears pricking the back of my eyes.

His eyes soften so that they look like they're glowing. "I know I might not be what you originally wanted, but I need you to know that I'm always going to make you my priority, and I'm going to try—"

"You're everything I want, Jax. I know what I really want now, and it's you." I smile up at him, my eyes still teary but my heart soaring. "You're my perfect man."

"The perfect man still doesn't exist, Hollywood, so I can't promise perfect. But what I *can* promise is to be your partner. Your co-pilot. Your equal. To choose you, every single day, always."

"I choose you too, Jaxon Grainger."

With a sudden grin, I reach into my purse and pull an old, crumpled piece of paper out of a side pocket. A piece of paper I've been holding onto since that night I first came to the bar to ask for Jax's help, the night that put everything into motion that rewrote my happy ending to be here, in this place, with a guy who might not be perfect, sure, but is perfect for *me*.

"Check it out, I made some edits."

Jax gives me a curious look before unfolding the paper. I lay my head on his chest and look down at the changes—no, *corrections*—I wrote on my hit list when we came home from the mountains a week ago:

1. ~~He must be over 30 and under 45~~ *He must be mature, and wise, and full of great advice beyond his years*
2. ~~He must have stable employment~~ *He must favor happiness and quality of life, and not always put his career first*
3. ~~He must want a family~~ *He must make me feel like we can conquer the world together, as a team*
4. ~~He must be looking for a long-term commitment~~ *He must support my dreams and allow me to support his, but we must always prioritize each other, too*

When Jax finishes reading, he turns to me with a look of wonder in his eyes. "Holly, this is... everything."

I squeeze him tight. "Bonus points if he has a van with a

girl's name, a dog who likes to ride shotgun, and space in said van for one more on his next adventure."

He frowns at me. "Wait, don't you have to work? In fact, what are you doing outside?"

"Well, I added one last thing to my quit list."

His eyes glint. "Oh, yeah?"

"Quit tying myself to my past when I've got my future right in front of me."

"You quit your job?"

"I did. So, if it's okay with you, I'd very much like to accompany you to the cabin today. I won't be much help but I can chat to the guests and regale them with fascinating tales of Sasquatch sightings."

He scoops me up into his arms and begins striding towards Edna.

"Is that a yes?" I laugh.

"It's a hell yes!" he practically yells. Then, he looks down at me, all smiles. "But outside of spying on me when I'm in the shower, what are you going to do now?"

I think about this. And honestly, it doesn't matter. The right thing will come, and in the meantime, I have everything I could ever want and need.

"Well," I say as I look up at him. "Let's just say that I'm seeing how it goes."

EPILOGUE
HOLLY

6 months later...

"Come on, Holly, get that sexy butt in gear!" Jax calls from outside the cabin.

"One sec and I'll be ready," I call back with a smile, then turn back to my laptop, where I'm captioning an image and scheduling it to be posted.

I'm beyond busy at the moment, and loving every second of it.

Hollywood Marketing & Creative was born after I quit my job at the Pinnacle. Jax asked me then what I *wanted* to do for a career, and I realized very quickly that what I desired was to take a chance on something I loved.

Jax has been my biggest supporter, even building me an office space to work from when I'm at the cabin, complete with a comfy chair, a desk next to a huge window overlooking the forest, and a big-ass sign hanging on the wall that says, "Because I'm the Boss, That's Why."

And I have to say, I love being my own boss.

Once my business was up and running, Grainger Guides was my first official client. And after a very successful marketing campaign that brought Jax a ton of bookings, I have since acquired five more clients. I'm unbelievably grateful for each and every business that took a chance on using my brand new agency for their marketing needs.

It's my dream job—made even dreamier by the fact that I can work from anywhere I like. And I *like* to work here at the cabin, taking full advantage of the satellite internet, the incredible scenery, and, above all else, all the time I get to spend with my boyfriend:

Jaxon Grainger. AKA the hottest wilderness guide the world has ever seen.

He's gone from strength to strength in his guiding. As I once predicted, he now has a score of rave reviews on Google, and (thankfully) has had no more encounters with rogue LARPers on the trail.

I close my laptop, then bend to pet Rick, who's sitting at my feet. "Come on, boy. Let's go see what your daddy wants."

This week, we have a rare breather where Jax doesn't have any guests and we are enjoying the time alone, taking pleasure hikes together. And, of course, cramming in all the waterfall swims we can before winter hits and the water gets too cold to make out in (as warm as he always keeps me).

I step outside and soak in the sight of the man I love standing in the afternoon sunshine. He's wearing all black, emphasizing his tanned skin—he's more tanned than ever after a summer spent outdoors. He's got a daypack slung on his back and looks entirely gorgeous—this guy is the full manly-man package, and he's all mine.

"Where are we off to today?" I ask as I hop down from the deck and come towards him.

It's only once I'm closer to him that I notice he's shifting from foot to foot, looking almost nervous.

Which is unlike him.

I hope that he's not nervous about taking me on whatever hiking route he's chosen today. He loves helping me push my limits and is always showing me what I can achieve when I put my mind to it. It's one of the things I love most about him—for so long, I believed the man was saving me, but ultimately, while he still catches me whenever I fall (both figuratively and literally), he's done so much more than save me.

He's helped empower me so I can save myself.

He's my biggest cheerleader, and I'm his.

Now his gray eyes crinkle at the corners and his expression softens as he looks at me, all signs of potential nervousness melting away. "Hi, beautiful. And it's a surprise."

"I like surprises," I tell him as I place my hand in his and stand on tiptoe to kiss him. I'm expecting a peck, but he threads his hand through my hair, sliding to the nape of my neck and anchoring there as he kisses me until my head is spinning and I can't catch my breath.

After six months together, the sparks and fireworks and romance aren't just present, they're bigger and better than ever.

"What was that for?" I gasp when he finally releases me.

He grins that irresistible grin of his—the one that's sweet and overconfident and sexy and brave and bashful and teasing and genuine, all at once. "Because I love you."

I never knew I could be this happy, this content... without any kind of plan.

We're both working on our businesses every day, enjoying the satisfaction they're bringing us, but choosing to put each other first. We make sure we are prioritizing our relationship, while still working on ourselves and our dreams.

And let me tell you—it works.

I spend my time between the cabin and Atlanta, going back to the city every time I need to meet a client. Or if I miss Mindy, Aubrey, my niece and nephew. Or if I'm simply craving a McDonald's milkshake.

Jax comes with me when he can, and on those trips, we go see Maddie and Seb too.

He, in turn, spends his time between the cabin and taking guests on multi-night hikes. Sometimes I join him, sometimes I go back to the city when he's out on an excursion.

We miss each other when we're apart, but we know that the distance will make it all the sweeter when we're reunited.

Our relationship isn't perfect—because, as Jax says, perfect in itself doesn't exist—but it's perfect for *us*, because we're perfect for each other. And that's what matters.

"What're you thinking about?" Jax asks me with a half-smile as we make our way down the trail, hand in hand. Rick trots in front of us as the afternoon sun warms our shoulders. "You seem so lost in thought right now."

"Just thinking about how happy I am," I tell him, and he squeezes my hand.

"I'm happy, too. The happiest I've ever been."

I squeeze back. "Do you feel like going back to Atlanta with me tomorrow? Maddie was asking if we'd visit her and Seb soon. She must be just about ready to pop."

"Three more weeks," Jax says with a look of mild concern. "Then, I will officially be a godfather."

"You'll crush it. You were so good with Sage and Sawyer when they came out here."

Jax snorts. "If you count Sawyer falling in the creek six times as me being good with kids, then sure."

I wave a hand. "He was wearing his life jacket, and it was only, like, three inches of water. Not your fault he has no balance."

"Toddlers can drown in just three inches of water, you know," Jax says gravely. I don't have a clue how he knows this, but it's adorable that he does.

"Good thing you were there to fish him out every time he face-planted."

He laughs, then murmurs, "Showing up when it matters."

"Exactly."

We continue the rest of our hike in the same manner, slogging slowly upwards as we talk and laugh and the sun dips lower in the sky on another beautiful day together.

A half hour later, the trail snakes around a corner, the trees part, and we pop out at the most beautiful sight I've ever seen. This viewpoint puts us high above the surrounding forest, and we can see for miles around. The sun is setting over the distant horizon, casting shades of pink and orange and purple across the sky like it's been painted.

I immediately move to the edge, soaking it all in. Jax comes to stand behind me, his broad, hard chest at my back, one arm circling my waist as he points with the other.

"See over there?" he asks, his arm outstretched towards the horizon.

I nod.

"That's the direction of Stone Mountain. The first hike we went on together, and the day I realized that you were so much tougher, so much stronger, than you gave yourself credit for."

He moves his finger, pointing at a spot below us. "And down there. That's our waterfall, where we kissed on our hike all those months ago. That was also the exact moment that I knew that I never wanted to let you go. That I didn't want to kiss anyone else again as long as I live."

Before I can respond, he points a ways further. "Over there is where we met those Viking idiots." I can hear the smile in his voice. "I was so mad, at first, that they cut into my time with you, but then I was grateful, because they gave me an excuse to spend the night with you. That night, I fell asleep to the sound of you breathing, to the feel of your heart beating, and when I woke up the next morning, I realized I was too far gone for you to ever turn back." He laughs. "Which was a good thing. Because turning back was never an option. I only want to move forward with you, Holly. Forever."

He steps away, and I immediately miss his warmth. I spin around, wanting to put my arms around his neck, draw him close, and tell him I feel the same way about him...

Instead, I find him down on one knee, looking up at me with those incredible eyes blazing.

My breath catches in my throat.

"I told you once to find a man who kisses you like he's going to move heaven and earth for you. Bring down the sun, moon and stars. But what I didn't tell you is to find a man who also *loves* you like that. Who wakes up every day in your corner. Who'll do anything for you, go to the ends of the earth for you."

He takes one of my hands in his. I feel frozen to the spot.

"But I guess I didn't need to tell you any of that, because you already had one. *Have* one." He pins me with his gaze. "And I want to continue to be that man for you until the day I die. I love you, Holly. You've changed my life and you're the center of my universe. I'm hoping that you'll do me the honor of being my—"

"Yes!" I practically scream, my head spinning. "Yes, yes yes!"

His grin turns crooked. "You didn't even hear what I had to say yet. What if I was about to ask you to be my date to the annual Wilderness Guides of America ball this fall? Or, even better, to be my DD that night in case Morris plies me with margaritas and I end up wearing a Hawaiian shirt while singing Jimmy Buffet and embarrassing myself over—"

"Jax?" I cut him off again, my smile a mile wide and my heart thumping a million miles a minute.

"Yeah?"

"Shut up and kiss me."

The man I love with everything in my entire being doesn't need to be told twice. He jumps to his feet in one smooth motion and picks me up. Spins me around before setting me down slowly, my body sliding sensually against his until my feet finally hit the ground. He turns those slate eyes on me, full of heat and passion as the pad of his thumb runs along my lower lip, making me gasp.

"Anything for my future wife," he says with conviction.

And then, his lips are on mine and I'm melting into his kiss —into him—and it's absolutely perfect in every way.

A NOTE FROM KATIE

I hardly even know where to begin with this note—this book was a journey and a half, and I have SO many people to thank: First of all, thank you, reader, for spending time with Jax and Holly. I hope you fell in love with them as much as I did! They were complicated characters to get to know, and it took me a long time to figure out who they were as people, but in the end, I really do think that they were completely (and unexpectedly) perfect for each other.

I also want to say a huge thank you to my best friend and business partner and all around badass SJW, AKA my savior when it came to this book. You're like the Jax to my Holly, always pushing me to do better and making me believe I can do it when I think all hope is lost. I love you always.

To Madi—your ideas are always on point and I'm so grateful you make time for me and my stories in your insanely busy schedule. You're the best and everything you do helps make my books better, too.

Jen, you're the most amazing PA ever and you've been a

great help in this book. I love you and your endless encouragement and your love for Jax and Holly.

To Dawn, Bethany and Megan. What an AWESOME bunch of beta readers! I feel insanely lucky to have had your thoughts and feedback added to this story to make it better.

Abby and Suzan, thank you for all your work with catching final typos. I appreciate you both!

To Emily S and Emily W—the best pair of Emilys the world has ever seen. Thank you for supporting me and my books and for all of your work with the book tour for this one :)

A huge thanks to my launch team for helping me spread the word about Jax and Holly, and my wonderful ARC readers, for taking the time to read and review this book!

Thank you to Cindy, for your beautiful cover art, and to my incredible author friends for being such a great community of women supporting women. You are all so inspiring to me, and I value all of your so much.

Last but definitely not least, thank you to my husband, for being the biggest support ever to me as I wrote this book, for having grace with me when I was grumpy and stressed and tired, and for being my IRL perfect person and cheerleader. You are everything on my hit list and so much more.

Love always,

ALSO BY KATIE BAILEY

The Cyclones - Holiday Hockey Rom Com

Season's Schemings

Donovan Family

So That Happened

I Think He Knows

Only in Atlanta

The Roommate Situation

The Neighbor War

Printed in Great Britain
by Amazon

40344594R00199